'It's a great story . . . accessible, interesting and incredibly well-written . . . *The Soldier's Song* speaks as a welcome new voice in Irish writing'   www.theladylovesbooks.blogspot.com

r . . . Devoid enerals, and stated, *The* ad, and will *Daily Mail*

)2 Hennessy *he Soldier's* ely readable *Irish Times*

Independent

l told' *ning Herald*

s to Barker, n this series. servedly find *usiness Post*

and it's well written, engaging and highly readable. And the Dublin setting obviously gives it great potential to be the first bestseller of 2010 for us'   Bob Johnston, owner of The Gutter Bookshop in Dublin, *Bookseller*

THE SOLDIER'S SONG

Alan Monaghan

PAN BOOKS

First published 2010 by Macmillan

This edition published 2013 by Pan Books
an imprint of Pan Macmillan, a division of Macmillan Publishers Limited
Pan Macmillan, 20 New Wharf Road, London N1 9RR
Basingstoke and Oxford
Associated companies throughout the world
www.panmacmillan.com

ISBN 978-1-4472-5630-4

Typeset by Ellipsis Books Limited, Glasgow

Printed and bound by CPI Group (UK) Ltd, Croydon, CR0 4YY

Visit www.panmacmillan.com to read more about all our books
and to buy them. You will also find features, author interviews and
news of any author events, and you can sign up for e-newsletters
so that you're always first to hear about our new releases.

Part One

I

Mr & Mrs Richard D'Arcy politely
request the company of

STEPHEN RYAN ESQ.

On the occasion of the 21st birthday
of their daughter, Mary

at the King's Ballroom, Dawson Street on:
Tuesday 4 August 1914 at 8.00 p.m.

RSVP: RYEVALE HOUSE, LEIXLIP.

The kids in the street were fighting again. They were always squabbling over something, but this time it was serious. He heard scuffling and shouting, and the high-pitched voices rising to a crescendo – then a distinct slap, and the wail of a child crying. As he bent to look out through the lace curtain, he saw some of them darting into the gloomy hallway of the tenement building across the street. A welter of skinny legs and heads shaved for nits. Running to mammy, he thought, smiling to himself, though they'd probably all get a clip round the ear for their trouble. That was the hardest lesson they'd learn; that she didn't care what side they were on.

He was still smiling as he turned back to the mirror and finished fastening his cufflink. He straightened his cuffs, enjoying the feel of the heavy, luxuriant cloth around his wrists, and then took the jacket from the back of a chair and slipped it on. Nearly ready now. He plucked the invitation from the shabby gilt frame of the mirror and looked at it for a few moments before slipping it into an inside pocket. Not bad, he, thought, standing up straight and sticking out his chest as he surveyed himself in the glass. Quite elegant, in fact – although he couldn't resist tugging the tie just a little more to one side.

He glanced down at the table, stacked with books, and thought about all those evenings he'd spent teaching sweaty, dull-eyed young lads to bluff their way through the civil service exams. The tedium, the endless bloody repetition. But it had been worth it at a bob a time. The suit was the only thing he'd ever had tailored, and he smiled to himself again as he admired it in the mirror. It was a good suit and he carried it well. At nineteen he still had the gangly limbs of an adolescent, but he was tall and well propor- tioned and there was a certain grace in his bearing. With his fair hair brushed and his face freshly shaved, he thought he looked presentable, if not downright handsome. And definitely elegant. He could easily pass for a gentleman.

'Stephen!'

The reedy voice barely carried down the stairs, but Stephen's face fell at the sound. What was it this time? More tea? Or a mug of porter? Or did the chamber pot need emptying again?

'Stephen! Stephen!'

He walked out into the narrow hallway in his stockinged feet. 'I'll be up now!' he shouted up the stairs, and scowled to himself as he went down the passage into the kitchen. Why couldn't Joe see to him? He'd heard him come in from work hours ago – the slam of the hall door and then his heavy boots on the stairs as he went straight up to bed. The late nights were catching up on him. He'd been out until the small hours again last night, over in Liberty Hall with his union pals. That was all very well, but he still had to be up at the crack of dawn to queue with the corner boys and bowsies looking for work on the docks. If the Da was in better health he would have had something to say about that. Joe could do better. He'd been an apprentice coachbuilder before they were all locked out – regular work and good prospects. Now he was lucky if he got three days a week.

Stephen's shoes stood on a sheet of newspaper on the kitchen table. They were his old shoes – the money from the lessons hadn't stretched that far – but they'd been polished until they seemed to glow in the shaft of evening sunlight that came in through the scullery window. As he sat down to put them on, he wondered if it suited his brother not to have a regular job. The lockout had ended a year ago, and he could have gone back to work with all the others, but Joe said he wouldn't lower himself. He'd found his niche in the trade union – working in the soup kitchen at first, then helping to organize pickets and rallies. Now he was a sergeant in the workers' militia. Stephen had laughed when he heard about that. A soldier in Jim Larkin's ragbag army? Much good they'll do, armed to the teeth with stones and bottles! But that was before he found the gun.

A real gun – a rifle. He walked back up the dingy passage, his shoes ringing loudly on the cracked lino, and stopped at the foot of the stairs. He'd left the parlour door open and he could see the sideboard against the far wall. That was where he'd found it, when he went in there to fetch a book. It was wrapped in a potato sack and stuffed underneath the sideboard. The sacred bloody front parlour of all places – their mother would be spinning in her grave! But more worrying was where it came from: the Irish Volunteers had landed hundreds of rifles from a yacht the Sunday before, and there had been trouble when they smuggled them back into the city. A riot, shooting on the quays, and four civilians had been killed. Joe had been out all day Sunday, coming home sunburned but unusually quiet. Now Stephen knew why.

The gun was gone when he brought the book back the next day, but he had a feeling it hadn't gone far. It gave him pause for thought. Joe was always on about fighting for the rights of the workers. Maybe they were doing more than just talking up a revolution over in Liberty Hall.

'Stephen! Stephen!'

'I'm coming, Da!'

He dreaded going back up. He'd been up there half the afternoon, and he still hadn't got over watching Phillips unwind the bandage; the smell that filled the small room, the purple, puffy look of the mangled leg. His father had borne the indignity without a murmur, keeping his face to the wall, but even Phillips had winced when he saw the wound. He was enough of a doctor to know the agony it must be causing.

Watching the examination, it seemed to Stephen that the pain had shrunk his father physically. Every time he walked into that room he was shocked to see how frail he had become. Perhaps it was because he'd been so hearty before. A blacksmith, with a blacksmith's arms and chest. Stephen could barely remember his mother's illness, but he thought it had been different for her. Where his father had shrunk, she had faded away. Even her red hair had lost its shine as the disease consumed her, turning her greyer and greyer, until finally it seemed the only colour left in her was the scarlet flecks of blood on her lips. His father had been strong then. Every evening, he'd carried his two sons up to bed, one on each arm, and then gone back down to tend to his dying wife. Now he could hardly raise himself up in the bed to piss.

Stephen stood silent, listening, hoping he'd fallen asleep.

There was a soft tread above and Joe appeared on the landing. His shirt was open and his face puffy with sleep. He was shorter than his older brother, but as stout as his father had once been, with a barrel chest and muscular arms. His hair was jet black, and clung to his round skull in tight curls.

'He's asking for you,' he said, with a jerk of his head. 'He wants to see the suit.'

So that was it. Stephen sighed as he went up the stairs, feeling his brother's eye on him. He could feel another row brewing, but he was in no humour for it tonight. Joe held his peace too. The bedroom door was open and both of them had enough respect for their father not to let him see them fighting. Joe waited until he came up and then squeezed past him on the narrow landing and started down the stairs, his face stony. Stephen straightened his jacket and touched his tie. He could already see the childlike smile on the ravaged face, the withered hand patting the bedspread, telling him to sit. He loved his father, but he hated to see him like that. Still, it had to be done. A deep breath and a false smile, and he walked into the darkened room.

By the time he came back down, Joe was in the kitchen, sitting at the table with a mug of stout and a plate of bread and cheese. The sun had sunk out of sight, and the kitchen was gloomy again. Stephen's top hat stood on the table, freshly brushed and gleaming.

'Did your man come and have a look at him?' Joe asked. Your man was Phillips.

'He did.'

'And what did he say?'

'He said there's some infection that we need to keep an eye on. He put on a fresh bandage and said we should change it every other day and wash the wound while we're at it. He put some iodine on it and left the bottle.'

'That's all he did? He put on a fresh bandage?'

Stephen picked up his hat from the table and brushed some crumbs from the brim.

'Yes. That's all he could do.'

'Ah, my arse, that's all he could do! Could he not give him something for it?'

'What do you mean, could he not give him something for it? What could he give him? He's only a doctor, not a miracle-worker.'

'He's not even a doctor!'

Stephen's mouth tightened into a grimace. It was true; Phillips was still only a medical student – which was why he didn't prescribe anything. But he knew his business and he would take hardly any money. Joe liked to sneer at him, but he wasn't the one who was paying.

'Well, he will be a doctor, and he knows more about medicine than that quack chemist of yours with all his powders and potions.'

'Sure, if he knows that much, why can't he help our Da? All he ever does is put iodine on it and change the bandage. Why can't he make him better?'

Stephen had to put the hat down to keep from crushing it in his hands. He could feel his colour rising and anger swelling in his chest. That was Joe all over: always black and white, yes or no, nothing in between. Always going at everything like a bull at a gate. Did he really think his father's leg could be mended just like that? As if it was ever that simple.

'You know why, Joe! You know damn well nothing's going to make him better. Have you ever seen the state of his leg? Have you? Have you ever looked at it with the bandage off? Phillips said it's a wonder he never got gangrene. And I'll tell you what else he said to me. He said he'd have been better off if they'd amputated it. He'd have had a chance then. But he's too weak for it now – the operation would finish him off altogether.'

Joe had never seen his father's leg – not because he was squeamish, but because he couldn't bear to even think about it without blaming himself. He shifted uncomfortably in his chair. He was the one who'd dragged him down to the rally on Sackville Street during the lockout. The old man had never had much time for trade unions, but he'd let his son talk him into coming down to support them. Joe had told him the only way he might get his job back was if all the workers would unite and show the employers that they couldn't just be shut out on the street. He wasn't to know that the police would charge the rally, or that a police horse would run his father down as he tried to get out of the way. He'd wept as he helped to carry him to safety, the poor man screaming in pain every time they moved his leg. It wasn't his fault, everybody kept telling him; it was those bastard coppers. But he knew who was really to blame.

Stephen had picked up his hat again and watched his brother take a long swallow from his mug of stout. He knew the guilty look, but he knew also that Joe was obstinate. This was his way if he was on the back foot; he'd clam up, grow surly. He wasn't finished yet, not by a long chalk. There was a palpable tension as Stephen settled the hat on his head and picked up his cane from the corner. Joe eyed him with barely disguised contempt.

'Go on so, go out and enjoy yourself,' he muttered, as his brother stepped into the hallway.

Stephen turned to give him an angry stare. 'I will. And why wouldn't I?'

'Why wouldn't you? Your own father's lying sick in his bed and you're off to a party with your college chums. Have you no shame at all?'

Shame? Stephen had to master the urge to hit him with the cane. He'd a hard neck. He pointed furiously at the ceiling.

'He's only after telling me to be sure and enjoy myself,' he hissed. 'He's sick, sure. He's been sick for a year. What good will it do to have me sitting here all night? Anyway, wasn't I here last night? I'm here most nights while you're over in Liberty Hall playing with your new gun.'

Joe's mouth fell open as if he'd been slapped, but then he flushed angrily. 'That's none of your business.'

'You're right, it's not. And what I do is none of yours, so keep your nose out of it!'

'It's none of my business, is it? I'll tell you what, it's my business if you're going to a party thrown by Richard D'Arcy.'

'How is it your business? What's he to you?'

'He's nothing to me – only one of those greedy bastards who put honest men out of work for fear they'd have a union. And the worst of them at that. The richest man in Dublin and the first to have scabs in. And him after locking out men with twenty years' good service.'

'Ah, will you ever cop on to yourself!' Stephen shouted. 'The lockout's over. It's finished, and it failed. Most of the men have gone back to work and they're glad to take money from the likes of Richard D'Arcy. If you want to carry a grudge, then go ahead, but I won't help you. It's his daughter's birthday party. I know her, and I'm going.'

He turned on his heel and walked down the hall to the front door.

'You're as bad as a scab,' Joe called after him.

'I don't care, I'm going.'

'I hope you choke on the cake,' he heard his brother shout, before the front door slammed behind him.

The bang of the door echoed around the empty street. The kids had all gone in for their tea, and the only thing disturbed by the noise was an old dog that sat up on the steps of the tenement house and then busily set to scratching himself.

Stephen stood for a moment and took a few deep breaths. Always the bloody same, always a flaming row. Why couldn't Joe just keep his flaming mouth shut? But to hell with him! He decided he wasn't going to let his brother spoil the evening. Straightening the hat on his head, he turned and went on his way, enjoying the quiet and the smell of roasting hops that the warm breeze carried down from Guinness's brewery.

It took him a little while to realize that something wasn't right. It was a nagging feeling that grew on him as he walked towards Trinity College. He had lived in Dublin all his life and he was familiar with the rhythms, the heartbeat of the city. He knew it was the August fortnight and many people were on holidays – but this was too quiet. Not a soul stirred as he passed along the empty streets, not a tram or a cart. Nothing, until he walked past the train station at Westland Row and saw the soldiers outside. That jarred on him. They weren't lounging outside having a fag and a laugh, but solemnly standing guard, rifles at the slope. There were more at the railway bridge; stiff, silent, but eyeing him as he passed. Next he saw an empty news-stand still blaring the morning headline:

WE CANNOT STAND ASIDE

Finally, the penny dropped: that was it. War was looming, and the city was holding its breath.

Only when he walked through the front gate of Trinity College did Stephen feel any sense of relief. It was as if those high walls could keep anything out – even the threat of war. The Front Square was quiet and peaceful, with birds singing in the trees and the evening air as still as water. Five minutes from his house, and it was as if he'd walked into another world.

But it wasn't his world, not really. Even now, he felt like an interloper, a thief, stealing across the square. He tried to walk with a measured, regal step, following the tap-tapping tip of his cane across the cobbles, but he couldn't shake that feeling. Three years as a student and he still wasn't at home, though Joe thought he was. Joe thought he'd climbed the golden ladder to a toff's paradise and turned posh the minute he walked through the gates. But he was wrong: it wasn't like that. Stephen wasn't posh. He was among toffs, but not like them. And they had an innate sense for these things. They could tell he was from below the salt.

Then again, he wasn't like Joe either – not any more. This place had marked him as far as his own class was concerned. They respected learning, but suspected it also. Education was the province of others, of owners and bosses. In coming here he'd changed sides; he'd left his own people behind and he could never go back. They had an innate sense of these things too.

But he'd known that would happen. He'd known damn well and still he'd fought his way in here. In the end it came down to talent and sheer bloody-mindedness. He'd provided the one and Mr Keogh, his maths teacher, the other. Mr Keogh was the one who'd put the idea in his head, who'd told him not only that he *could* go to university, but that he *should* go, he *must* go – it would be a terrible shame to waste the gift he'd been given.

'They can't keep you out, not with what you have in there!' Keogh used to say, and he would rap his bony knuckles on Stephen's skull as he pored over a book. But it wouldn't be easy – his father could never afford the fees. He would need a scholarship, or a sizarship as they called it at Trinity. Two years of hard work followed, and old Keogh had brought him to the entrance exams himself, standing behind him like a cat on hot bricks while Stephen signed his name in the roll, and solemnly shaking his hand before he went into the hall. As he sat at his allotted desk and waited for the examination paper, he wondered if Mr Keogh had once sat here. He had never gone to university himself, but had he tried? Had he tried and failed? Stephen had never considered failure, but now that the moment had arrived, now that the invigilator was coming down the line of desks with a sheaf of papers, he felt his throat go dry and his palms turn clammy.

Keogh was dismayed that he came out so quickly. He should have stayed in, checked his answers, made adjustments. Even after he'd gone through the paper line by line, Keogh wasn't satisfied. Was he sure? Had he done everything he could? It wasn't enough just to pass – any fool could pass. He had to excel. But Stephen knew he'd excelled, and wasn't surprised when he opened the letter from the university. Keogh had wept with joy when he showed him the result. A sizarship to study mathematics at Trinity College. It was his greatest achievement in twenty years of teaching, and his greatest victory in a lifelong battle with the Christian Brothers. But they conceded it only grudgingly. Noses were turned up and disapproving stares directed at Stephen. The boy had a gift, no doubt, but why couldn't he go to the Catholic university? Surely the Protestants would corrupt him. As the pressure mounted, Stephen had wavered, but Keogh remained defiant: 'Don't you listen to them, Stephen: they're only jealous, the small-minded bastards. You'll show them. You'll be better than they ever were.'

'Stephen! Up here!' The shout rang around the square, and Stephen looked up to see a moon face thrust under the sash and an arm waving furiously from a window on the top floor of the Rubrics. Billy was in his new lair – one of the corrupting Protestants. He smiled to himself. If they only knew, the Christian Brothers would be in like a light, dragging him out by the scruff of his neck. He waved back.

'Come up! Come up and see!'

He went up by the narrow winding stairs. The Rubrics was the oldest building in the college and it smelled like it. The top floor was like something out of a tenement, with low ceilings, warped floorboards and patches of horsehair showing in the walls. As he came up to the landing he could hear pigeons cooing in the attic above and he wondered how long Billy would last this time? Every year he took rooms in college and every year, when the damp and the squalor became too much, he vacated them by Christmas. When this happened he went back to his aunt's mansion in Rathgar, but he could never settle there. Billy wasn't comfortable in the bosom of his family, and by Easter he would be dreaming of a poky little room he could call his lair.

The last door on the landing stood ajar, and when Stephen looked inside he saw Billy's round face looking back at him from the oval mirror of a dressing table.

'Come in, come in,' he beamed. 'Don't be shy.'

Stephen stepped through the door and stumbled over a suitcase lying open on the floor.

'Oh, dear me, Stephen. Are you all right? Do excuse the mess. Just moving in, you know. What do you think of the place?'

Straightening up, he found his head almost touched the ceiling, which was cracked and yellowed and cobwebbed in the corners. Apart from the dressing table, which seemed to double as a desk, the only furniture was a chair and a narrow bed, both of them covered with suitcases and clothes and stacks of books and papers. A white silk evening scarf hung over the reading lamp and Billy stood in a clearing at the window, doing something with his tie.

'It's a bit small, isn't it?' Stephen answered dubiously.

'It's cosy, Stephen. That's the word you were looking for. Cosy – not to mention well appointed.' He gestured out the window, where the Front Square lay before him. 'I have the most agreeable view in the college and the bathroom is just next ... Stephen, why are you making a face?'

'What's that smell?'

'Oh, that? Mothballs, I believe. Or turf. The previous tenant was of a rustic persuasion and used to burn it in the grate. The discerning palate may also detect a hint of damp, I admit. But it's not so bad once you get used to it.'

Stephen knew what mothballs smelled like, and he was familiar with turf smoke. This was neither. 'It smells like a dosshouse,' he said bluntly.

The grin faded from Billy's face. He sighed.

'You're right. It does pong a bit, doesn't it? I suppose I shall have to leave the window open for a while to air it out. And those flaming pigeons had better go to sleep at a reasonable hour!' He stopped fiddling with his tie and turned away from the mirror, 'Can you do something with this, Stephen? I have the fingers of a navvy.'

Stephen dropped his top hat and cane on the bed and set to work on the knot while Billy obediently stood still and looked past his shoulder. Billy was a good deal shorter than he and much broader around the waist. He had sparse blond hair and bright little eyes that shone out from behind his round spectacles.

'So how are things chez Ryan?' he asked, 'Everything all right?'

'Billy, this would be much easier if you didn't talk.' The collar stud had come undone and he deftly closed it without letting go of the tie.

'Sorry.'

The stud popped open again.

'Billy!'

A mute apologetic smile as Stephen closed the stud again and swiftly whipped the tie into a neat knot.

'Since you ask, things are not good chez Ryan,' he said grimly, adjusting the tie so it sat straight under Billy's chin, 'As a matter of fact, everything is far from all right. I've just had another row with my flaming brother.'

'Hmm?'

'You can talk now.' Stephen put a hand on each shoulder and turned him back towards the mirror.

Billy admired himself for a few seconds before he asked, 'When was this?'

'Just now, before I came out.'

'Oh dear! He's not still moaning about you going to college when you could be earning an honest wage, is he?'

'A variation on that theme. He told me I should be ashamed of myself, going to a party with my father lying sick in his bed.'

'But your father's been sick for ages. I don't see how donning the sackcloth and ashes is going to make him any better.'

'That's more or less what I said. But I don't think it's the party he objects to as much as who's throwing it.'

'Ah, of course!' Billy took his jacket from a hanger and shrugged it on, 'Old man D'Arcy was no friend to the workers during last year's unpleasantness, was he? To a trade union man like your brother I'm sure it looks very much like you're supping with the Devil. But I'm sure he'll get over it eventually. And how is your father? Bearing up?'

'Hanging on is more like it,' Stephen said bleakly, and he sat down on the edge of the bed and told Billy about Phillips's visit and what he'd said about his father's leg.

Billy listened attentively, watching him as he talked. Strange how he chose to confide in him of all people – after all, they'd only known one another for three years. But what a change Billy had seen in that time. He remembered the boy he'd seen on his first day in college: an ungainly-looking creature in a threadbare suit and heavy boots. But the suit, though ill fitting, was clean and freshly pressed, and the boots were polished to a high shine. He didn't have much, but he made the best of what he had. There was a dogged pride in his bearing – he knew he couldn't match all the blazers and bowlers and silk ties, but if he didn't come up to scratch it wasn't his fault. Still, there was no mistaking another misfit, and one painfully aware of it too. It was that which had drawn Billy to him in the first place; a mixture of pity and curiosity propelling him across the square to where Stephen stood eating thick sandwiches from a parcel of newspaper. To look at him now, with his silk topper and silver-topped cane, was to see the butterfly emerged from the chrysalis.

Still, he often wondered how they had become such close friends. They had little enough in common – different backgrounds, different classes and one enormous difference that Billy still quailed to think of. That misjudged kiss. God! What was he thinking? It had happened in a dingy little room just like this one, after they'd whiled away half the evening talking and joking together. A few glasses of sherry and he'd seen the shy, reticent scholarship boy melting away and the real Stephen opening like a flower. He thought he'd seen something else too, but in the giddy heat of the moment he had misjudged it. Oh, he was sure he was being so bloody cosmopolitan, chattering on about Oscar Wilde. A former student here, did he know? Of course he knew. He was anything but stupid. Of course he'd read the plays – and the poems, and the prose – but not out of any devotion to Wilde. He'd read them because he read everything he could get his hands on, but Billy never thought of that. The sudden urge that came on him had blotted everything else out. Their friendship was barely two weeks old and he'd nearly wrecked it with that foolhardy, hasty kiss. He knew it the moment he felt Stephen pushing him away and standing up. The look of shock on his face nearly stilled his heart. He was still sitting on the bed, his legs still crossed, one sweaty hand on the coverlet, but he almost fainted at the thought of what might happen next. An appalling vista opened before him; shame, rejection. He would be sent down at the very least, his life ruined. But Stephen had stopped with his hand on the door. He was disconcerted, but not disgusted.

'I'm not like that,' was all he said, and sat down again.

Listening to him now, Billy realized that any guilt he might have felt was as nothing compared to Stephen's. Poor devil, he thought. The Christian Brothers had done a right job on him in that department. *Mea culpa, mea culpa, mea maxima culpa.* What could he do for his father but make the best of his gifts? He had a talent for mathematics – a rare talent if the reports were true – but guilt would eat it all out of him if he wasn't careful. And his flaming brother didn't help. He had a neck, accusing Stephen of living it up when he paid the rent and put food on the table by giving lessons and tutoring schoolchildren. But Joe's words had hit home and hurt; Billy could see it even in the way Stephen sat on the bed, perched on the edge, not quite at ease.

'Very moral, your brother,' Billy said when Stephen finished talking. 'And I don't mean that in a good way. Look where morals have brought us now, look.' He picked up a newspaper from the cluttered desk and handed it to Stephen, who read the headline:

GERMANY DECLARES WAR ON RUSSIA

Stephen gave him a sceptical look.

'Moral? I'm curious to hear how you think war is moral.'

'It's not! Of course it's not!' Billy called over his shoulder as he rummaged around his desk, 'But I bet you'll find that all those top-hatted buggers who started it are terribly moral. Fine, upstanding, churchgoing men one and all. Men of honour, I'm sure they'd say. They honour their stupid bloody terribly moral treaties – for

Brutus is an honourable man! I dare say they'd stand by a bargain with the Devil. I mean, there's Germany going to war with Russia because one's got an agreement with Austria and the other with Servia. No other earthly bloody reason to fight, but they'll do it anyway because a couple of old farts shook hands on it. And we'll be in it next – you mark my words. We cannot stand aside, they say. We're all chained together by flaming agreements, the whole bloody lot of us. Ha!' Billy triumphantly held up a half-bottle of Bushmills and shook it at Stephen, 'What about a snifter before we walk up?'

'Why not?' Stephen threw the newspaper on the bed, but his eye was drawn to it as Billy went looking for glasses. 'I'm sure it'll all blow over,' he said, absently reading the words again. 'It's all just bluster. They'll sort something out.'

'You must be bloody joking,' Billy chuckled, and Stephen noted the high colour in his cheeks. He always flushed when he was excited, though that was usually only when he got started on Home Rule. 'It's gone too far for that now. They're bombing Belgrade already. Did you hear what Lord Grey said in the Commons? About the lamps going out all over Europe. Well, when the Foreign Secretary starts talking doom like that, you know the game is up. King Solomon couldn't sort this one out. We'll be at war next week, no two ways about it, and God help us all.'

He picked two glasses from a drawer, cleared a spot on the desk and poured a generous measure of whiskey into each. He handed one to Stephen and raised his own.

'Well, here's to all those moral people and the trouble they get us into.'

'Here's to them,' Stephen agreed, and swallowed half his glass, wincing as the whiskey burned his throat. He shook his head as if to clear it, and added, 'Though I'm not sure if Joe is as moral as all that. Did I tell you he's got a gun?'

The sombre look that had settled over Billy's face cleared in an instant. 'A gun?' he asked disbelievingly, 'What sort of gun? And where did he get it?'

'Howth, I imagine,' Stephen said with a shrug, and went on to tell him about finding the rifle in the parlour, and how he had sprung it on his brother before storming out.

'Bloody hell!' Billy exclaimed, 'But how do you know it was part of the Howth shipment? Are you sure?'

'I know a thing or two about guns, Billy. It was a single-shot rifle, rather old, German-made. I'd say it fits the bill, according to what I read in the newspapers.'

'Well, well, well! A smuggled rifle!' Billy broke into a delighted grin and sat down on the bed beside Stephen, 'Not that there's anything unusual about that. I mean, every dog, cat and devil seems to be smuggling guns these days, but still! Where is it now? Has he still got it?'

'If he does, he's moved it out of the house. And good riddance – it damn near ruined my suit with all the grease.'

'But how did he get it? The National Volunteers brought in those guns. Your brother's not in the Volunteers, is he?'

'No, the Citizen Army.'

'But I heard they didn't get on with the Volunteers.'

'Well, they didn't before. But I dare say with the Unionists smuggling in their own guns and the war coming, they didn't want to be left out. Anyway, according to Joe, his friend Connolly is the coming man in the Citizen Army, and he's much more of the Volunteer way of thinking.'

'God's my life,' Billy sighed. 'All these guns. It's bound to end in a fight!'

II

The richness of the scene was overpowering: candlelight and the rustle of taffeta and the thump of dancing feet and the swish of dresses whirling past. The air was heavy with the smell of perfume and cologne and hummed with polite conversation. It was making him dizzy.

'I suppose it hasn't occurred to your brother,' Billy was saying, 'that you are striking a blow for the workers simply by being here.' He paused to gesture as expansively as he could with a champagne flute in one hand and an overflowing plate in the other. 'I mean, every morsel of food you eat comes directly from the coffers of old man D'Arcy. And since he's usually as tight as the proverbial duck's arse, the fact that our cups overfloweth at his expense makes it all the more tasty, if you ask me.'

Stephen smiled and rocked back on his feet. He wasn't terribly drunk, but he was drunk enough to feel his face flushed and his skin prickling. He should never have let Billy talk him into polishing off that bottle of Bushmills. Whiskey had never agreed with him and he'd felt a sullen heaviness settle on him after the first glass. When it finally came time to leave he felt muzzy and tired and it took an effort just to get up off the bed. Billy was still rattling away fourteen to the dozen about the war and Home Rule and how it was all such a mess, but Stephen could hardly hear him. When he got out onto the landing, a wave of nausea washed over him and he had to steady himself against the wall as Billy bent down to lock the door, taking an inordinately long time to insert the big iron key.

The short walk up to Kildare Street had done little to clear his head. As they crossed the patio to the ballroom, the music blared out at him, unnaturally loud, and he stopped at the door, dazzled. The band was playing a waltz, the floor filled with whirling couples, and the golden light of hundreds of candles was reflected in a rolling sea of sequins and shining silk. He wasn't ready for this, he thought; he was an impostor, a costumed fool who'd be found out the moment he opened his mouth. He felt his resolve failing, and he had to overcome the urge to turn around and walk away. It was all right for Billy – he was born to this. He was already inside, gazing around and laughing, completely in his element. But fearing Billy might slip away into the crowd, Stephen found himself hurrying after him, automatically straightening up and squaring his shoulders.

'Sigh no more, ladies.' He grinned, when he caught up.

'Speak for yourself.' Billy hardly looked at him. He had spotted the buffet table, which stretched the whole length of one wall, 'I don't know about you, but I'm famished. What about a bite to eat before we start?'

That was twenty minutes ago and they were still at the table. Billy was on his second plate of smoked salmon and vol-au-vents, but Stephen had no appetite. He had tried a single sliver of ham on brown bread, but found it turned to ashes in his mouth. Even the champagne tasted sour and fizzy. He was feeling more and more unwell, and all he wanted to do was to sit down somewhere quiet for a while.

But the rhythmic motion of the dancers was hypnotic and he felt himself slipping into a trance as he watched them fly past.

Now and then a familiar face appeared in the throng. There was Mary D'Arcy herself, flashing by in a turquoise gown and diamonds. He followed her for a few moments, watching the bob of her head and the flash of her smile. *Ah, Mary, Mary, quite contrary!* Strange how little she moved him now. He remembered the first time he ever saw her, how smitten he was. He thought she was the most beautiful creature he'd ever set eyes on: as small and delicate as a doll, with a porcelain-white face and dark green eyes. He'd craved a smile, a look, anything to show that she had noticed him, but eventually he realized that it would never come. He'd screwed up his courage once and bid her good morning, braving the curious looks of her friends as they walked to an early lecture. She'd smiled at him then, but it was merely polite, nothing in the eyes, and when he walked away he'd heard them laughing behind his back. He'd hated her then, but even that had faded and now he realized that she meant nothing to him, neither good nor bad. It seemed to him that she hadn't changed in three years. She was made up differently, she wore a different dress, but the essence hadn't changed. He heard her high trilling laugh and knew it was the same laugh he'd heard before. *Exactly* the same – like the call of some exotic bird. There was nothing else to her, he reflected. All she had was her looks and her laugh. Nothing more. She *was* a doll.

The band finished their tune with a decisive double note and the dancing couples came to rest, breaking apart and applauding. The sudden stop brought Stephen to his senses. He saw Mary again, clapping madly, and then her father appeared behind her, bending to whisper something in her ear. Impeccably dressed and plump as a pigeon, he had the smooth well-fed look of enormous wealth. A self-made man, by all accounts. A barrow-boy who'd managed to become the biggest bonded merchant in the city. But there was something faintly reptilian about him, something that made the flesh crawl. Maybe Joe wasn't far off the mark: D'Arcy would buy and sell anybody to get what he wanted. But Stephen put that from his mind. It could be he was looking at his future over there. He would graduate next year and then he would need a job – and Richard D'Arcy might be the man to give him one. Actuarial work, he thought, and his heart sank. He'd be a glorified bookkeeper. He saw a small office with grimy windows and endless rows of figures stretching away into despair and middle age. It didn't appeal to him in the least, but what choice did he have?

'You are not keeping your end up, Stephen,' Billy broke in, wiping his mouth with a napkin. 'What's the matter? Are you off your hay?'

'I'm not hungry.'

'Oh? Well, it's your loss, because this grub's lovely. What are you staring at? Well, well, if it isn't the Belle of the Ball herself? Thinking of asking her for a dance, were we?'

'No fear,' Stephen said, without taking his eyes off her, and Billy nodded slowly to himself. Although he'd never said anything, he knew Stephen had once had notions about Mary D'Arcy. Foolish notions, to be sure, but perhaps all the more vulnerable for that.

'Just as well, because she's already spoken for. She is – what's that word? Affianced. Yes, that's it. The dear girl is soon to be married.' He said this knowing full well it would get Stephen's attention, and smiled complacently at the look of wide-eyed disbelief. 'What? Don't tell me you didn't see the engagement notice in today's *Times*?'

Too late, Stephen tried to mask his surprise. 'I don't have time to read the engagement notices,' he said gruffly. 'Some of us have better things to be doing.'

'Well, I'm surprised you missed it. It was practically on the front page. Mr and Mrs Richard D'Arcy, of New Money and lots of it, are delighted to announce the engagement of their daughter, Mary, to Mr Alfred Devereux, of Old Money . . .'

'Alfred Devereux?' Stephen grimaced, 'The man's an ass!'

'Yes, he is. And she's a vapid little vixen, so it's a match made in heaven if you ask me. But don't tell me you're surprised – the pair of them have been knocking around together for years. Besides, his family owns half of Waterford, not to mention all those newspapers, and everybody knows Daddy D'Arcy is a very shrewd businessman. You didn't think he'd let his only daughter marry the first young chap with a twinkle in his eye, did you? Oh, and speak of the Devil, there's Devereux himself, trotting after his future father-in-law like a good little lapdog.'

This brought a smile to Stephen's face as he spotted Devereux, bending down to snatch a kiss from his fiancée. Lapdog? Bulldog was more like it. He wasn't very tall, but he was broad-shouldered and so powerfully built he looked as if he could crush her in his fist. Handsome too, Stephen had to admit; dark and deep-voiced, and exuding an air of barely contained energy. He was captain of the rugby team, platoon leader in the Officer Training Corps, and the heir to a fortune. Billy was right: he shouldn't have been surprised. If ever there was a husband for Mary D'Arcy, it was Alfred Devereux.

'It's been quite a week for him, between one thing and another,' Billy went on. 'Apparently he's taken a commission in the army as well. The way things are going, it looks like he'll soon be off to bash the Hun for King and Country.'

'No surprise there,' Stephen observed. 'His uncle's a general or something on the Imperial Staff. I've often heard him bragging about him.'

'Haven't we all? God help us, Stephen, the chap's already a world-class bore. Can you imagine what he'll be like if he joins the army? If he doesn't get killed he'll come home laden with medals and tales of derring-do. Just when you thought he couldn't be any more unbearable, eh?'

Billy chuckled to himself and shoved his glasses up on the bridge of his nose as he scanned the room for more targets. His eye fell on a tall girl in a black dress who stood alone near the far end of the buffet table. He nudged Stephen with his elbow.

'Now there's someone who's much more up your street.'

Stephen followed his look and frowned. 'Lillian Bryce?' he murmured in surprise, 'She's the last person I expected to see here.'

Even more surprising was the transformation. Billy had once mockingly described her as a Protestant nun and, like most of Billy's little barbs, there was truth at the heart of it. With her short hair and thick glasses, and always dressed in black from head to toe, she had an aura of austerity that didn't invite a second look. But not tonight. She still had the glasses, and her dress was still black, but it showed off her slim figure and long limbs and was set off perfectly by the emerald pendant around her slender neck. Quite the revelation, Stephen mused, looking at her. He felt he was seeing her at last as she really was. She might not have had the doll's face and pert figure of Mary D'Arcy, but there was something else about her, something that intrigued him.

As he watched, she turned her head towards him. Their eyes met for an instant, but they both looked away quickly. He smiled to himself, embarrassed, but thrilled. *She's just as bad as I am.*

'Why don't you go and try your charms on her?' Billy suggested, as the band struck into another tune and the whole floor began to move. 'Come to think of it, you'd be a perfect match. Two mathematicians! The pair of you could jaw on about logarithms and theorems until you're blue in the face.'

Stephen threw Billy a sharp glance. That was a bit close to the mark.

'Since when did you go into business as a matchmaker?'

'Ooh! Have I touched a nerve?'

'No.'

Liar. He risked another glance in her direction. Strange that he'd hardly paid her any attention before. Of course, he'd noticed her, but thought it was kinder to ignore her. She got enough attention from the old-fashioned element – the diehards who still thought women shouldn't be admitted to college. They were the ones who jeered her into every lecture, knuckles and books drumming on the desks until she sat down. Small wonder she usually came in early, took a seat in a quiet corner and left as soon as the lecture was finished. He had to admire her for that. It took strength to put up with it, day in, day out. He wouldn't have done it.

Billy looked him up and down, amused. 'Dear me! Don't tell me you're still smarting after that drubbing she gave you last term?'

Stephen turned his head and glared at Billy.

'That was not a drubbing,' he said primly. 'She pointed out a flaw in my paper and we worked out a solution between us. It was more in the way of a debate.'

'A debate, was it? I heard she cut you off at the knees. And whatever you want to call it, it can't have been pleasant having the wind taken out of your sails by the only girl in the class.'

'The only girl in the class happens to be an exceptional mathematician.'

He could say that now without reservation. But how had he not seen it before? He'd thought her interests lay closer to astronomy than pure mathematics. Apparently, she had written a paper on Professor Einstein's special theory of relativity that Professor Barrett had rated as very good, but a shade too radical for his taste. He knew she was able – probably more able than the men who booed and heckled her – but he'd not suspected such deep insight, such penetration.

But then again, he'd grown too complacent. After all, he was Professor Barrett's golden boy, and not prone to errors. Every year was the same: another prize, more accolades. But this year he'd slipped, and slipped in a way that was so subtle, so barely out of line, that nobody noticed. Not him, not Professor Barrett, not the rest of the class. They had listened to his paper with polite attention, and applauded when he was finished. Delighted and embarrassed all at the same time, he'd hardly noticed this tall girl standing up at the back of the room.

'Exceptional, indeed?' Billy gave him a sidelong look and smothered a laugh. 'So, you had just presented this paper of yours – what was it called again?'

'On Lucas numbers and Mersenne primes.'

'And fascinating I'm sure it was. But in any case, she stood up and said it was a load of rubbish . . .'

'She didn't say it was rubbish. As I said, she pointed out a f—'

'I rest my case.'

Stephen rolled his eyes. Billy was studying law; training to win the debate at all costs. The concept of refining a proof through argument was alien to him. Still, he wasn't far out in one respect: Lillian had caused such a stir when she stood up that she might as well have said he was talking rubbish. As the applause died away, he'd heard a polite cough, and then, 'Excuse me?'

The lecture hall fell into a deep hush, and Professor Barrett turned around in his seat to examine her over the top of his half-moon spectacles.

'You have something you wish to add, Miss Bryce?'

'I believe Mr Ryan has made a mistake, sir.'

'I even heard old Barrett sent someone to round up the freshmen – so they could see a genuine mathematical prize fight,' Billy added.

'Well, that was later on.'

Barrett had continued to stare at her for several seconds. Stephen looked from him to her and back again, while Lillian stood her ground, her eyes fixed on the blackboard where Stephen had written his proof. At last Barrett gave a puzzled grunt, and gestured towards the blackboard.

'Then I suppose you had better explain your contention, Miss Bryce.'

There was no jeering or booing as she came down to the board. This was so unprecedented that he could hear the creaking of chairs as everybody leaned forward in anticipation. Stephen handed her the chalk, wondering if this was some sort of elaborate stunt – was she trying to make a fool of him? But her eyes were fixed on the board. She considered it for a moment and then, in three short sentences – punctuated by swift, sure strokes of the chalk – drove a stake through the heart of his proof.

The first thing he realized was that she was absolutely right. Once she'd turned on the light, it was blinding. One look at Professor Barrett confirmed it. His eyes were wide behind his glasses, and his look was a mixture of shock and amusement. This was indeed unprecedented.

'Mr Ryan, can you find fault with any of those statements?'

Even though he already knew the answer, he made himself study the blackboard for almost a minute, his hands thrust deep in his pockets, trying his best to appear nonchalant, unperturbed. But his mind was racing. The moment he'd seen what she was driving at, he had started working, building a solution; moving the pieces, rearranging things, patching his proof. Two of the problems were easily fixed and as he studied the board he thought he saw a glimmer of hope for the third. It was enough. He turned around.

'No, sir, Miss Bryce is quite correct in her assertions. However, if you will permit me, I believe I can modify my proof in order to satisfy all conditions.'

'I should bloody well hope so,' Professor Barrett muttered under his breath. Then, in a louder voice, he added, 'Very well, Mr Ryan. Let's see it. Miss Bryce, please remain where you are. We shall rely on you to make sure our friend doesn't stray any further from the truth.'

She turned and handed him the chalk, looking at him steadily with her grey-blue eyes, a faint smile playing about her lips. She was enjoying this.

He could feel her eyes on him as he wrote out the first rebuttal, and knowing before he had even finished where it was weak. She knew it too, she knew it very well – that much was obvious. But instead of attacking again, she proposed an alternative, and he countered it, and so it went – the best hour's work he'd ever done. It was feverish, the two of them working at the blackboard, completely absorbed, completely unaware of the crowd that was filling the lecture hall. When it was done, Stephen's original proof had expanded to fill two blackboards and taken on a beautiful life of its own. It was much more complex, but it was also elegant and perfect. The lecture hall stood completely silent for almost a minute, and then Professor Barrett was on his feet, leading the applause.

A gentle nudge from Billy's elbow brought him back to the present. 'Aren't you going to ask her to dance? She won't stay there all night.'

Stephen's stomach turned over. 'Dance?' he stammered, seized by doubt. 'No. Why would I ask her to dance?'

'Oh my God. I've come out with a wallflower.'

'But she's a suffragette. She probably doesn't like to dance.'

'Dear Stephen, let us forget for the moment that I'm probably the last person you should be asking about women . . .'

'But I didn't ask you.'

'Yes, well, not in so many words, perhaps,' Billy puffed up his chest and brushed a few crumbs from the front of his jacket. He often liked to imagine himself in a courtroom, 'But let us examine the facts of this case in a cool and rational fashion. First of all, the girl is a suffragette – she gets it from her mother, I understand, but that's beside the point. She is an advocate of women's rights, not a flaming nun! Second, this is a ballroom, a place of dancing, and she is standing in it. Ergo, of course she flaming well wants to dance. Furthermore, she is a woman, and convention dictates that she cannot dance unless invited to do so by a man. You are a man, are you not, Stephen? You can help her out of her predicament.'

'I can't dance,' Stephen said, shaking his head.

'Are you afraid of her, Stephen?' Billy asked earnestly.

'Me? No, of course not.'

'Then what the bloody hell are you waiting for?'

'I don't think she likes me.'

'Oh, don't be such an ass. Of course she likes you. She's been making eyes at you for half the evening.'

'No she hasn't.' Stephen felt his cheeks beginning to redden, 'She's probably looking for her sister.'

'Oh, balls, Stephen,' Billy laughed and clapped him on the shoulder. 'You're a terrible liar. You are afraid of her, aren't you? Go on, admit it.'

This was more than he could bear, and Stephen set his glass down and straightened his tie. 'All right,' he muttered, 'I'll ask her to dance.' His mouth was dry but his mind was set. How hard could it be? Just go up to her, smile, say good evening, and take it from there. It couldn't be easier.

'Not that I'd blame you if you were. Those votes-for-women gals can be a bit fierce. Did you know her mother was arrested for breaking the windows of one of the Devereux newspapers?

Apparently, they printed an editorial that more or less said women should stick to needlepoint and having babies, so Mrs B dashed off a stinker of a letter to the editor. They refused to print it, so she took the train down to Wicklow and marched around to demand an explanation. The editor wouldn't even give her the time of day, never mind print her letter, so she went back outside, wrapped the letter around a brick and heaved it through the window. Hell hath no fury, and so forth. But Bryce *filia* has a bit more charm, don't you think? I see her as a Spartan woman: fierce, warlike, but loyal . . .'

'Shut up, Billy.'

'That's not to say she won't bite, however.'

'I said, I'm going to ask her.'

But his timing couldn't have been worse. The music died away once more, and the bandleader announced a short break. In moments, the buffet table was crowded with hungry dancers. A solid wedge of young men came in at a rush, and he recognized a coterie of Devereux's friends from the rugby team. Devereux himself was in the lead, rubbing his hands and grinning wolfishly.

'Come on, boys, we'll be at war soon, and then it'll be bully beef and cold tea. Let's make hay while the sun shines!'

He snatched up an éclair and devoured it in one bite, smearing his lips with crumbs and cream and chomping it down with his eyes bulging. Following his lead, his friends set upon the food like wild dogs.

'Bloody hell,' Billy muttered, watching them with some distaste. 'It's like a Roman orgy.'

Then they heard Devereux exclaim in a loud, drunken voice:

'Good God. It's the Bryce girl. I didn't think they'd let her sort in.'

'Votes for women!' One of his gang called out, in a high falsetto, followed by a snort of laughter.

Lillian looked away, ignoring him, but Devereux wasn't to be put off. He swaggered up to her, laughing. 'You'd better behave yourself tonight, Bryce. We'll have none of your suffragette tricks here. This is a civilized occasion.'

She didn't answer, but only gave him a stony look as he closed in and started to circle her. He looked her up and down like a farmer might assay a head of beef, but she refused to play his game. She turned with him, watching him silently, warily.

'Well, at least you've cleaned yourself up a bit. You know, you don't look too bad when you make an effort. Still a bit mannish, if you ask me, but I suppose that's the intention with you suffs, eh?'

'I can't watch this,' whispered Stephen, 'he's making a show of her!' He made to push his way through the throng that cut him off from the grubby scene, but Billy stopped him with a hand on his arm.

'Steady on, old man,' he murmured, nodding at the broad backs of the rugby team. 'Don't forget you're in the lion's den. Besides, I don't think she needs your help. She is a Spartan woman, remember? And she has the look of a cornered she-cat. Have no fear, she's well able for *him*.'

This was becoming clear, even though Devereux was still circling her with his hands on his hips. His audience was getting restless and he was coming off badly against Lillian's silent dignity.

'So why are you here, Bryce? Trying to snare yourself a man, perhaps?' He turned to his friends, 'What about it, boys? Any takers? No? You see, Bryce, you can dress up all you want, but you're not fooling anybody. What man in his right mind would go with a suffragette? Eh? I mean, just look at your father. He didn't hang around once he'd realized his mistake. Daddy went running away to sea and never came back and who could blame—'

She cut him off short with a slap. It was so hard that his head

33

turned half around and he staggered backwards a few steps. The crowd gasped, but Lillian made no sound as she turned on her heel and walked towards the door. Her head was high and proud, but she was barely in control of herself. She looked as if she might cry. The crowd parted to let her pass and Devereux watched her leave with his hand to his cheek, his friends looking at him as if they wanted to laugh, but were afraid to.

Billy had no such qualms. He chuckled gleefully and poked Stephen with his elbow. 'What did I tell you?' he whispered, 'A Spartan woman.'

Stephen hardly even noticed. He was staring at Devereux, who was still rubbing his cheek, but laughing it off with his friends.

'That man is a pig,' he said.

'Indeed and he is. But she certainly put him in his place. Did you see that smack she hit him? God, I nearly felt it myself. But what was that crack about her father? I didn't quite catch his drift, though she clearly did. Bang! Right on the kisser. That softened his cough, didn't it?'

'Her father was a sea officer with the White Star Line,' Stephen explained. 'He went down with *Titanic*.'

'Oh?' Billy stopped laughing and his face turned serious as his eyes darted from Devereux to Lillian, who had almost reached the door. A few curious heads turned in her direction, quite unaware of what had happened. 'Well then, he certainly had *that* coming, the ignorant swine. All the same, I'm afraid he's rather dished your chances of getting a dance. She won't be back now – and more's the pity. You couldn't go wrong with a girl who has such a good right hook.'

Stephen wasn't listening to him. The crowd was dissolving, the tension easing, but he still felt it coiled up inside him. His head was clear now, his muscles tense. He'd never had anything to do with Devereux but he knew what he was like. He'd heard some of the talk that went on behind his back and he knew Devereux despised him, as he despised everybody who didn't fit into his social circle. It could as easily have been Stephen he picked on instead of Lillian Bryce, and now Stephen wished he had. He was angry. Was this what burned inside his brother? This rage against injustice? Was it that hot? But Joe had it wrong. Joe was seeking to turn the world on its head, to pull down the pillars and let the roof come crashing down. That would never happen. It was just too big, too grand a scheme for mere men to manage. Devereux's kind would endure. They would live through storm and flood, through war and revolution. The only way to deal with them was one at a time.

The way cleared in front of him, and he picked his way through the crowd to where Devereux stood. He was still rubbing his cheek, but he was regaining his composure, holding court.

'I knew they shouldn't have let that Jezebel in here,' he declared, as Stephen stepped in front of him. He was taller than Devereux, and held himself dead straight, his arms down by his side, his fists clenched. Despite the difference in height, Devereux still looked twice his size.

'What do you want, Reilly?' he sneered, 'What's the matter? Is the free food not up to scratch?'

'My name is Ryan,' said Stephen coldly. 'And you're a pig, Devereux.'

'Oh? And you can talk,' Devereux grinned at his friends, who were still loosely crowded around. 'I'm sorry; did I offend you by teasing the suffragette? Well, maybe I spoke too soon. Maybe she can get herself a man after all – if she doesn't mind taking one from the slums.'

Stephen's voice was barely audible through the guffaws from the others. 'You watch your mouth.'

'Why? Are you going to make me?' Devereux pushed himself

closer, his eyes going hard. 'Come on then, let's have it.' He placed his hand on Stephen's chest and pushed provocatively.

'I wouldn't waste my time.'

'Oh, well I would,' Devereux said, and punched him low in the stomach.

It wasn't a very hard blow but Devereux knew what he was doing, and the breath went out of Stephen in a loud whoosh as he doubled over. Pain and nausea washed up from the pit of his stomach and for a moment he teetered on the brink, thinking he might actually throw up. But then he seemed to regain equilibrium. The nausea passed and he felt cold anger driving him upright again. Devereux wasn't expecting that; he'd already started to turn away, and only saw him out of the corner of his eye. Stephen swung back and hit him as hard as he could on his exposed left cheek. The blow wasn't as expertly delivered as Devereux's, but it was much, much harder. It connected with his jawbone and sent him staggering back against the table.

Stephen watched him go down and felt the first stirrings of triumph, mingled with disbelief. Then something heavy hit him in the back and he went down himself, falling to the floor under a welter of bodies.

After the heat and press of the ballroom, the cool air of the patio felt refreshingly clear. There was a stone seat near the doorway and Lillian sat there for a few moments, wiping her eyes with the back of her hand. She was glad she'd got out before the tears came. She hadn't cried since – well, since the White Star man came to tell them her father's ship was lost.

Even then she'd managed to hold it in. She'd known the moment she saw him standing on the doorstep. He was a little nondescript man in a grey raincoat, but she'd known before he ever opened his mouth that something dreadful had happened. Still, she kept

36

her composure. She showed him into the sitting room and offered him tea, and sat with her mother and sister as he told them the ship had struck an iceberg and sunk. When he finally explained that her father was not among the survivors, that there was no hope, none at all, the other two had broken down crying, but not Lillian. She had asked the questions that needed to be asked. Was there a body? What about the funeral?

Afterwards, when she was alone in her room, she cried for her father. She cried until the tears wouldn't come any more. He'd been away at sea for most of her life, but that made the time he was home all the sweeter, and she'd grown used to waiting for him; the pleasurable anticipation, the knowledge that every voyage out had an inevitable return. But not this voyage. To think he'd died alone and cold in the water was almost more than she could bear. The man said he'd done his duty; remained calm, helped people and probably saved lives, but that was small comfort to her. Small comfort, too, to know that she'd behaved as he would have wished – the calm one, the rock in the midst of the storm.

But damn Devereux for . . . Damn his impertinence! She was trying to calm herself, but she knew she was in a proper state. Her hand was still smarting from the slap – though she wasn't sorry about that. No, she was only sorry she'd let it get that far. She should have just walked away when she saw him coming. At least she would have saved herself the embarrassment.

In fact, she thought, she should never have come. And she wouldn't have, either, if Sheila hadn't kept pestering her. She'd been dying to go ever since she first heard about it, and Mary D'Arcy's birthday party was the talk of the town. She couldn't believe Lillian had an invitation and wasn't going to use it.

'But *everybody's* going, Lillie.'

'That's because everybody was invited, Sheila. It's only showing off they are.'

'But you *have* to go. You've known her since she was small. Sure, didn't you go to school with her?'

Lillian just smiled and said she'd see. The truth was that she didn't have fond memories of going to school with Mary D'Arcy. She would much rather have stayed at school in England, but her father's posting there had come to an end and they had decided to move back home to Dublin. So, at the age of thirteen, Lillian had found herself in a new school, a head taller than any girl in her class, and with an unmistakable trace of London in her accent. She was an easy target for Mary D'Arcy and her gang of privileged harpies. They called her lanky first, and then spotty because of her freckles, and mocked her accent, telling her it belonged to neither one place nor the other, but in the middle of the Irish Sea. Then she was specky for her glasses, and finally, teacher's pet, brainbox, know-it-all.

Recalling this litany of names did little to calm her down. In one sense the party was just what she'd expected from Mary; showing off her privilege, shoving Daddy's wealth down everybody's throat. Oh, she was better at it now, more subtle by far, but she was still a spiteful little bully.

But what was done was done, and no point in crying about it now. She tried to think what to do next. She'd left her sister inside – and her good shawl too – but wild horses wouldn't drag her back in there to fetch them. Not while that ape Devereux and his friends were still at large. She should go now, go home and get out of it. Her sister was old enough to make her own way home and she could come back for the shawl in the morning. But that wouldn't do. A cup of cocoa and a book in bed? That would be running away. But she wouldn't go back in. She would wait. She would . . . Oh! What was she thinking? Sitting out here in the dark, sulking. Pride is your sin, girl, she chided herself. What were you like with that poor Ryan boy? Giving him the eye one minute and then looking away like Cleopatra when he smiled at you. You need to make up your mind, or you'll be left. And now you're starting to sound like your mother.

She stood up and wiped her eyes with her handkerchief, but she still couldn't make up her mind what to do. Go home or go back in? She was about to sit down again, when there was the sound of a commotion from inside. The band had not yet resumed playing, and the peace of the patio had barely been disturbed by the low hubbub of polite conversation and the occasional peal of laughter. But here was a confused thunder of feet coming to the doors. They burst open and a knot of young men staggered out, wrestling with something between them. She recognized Richard D'Arcy's voice coming from behind them, sharp and shrill and raised to an angry pitch:

'Get him out! Get him out!'

And they threw down their bundle on the flagstones before turning back and pulling the glass doors behind them.

For a moment she just stared in disbelief at the dishevelled figure as he pushed himself up on all fours.

'Oh my goodness,' she cried, hurrying over. 'Mr Ryan? Are you all right?'

He was so dazed that he flinched when she put her hand on his shoulder. She drew back and looked at him uncertainly, horrified when he turned his face up to her and it was streaming with blood.

'Miss Bryce?' he said groggily, and tried to get to his feet. 'What are you doing here? I mean, I thought you'd gone home.'

'I was about to,' she admitted, watching him with some concern as he finally got up and stood swaying on his feet. 'But never mind me. What on earth happened to you? Your face – your nose is bleeding.'

'It probably looks worse than it is,' he said, and winced as a sharp pain stabbed through his ribs.

'I doubt that, somehow.' She took him by the arm and guided him over to the bench. 'Here, sit down and let me have a look at you.'

The light spilling out through the doors showed blood trickling over his lips and one eye already starting to swell. And from the way he grimaced as he sat down, she knew there was more that she couldn't see. She pulled her handkerchief from her sleeve and dabbed gently at his nose.

'Those were Devereux's friends, weren't they?' she said. 'I recognized a few of them from the rugby team.'

'I think so. I didn't get a very good look at them. They came at me from— Ow!'

'Oh shush, Mr Ryan. And hold still.' She took him by the chin and continued dabbing, though more gently. 'Really, you're the last person I expected to see fighting. I thought you had more sense.'

'Well, you started it.'

'I did not!' She felt herself blushing to the roots of her hair. 'Alfred Devereux was being very disagreeable. I simply gave him a piece of my mind.'

'Yes, and so did I.'

'Oh, no.' Lillian stopped dabbing and looked him squarely in the good eye, 'Mr Ryan, don't tell me you picked a fight with Alfred Devereux on my account.'

'Well, not just on your account. As you said, he was being very disagreeable . . .'

'But look at you,' her gesture took in not just his battered and bleeding face, but the ripped sleeve of his jacket, and the collar of his shirt torn away from its studs and splashed with blood. 'Look at you. Your suit is ruined, and your face . . .' A gush of blood had run from his nose, over his lips, and was starting to drip from his chin down the front of his shirt. Lillian tried to wipe it up as best she could but her lacy little hankie was already soaked through. 'Oh, for God's sake, Mr Ryan. A handkerchief? Do you have a handkerchief? This one is no use.'

He pulled the handkerchief from his breast pocket and handed it to her. She quickly folded it, wiped away the worst of the gore, and then pressed it under his nose.

'I never thought I would say this, but you are a fool, Mr Ryan. An idiot.'

'Why thank you,' he answered, his voice muffled by the hand-kerchief. 'You're very welcome.'

'I'm perfectly capable of fighting my own battles, you know.'

'So I noticed.'

Lillian didn't answer, but looked away for a few moments. She was trying to be angry with him, but she just couldn't manage it. The people she was really fuming at were Devereux and his thugs. She had half a mind to get up and storm back inside. She would make a show of them if they had to drag her out like a mad woman. Be damned to Mary D'Arcy and her birthday and all her snobby friends. She would give them what for . . . But no, that wouldn't do. They'd only laugh. She sighed and turned back to Stephen.

'Let me have a look at that eye,' she said, and gently turned his face towards the light. The lid was already half closed, and only a thin line of blood red was visible beneath it. 'Ice. We need ice. That will help, anyway. Though I'm afraid you'll still have a shiner in the morning.'

Stephen nodded his agreement as best he could, though the whole side of his face was numb. With his good eye directed over her shoulder, he saw the door open and Billy's head appear, turn from side to side, and then frown directly at him. His face cracked into a broad grin, gave him a knowing wink, and then disappeared inside again.

Much bloody help you were, he thought, but he didn't really mean it. What could he have done? It was his own bloody fault for picking a fight with Devereux when all his friends were so close at hand. Then again, it hadn't worked out entirely to the bad. After all, here he was, alone with the girl, and her looking into his eyes and furrowing her brow. The pain wasn't so bad for the moment, though he had a feeling she was right – he'd know all about it in the morning.

'Let me see,' she said, and gently took the hankie away, quickly folding it again to expose the dry parts. 'Here, hold this again. And tilt your head back. I'll just pop inside to fetch some ice. I won't be a minute.'

She got up and walked towards the door. Wild horses? But she couldn't leave him bleeding. No, she'd go back in and let them stare all they wanted. She was reaching for the handle when the door opened in front of her and her sister was standing there, blinking at her in surprise.

'Lillie!' she squealed. 'What on earth are you doing out here in the dark? You're after missing all the excitement. There was a big fight and some drunk fella . . .' Her eye strayed to the bench. 'Oh.'

'Be a good girl, Sheila, and bring out a few napkins and some ice. This gentleman is a friend of mine from college. Mr Ryan, this is my sister Sheila.'

'How do you do?' Stephen enquired from under the blood-soaked handkerchief. With his head tilted back, all he could make out was a bundle of coral pink silk standing in the doorway. He raised his hand in a sort of wave.

Sheila's expression changed to one of concern, and she brushed past her sister and bent over him, peering intently. She was shorter than Lillian, and her hair was longer and closer to blonde, but there was no mistaking the resemblance. They had the same cheekbones, and the same bright, intelligent eyes.

'What's the matter with him?'

'His nose is bleeding.'

'Oh, Lillie! You're an awful thick. It's head forward for nosebleeds. Forward, or he'll choke on the blood. And pinch the bridge of the nose.'

'Well, how on earth was I supposed to know that?' Lillian asked. 'You're the nurse.' She shot Stephen an icy look, 'What are you smirking at, Mr Ryan?'

'Nothing, nothing. Don't mind me.' He obediently tilted his head forward and pinched the bridge of his nose.

'Keep him like that while I fetch some ice for his eye. I'll be back in a minute.'

Sheila picked up her skirts and darted back through the door and Stephen sat quietly for a few moments. He could see very little with his head bent down, but he was aware of Lillian sitting down beside him again. 'She seems like a very capable young lady,' he said. 'Is she really a nurse?'

'By capable, I take it you mean bossy,' Lillian answered, with affection for her sister showing in her voice, 'and yes, she is a nurse – or she will be shortly. She's been training with the Red Cross for the last three months, in case the war breaks out. I think she'll be quite put out if it doesn't.'

Just then, an urgent chiming sound came from inside – like a bell, but more clamorous.

'Is that a dinner gong?' Stephen asked, frowning. Then they heard Richard D'Arcy's voice, loud and clear enough to carry out to them.

'Ladies and gentlemen, may I have your attention please.' He paused, and there was the hiss of the crowd shushing one another.

43

'Ladies and gentlemen, I'm sorry to interrupt your entertainment, but I have just received a very important telegram from London. In short, it informs me that since the Foreign Secretary has received no reply from the German Ambassador regarding his ultimatum, a state of war now exists between Great Britain and Germany.'

This statement seemed to drop into a pool of silence. Stephen brought his head up and saw Lillian's face glowing like a pearl in the light from the doorway. After a few moments she shook her head sadly. But the ballroom exploded in applause, followed by loud cheering. Then the band struck into 'God Save the King'.

'Well, it looks like your sister won't be disappointed.'

'No, I'm rather afraid she won't, Mr Ryan,' she gave him a wan smile and added, 'God save us all.'

III

'My dear Stephen, have you gone completely mad?'

They were walking in Phoenix Park and Billy had stopped, leaned on his cane and given his friend a disbelieving stare. It was the Saturday after the ball and Stephen still bore the scars. His nose was swollen and tender, and his left eye was at the centre of an enormous bruise that was starting to go yellow around the edges.

'I mean, did that bang on the head knock your wits astray? Or have you actually taken leave of your senses?'

Stephen walked on a few paces and turned around with his hands in his pockets. 'I'm perfectly fine, Billy. I know exactly what I'm doing.'

He could say that with conviction now, but only because it was too late: it was done. He hadn't been half as confident yesterday – not after nerves had kept him awake half the night and then caused him to draw blood from his bleary face when he shaved. His everyday suit, which fitted him like a second skin, had felt tight and scratchy and he had a queer feeling in the pit of his stomach as he rode the tram across town. He kept patting his pockets for the letters he had got from the college. One was a deferral, promising him his place would be kept until he returned. The other was a letter of recommendation from Captain Wheeler, the adjutant of the university Officer Training Corps. Wheeler didn't know Stephen from Adam, but if he was a university man then, by God, that was good enough for him. He'd signed the letter with a flourish and stood up to shake Stephen's hand. Now that the war had started, Wheeler's time had come and he was handing out letters like benedictions.

But two letters didn't feel like much when he stood outside the barracks, feeling dwarfed by the high walls and with the sentry staring at him from his box by the gate. When he eventually managed to explain himself he was directed to the adjutant's office, but as he walked under the deep archway to the barracks square he was assailed by doubt. Last chance to change your mind, he thought. It's not too late. He looked out across the quays, at Guinness's brewery and all the barges and carts milling around the river. Normal life. But damn it, you've come this far, he told himself, and took a deep breath, and stepped out into the square.

The enormous space was filled with ranks of new recruits still in civilian clothes. Hundreds of men just like him, clumsily drilling under the merciless eyes of khaki-clad drill sergeants.

'You call that a fucking straight line?' one of them screeched, spittle flying, 'What the fuck are you looking at, son? Did I say "eyes front"? No, I fucking well didn't!'

The ferocity of that nearly did for Stephen there and then, but he put his head down and hurried around to the adjutant's office. Here, he found an elderly officer with grey side whiskers sitting behind a desk stacked high with paper, some of which had overflowed onto chairs, side tables and cabinets – not to mention filling most of the floor. The adjutant looked as if he hadn't slept well either, but he spoke politely:

'Good morning. Can I help you?'

'Stephen Ryan, reporting for duty, sir,' he answered smartly, and handed the adjutant Wheeler's letter.

'A university man, eh? Very good.' He nodded at the headed paper but gave the letter no more than a cursory glance before rooting around on his desk until he found a tattered brown envelope covered with spidery handwriting. 'I think I can fit you into the Seventh Battalion – the Sixth is already full. How would you like that, eh? What do you say to the Seventh Dublin Fusiliers?'

Stephen had heard of the Royal Dublin Fusiliers, but didn't know one battalion from the other. He shrugged.

'That would be fine, sir.'

'Very good. I'll put you down for the Seventh, then.' The adjutant made a minute annotation on the corner of the envelope, and asked offhandedly, 'You wouldn't happen to own a revolver, would you?'

'No, sir, I'm afraid not.'

'No? Well, I'm afraid you'll have the devil of a time getting hold of one. They can't be had for love nor money these days. What about a sword?'

'A sword, sir?'

'Yes. Didn't they give you one in the cadets?'

He was on the point of replying that he hadn't been in the cadets when he pulled himself up short. Not wise with Wheeler's letter lying open on the desk.

'No, sir.'

'Well, you'll need one of those as well. Take this chit to the paymaster. He'll give you your equipment and uniform allowance, and an advance on your pay. You'll have to make up the rest yourself. Report back when you've got yourself kitted out and I'll write you an order for the Curragh. The Seventh is already forming, so you'll have to get down there pretty quick.'

'But you've gone and joined the army!' Billy exclaimed. He stopped at a park bench and they sat down. Billy took off his hat and mopped his brow with a handkerchief.

'Yes, Billy. I've joined the army.'

'You do know there's a war on? You realize that you'll be expected to fight.'

'Of course I will. As I understand it, that's what they do in the army. They fight.'

'Well, after your performance the other night, I'm sure the Kaiser has nothing to worry about on that score. But seriously, Stephen, I do fear for your safety. This is a proper war. People will be killed.'

'I thought you'd be all in favour of it. Isn't it going to get us Home Rule at last? Didn't John Redmond just get up and say every Irish Nationalist should join up, to show Britain that we can be trusted?'

'Oh, balls to John Redmond! He's too old to fight. And, besides, the Unionists are joining up in their droves as well – only they're doing it to make sure we *don't* get Home Rule. Who wins in that case? The ones who spill the most blood? It's not a flaming game, Stephen. There won't be any winners.'

'Well, I've thought it through, Billy. I understand the risks, and I think it's the best thing I can do right now.'

'But you haven't even finished your degree. One more year. Would that kill you? One more year and then you can bugger off and die with a baccalaureate.'

'Yes, but it's one more year at the pleasure of the senior fellows,' Stephen said. 'That's the whole point, don't you see? Look at my face,' he turned and thrust his wounded eye towards his friend. Billy quailed visibly. It was grotesque to see the bright blue of the iris gleaming out from the middle of all that puffy, bruised flesh.

'What do you think they would make of that? If I went in front of them next week with my cap in my hand, begging for my sizar-ship. Do you think they wouldn't notice? Do you think they wouldn't have heard that I was fighting with Alfred Devereux, of all people?

48

You know very well what they'd say: Brawling in public. Bringing disgrace on the college. I'd be out on my ear!'

But he knew in his own mind that it wasn't as cut and dried as all that. There were mitigating circumstances: he was a promising student who had never put a foot wrong before, and they had already invested three years in him. They would think twice before cutting him off now – particularly by the time Professor Barrett was finished eulogizing about him. He didn't need Billy to tell him the merits of his case; there was the fact that he hadn't struck the first blow, and what followed had been more in the way of a beating than a brawl. And then Devereux's behaviour was certainly not above reproach. But the fact was he didn't want to argue. He didn't want to beg and plead because he didn't believe it would be worth it. He had looked beyond his degree and all he could see was that grubby little office. Inky fingers, one tedious day after another. There had to be more than that.

Billy sensed it too. 'So are you telling me that joining the army is your way of atoning for your sins? Pleading forgiveness by fighting for King and Country? I mean, come off it.'

It was a fine day and the sun-dappled grass was dotted with children playing and courting couples enjoying the heat. The war seemed a million miles away, and yet, down the path came two officers on horseback. Their mounts moved at a slow walk but they looked all the more magnificent for that. The high sheen of the horses' polished coats, the creak of leather and the jingle of spurs as they passed, the stiff, upright bearing of the men.

'That's part of it, yes.'

But only part of it. Stephen's eye followed the passing officers and he thrilled to think he might be one of them soon. They belonged to a world he hardly knew existed and the chance of seeing it, of trying it for himself, was what he had taken. He didn't want to go to that nameless little office and grow old in it. He wanted to live, even if living brought danger and the threat of death. He'd had the first inkling when he offered to walk Lillian and her sister home from the ball. They declined at first; it was too much trouble, they wouldn't put him so far out of his way, but then they'd relented and he found himself – he, who'd never had a girl on his arm before – walking the pair of them down Baggot Street, with them laughing and talking across him. And all the while one part of his mind was wondering what might have happened if he hadn't taken that first reckless step. Half a dozen drinks with Billy, a good laugh and a few hellos to people they knew. But in the end he'd be letting himself into his house in the small hours, slightly tipsy but no further forward than he'd been when he set out. This was the other way.

'It's the only way,' he added, after the two officers had rounded a bend and were lost to sight. 'It's the only way I'll be able to see something of the world before I fall in step with everybody's expectations.'

'It's the only way you'll be able to get bloody killed.'

'You think I haven't thought of that, Billy? Trust me, I have. I've thought about little else since I made my mind up. But I still think it's worth it. I'd say the war should last a year at the most, and when I go back before the fellows I'll have done my bit. They won't be able to argue with that. All it will cost me is a year, and who's to say I won't enjoy myself?'

Billy thought about this for a few moments.

'There is a certain logic in what you say,' he admitted. 'But I still think you're cracked. This is going to be a real fighting war. It might last a year or it might be all over by Christmas, as some people think. But I'll tell you this: it's been so long coming that they won't pack it in until there's been some proper bloodletting.'

'It's all the one, Billy. I could be run over by a tram tomorrow. But I'd prefer to live before I die.'

'Well, my only hope is that you get the chance, my friend. But tell me, what does your family make of this sudden change of tack? What did your father say?'

'Oh, he's delighted. He was always a Home Ruler, even back as far as Parnell. He makes me read Redmond's speeches out of the newspaper for him, and when I told him I was going to join up, he shook my hand and told me I was doing a great thing for my country.'

Stephen's voice trailed off. While what he had said was true, it wasn't the whole truth. He didn't mention the other things he had to read from the newspaper: the accounts of the German invasion of Belgium, of Austria-Hungary's attacks on Servia. His father had never had any interest in international politics, nor had he paid any attention to the long drawn-out series of events that had culminated in war. But the moment war was declared he had shown a sudden and childlike fascination with it. He couldn't hear enough about it, and writhed in his bed when Stephen read out accounts of atrocities, or even shelling. In particular, he'd conceived a hatred of Kaiser Wilhelm, and made a face whenever his name was mentioned.

'That fella's the Divil!' he often spat out, but when Stephen stopped reading and looked self-consciously at the floor, he would urge him on, 'What else? Is there more? Read it again. Tell me about the fighting.'

It was distressing for Stephen, and he had taken to lying or skipping over large tracts of the newspaper articles. His father had always been mild-mannered and gentle to a fault. But had this viciousness, this spite, always been in him? Was this mere raving, or was it the real man he was seeing? He was afraid it wasn't pride that made his father's eyes light up when he told him he was joining the army, but vengeance: all the bitterness and bile he'd built up lying sick in his bed spewing out unchecked.

'You'll show them,' the old man had whispered, his bloodshot eyes burning, and he held his son's hand so tight that the veins stood out under the parchment-dry skin. 'You'll get them back for what they did to us!'

'I'm sure he must be very proud,' said Billy, giving him a sidelong look. 'But what about your brother? What does he make of it?'

'He's disgusted,' Stephen answered, and smiled to himself. His brother had laughed out loud when he saw his face the morning after the ball. And he'd dined out on it too, smirking to himself the whole week long – until Stephen came back from the barracks on Friday afternoon. That had put the smile on the other side of his face. 'He nearly had a fit when he found out. "You're fighting the bosses' war for them," says he. "You're taking the King's shilling. You're spitting on the workers." But I think it sticks in his throat more that I'll be an officer.'

'God love him,' Billy chuckled, 'he must be the only socialist in the country with a brother who's a King's officer.' He stood up and pushed his boater back on his head, his face suddenly brightening as he pulled out his pocket watch. 'Come on, the pubs are open. We'll have to have a drink to celebrate – wet your commission or whatever it is.'

Stephen started to get up from the bench, but groaned and subsided again.

'Help me up,' he asked holding out his hand, 'my ribs hurt like hell whenever I try to stand up.'

Billy hauled him upright and looked him up and down with some concern. 'I know Kitchener's said every man should do his bit, and I'm sure they're probably taking all comers, but really – how did you get past the medical in that state? You look like you've already been in the wars. What did they say about all the damage?'

'Oh, there's nothing broken,' Stephen said cheerfully, as they set off towards Parkgate Street. But he still remembered the shock on the doctor's face when he pulled up his shirt. There were so many new recruits he'd been working flat out all week and he'd seen his share of rickets and TB and the mange. But he'd not seen anything to match the yellowish mottling that covered half of Stephen's ribcage. 'It's just bruises. The MO said they should clear up in a week or so.'

'But wasn't he the least bit curious as to how you came by them? Didn't he ask?'

'Of course he asked. I told him I got them playing rugby.'

'And he believed you?' Billy laughed out loud, 'You cheeky sod! You lied your way into the army!'

'Well, whether he believed me or not is beside the point. He still passed me fit. Anyway, it's half true. Most of them *were* on the rugby team.'

'He must have thought you were a bloody awful rugby player.'

'I'm sure he did. He said I should think about taking up cricket.'

'Cricket?' Billy laughed again. 'For God's sake, you'll hardly have time for that. Doesn't he know there's a war on?'

The flat plain of the Curragh offered no shelter from the wind, and by the time Stephen got to the officers' mess it was snowing again. He could feel the flakes matting in his eyelashes and he had to kick the slush from his sodden boots before he went in. He'd been out in the open all day and was numb with the cold. As the afternoon slowly turned into night he'd started dreaming about the warmth of the mess and now he could hardly wait. The fire had been burning in there, day and night, for the last week, and the moment he stepped inside he felt his ears begin to burn and his eyes water. The familiar reek of turf smoke brought a smile to his pinched face, but his heart sank when a figure turned to look at him from the ragged armchair near the fireplace. The good armchair.

'Ah, there you are, Ryan. The CO is looking for you.'

He might have known Hamilton would already be there. He'd hoped to get a few minutes warming himself by the fire, but Hamilton had beaten him to it. Doctor's orders. He had a blanket around his shoulders and his feet in a basin of water. Frostbite in three of his toes. Half the mess had already come by to see him – partly as an excuse to bask in the heat for a few minutes, partly out of morbid curiosity. Frostbite in Ireland? Who'd have believed it? But who would have believed the weather could be so appallingly bad, and for six weeks with no respite. Day after day the freezing north wind had brought more snow and ice. Trees were falling down under the weight of it. The drifts were thigh deep in places, and the latrines needed boiling water tipped down them to melt the ice.

But they couldn't let the weather stop them, not when they were this close. They were at the tipping point: on the cusp of becoming soldiers. Spring was just around the corner, and then they would be going to war. So with only a two-day break for Christmas they'd stuck it out: standing guard through the frozen nights, drilling together, digging trenches in the iron earth. They learned to ambush and skirmish in the snowy heather. They went on route marches across the frozen plains, and they climbed into the Wicklow Mountains with the cold pinching their faces and the icy wind howling around their ears. Maybe it wasn't so shocking that Hamilton had come down with frostbite. Perhaps the real surprise was that he was their only case.

On foot of Mr Hamilton's condition – when he read out the order that morning, the adjutant had paused to let the joke sink in, then repeated it just to be sure – on foot of Mr Hamilton's condition, feet were to be inspected at the end of every day. Consequently, Stephen had just made the rounds of his platoon – all twenty-five of them sitting on their haversacks with their socks off and their feet held up for him to peer at. Remarkably varied, he thought, as he moved from one pair to the next; one man's feet were as different from another man's as his face was. But even though the feet were all scarred to one degree or another – mostly pocked with the fleshy craters of old blisters long since hardened over – there was no blackness, no sign of frostbite. He was relieved and glad to get it over. No weather to be lying on your arse and waving your bare feet in the air. By the time he got to the end of the line his own feet were like blocks of ice and he craved warmth. He wanted heat and he wanted food, but Hamilton had beaten him to the good armchair, and the CO wouldn't be kept waiting.

'He was here not five minutes ago wanting to know if you were about,' Hamilton added helpfully. 'Said to send you over to his office if you showed up.'

'Oh, right-oh. I'd best see what he wants.' He turned towards the door but hesitated. To linger in the warmth for even a few seconds was a balm, 'How are the feet?'

'Much better, thanks. Hurt like buggery when the circulation came back, but I can wiggle my toes now.' Hamilton lifted one foot out of the water and wiggled.

'Good for you!' Stephen fastened the neck of his greatcoat and turned the collar up around his ears. 'Well, see you in a bit,' he waved, and then plunged back out into the frigid air.

Colonel Downing's office was on the far side of the barracks square, its window a warm yellow beacon in the dark. But getting there was no simple matter. The square had been shovelled clear of snow that morning, but it was already covered again – though so lightly that the treacherous undercoat of black ice still gleamed in the moonlight. He decided to go around by the wall, picking his way past windows rimed with frost and open arches hung with fangs of ice. Better to go the long way than to risk his neck on that flaming skating rink. As he worked his way around he started to examine his conscience. Was he in trouble? Back in the autumn a summons to the colonel's office was like a death sentence for subalterns. Three had gone in there and got their marching orders before September was even out.

But that was months ago, and once the obvious no-hopers had been weeded out the sackings had stopped. Stephen had found army life to be more agreeable than he expected. Perhaps it was because, apart from the small cadre of regular soldiers drafted in to train them, the battalion was entirely composed of volunteers. There was a sense of common purpose about them, a camaraderie that he had not known in college, and for the first time he felt as if he belonged to the majority. It helped that he had proved himself to be a useful officer. He was competent, clever and popular with his men, but better than that, he could shoot – and the regulars prized this skill above all others. On his first day at the rifle range he emptied his ten-shot magazine into the bull's-eye at two hundred yards. He didn't even have to turn his head to know that most of his fellow lieutenants weren't doing nearly as well. The angry bellowing coming from down the line told him that most of them were struggling to put even one shot in the paper. But when he heard the tread of the musketry sergeant behind him, there was only a surprised snort, and then:

'Reload!'

Stephen deftly reloaded and snapped the bolt shut.

'Fire!'

He brought the rifle up, steadied the sights, and squeezed the trigger. It was all easy and familiar to him; the butt thumping hard against his shoulder, the smooth flow of his right hand from bolt to trigger, the crack of each round and the tinkle of falling brass. With the last shot he lay still and smiled to himself. Even before the flag went up he knew he'd done it again. There was a stunned silence from Sergeant Townsend.

'Where the fucking hell did you learn to do that, Mr Ryan?'

'My grandfather taught me, sergeant.'

'Was your grandfather an army man?'

'No, sergeant, a gamekeeper.'

'I dare say he would've made a fucking good poacher, Mr Ryan!'

This cold weather had brought his grandfather to mind again. He'd have it hard in his small cottage in Mayo, miles from the nearest village. The hardiest man he ever met, but so old that he had to worry about him. For the first few years of Stephen's life he'd been so remote, so deep in the country that he had barely been aware of his existence. But when Stephen's mother died the old man had made the long journey up to Dublin to see his daughter buried. Stephen had felt an affinity for him from the moment they met. Even though he had barely turned seven, he thought he felt the roots of himself in this tall man, with his neatly combed silver hair and his heavy tweed suit. He thought he could see himself grown old.

That summer, when their father had sent them down to stay with him for the first time, it was like heaven on earth. A whole month in the country. Joe hated it; after the noise of the city, the endless silence and the vast open sky frightened him. But Stephen was in his element. His grandfather had taught him to hunt and fish, to read the weather and find his way by the stars, to row a boat, and a thousand other smaller things. But the one thing he had taught him above all was the power of nature. He'd always said, you can read the weather, but you can't change it. Stephen couldn't help thinking that he was an old man then and he was older now, and it would have been cold in that cottage these last few weeks.

The last few yards were badly iced, and Stephen had to grab onto the door handle to keep his balance. When he went inside he found Colonel Downing's orderly hunched over his desk in a greatcoat and fingerless gloves. He looked up beseechingly at the blast of freezing air and Stephen obligingly closed the door and kicked the snow off his boots.

'I believe he wants to see me.'

'Yes. Lieutenant Ryan. Just a minute, sir.' If the orderly knew what this was about he knew better than to give it away. It was impossible to get anything from his inscrutable face as he went and knocked at the inner door. Then he deliberately averted his eyes as he held open the door and Stephen marched past him, stamped and saluted.

Downing's office was much warmer than his orderly's. A wave of dry heat washed over Stephen as he stood at attention, making his cheeks burn after so long in the cold. There was the strong smell of paraffin from the little heater by the desk, and undertones of beeswax and stale sweat. Downing was working at his desk and his face was beet red as he looked up.

'You wanted to see me, sir?'

'Yes, Ryan, I did. Please, sit down, sit down. That will be all, Higgins.' The colonel waited until the door closed again, 'I'm afraid I've got some rather bad news for you, lieutenant. There's no easy way to say it: We received a telegram this afternoon. It's about your father.'

'My father, sir?'

His father, not his grandfather? His father, whom he'd seen at Christmas? Who'd fairly beamed when he saw his son in his uniform, and whom they'd carried down the stairs on a chair so he could share their dinner and nod off over a glass of stout afterwards. But then, he didn't need to hear the rest. There had been something a bit false about Christmas. Something had been lost – there was no more raving about the Kaiser, no fire left in him at all. He was no weight at all to carry down the stairs, and he had hardly touched his Christmas goose, or even his stout. When he nodded off at the table, it wasn't because he'd eaten his fill; it was because he'd used up all his strength just getting through the day.

Stephen listened to Colonel Downing's sympathetic voice but didn't hear the words. He accepted the glass of brandy that was offered, and then the colonel's handshake and the car that took him to the station. When he finally came to himself he was on the train to Dublin. It seemed like only yesterday that he'd been on the same train, looking out at the same ghostly night landscape, the same frozen tracery of icy tree branches flashing in the lights. It was more boisterous then. Standing room only, the train packed full of men going home for Christmas. In the corridors they were singing a raucous mixture of carols, marching songs and the filthy ditties they had taught each other in the barracks. Now it was silent. He had the compartment to himself and only his own reflection in the dark glass for company.

It was when he got down from the train that he realized how overwhelmed he was. Other hands had pushed him this far, but now he stood alone on the empty platform with his valise at his feet. What did he do now? How did he get out of here? He felt the upset rising in his chest and had to take a deep breath and master it, push it down. He had to take control. Move. Do something.

It was a half-hour's walk to his house, but it was dark and the quays would be icy. Hang the expense. He took a cab and closed his eyes to the bumping, the sounds and the lights of the city. When it shuddered to a halt he walked the last few yards down the empty street. He recognized his house, but it had never felt quite like this before. For the first time it felt as if he was going instead of coming – that this wasn't his home any more.

He stopped in the darkened hallway and tried to breathe in some sense of the place. Small things seemed familiar; the crooked dowel in the banister, the spidery cracks in the ceiling. There was a light burning in the kitchen and the dimmer glow of candles from the front parlour. His father would be laid out in there, pennies on his eyes, his hands crossed on his chest. Stephen averted his eyes as he passed. He didn't want to see that, not yet.

Joe wasn't in the kitchen. Instead he found three women; a coven of black shawls keeping the death watch. He recognized Mrs Byrne from next door, but the others were strangers to him. They might as easily have been her sisters or supplied by the undertaker. They were made for this job: the same lined faces, the same steel-grey hair. There was a kettle steaming on the stove and the acrid smell of tobacco in the air.

'Oh, there you are, son! God love you! Are you after coming up from the camp? You must be half dead with the cold.'

He felt the weight come off his shoulders as they pulled him in, sat him down, fed him tea and cake. His annoyance that they should be there, strangers in his house, gave way to relief that they had everything in hand. He had not been sure where to begin, what to do. Where did you start? Gradually, he found himself coming to grips with it. The three women tried to be kind: they told him his father had had a lovely death, very peaceful in the end. He smiled and nodded, but didn't make any reply. How could they say that? How was death lovely? Then with hardly a pause, they turned to the practicalities. His brother was at the undertakers, sorting out the carriage for tomorrow. He'd already seen to the church, and food for afterwards. And he'd organized a hall just over the river. Very good, his brother. Oh, and the priest had been and said some lovely things about his father. He'd been a good man all his life; he had no fear of being left in purgatory. Would Stephen like to see him?

This stopped the teacup halfway to his lips. What was he afraid of? He was no stranger to death; he'd seen his mother laid out in the same parlour. But that was when he was young and didn't understand. He'd thought she was sleeping. That's what his father had told him; she's gone to sleep in heaven. Now he knew what death was, he didn't want to face the finality. But he would have to do it sooner or later and he'd rather get it out of the way. He set down the teacup and, with the eyes of the women on him, he walked down the hall to the front parlour.

The room had been cleaned, dusted, tidied and a space cleared for the coffin to lie on its bier. There was room for precious little else, and the candles that burned at the head and feet made the space seem even smaller, gleaming in the glass of the cabinet by the window and throwing long shadows that flickered across the ceiling.

He stood alone with his hands clasped and his back to the door. He wasn't praying. He didn't much believe in it, and he didn't think the rote-learned prayers he knew would do much good. Instead, he looked down at his father and thought about him. He looked more solid in death than he had at the end of his life. His face was pale and his cheeks were sunken but there was some form under the waxy skin that had been harder to see before. It was as if death had solidified his spirit, gathered it together and set it at rest inside his frame. Stephen looked from his face down to the fingers with the rosary beads twined around them. Good fingers, long and strong. All his life he'd worked with his hands. But what had they brought him? Nothing – only hardship and misery. A wife who died before her time, and two sons who could do nothing but fight with one another. And then to live the last year in such pain and to die in the dead of winter, in the cold and the dark. Maybe it was peaceful after all. Maybe he was glad to be out of it.

Stephen heard the front door open and Joe's heavy tread go down the hallway to the kitchen. He would have to see him soon and face the recriminating look. While you were away playing soldiers . . . He didn't want to hear it. It was no good wishing to change anything. What was done was done. But if he could wish to see it different, he would wish he'd stayed in college, just for his father's sake. He'd wish his father another few months of life – just long enough to see him graduate. That would have been one bright thing in his life. That would have made him proud.

He reached out and touched the fingers, feeling the waxy cold skin and the harder texture of the rosary. Then he turned and went down to the kitchen to face his brother.

The smell of incense and candle wax. The freezing church echoing with Latin prayers and incantations. Stephen watched the priest sprinkling the coffin with holy water, thinking he looked a bit like a Roman emperor with his robes and his hooked nose and his purple veiny face. He was nearly finished. With slow, deliberate movements, he clasped his hands, bowed his head and advanced on the front pew.

Stephen steeled himself. This was the part he hated: the condolences.

'I'm very sorry for your trouble, boys,' the priest murmured in wearily sympathetic tones, shaking first Joe's hand, then Stephen's. The long line was already forming down the side aisle, faces full of regret, ready to shuffle past and whisper variations on the formula:

'I'm sorry for your trouble.'

'I'm terrible sorry.'

'He was a good man.'

Stephen shook their hands, one after the other. Most of them were strangers to him, and the few he did remember had grown old since he last saw them. He mumbled the platitudes, listening to Joe following him like an echo.

'Thank you.'

'Thanks very much.'

'You're very kind.'

He felt his attention wandering. He wondered about his men, about what they might be doing. Rifle drills, marching. He could see their faces and he knew their looks and their weaknesses. He knew them better than most of these people. Then he found himself looking into the face of Billy Standing, who wore such a woebegone look of regret that it was almost comical.

'Hello, Billy. Thanks for coming.'

'Of course. The least I could do.'

Another couple of barely familiar faces, and suddenly he was holding the hand of Lillian Bryce.

'My deepest sympathy, Mr Ryan,' she murmured, and he was so flustered that he couldn't even get out the stock reply before she had passed on to his brother.

At last the stream of mourners trickled out and the funeral continued in its course. Shouldering the angular weight of the coffin out into the snow. Stephen no longer thought of it as containing his father; it was just a symbol, just something that had to be there. They picked their way after the hearse, sliding on the treacherous cobbles. The cold weather thinned the crowd from the church, so only a handful stood around the open grave, like a dark scar in the white earth. It lent some urgency to the priest, too. With his surplice flapping and blowing up into his face and flurries of snow whirling over the polished wood of the coffin, he pronounced the final words hastily, shook hands once more, and was gone.

Stephen sighed when it was over and the others started to leave. He stayed hunched against the cold until he thought everybody was gone, but when he turned around there was Billy, leaning on his cane and with the collar of his astrakhan coat turned up around his ears.

'How are you holding up, Stephen?'

'I've been better. I suppose I'm glad it's over.'

Billy nodded and briskly rubbed his gloved hands together. 'What do you say to a cab? This is no weather to be walking anywhere.'

He was glad to sit in the back of the cab, feeling as if he had survived an ordeal, as if ordinary life was now slowly starting again. Billy watched him, trying to gauge his mood, but without much success. His face was closed and yet he seemed to be taking an interest in his surroundings, watching the people they passed, the children playing in the snow, old women carrying bundles of firewood.

'Was that Lillian Bryce I saw in the church?' Billy asked at last.

'Yes.'

A flicker of interest. Perhaps even a hint of self-consciousness. Was that embarrassment colouring his cheeks, or just the cold?

'Rather good of her to come.'

'Yes, it was. She's a nice girl.'

A smile, no doubt about it. Billy's face broke into a broad grin.

'You sly old dog!'

'Shut up, Billy!'

In this weather, the small fireplace couldn't hope to heat the big room in Liberty Hall. Frost spangled the inside of the window panes and the normally gloomy space was bathed in white light reflected from the snow in Beresford Place. The few remaining mourners gathered in knots around the room, still in their over-coats. Stephen stood apart from them, staring out of the window at the icicles hanging from the iron lattice of the railway bridge. Billy had brought him sandwiches and a bottle of stout from the trestle table near the fireplace, and he ate mechanically.

'I agree with you entirely!' he heard Billy say from somewhere over near the fireplace, 'But I really do believe that Home Rule is the best we can hope for at this stage. You see, you have to be realistic. It's all very well looking for complete independence for Ireland, but is that a practical proposition? I mean, particularly with this war on. Do you really think that Britain would allow it so close to home? What do you think that would say to the colonies, to India in particular?'

There was a rumble of discontent. Then a deep Scottish voice spoke up strongly: 'The whole concept of colonies is founded on inequality. No man should have to live under the colonial boot.'

'Yes, yes, that's all very well in theory – but a lot of people don't see it that way, do they? And let's not forget that Ireland isn't a colony as far as the Unionists are concerned. They might regard themselves as British, but since they were born in Ireland and they live in Ireland, they have as much right as you or I to say what becomes of it. As it was, they nearly went to war over Home Rule. That's why the King didn't sign the Bill. He knew there'd be bloody murder if he did. So imagine what it would be like if you tried for full independence: pandemonium! Which is another reason why it can't be countenanced right now. Britain is already up to her neck in a war with Germany – the last thing she needs is a civil war in her own back yard! But that's not to say that the Unionists are completely intractable. They fear change, of course, but they can be brought around. As long as it's done the right way, as long as it's introduced gradually . . .'

Stephen smiled to himself as he listened. Trust Billy to get into an argument at a funeral. But he had to admit he could hold an audience. When Stephen looked across he saw a group of men sitting on hard chairs near the fireplace. Most of them were young, and he recognized a few as friends of Joe's. Billy stood in their midst like a preacher, watched like a hawk by one of the older men, who sat bolt upright in his chair with his near-empty glass held firmly on his knee. That was Connolly. Stephen had never met him, but he had seen photographs. There was no mistaking him: in the flesh he was a dark, intelligent-looking man who appeared to relish an argument, and he was undoubtedly the leader of the group. As Billy spoke the others shook their heads or murmured their disagreement, but when it came to speaking against him, Connolly was the one who made the argument.

At length, their debate garnered more and more laughter. Billy was playing the clown and was certainly slightly drunk. It was of no matter. Connolly and his men had taken a liking to him, and by the time Stephen finally made his way across, he was sitting among them, his face flushed and pink from laughing.

'Stephen!' he called out. 'Come and meet these fine gentlemen. They've been trying to bring me around to the right way of thinking. Not with much success, I'll admit, but it was a game attempt . . .'

Despite the gaiety in Billy's voice, Stephen was aware of the chill that settled over the group as he came closer. He'd caught a few guarded glances at his uniform in the church, and he knew it didn't sit well with these men. Seeing a cloud pass over Joe's face, he had the feeling that the truce that had kept them civil these last few days might be drawing to an end. The chatter dried up and they all looked at him uncomfortably, but then Connolly stood up and offered him his hand.

'You'll be Joseph's big brother, then,' he said, and Stephen bowed as they shook hands.

'I am. Stephen Ryan, sir. At your service.'

Connolly's eyes narrowed as he peered at the bronze bomb on the lapel of Stephen's tunic. 'A Dublin Fusilier, is that right?'

Out of the corner of his eye, Stephen thought he saw Joe's expression change. It was a hostile look, as if Joe resented all this attention being lavished on his brother, but was there something else to it?

'That's right. Seventh Battalion.'

'He's an officer,' Joe blurted out suddenly, and Stephen knew from the slur in his voice that he was drunk. It amused his friends.

'Yeah, and you're only a sergeant, Joe,' one of them whispered, and the sniggering caused him to blush.

'I was in the army myself, for a while,' Connolly said amicably, trying to ignore the obvious ill feeling. 'From what I hear, you must have nearly finished your training.'

'I hope so. We'll be ready to fight come the spring, they say.'

'Aye, I bet you will.' Connolly's eyes twinkled as he sat down again, 'And tell me, did you see our little banner outside?'

Stephen smiled. Of course he'd seen it. It stretched across half the width of the building and proclaimed: We serve neither King nor Kaiser, but Ireland.

Billy had looked up at it after they stepped down from their cab. On the way across town they'd been talking about the Italians; whether or not they might come into the war, and whose side they were likely to take.

'Well, at least we know where *they* stand,' he had observed, with a grin.

'I saw it,' Stephen said.

'And who do you serve, lieutenant? Who will you be fighting for? For your King?'

'For my country.'

Connolly's eyes narrowed again, and he gave a little smile as he nodded. 'And what country is that?'

'Ireland.'

'Bollocks he's fighting for Ireland,' Joe exploded, leaping out of his seat. 'He's fighting for the King. It's the King's commission he has, the King's uniform he's wearing.'

'You sit down, sergeant!' Connolly snapped, and Stephen was impressed at the calm authority in his voice. They all fell silent as he drained his glass and wiped his moustache with the back of his hand.

'I must be away now,' he said softly, the Scottish burr plain in his voice. Then he shook Stephen's hand for the second time, 'My condolences, again, son. Your father was a good man. I'm sure he'd be proud of you.' A significant look in Joe's direction, 'I'm sure he'd be proud of both of you.'

Springtime, and the air was warm and clear. A thousand men were formed up in the barrack square, but they stood in such complete silence that he could hear the pigeons cooing high up under the eaves. The men were holding their breath, waiting for the order. Stephen turned his head a fraction so he could look down along the line of his platoon. They had just passed a general's inspection and they were perfect: buttons and buckles gleaming, rifles exactly sloped, faces stony. Soldiers at last – even Kinsella, of whom they'd all despaired. Kinsella of the two left feet, they'd called him. And probably just as well, because he didn't know left from right. A bloody miracle in some respects: after his first week of training he'd been marked out as an obvious no-hoper. He couldn't march, he couldn't hold a rifle, and he certainly couldn't shoot. The NCOs had latched onto him with ferocious glee, and he'd endured more punishments than Stephen could remember, but, somehow, he'd survived. He'd taken it all with a sullen determination, and he'd learned. Slowly, painfully, he'd turned himself into a soldier, like his brother in the Second Battalion. Stephen had overheard him saying, with an unmistakable note of pride, that his brother was already killing Germans, and that's what he was going to do too. Now here he was, chest out, back straight, ready to go over to France. Only that wasn't where he was going. At least, not according to the rumours.

The closer they'd come to actually going to war the more rumours had appeared. If it wasn't German spies putting arsenic in the water, it was the King and the Kaiser meeting on a battleship to agree an armistice. But the one about the Mediterranean had lasted a bit longer than most and it had the mundane ring of truth. There was a new front just opened there: a bold attempt to take the Dardanelles and put Turkey out of the war. The First Battalion had already gone ashore with the Twenty-Ninth Division, but there was heavy fighting and the Turks were keeping them hemmed in on the beaches. Another division would surely do the trick, and here was the Tenth Division, freshly trained, and ready for anything. There wasn't a single scrap of evidence to support it, nothing in their orders, training or equipment, but about half the men were convinced that they were going to the Mediterranean. The others still thought it would be France, and since the division had moved up to Dublin – a sure sign that they would soon be shipping out – the debate had raged hotly.

I bet they know, Stephen thought, as he watched General Mahon and Colonel Downing return to their starting point near the gate. Mahon looked pleased, but not half as chuffed as Downing, who was beaming with undisguised pride. At a nod from the colonel, the regimental sergeant major marched forward and spun around on his heel.

'Atten . . . shun!' he shrieked at the top of his voice, and hundreds of hobnailed boots crashed down as one.

Stephen didn't mind where they went as much as some. He had never been abroad before, but he thought the Mediterranean might be a bit more exotic than plain old France. At least it would be warmer, and after the arctic winter they'd just endured, a bit of heat wouldn't do them any harm. But he was in the minority among the officers.

'The Med means fighting the bloody Turks,' one of the older ones had complained at breakfast that morning, 'filthy beggars!'

Most of the others didn't put it in quite those terms, but they believed that the Mediterranean was only a sideshow. They didn't think taking the Dardanelles would make a blind bit of difference to the war because the Turks were bloody useless anyway. France was where the real action was because France was where the Germans were. Many men had lost brothers or fathers or uncles over there – and the bayonet drills had rung with screams to 'Stick it in that fucking German! Kill 'im! Kill 'im!'

'Fiiiiix bayonets!'

This command was anticipated and, while it was still an echo, bayonets flashed out and onto rifles in a series of well-practised movements. Click, click, click – like a machine. Nobody dropped either rifle or bayonet, and Stephen drew his sword, relishing the menacing grate of the blade in the scabbard. As he held it up, the April sunlight reflected from the polished steel and dappled his face.

Another order, and a thousand rifles were shouldered with a single crash. A forest of glittering needles pointed to the sky as the band struck up the first rolling beats of a march. Then came the crunch of boots as the men wheeled around the square and marched solemnly out of the barracks. It was pure clockwork. Hundreds of miles they'd marched together, and now the rhythm came to them as easily as breathing. Out of the gate and onto the quays with the band striking into 'The Girl I Left Behind Me', and the tugs and barrel barges of Guinness's brewery piercing the music with their steam whistles. The quays were lined with cheering crowds as the soldiers marched past the Four Courts and on into the heart of the city. They crossed the Liffey and marched up Parliament Street, the crowds growing thicker, and here they were joined by swarms of small boys running barefoot alongside, trying to keep in step as they sang:

> *Left, right, left, right, here's the way we go,*
> *Marching with fixed bayonets, the terror of every foe,*
> *A credit to the nation, a thousand buccaneers,*
> *A terror to creation, are the Dublin Fusiliers.*

'You fuck off, you little bastard,' Fusilier Kinsella snapped, as one of them tried to grab his rifle. Stephen turned sharply, ready to reprimand, but Kinsella hadn't broken step and was once more marching in perfect time like a toy soldier.

They turned down Dame Street and the familiar West Front of Trinity College grew closer, closer. Stephen felt the bite of nerves all of a sudden. This might be the last time he would see these streets. They were marching down to the docks to sail for England, and after that, who knew? It could be France or it could be the Med. Either way, it was certain that some of these soldiers wouldn't be coming back. And he might be one of them. He regretted not writing that letter to his brother. He'd been trying to for days, but he couldn't think of anything to say. It seemed that the connection was finally broken now. They hadn't spoken since the day of their father's funeral. No goodbyes, no regrets. He'd just got up the next morning to find the house empty and the kettle still warm on the kitchen stove. He packed his things and went back down to the Curragh to continue training with his men. They were his family now, and he didn't expect anybody else would be coming to see him off.

71

But Lillian Bryce had come to see him off. She stood at the bottom of Dame Street, outside the gates of Trinity College, in the midst of a throng of cheering students. She watched the parade approaching and hoped her sister wouldn't see her. But if Sheila were watching, she would be further up the street, outside Dublin Castle. She'd been working in the army hospital there these last three months, which was where she'd learned about the parade.

'We're all going out to cheer them off,' she said excitedly, over dinner the night before. 'What about you, Lillie? Are you going to give them a cheer? They'll be marching right past the college.'

'I have to study, Sheila. My exams are coming up.'

'Oh, but it'll only take you ten minutes, Lillie. Will you not come out to see your friend off?'

'Friend?' their mother stopped her fork halfway to her lips and looked from one daughter to the other, 'What friend is this?'

'A lad who used to be in my class,' Lillian admitted coyly, looking down at her plate.

'It's that boy who walked us home from the party, Mam,' Sheila gushed. 'He joined the army and he's going away to the war tomorrow.'

'Really? You never said, Lillian.'

'Lillie's sweet on him.'

'I am not!' she said indignantly, feeling her cheeks flush bright red. 'I hardly said two words to him all the way home.'

'But I saw the way you were looking at him, Lillie,' Sheila shot back, with a broad grin. 'You're sweet on him, and I bet you'll go out to see him tomorrow.'

Suddenly, she was looking at him again. As the parade wheeled around College Green, the throng of wives and sweethearts and children finally overwhelmed it. The marching men came to an untidy halt and civilians ran freely between the soldiers, hugging, kissing and crying. As she scanned the ranks, she saw him laughing as he sheathed his sword and then looking startled as a young woman dragged his head down and planted a kiss on his cheek. Then, out of the corner of her eye, she saw Billy Standing waving his hat.

'Stephen! Stephen!'

And he turned to see his friend beaming at him.

'Do come back, there's a good chap.'

Stephen said something in reply, but she couldn't catch it over all the cheering and noise.

'Mr Ryan!' She called out, waving, but she was at the back of the crowd, almost against the railings, and she knew he couldn't hear. The order was passed to reform ranks and the lines of men were straightened and some semblance of military order was restored. It was only as he took his place in front of his platoon that his eyes met hers and he smiled. Feeling her heart beating harder, she raised her hand.

'Good luck!' she called out, louder, and he bowed his head and touched the brim of his cap. He shouted something in return, but once again his words were lost in the rolling of drums and blaring of trumpets as the band struck into a march and was answered with a deafening burst of cheering and applause that saw them off to their ship.

IV

At last I have the chance to use my notebook. I bought it in Basingstoke with the intention of keeping a journal of my Mediterranean travels, but the voyage out was far too bloody tedious to bother with. However, that all changed this morning.

We sailed from Limnos last night, the whole battalion packed like sardines into a tiny minesweeper. It was an uncomfortable trip, what with the heat and seasickness and all the tension because we knew we were finally going into battle. I thought we'd have further to travel, but when the sun came up the Turkish coast was less than a mile away and we lay off a shallow bay packed with ships. But it was Terra Incognita to us. We hadn't been issued with maps, and had to borrow the ship's chart to put names to the features on shore. Did I say names? I meant tongue-twisters – more like something out of a fairy tale. We eventually learned that the little round hill on our right was Lala Baba, and the high cliffs straight ahead of us were called Kazlar Dagh. The bay was called Suvla Bay.

It was certainly a noisy spot. The battleships were bombarding the shore from further out to sea and their shells sounded like trains thundering overhead. Orders had to be shouted over the

74

din, and it was pandemonium when our time came to go ashore and we had to get everybody over the side into steam launches. Luckily, many of the men in my platoon worked on the docks before the war, so we managed it without anybody falling into the sea.

The launch was a bit like a charabanc, with the little steam engine chugging away and the men laughing like excited schoolboys as we weaved through all the shipping to get to the shore. Then something exploded in the sea right beside us, and a big spout of foam collapsed into the boat, drenching us all. Everybody cheered. Abdul will have to do better than that if he wants to put us off.

There was less laughing after we landed. Another launch was grounded on the beach and it had clearly suffered a direct hit. The planking in the bow was all splintered and the water around it was red with blood. Men were being lifted out, arms hanging loosely, heads lolling. Then, almost the moment we splashed into the shallows, a stream of walking wounded appeared from between two small hills and started to fill our boat.

And so far, that's all I can report. We've been ashore for four hours now, but all we are doing is sitting in the sand, waiting for orders. The beach smells of thyme and guncotton. We can hear fighting going on a bit further inshore, but nobody knows when we'll get into it. We have no maps and no orders, and I'm getting a bit worried because we are drinking so much water and I think my legs are getting sunburned. It was a long night and I'm tired now. If I can find a bit of shade I might try to get some sleep.

7 August 1915 (Night)

Well, I didn't get much sleep earlier on. I'd no sooner rigged myself a little awning with my groundsheet than a runner came looking for Colonel Downing. At last, after half the day was gone! Soon the order was passed to form in threes and we set off around the bay, the old boy at the front with his blackthorn stick, and everybody sweating and grunting along under the blazing sun. It was clearly too hot to be marching with full packs so, to lighten the load, we dumped all our kit except rifles and a day's rations. Then it was on again, past piles of stores and men lying on the beach or bathing in the sea.

After about a mile we reached a deep gully cutting down to the sea. It was a natural choke point, and the Turks were shelling it sporadically. It was here that I lost my first man: a shell landed in the gully as he was scrambling out and he toppled back in. His name was Kelly. The blast must have killed him because I could see no wound, but the MO pronounced him dead and we had to leave him and keep marching.

We were headed for a little hill that the CO called Chocolate Hill. We could see it by now, and we could also see the Turkish trenches criss-crossing the top. To reach it, we had to cross the bed of a dry lake. I suppose when it rains this is a real lake, but now it was just dry mud with a salty crust that broke under us as we marched across. At every step we sank up to our ankles in a dusty mixture of salt and sand. The dust clogged our throats and worsened the thirst, but I was grateful for the cover it gave because the Turks had spotted us and opened fire. This was something I hadn't heard before: the crack of a shot passing overhead, and the thud as another hit the ground nearby. The urge to lie down was very strong.

It was a relief to reach the scrubby ground on the far side. As we closed on the hill, the Turkish fire got heavier. A man was shot in front of me, but I stepped over him with little more than a glance. We had to keep moving and we were soon advancing by rushes through the long grass. It felt safer now that we were shooting back, and at least directing my men gave me some sense of control.

With one last dash we tumbled into the Turkish trench at the foot of the hill as the former tenants ran away under cover from their friends at the top. They left a few corpses behind, which we tried to ignore – though it was hard to avoid walking on them. While we waited for the navy to shell the top of the hill I decided to have a bite to eat. The hard tack was very dry in my mouth and the warm water tasted gritty and stale. My stomach was closed with nerves and I was surprised to see the sun already setting behind Kazlar Dagh.

Suddenly the shelling started. The whole top of Chocolate Hill was covered in smoke and flame and the noise was tremendous. It went on for about half an hour and then, just as suddenly, it stopped. The command was passed to fix bayonets and I reloaded my revolver. Many of the men blessed themselves as the CO jumped up on the parados, waving his stick, and called for three cheers for the Dublins. At the last hurrah he pointed up the hill with his stick, and the whole battalion charged out of the trench, howling and screaming like savages.

We went flying right over the summit of the hill, hurdling empty trenches like thoroughbreds. When at last we stopped, puffed out and laughing, we had chased the Turks halfway across the grassy saddle between this hill and the next. We trudged back and found the CO looking hungrily at the other hill – Green Hill on his map. The Turks had vanished down the other side and for all we knew they were still running. We reckoned we could take it with another charge, but Downing was more prudent. It was almost dark and he had strict orders not to push too far forward for fear of being cut off.

So here we stay – in shallow scrapings and shell holes, the remains of the Turkish trenches. We have lifted the corpses out *and laid them on the parapet. Apart from the sentries, everybody is trying to sleep, but the excitement of the charge is still coursing through our veins and most are talking quietly or sharing food. I'm writing by the light of a Turkish candle I found in the trench. I see I've half filled my notebook already, so I'll have to be less long-winded if it's to last me past the end of the week.*

* * *

The scream brought him snapping awake. But when he opened his eyes there was silence, nothing but the whispering breeze. And yet he was sure he had heard a scream; there was anguish in it, real pain. What would make somebody scream like that?

He cocked his ear and strained his eyes into the darkness. Still nothing. Maybe it was in his head. But the smell was real enough; there was no getting away from that. Even though the fire was long out, there was still smoke wafting into the trench and sometimes an eddy in the breeze brought the sweeter stench of burning flesh that turned his stomach. The sights and sounds he remembered were all nothing to that. That was the stink of war and he'd have it with him for as long as he lived. He had known those men, talked to some of them, but now they were just blackened lumps lying out there in the burned grass.

It had been such a perfect morning that they'd had no inkling of what was to come. As the night faded over the Anafarta plain, the rocky hills rose like islands out of the gloom and the sky gradually turned pink and then blue. The men were scattered around the hilltop, lying in crevices and corners, sleeping with the sun on their faces. All silent save the clink of a tin mug, or the rattle of stones as a sentry shifted his weight. And all around them dry grass rustled as the night breeze slithered down to the sea. It was peaceful until a hoarse docker's voice broke out.

78

'Stand to arms! Stand to arms! Come on, you lazy buggers, let's be having you.'

Men stretched and yawned and stood up to look over at Green Hill. Then a bullet cracked off a rock and went zinging away in an angry ricochet, and they remembered where they were and bolted for cover. The reality of their situation robbed the scene of all its beauty as the first privations made themselves felt. Breakfast was a few dry biscuits and a sup of water. Yesterday's sunburn was starting to sting.

It was obvious that they were going to have to attack Green Hill, but the night had stolen their appetite for a fight and the impetus of the last evening had evaporated entirely. More worrying, it was clear that the Turks had brought up reinforcements. They had grown bolder and were sniping at the carrying parties bringing up ammunition and water. A clever stroke, since most of the men had exhausted their canteens and as the sun got higher and hotter it was hard to think of anything but a long cool drink.

Colonel Downing went down to the beach after breakfast and didn't return until lunchtime, puffing back up the hill under a hail of fire from the Turks.

'Those saucy buggers were shooting at *me*,' he exclaimed, when all his officers had been assembled, but there was a wild gleam in his eye as he went on: 'Well, gentlemen, the time has come. We're going to put a stop to Abdul's capers for once and all. Division's finally got the finger out, and we shall be attacking this afternoon. That bloody hill,' he pointed at Green Hill with his blackthorn stick, 'that's the key to this whole place. If we can clear them off there, then we'll finally have secured our beachhead. So the honour falls to us, gentlemen, with the Munster Fusiliers supporting us on the right. We'll have to move damned quickly, so it'll be rifles only. Leave the haversacks, but make sure your chaps have got plenty of ammunition. I have a feeling they won't give up that hill as easily as they did this one.'

After lunch, the battalion formed up just below the crest of the hill. Stephen lay with his men, feeling the heat of the sun through his shirt and weighing his heavy revolver in his hand. Kinsella was grinning at him from a few feet away, his face already burned red by the sun, but the rest of the men seemed distracted. Some of them were looking at the ships in the bay, some at the Munster Fusiliers forming up on the eastern side of the hill. When everybody was in position, a whistle shrilled at the far end of the line and they scrambled out of their trench and set off across the broad grassy saddle.

Even the first few yards seemed harder than the night before, the ground rougher and the going slower. But not a shot was fired, and only the swishing of the long brown grass around their bare knees broke the uneasy silence. Then, when they were about half-way across, the Turks hit them hard. Mortars, artillery, machine guns. Men fell like ninepins and the rest instantly dropped flat, crawling and twisting like rabbits through the grass. Stephen scrambled behind a rock not much bigger than his head, and a bullet cracked into it, fragments flying into his eye. Half-blinded, he looked around for his men; there were khaki lumps scattered through the grass, whether dead or alive he couldn't tell.

'Pull back! Pull back!' he shouted, crawling towards a shallow gully a few yards behind. Bullets were whipping through the grass and it was a queer feeling to be crawling like that, head down, back exposed. Then he slid into the gully and found it already full of men cowering down under the solid thatch of bullets snapping overhead.

'Don't just lie there!' he burst out, unsettled by the fear that was plain on their faces, 'Shoot back! Fire, for Christ's sake!' And he snatched up a rifle from a wounded man, drove home the bolt and emptied the magazine at Green Hill. He couldn't see a thing, but it had the desired effect. Stung into action, the men followed his lead and soon they were lining the edge of the gully, shouting and cursing and blazing away.

If it was only bravado, at least it distracted them from the danger they were in. Their shelter wasn't more than a foot deep and every inch of it was covered in khaki; some men living, some dead, many wounded. One shell in there would kill them all, but they were pinned down and they would be cut to pieces if they tried to get back to their trenches on Chocolate Hill. Their only chance was another naval bombardment to give them cover, but they might all be dead before anybody thought of that.

'Jesus, Mary and Joseph. It's on fire,' Kinsella shouted in his ear, and he pointed to the right.

'What?' Stephen was in the middle of reloading a magazine and found the brass cartridges greasy and slippery with sweat. It didn't help that his hands were shaking.

'The grass is after catching fire. Look!'

His eyes followed the pointing hand towards the centre of the saddle. The Turks had concentrated their mortar and artillery fire there, and some of the shells had set the dry grass on fire. Fanned by the hot wind, the flames were spreading quickly, covering everything with thick smoke. Stephen watched with a mixture of dread and hope. If the flames spread over here they would be cooked alive. On the other hand, the wind was blowing the smoke in this direction. He waited, waited, watching the black pall spread across the spotless blue sky, and then scrambled to his feet.

'Fall back,' he shouted, and he could hardly see the men in front as they ran through the smoke. In minutes they were back in their own lines, Turkish bullets flying high and wide. Small comfort to the hard-pressed men, most of them terrified and shaking. It took grim determination to pull together the remains of his platoon and make them dig in and prepare for a Turkish counterattack. After half an hour it was plain that the Turks wouldn't come, but lying there doing nothing was almost worse. Fuelled by the fitful breeze, the fire consumed the whole saddle, smelling like the stubble burning in the fields back home. They could see nothing, but as the flames spread they could hear the screams of the wounded men who had been left lying in the grass. Terrible sounds, wrenching at already strained nerves, and more unbearable because there was not a thing they could do to help them . . .

Stephen's head nodded forward again and he snapped awake in the dark. Still quiet, but that seemed even more ominous. Sitting curled up in a corner of the trench, he felt completely alone, bereft; no human voice for comfort, no friendly light, and after a while he found himself stumbling over a prayer. He hadn't prayed in years, and he could hardly remember the words, but they came to him after a while and he mumbled them fervently. He felt a hypocrite, praying to keep from falling asleep, but anything was better than hearing those screams in his head.

* * *

Dublin,
15 August 1915

Dear Stephen,

You really must write more! There was such a hiatus between your last two letters that I thought you'd fallen off the edge of the world, or worse. But I mustn't complain. I was so delighted to receive your last letter that it put a spring in my step. I am amazed that you have finally landed in Turkey. I never thought I'd see the day. We've been fighting our wars in Flanders and Picardy for centuries, and this sudden change to an away fixture is quite beyond me.

To be serious, the thought of your fighting over there chills me to the bone. It seems that every day another familiar name is added to the roll of honour. The latest was Ernest Julian – my old law professor – and as I know he was in your battalion, I hope and pray you are doing everything you can to stay out of danger.

You asked for news of home. Well, you will be shocked and amazed to learn that I have graduated with a second-class degree. After many broad hints from my father I have taken up the family trade and I am to become a barrister. I have just started devilling for a KC called Percival Barton, who is a terribly clever old chap, though exceedingly fond of a drink. You will probably laugh when you read this, but I am very much the sober half of the firm. Apart from my other duties, I am responsible for retrieving the gaffer from the pub after lunch, nudging him awake during the long afternoon sessions, and checking him if he seems about to say something he will come to regret.

Which reminds me – who did I see last week, only your brother. We were just going into court when a group of militia came marching down the quays – you can spot the Citizen Army a mile off because their uniforms are a very dark green – and there was young Joseph, marching at the head and giving it the old left, right, left. Unfortunately, old Barton (who is a dreadful Unionist, particularly after a few brandies) let fly at them with a torrent of abuse that would make your hair stand on end, the gist of it being that they should be in France fighting for King and Country instead of prancing about like a troop of Boy Scouts. The last time I saw them, the Boy Scouts weren't armed to the teeth with rifles and revolvers so, needless to say, I took a firm grip and ushered him off stage before Joe and his friends could get in a reply.

More recently, I bumped into your old pal Lillian Bryce. Did you hear she got a gold medal in the senior mods and won a studentship? So next year she'll be doing postgrad work, as well as giving lectures and tutorials. More luck to her, I say. In a few years she could well be the first-ever woman fellow. And she's such a charming girl; I don't know why she's got a reputation for being a bit peculiar. We had a good old chinwag and she made a particular point of asking after you. (Hint: I shan't be too upset if your next letter heads in her direction.)

Nevertheless, I can't help thinking she is stealing your thunder. That medal would have been yours for the taking if only you hadn't gone off to play soldiers! But there it is; you have gone off and I can only hope you will not take as long as Odysseus to return home from those parts.

Please write again soon, to let me know you are alive and well. I remain,

Your Friend,
William Standing (BL!)

16 August 1915

I don't know what I can write about last night. I've been staring at the page for an hour, but I'm still not sure where to begin. The sun is up and I can see the rocks of Kiretch Tepe Sirt as I sit with the handful of men I have left – the rest are still lying up there.

We lost a lot of men but the officers were nearly wiped out. Colonel Downing was hit in the foot by a sniper before we even got to the top of the ridge and Major Harrison, who took over from him, was blown to pieces by a Turkish bomb. The list goes on and on: in my own company, Hamilton and Leschalles were both killed, and Robinson badly wounded. That means I'm the only officer left in B Company, so the command has fallen to me. Captain Fitzgibbon from A Company is the senior surviving officer and has taken temporary command of the battalion. He has gone off, shaking with anger, to see why we were never given the order to withdraw.

It is hard to describe the fighting itself because it was all just flashes in the dark. I had a bad feeling about it from the start. The sky was clear and there was a full moon and I was reminded of the first time Granda took me out hunting at night. We hid ourselves down low in a hollow, and when the moon rose he touched my shoulder and pointed up the valley. The crest of the hill was cut sharp and black against the moon, and even as I watched I saw a fox dart out from cover and trot across the sky, so clear I could see his legs and his head as he raised his snout to sniff at something on the air.

We must have shown as clearly to the Turks as we crept along the ridge past the Pimple. When we got as far as the knobbly peak of Karakol Dagh the machine guns on Kidney Hill opened up on us and we had to crawl forward, hugging the sharp rocks for cover, chips flying around our ears. We should have turned back – all surprise was lost, they could see us plain as day – but still we crept doggedly on. Then, just as we reached the extremity of our lines, the Turks counterattacked, working their way along the ridge below us. Below us, for God's sake! Our height should have given us the advantage, but instead it was killing us. We were silhouetted against the sky while they were hidden in the moon shadow – and doubly protected by the overhanging cliff, they could get right in and lob their bombs up among us.

These were wicked little things about the size of a cricket ball, with a fuse that they lit with a cigarette. They came fizzing out of the void a dozen at a time and we had no cover against them and no bombs of our own to reply with. Sometimes we threw the Turkish bombs back down on top of them; Wilkins threw down five but the sixth blew up in his hand. Some men pushed rocks down onto them – it was fatal to try to shoot, as you had to lean out and show yourself against the moon. I found a notch where I could fire down with my revolver without exposing myself, but

85

it was difficult to see; I had to wait for the glow of the cigarette, and by then the bomb was already on the way up.

A couple of hours of this and the Turks were starting to wear us down. Far from achieving our objective of pushing them off the end of the ridge, we were in danger of losing the whole thing. Dead and wounded men littered our position and the air was thick with the stink of gunpowder and blasted rock. Major Harrison scrambled about, calling for men to mount a charge down the side of the ridge to clear out the bomb throwers. They disappeared over the edge and that was the last we saw of them. A gallant act, but it cost us dear; I have a vivid picture in my head of Harrison silhouetted in the blinding flash of a bomb. Three more officers were killed in the same charge and a fourth shot through the head as he crawled up to see if any of them had survived.

After that, I don't know how we held on. I think the only reason the Turks didn't overrun us was because it was easier to leave us there while they cut us to bits. We had no relief or reinforcement, no orders, no objective. We just lay there losing men by the hour, until eventually we were relieved and crawled away as the sun was coming up. It was the worst night I have ever endured.

But I would be lying if I said it has not had another effect on me. I have survived, and there is a little sense of triumph there. I have survived, and the sky never looked so blue, nor the ground felt so firm.

16 August 1915 (Afternoon)

Captain Fitzgibbon came back from Brigade HQ in a terrible state. He was cursing General Mahon – calling him a f—ing murdering bastard and wishing him to hell. I had to lead him out of earshot before somebody heard him. A mug of tea calmed him down a bit, but still his hands were shaking and there were tears of rage in his eyes. Eventually, he explained to me why we weren't allowed to withdraw last night.

It starts with General Hamilton, who is in charge of the Turkish campaign. Unhappy with how things are going, he sacked a few of his subordinates, including General Hammersley our corps commander. General Mahon, who commands our division, was next in line to replace him, but Hamilton promoted DeLisle from the Twenty-Ninth Division instead. Mahon resented being super-seded and resigned, marching out of his headquarters in a sulk just as the Turks launched their counterattack against us. This meant there was nobody to answer our calls for help or to send support until DeLisle arrived a few hours later. The moment he realized what was happening, he pulled us back, but by then the damage was done.

As Fitzgibbon finished his story, I looked at the top of the ridge. There are a lot of men rotting up there for the sake of Mahon's pride. I hope they haunt him to the end of his days.

*   *   *

They were led down to the shore in the dead of night. There was no moon and lights were forbidden for fear of betraying their withdrawal – for fear of betraying their failure, because from here to Cape Helles hundreds of boats were plying back and forth, gradually thinning the ground they had fought so hard to take.

Stephen felt no regret that they were leaving, but no elation either – he was too sick and exhausted for that. He simply felt hollowed out, and it took all his strength just to walk down to the beach, invisible hands as weak and trembling as his own steadying him when he stumbled against the guide rope. When he finally reached the beach he collapsed onto the still-warm sand and listened to the sighing of the surf. It seemed very peaceful, until an electric white flash lit up the whole horizon, and he saw the men scattered around him; a hundred of them covered in scabs and suppurating sores, weakened and wasted with dysentery. Then the ground trembled and the sky shrieked as the naval shells thundered over.

As his eyes grew accustomed to the dark, he noticed sailors moving about the beach with shaded lanterns, counting heads. They looked fit and strong in the dim light, towering over the soldiers like giants as they handed out cigarettes and chocolate. We must look like scarecrows to them, he thought – husks of men, sick and broken. When his group was called forward they climbed painfully to their feet, helping one another stand on swollen joints, and stumbled out along the jetty, led like cattle. There had been no jetty here when they came ashore at the beginning of August, but that seemed so far away now he might have dreamed it. His head swam when he thought of that first day, when the warm air was heavy with the scent of thyme. Then a wave of nausea washed over him and he felt faint, weak, white patches flaring in front of his eyes.

'Easy there, mate,' a sailor whispered, catching him before he stumbled into the inky water. He felt himself being lifted into the boat and tried feebly to help, but his arms had no strength and his two legs knocked together like dry sticks. He slumped onto a seat and weariness washed over him, his head drooping with fatigue. He needed to sleep; two hours a night was all he'd had these last weeks, and that had only been a light stupor with bad dreams and night sweats. The daytime was worse; even in a rest area there was still the unbearable heat and the stink of shit and corpses, the stomach cramps and diarrhoea. No rest, no relief, and it soon started to tell. The strain had been building up inside him for weeks, winding tighter and tighter like a clock spring, and after he shot the sniper it overpowered him entirely.

How long ago was that? A week? Two? He couldn't even count

the days. All he could remember was the thirst, growing inside him like a tumour. It was the one thing that preoccupied him day and night. He'd seen it drive men mad. They craved water, craved it with every fibre in their bodies, but the searing sun was merciless, and the meagre supply of water the navy sent ashore came nowhere near slaking their thirst. In desperation, they tried to supplement their ration with water from the little brackish wells that dotted the hills, but that could only be had at a price. The Turks knew about their thirst. They knew they had their enemy pinned to the undrinkable sea, and they posted snipers to cover every well within sight of their lines.

That made Scimitar Hill the worst possible position to hold. At a mile inland it marked the furthest penetration of their lines, and if any water carriers ever made it that far, they did so only after everybody else had taken their dip. The trench was exposed too, hewn into a rocky hillside, devoid of shelter from the sun and a long way from the cool sea breeze. There was only one well and that was in a green hollow a few yards behind the trench. Before they even set out, Stephen had started to feel ill, and by the time he reached the position after the long march up from the shore his mouth was dry and cracked and he was seeing black spots in front of his eyes. His knees were trembling with the effort, and he had to steady himself against the wall of the trench for a few moments. Then he saw Kinsella, beaming at him like a friendly dog, seemingly impervious to the heat.

'All right, sir? What about a drink of water?'

Stephen nodded, but suddenly lurched forward, pushing past Kinsella. He could smell the water but he couldn't stop – his guts were in a knot again and he had to run to the slimy notch in the wall that served as a latrine. He hadn't been there long when he heard the crack of a rifle and then the frightened shouts of his men.

They were crowded in the trench near the hollow, and it didn't take long to see why. Feeling their eyes on him, Stephen crept along the trench and darted his head up just long enough to see what he had feared. Nailed boot soles, sunburned calves, and a sweat-soaked shirt with a ragged hole just below the collar. Kinsella lay stretched in the hollow, his tin mug clutched in his lifeless fingers as if he was still trying to fill it at the well.

'I think he's in them olive trees, sir,' Sergeant Toolan said, when he dropped back into the trench.

Stephen nodded in agreement. The well was hidden from the Turkish trench, but there was an olive grove in no man's land and the stunted trees could easily give a sniper the elevation to get a shot at the well. Stephen's heart sank. The trees would also give the sniper the cover he needed to stay there all day.

The men knew it and they were taking no chances. They huddled in the bottom of the trench and looked at Stephen with wide, expectant eyes. His mind raced. He had to do something: in one stroke, the sniper had denied them the well, leaving Kinsella's body as a grim reminder of his power. But they needed that water. He wasn't the only dysentery case, and he doubted they could last until nightfall without dehydration taking a toll. It was barely ten in the morning and already the sun was unbearable, the baked walls of the trench hot to the touch and black flies swarming over everything.

But as he squinted into it, shielding his eyes with his hand, he wondered if that blazing sun might not save them. He tried to gauge its track, his mind working all the time. It depended on the sniper; if he was bold enough to stay in his post, then the sun might betray his position – but only if he was using a scope. That was a lot of ifs, but he didn't see that he had any choice. It was a slim chance, but better than doing nothing.

'Let's get our sentries up, sergeant,' he said, in an officious voice, trying to make it sound as if he wasn't rattled. 'Make sure they have periscopes and change the sentries on the hour. Heatstroke is the last thing we need in this godforsaken spot.'

'Very good, sir,' Sergeant Toolan said, looking relieved that somebody had given orders; that something was being done.

'And I shall need a rifle, sergeant,' he added, in a lower voice.

'Right you are, sir.'

He took the weapon that was silently passed to him and walked along to the sap that cut into no man's land near the northern end of the trench. This was a crude scrape that had been dug to allow patrols and listening parties to crawl out into no man's land. It wasn't very deep, but at least it was covered. With the worried eyes of his men still on him, Stephen crawled into the sap. Creeping slowly on his elbows – he couldn't make a sound, even under the cover of the brushwood roof – he reached the end and lay dead still, watching the green leaves of the olive grove a hundred yards away.

The heat was overpowering, smothering, lying over him like a thick blanket, but he didn't move a muscle. He thought of the hours he'd spent hunting with his grandfather, learning patience, stillness. He used to let his mind roam where it would, almost free of his body, and soon he would be only dimly aware of his grandfather, sitting like a stone beside him. But they had always done their waiting in a mossy ditch or on the riverbank, with the mist curling around them and no sound but the lap of the water and the distant boom of a bittern. Now he was in a reverberating stone oven with his face pressed into hot rock and his guts heaving and knotting spasmodically. His tongue felt swollen and furry and he was bathed in sweat just lying still.

What made it worse was the exposure. The end of the sap was open to the Turkish trench, and his only cover was the deep shadow from the roof. He couldn't move or make a sound; not when the heat grew so intense that his head swam and running sweat blurred his eyes, nor even when his bowels gave an intense spasm, as if a giant hand had twisted them. *Bloody stupid idea.* Slowly the sun swung through the sky, the heat building mercilessly through the afternoon, growing hotter and hotter, until he thought he would suffocate.

Then he saw it – a white flash in the green of the trees. He waited, holding his breath, and it came again, steadier, the twinkling of sun on glass. He eased the bolt closed and brought the rifle up. His grandfather was beside him again, whispering to him to move steady and sure. *Take your time.* He blinked the sweat out of his eyes and then, with one last long breath, heaved himself out of the shadows and into the blinding sun. The rifle came up snug against his shoulder and he pushed the barrel against a rock, pivoting, swinging the sight onto his target as he hissed half his breath away and felt the trigger giving under the pressure of his finger. Crack! He saw branches nodding in the olive grove. Something thumped to earth, but he was already scrambling back through the sap, feet first, pushing with his elbows.

He had no time for congratulations, but dropped his rifle and ran back to the latrine. When he came out again there was a mug of water waiting for him, and a different feeling in the trench. The curse was lifted. The men were still sunken-eyed and filthy, but they were soldiers once again.

But just as he emptied the mug, the screaming started. It came from the olive grove: a low moan that rose to a high-pitched shriek before dying away and starting low again. A white flag appeared over the Turkish trench and two stretcher-bearers came out, but a volley from the sentries sent them scurrying back again. Normally both sides let stretcher-bearers go about their work unmolested – but not for snipers. Snipers would die where they fell.

This one was a long time dying. The screaming went on all

through the afternoon, grating on his nerves and turning his triumph to unease. He ordered the sentries not to fire if the stretcher-bearers came out again, but with little hope that they would try. Finally, just after sunset, it stopped – but the silence that followed was almost worse. When it was fully dark he ordered Sergeant Toolan to take a patrol out to the olive grove and burn it.

He had no appetite, but he made himself sit down to his dinner of bully beef and biscuit. He knew he had to eat and, besides, there was the letter to Kinsella's mother. As he ate, he wrote – mechanically brushing the flies from the paper and then his plate with one long-practised gesture. All he knew about Kinsella was that he had an older brother in the army, and he hoped to God this wasn't the second letter the poor woman was getting. As usual, he wrote that her son had died quickly – it was the truth for once – but in the quiet of the dugout he couldn't get the sniper's screams out of his head. He'd probably killed men before, but this was the first time he had done so deliberately, coldly. May you die roaring, said the old Irish curse, but it bothered him now. He was still in a daze, with his pen poised over the paper, when Sergeant Toolan coughed politely outside and asked if he would come and have a look at the sniper.

Something was amiss: he could tell from Toolan's diffident manner, from the way he dropped his eyes as Stephen came out of the dugout. The scene in the trench was like a wake, with the corpse laid out by candlelight and the eerie orange glow from the blazing olive grove. But he shuddered when he saw the body; it was unmistakably feminine, a young woman – almost a girl. Her bare legs stuck out from a rough canvas smock that was soaked with blood around her midriff. That explained all the screaming. There was no worse way to die than from a stomach wound.

But, Christ! He'd shot a woman – killed her. Was she a civilian, a shepherd who wandered into no man's land? Relief flooded through him when he picked up the rifle lying beside her – a modern German Mauser with a Zeiss telescopic sight. She was the sniper all right, no doubt about it. She had shot Kinsella, and God knew how many before him. But there was an uneasy guilt in the faces of his men, as if they had conspired in murder. He might have shot her, but they had condemned her when they fired at the stretcher-bearers. He knew he ought to say something, offer some justification – but what? Curious, he brushed hair away from her face and caught his breath. What had he hoped to find? Some evil cast to her dead eyes? Some sign that marked her a murderer? But even filthy and bedraggled and sunk in death, she was beautiful.

He laid the rifle down and turned away, and the men simply nodded sympathetically. Mahony knelt beside the firing step and started whispering an act of contrition into her ear, his rosary beads clicking in the silence that filled the trench. He wanted to tell him not to bother, that she was most likely a Muslim, but he held his tongue. There was a kindness that not even the war could root out; they were only giving her what they would wish for themselves, and it was best to let them have their rites.

Inside the dugout, his unfinished letter to Mrs Kinsella was still on the table, but he couldn't face it. He lay down on the bunk and closed his eyes, but he could hear the girl screaming. Even when he put his hands over his ears he could still hear it, and as sleep crept up on him, he could taste the bile rising in his throat.

Part Two

V

By the time Stephen got home he was sick of hospitals. The one at Lemnos had been welcome because it was the first. After the torrid heat of Turkey it was clean and cool and peaceful, but he didn't have long to enjoy it. Fever struck on his second night and for the next week he was racked by shivers and sweats and delirium, so the next thing he remembered was waking in Malta, in another hospital; another long room with distempered walls and a cool breeze whispering between the beds.

A week passed before he was fit to move again – a week of staring at the ceiling and wondering if this was real, or if he was just asleep in a roasting hole in Turkey and would shortly wake to the filth and flies. But reality slowly gained ground. On the voyage south he was able to taste the fresh scent of the sea, and when the hospital ship docked in Alexandria he could feel the pulsing chaos on the quays before he was plunged bodily into it on his stretcher, carried shoulder high through teeming hordes of urchins thrusting their wares at him, 'Eggs a cook! Eggs a cook!'

Then another hospital, but the same distempered walls and long rooms. He began to wonder if they built these places to a pattern. It was evening when he arrived, and there was a monastic liquidity to the silence that seeped out of the shadows. When they left him he closed his eyes and felt himself sliding into it, as if he were sinking into water. Opening them again, he found it was morning, bright sun piercing the windows. A doctor was sitting beside his bed. He was poring intently over a chart, and his bare brown knees stuck out through the open front of his white coat.

'G'day, lieutenant,' he said, with a flat Australian twang. 'How are you this morning?'

Stephen blinked at him. For the first time he had slept right through the night, a deep dark sleep undisturbed by fever or nightmares. He felt refreshed, but at the same time frail and disoriented.

'Where am I?' he croaked.

The doctor smiled. 'The Australian Military Hospital in Alexandria. You've been very sick, but I think your fever's broken now. I bet you'd like a drink of water.'

Stephen pushed himself up in the bed, licking his dry lips. Water! Good clean water, in a glass! He gulped it down like a greedy baby until the doctor gently pulled the glass away.

'Easy there, mate. You'll make yourself sick. Why don't you leave some for later, eh?'

He sank back against the pillows. The ward was noisier now, with men walking about in dressing gowns and pyjamas, and blue-smocked nurses working around the beds. But his companion didn't seem in any hurry to leave. He picked up his chart again and started making notes, humming quietly to himself.

'What's wrong with me?' Stephen asked at last.

'You've had malaria and dysentery, lieutenant,' the doctor answered cheerfully, signing something with a flourish, 'and you're bloody lucky to be alive, if you ask me. Not many survive that combination. But you're past the worst of it now. We'll have you on your feet in no time.'

Lucky? He didn't feel lucky. He felt weak and tired. He wanted to sleep again.

'What about my battalion?' he asked, feeling as if the room was fading away from him. He had to make an effort to regain his grip on it. The doctor leaned closer, frowning, and he felt strong fingers on his wrist.

'What was that, mate?'

He couldn't find the breath at first, but somehow he managed to push the words out in little gasps.

'Seventh Dublins . . . Tenth Division . . . where are they?'

'Oh, they're in Salonika, mate. Gone to Greece to fight the Bulgarians. But don't you worry about them. It's home for you now. A few weeks' rest and then straight back to Ireland.'

And home it was – home to Dublin at the bitter end of January. They'd kept him in hospital for two months, followed by another month of light duties. It was only then that he realized how sick he'd been. His arms and legs were gone to bone, and if he climbed a flight of stairs he had to stop and wait for the dizziness to pass. Even when they sent him home he was still weak, still dosing himself with quinine and camphor, and the cold cut him to the marrow. He stayed in barracks and went to bed early every night, clutching the hot-water bottle to his chest and wondering if he would ever feel warm again.

When spring came and the weather grew warmer he felt his strength begin to return. In March he saw his first medical board – a panel of stone-faced doctors who prodded him as if he was a laboratory specimen, muttered to each other about his liver, and at length pronounced him fit for home service.

But if his body had shrugged off the worst rigours of his ordeal, his mind still bore the scars. Part of him was still in Turkey. Some nights, when he was on the edge of sleep, he thought he could hear the distant boom of the naval guns, or smell the sickly stench of sun-bloated corpses. In his waking hours he would often shiver if the sun caught his eye just so, or the breeze rustled the leaves in the park. Even sitting in the breakfast-time clamour of the Empire Café, he found his eye drawn to the white twinkling of the sun on a glass and it was only when he felt a touch on his sleeve that he came to his senses.

'Penny for them, Stephen?' Billy asked.

Stephen smiled, embarrassed. Nothing could be further from Turkey than the sight of his friend in his striped blazer and straw boater. They were going to the Easter races at Fairyhouse and Billy's face was already glowing with excitement.

'Sorry, I was miles away. You were saying?'

'I was saying you should really make another effort to see your brother. I mean, since you're going away again next week. It might be your last chance.'

'Oh, come on, Billy. They're only sending me to Gravesend – not Timbuktu.'

'Yes, it's Gravesend next week, but then where?'

Then France, he admitted to himself. He was due another medical board in a few weeks, and he would almost certainly be passed fit for overseas service.

'Well, I already went to his—' the word was on the tip of his tongue, but he pulled himself up short. House was overstating it. Joe lived in a tenement room in Bull Alley, near Christchurch. 'I already went to his place, but he wasn't there.'

'Well, go again! He's only up the road now – but he'll be a damned sight further away when you're in Gravesend.'

Stephen didn't answer. He wanted to tell Billy it was none of his business, but he kept his mouth shut. Billy literally didn't know the half of it. He didn't know that before he'd tracked him down to Bull Alley, Stephen had first gone to their family home in Sandwith Street. Only it wasn't their family home any more. The first he knew about it was when he found it occupied by a family of strangers. He was so shocked that the first thing he did was walk away, determined to have it out with Joe. But then reason prevailed: Fool! Where had he gone? And he went back and knocked on the door of Mrs Byrne, the neighbour. It was she who gave him the address, as well as a box of books that Joe had left with her. He had taken some of the furniture with him and sold or given away the rest. Stephen listened to all this with as much equanimity as he could muster, and when he took his leave he thanked her for her trouble. But inside he was fuming. The cheek of him to take off like that without a word. To give away half their things and take the rest! He would kill the little bastard.

Encumbered by his books, Stephen had to go back to the barracks, but he went straight to the tenement house the next morning. As he walked through the courtyard, criss-crossed with lines of washing, he saw small children and young women staring at him from the corners and lower windows. It was the uniform. In that place, an army uniform only ever meant bad news or trouble.

The second-floor landing was gloomy and worn, but spotlessly clean. One of the doors was open, and his eyes met those of the stout woman who was inside on her hands and knees, scrubbing the floor.

'Good morning, ma'am. I'm looking for Joe Ryan.'

She stopped scrubbing and looked at him warily. 'Why? Is he after running?'

'Running?' It took a moment for him to realize it was the uniform again, 'Oh, no. It's not army business. I'm his brother.'

'He's out working.'

'Do you know where?'

'Down the docks.'

With one last suspicious glance at his uniform, she went back to scrubbing, but Stephen thanked her as he went down the stairs. He'd made up his mind before he even reached the doorway and walked back out into the yard. He stopped on the street and looked back at the building. It was completely alien to him – it could have been anywhere. There was no link between him and Joe now, no common ground. He wouldn't trawl the docks looking for him. They were finished. He turned on his heel and went back to the barracks.

Billy had probably guessed at least some of this from Stephen's silence, but he didn't press it, and instead gave him a steely look as he buttered a slice of toast.

'And whatever about him, I can't believe you didn't go and see Lillian Bryce.'

He felt his cheeks redden. 'Why would she want to see me?'

'God only knows, but, do you know what? I saw her not three weeks ago and she was asking after you again. I hadn't the heart to tell her you were home. It amazes me that you didn't even write to her from Turkey. If you're not careful you'll miss your chance with that girl.'

Once again, he was tempted to tell Billy it was none of his business. What did he know about girls, in any case? But what he didn't tell him was that he *had* written a letter to her. He'd written it the day after he came down from Karakol Dagh. He'd stuffed it with some of the elation he felt at having survived and thought it was the best thing he'd ever written. It was witty, effusive, bound to strike the right note. But that night they'd brought down the bodies from the ridge. They'd got a short truce to collect them before they bloated in the sun. More and more and more came down until there were hundreds of blanket-covered bundles lying on the sand. Some of the survivors prayed for their friends, but Stephen just sat there and looked at them until he started to shake. The next morning he was in charge of one of the burial parties. He tore up his letter and threw it into the shallow grave.

'I'm sure she was only being polite,' he answered evasively. 'She's a good-looking girl. I bet there's no shortage of chaps asking her out.'

'Well, that's where you're wrong. They're all afraid of her, same as you,' Billy said acidly.

'I'm not afraid of her.'

'And yet you think she's a good-looking girl?'

'Well, she is, in her own way.'

'Then why haven't you been to see her?'

Why not? That was a question he asked himself often – every day, now that his departure was imminent. He had recently returned to studying mathematics by himself; partly because he now had a box full of books in his Spartan room at the barracks, partly out of boredom. His day job was a mind-numbingly dull round of reports and summaries, and he spent half his time working out problems in his head before sitting down to write them up in the evenings. It was refreshing to return to the subject, and a relief to find that he hadn't lost his touch. By now, he had accumulated a thin sheaf of papers that he'd thought worth keeping. Nothing groundbreaking, but they might be of interest to the right person. He'd thought of sending them to Professor Barrett before he went away, but decided that would be far too formal. Besides, he'd soon realized that the person who most came to mind as he worked wasn't his old tutor, but Lillian Bryce. She seemed so close, and yet – when he glanced at the sun-bleached haversack he'd brought back from Turkey, with his tattered diary and other knick-knacks – so far away. It would never do. He knew it, and it pained him to think about it. It pained him that Billy kept asking about it too, but he did his best to mask his irritation with a smile.

'Don't be cross-examining me, Billy. It's your day off.'

But Billy wouldn't be put off. He merely changed his tack, carefully wiping his lips with a napkin before folding it and placing it on the table in front of him. When he spoke, his voice was measured and serious.

'I'm not cross-examining you. It's a simple enough question. Why don't you go and see her?'

'I don't want to burden her,' he answered, and grimly faced down Billy's incredulous look.

'What do you mean, you don't . . . ?'

Suddenly a man burst into the café.

'The Shinners are after taking over the post office!' he shouted, and dashed out again.

Along with most of the customers, Stephen twisted around in his seat to stare at the empty doorway. As he turned back he saw a policeman running past the window.

'Good Lord!' Billy exclaimed, 'What do you think that's about?'

'I honestly have no idea. Do you think it's a joke?'

Billy drained his coffee with a gulp. 'Come on, let's go down and have a look.'

'Ah, Billy,' Stephen looked uncertainly at his wristwatch. 'We'll miss our train!'

'Not if we're sharp about it. We can go down to Sackville Street, have a peek, and then hop across to Amiens Street Station. Come on, Stephen, it could be a laugh. We'll be at the course before the 12.30, and I'll bet you now it's not the Shinners at all – probably some students pulling a holiday prank. It might even be somebody we know.'

There was something going on in the bakery. Every day on her way to college Lillian passed the open gates, and she liked the warm yeasty smell that wafted out – but this morning the gates were locked and there was no such smell.

It was the first tangible clue she had that something was amiss. She stopped her bicycle and listened. The gates might be closed but there were definitely people inside. She could hear them running about, shouting, and then a steady hammering that echoed over the quiet streets. Maybe Mr Purcell had been right after all.

Mr Purcell was their next-door neighbour, a shy old gentleman who was a retired solicitor and sounded like it – dull, prosy and precise. He had knocked on the door just after the breakfast things had been tidied away and, in his roundabout rambling way, told Lillian and her mother that he had just come up from town, where he had gone to meet his friend, Mr Donohue. Here, Mrs Bryce's face took on a look of bored indifference to both Mr Purcell and his friend, but it soon changed to consternation when he explained that he had seen men in uniforms taking over the post office and heard shooting coming from Dublin Castle. A lot of shooting – it sounded like a proper battle. And wasn't young Sheila on duty up there this morning?

Young Sheila certainly was on duty up there this morning, and Lillian saw the blood drain from her mother's face at the mention of shooting. Mr Purcell carried on blithely, trying to console them with the thought that it probably wasn't the Germans, but Sinn Fein, or perhaps the Volunteers. There were far too many people going about with rifles, in his opinion. Lillian cut him off with a polite but firm thank you, and practically bundled him out through the hall door. When she came back into the sitting room she was buttoning up her cardigan.

'And where do you think you're going?' her mother asked, though she never stirred from her armchair. She wouldn't have called her oldest daughter headstrong, but she could be very determined. Once she had decided to do something, there was no stopping her.

'I'm going into town to see what's happening, Mam.'

Her mother nervously twisted a handkerchief between her fingers. 'If there's trouble, I don't want the pair of you out in it.'

'Don't worry about either of us, Mam. Sheila's in the castle, and there's no safer place in the city. I'll try to get up to see her, but if I can't, I'll go back to the college. It'll be safe enough there.'

'If there's any trouble I want you to come straight back here. Don't be taking any chances, now.'

'Don't worry, Mam. It's probably only the Volunteers having another drill. They're always taking over places.'

But she had to admit that it felt different. Even standing out on the street in front of the bakery – not five minutes from her house – she could feel a quiet tension in the air. She almost jumped at the sound of cartwheels grinding close behind the wooden gates. There was a bump, and then a young man's head appeared above the wall. He was wearing the light green slouch hat that she recognized as part of the Irish Volunteer uniform.

'Good morning, miss,' he touched his hat politely when he saw her.

'Good morning.'

'I'm sorry, miss, the bakery is closed. No bread today.'

'Why? What are you doing?'

'We're taking over,' he answered with a grin.

'You're taking over the bakery?'

'No, miss, the whole country.'

'Well, I hope it keeps fine for you,' she murmured, and started to remount her bicycle.

Rat-tat-tat! Three shots rang out a few streets away and she looked uneasily in that direction. So did the young man behind the gate.

'You should go home, miss,' he advised. 'There might be a bit of fighting.'

'I can't. I'm going to see my sister,' she said firmly, and cycled off towards the city centre.

It seemed to her that things became more normal as she went

along. There were certainly more people about, but there was an air of confusion too. As she cycled along Westland Row, she heard a distant crackling coming from north of the river, and saw knots of people stop to stare in that direction. Then they all started to move again, picking up the threads of conversations as if they hadn't heard anything.

She freewheeled around College Green, taking care in crossing the treacherous tram tracks, and then started the final push up Dame Street. Something cracked over her head, and she saw people on the pavement running to take shelter in doorways. A policeman came running out, waving her down as a tram shuddered to a halt with a squeal of brakes.

'You can't go up there, young lady,' the policeman warned. 'There's people shooting. Keep back down here where it's safe.'

As if to emphasize his warning there was another crack, and one of the tram's windows fell in with a crash. There were screams and muffled curses. People came running off the tram and shouldered their way into the meagre shelter of the shop fronts.

'It's not safe, miss. Go back!'

Billy stood alone in the small crowd in Sackville Street – alone, because Stephen had been nabbed as they walked past Trinity College. The heavy oak doors had opened a crack as they ambled past, and a uniformed cadet ran out and nervously saluted. Billy thought he was making fun of them until he remembered that Stephen was in uniform. He was surprised by the change that came over his friend. Whereas before he had walked in an easy slouch, with his hands behind his back, he straightened visibly and returned a smart salute before the young man breathlessly got out his request – the cadets were defending the college. They had already rounded up some Australians on sick leave – here he broke off and pointed to the roof, where they saw the silhouette of a man with a rifle – and if the lieutenant wasn't already under orders, they would welcome his assistance.

'Sorry, Billy – duty calls,' he said ruefully. 'I'd best go inside.'

Billy handed him the racing glasses slung across his shoulder. 'Here, take these. I dare say they'll come in handy for keeping watch and so forth.'

'Won't you need them at the races?'

'Oh, to hell with the races. It looks like all the fun's in town today.'

Looking at the high-columned front of the General Post Office, however, he was no longer sure if this was fun at all. There was a distinct earnestness about the men he could see, and they certainly weren't students – not the way they were putting out the windows and barricading them with books and furniture. Apart from that, they were all in uniform: most wore the leaf green of the National Volunteers, but there was a sprinkling of the darker green of the Citizen Army. After a while two flags broke out on the roof – one a tricolour of green, white and orange, and the other a plain green flag with a golden harp and some writing on it that he couldn't make out.

'Can you see what it says?' he asked the man next to him, who was shading his eyes with his hand.

'I think it's "The Irish Republic".'

'Well, well. Whatever will they think of next?'

If the republic was to be created by breaking windows then things appeared to be well under way. Otherwise there didn't seem to be anything to get excited about. The crowd had already started to break up when the front door of the post office opened and a man in a slouch hat and a long green overcoat walked out. He unfolded a sheet of paper and cleared his throat uncertainly, looking up and down the street as if he was afraid somebody would come and shoo him away.

'I know him,' Billy exclaimed, and racked his brains for a name. Was it Parsons? No, Pearse. Of course! Patrick Pearse. Old Barton had pointed him out one morning on Usher's Quay. Used to be a barrister, but had given it up for schoolmastering – among other things, by the look of it. Well, there was a turn-up for the books.

He listened attentively as Pearse started to read out his speech, but he wasn't alone in being barely able to make out a word of it.

'Speak up,' somebody shouted from the back, and when Pearse finished there was a half-hearted smattering of applause, and a couple of wags called out 'Encore!' to hoots of laughter.

Pearse ignored them, folded up his speech, and went back inside. Billy strolled over to Nelson's Pillar, where a Citizen Army man was pasting up posters.

By the time he got back to the college, the great oak door was locked once again. His pounding fist hardly seemed to make a sound, so he rapped on the wood with the head of his cane.

The door opened a crack and a face peered suspiciously out from the shadows within.

'What do you want?'

The voice seemed familiar. Billy peered closely at the white blur of a face and took off his boater.

'Harry Cardiff? Is that you?'

'Oh, what ho, Billy.' The door opened all the way and revealed the gangly shape of his former classmate. 'You'd best come in. Orders, you know. I've got to keep the door closed in case they try to get in here.'

Billy stepped inside and Cardiff bolted the door behind him.

'The Volunteers, you mean?'

'Yes. Apparently they're all over the place. They've already attacked Dublin Castle and I hear they're digging trenches in Stephen's Green.'

'Good Lord. I've just come up from Sackville Street and they're down there as well. Doesn't that mean we're surrounded?'

'After a fashion, I suppose. They're only taking over places at the moment. There hasn't been an awful lot of fighting per se.'

'Do you think they'll try to take the college?'

'I would, if I were them. Apart from anything else, we've got a pile of rifles and ammunition in the armoury. But they'll have a job getting in now. As well as the cadets, we've managed to round up a good few soldiers to mount a defence.'

'It's one of those I'm after. Do you remember my friend Stephen Ryan? He was a maths student, but he joined up when the war started, so it's Lieutenant Ryan now. He was shanghaied about an hour ago.'

'Oh, yes, I remember him. Tall chap, isn't he? I saw him earlier and I thought he looked familiar. I'd say he's probably up on the roof. Most of the regulars are up there.'

A few minutes later Billy put his head through the trapdoor leading to the roof of the West Front.

'Stephen,' he called in a hoarse stage whisper, 'permission to come up?'

Stephen turned from the low balustrade where he had rested Billy's racing glasses to watch the goings-on in Sackville Street.

'Yes, come on. Just keep your head down.'

Billy dashed across in a low crouch, clutching his hat to his chest. There were three other soldiers crouched in the corners of the roof, watching in all directions, but Billy's eyes were drawn to the rifle slung on Stephen's shoulder.

'Where did you get that?' he demanded, as he knelt down behind the balustrade.

'We've all been issued with rifles from the cadets' armoury,' Stephen answered absently, focusing the glasses on the space around Nelson's Pillar.

'Can I have a shot?'

Stephen took down the glasses and gave him a withering look. 'No.'

'Oh, go on. I've never fired a gun before.'

'Precisely, Billy. This is hardly the time to start. I can't just let you blaze away at the rest of the population. Besides, your eyesight's so bad you'd probably end up shooting me.'

'Spoilsport.' Billy made a face and folded his arms. 'I've a good mind not to tell you what I found out!'

Stephen gave him a knowing smile. 'You'd better tell me, or I'll have you arrested when martial law is declared.'

This appealed to the legal part of Billy's mind. He sat up with a grin.

'Martial law? Do you really think they'll declare it? I thought they'd just read the Riot Act.'

'Almost certainly, the way things are going. There was a lot of shooting going on around Dublin Castle a little while ago. I'd say they mean business, whoever they are.'

'Well, they're definitely not students. Most of the ones I saw were Irish Volunteers. The man in charge is a chap called Pearse – he runs a school out Rathfarnham way, would you believe? In any event, they've declared themselves to be the Provisional Government of Ireland. Pearse read out their manifesto in front of the GPO.'

Stephen frowned. 'They've declared themselves to be the government? On whose authority?'

'The dead generations, or some such. I don't know, I couldn't hear it very well. But they've got guns, Stephen. I suppose that's all the authority they need.'

'Well, they're going the bloody wrong way about getting Home Rule, that's for sure.'

'Home Rule? Don't be silly. These boys aren't looking for Home

Rule. It's the whole shooting match they're after: full independence for Ireland.'

There was a sound like a whip-crack overhead and Billy looked up.

'What was that?'

'A rifle bullet,' Stephen answered casually, and folded his arms as he leaned against the balustrade. His expression turned thoughtful. 'You're the legal expert, Billy. What do you think? Would you say this was treason? I mean, since we're already at war.'

'Are they shooting at us, Stephen? Hadn't you better sit down?'

'Oh, it was miles too high. I wouldn't let it bother you.'

'Really?' Billy gave him a curious look, 'Well, to answer your question, I suppose it depends on what happens next. True, there's been some shooting, but no actual *fighting* so far – at least from what I've seen. No doubt the government will make their move shortly, and if those chaps in the GPO and elsewhere come out with their hands up, then it'll be a few months in jail, a few fines, but no hard feelings. On the other hand, if they decide to scrap it out, if they actually mean to start an insurrection in time of war, then it will go very hard for them. I should imagine they'll throw the flaming book at them – and I'm sure I don't have to tell you what that might entail if martial law is declared.'

The words were hardly out of his mouth when a loud flurry of crackling came from the direction of Sackville Street. The air overhead was slit and cut by passing bullets, and Stephen whirled around and brought up the binoculars.

'Lancers,' he said, and then a few moments later, 'looks like they mounted a charge against the post office. There are horses loose, and some men lying in the street.' He slowly brought down the binoculars and looked at Billy, appalled. 'This is madness.'

'That's one way of putting it,' Billy agreed, and raised his head above the balustrade to try to see for himself. Dead men lying where he'd been standing not half an hour ago. Even the idea of it made him feel slightly sick. 'And I'm afraid there's something else you should know. The Volunteers aren't the only ones involved in this little caper. When I was down there I saw Citizen Army uniforms as well, and one of the names at the bottom of Pearse's manifesto was none other than Joe's friend, James Connolly. I could be mistaken, but I'm very much afraid that your little brother is in this right up to his neck.'

A troubled look came over Stephen's face. 'I might have bloody known!' he muttered. 'What has the silly bastard got himself into now?'

Brennan was talking again. He'd been chattering like a monkey all morning, but now he was starting to get on Joe's nerves. It must be the excitement, he thought, but he was in no humour for talk.

'For fuck's sake. Will you ever shut up?'

Brennan's face went slack and he glumly closed his mouth.

'Sorry, Joe.'

'Sergeant.'

'Sorry, sergeant.'

With Brennan looking at him like a slapped dog, Joe suddenly felt ashamed of himself. He was a decent lad, and he'd do anything you asked.

'Barricade the window with them books,' he said, but in a more conciliatory tone. Brennan obediently scooped up an armful of the books and started stacking them on the windowsill. Joe looked at them doubtfully. They might stop the odd bullet, but they wouldn't be much use against a good volley. He looked around the ransacked room, but there was nothing else they could use. For all his snooty protests and bluster, the editor of the *Dublin Mail & Express* didn't have much of an office.

But he did have a good view of Dame Street. Joe went to the window and looked out over the stack of books. Across the street he could see the main gate of Dublin Castle, with the big statue of Justice standing on top. Beside it stood the Grecian columns and green copper dome of City Hall. He got a thrill when he realized they were already in there. A couple of green-clad figures were moving around the roof, and the tall windows were starting to fill up with furniture and other odds and ends. It was a good spot. They'd have a clear shot right down into the castle yard from that roof, and that was all they wanted. That was the clever part. The Brits would be barricading themselves inside the castle, thinking they were under siege. But they didn't need to take the castle, just dominate it. The Brits would have to come out eventually, and when they did they'd know all about it.

When he turned his head and looked down the length of Dame Street, though, his delight turned to dismay. He found himself looking straight at the stone front of Trinity College and it made him anxious. With its high walls and iron railings it was well fortified, and if the Brits got troops in there they'd have a near-impregnable base right in the centre of the city.

And he knew that was exactly what they would do. As soon as they realized what was going on they would bring men in from all over, reinforcing and infiltrating and slowly putting a stranglehold on the city. They weren't stupid, and they wouldn't take this lying down. They would do whatever it took to crush the rebellion. Connolly had once said the British wouldn't use artillery in the city, but Joe thought he was wrong. They would. They would call this treachery and raze Dublin to the ground if they had to.

'We're in a great old spot here,' Brennan grinned, looking down the street beside him. 'We'll have them in a right old crossfire when they come.'

He was chattering again, but Joe let it pass.

'Just you keep your eyes on that gate,' he said, but he kept his own eyes on the college. It reminded him of his brother and he wondered where he was. He knew he was home from Turkey – Mrs Lyons had made sure the whole bloody building knew his brother was in the army – but he had no idea if he'd gone away again. Connolly had asked about him that morning in Beresford Place. They'd all paraded there – Volunteers and Citizen Army together – and Connolly had made a point of going around and shaking hands with his men before they marched off to their allotted positions. With most of the others it had been nothing more than a handshake, but he'd taken Joe by the arm and led him out of earshot.

'Have you heard anything from your brother, Joe?' he asked earnestly.

Joe shook his head.

'Well, is he still in the country? If he is, he might be sent against us. Have you thought of that?'

'Sure, of course I have.'

'And you might end up fighting him.'

Joe shrugged. 'We've been fighting one another ever since we were kids.'

'This is different, Joe. The next time you see him could be over the sights of your rifle.'

'Look, Jim, we're both grown men. He made his choice and I made mine. I'd rather not fight with him, but I'll do whatever I have to do if the time comes. You can rely on me for that.'

Connolly thought for a moment and then held out his hand.

'The best of luck to you, so. I'll pray God that you get through this.'

Joe forced a smile. That morning was the first time he'd ever seen fear in Connolly's face. Not for himself, he realized, but for the others, for the men who were following him.

'Sure, we'll all get through this,' he said, though his voice cracked on the words.

'No we won't,' Connolly replied, and with an unhappy shake of his head he quickly marched away.

'A soldier!' Brennan exclaimed, bringing Joe back to the present. He blinked and tried to follow a jabbing finger.

'Where?'

'Down at the gate. He's coming out, look.'

The castle gates had been opened about a foot and a khaki figure was crouched in the gap, carefully checking the street for signs of life.

'Well, what are you gawping at him for?' Joe asked, seeing Brennan's rifle still propped against the windowsill. 'Shoot him!'

VI

Stephen yawned, stretched and scratched the stubble on his chin. He needed a shave, and he'd better see to it before Captain Lawford came around. Lawford was a regular officer home on leave from France, and he'd been put in charge of the college defences. A sharp crack from over the roof told him he had nothing to worry about for the time being. Not content with merely organizing sentries, Lawford had installed himself at a window over the front gate and started sniping at the rebel positions around Dublin Castle. He'd been at it all yesterday afternoon and on into the evening until the light grew too dim. Now it was bright he was off again. Bloodthirsty little sod.

Stephen counted the little row of cartridges that lay on the roof beside him. Twenty, same as yesterday. He hadn't fired a shot.

But his men had. There were only three of them, all Australians here on sick leave from France. They'd tried a few shots when they saw the rebels fortifying the buildings on the corner of Sackville Street and eventually provoked a furious volley that sent them ducking down behind the balustrade as bullets spat and whizzed overhead.

'Fucking Irish bastards!' one of them shouted, laughing, but then looked aghast at Stephen, who pretended not to notice.

There was no sign of life in those buildings this morning, but the windows were still barricaded. When he slid Billy's racing glasses from one to the other he saw the corpse still lying below O'Connell's statue. There since yesterday. God knows how he wandered into the middle of it, but a sniper got him. As he watched the eastern corner, a figure walked into his field of view from further up the street. A young girl, barefoot, but wearing a fur coat and an oversized hat. The looters were growing bold now – not even a corpse would frighten them off. It was early yet, and there would probably be more as the day wore on. But nothing like the number he saw yesterday – hundreds of them pouring out of the tenements and rampaging through Dunn's and Nobbett's and Clery's. They'd cleared the place out and there was hardly anything left to loot, the street carpeted with glass and strewn with discarded clothes and cardboard.

He turned around at the sound of the hatch opening. He'd only sent his men down for breakfast ten minutes ago and they couldn't be back already. Perhaps it was Billy coming back. He'd gone down last evening when he finally got bored looking at the empty streets. But it certainly wasn't Billy. He was so startled to see a woman emerging that she was halfway across the roof before he recognized her.

'Get down,' he whispered, waving urgently. Lillian's smile changed to a look of surprise before she dropped into a crouch and hurried forward, her heavy skirt rustling.

'Sorry,' she said breathlessly. 'Are they shooting at us?'

'Not just at the moment,' he admitted, carefully scanning the strongpoints again before he put the glasses down. 'But I don't like to encourage them.'

'I brought you some breakfast.' She knelt down beside him and handed him a brown-paper parcel and an earthenware bottle that felt warm in his hand. 'Courtesy of your friend Billy. He's been drafted into the kitchen.'

He weighed the parcel dubiously. 'You mean Billy actually cooked something?'

'Well, I wouldn't put it as strongly as that. He's only making sandwiches and tea at the moment, though he says he has ambitions to try his hand at soup for lunch. May I?' She gestured at the racing glasses.

'By all means.' He took a bite from one of the sandwiches and chewed thoughtfully, watching her out of the corner of his eye. It was a year since he had last seen her and the time had been kind. Her face was fuller and her brown hair longer; it was now tied in a neat ponytail at the nape of her neck. She looked less gaunt and therefore less severe, a little more good-humoured. There was the faint trace of a smile on her face as she focused the glasses on the shattered shop fronts of Sackville Street.

'I heard you were back from Turkey,' she said, still looking through the glasses, and just as Stephen felt a jet of embarrassment burning his cheeks, she exclaimed, 'Oh! There's one. He just ran right across the street!'

Stephen swallowed hastily, glad of the change in subject. 'Which way?'

'Left to right – towards Clery's. Here, take a look.'

He took the glasses but found the street empty, as he expected. The corpse was still there, but even the little girl had vanished. All he could see was the sun glittering on broken glass.

'Probably a messenger,' he observed, 'Their headquarters is in the GPO, but they've got outposts across the street as well.'

'My goodness. They really have dug themselves in, haven't they? I imagine it will be quite difficult to get them out.'

Stephen nodded. 'Not without artillery, at any rate.'

'Well, it's funny you should say that,' she said. 'I saw some artillerymen earlier, digging a field gun into the lawn in New Square. Did you ever think you'd see the day? It's mad. The whole place is gone mad.'

'Strange days indeed,' he admitted, setting down the glasses and returning to his sandwich. 'But how do you come to be here? Did you come in this morning?'

'Not at all. I've been here since yesterday afternoon. I was trying to get up to Dublin Castle to see my sister. You do remember Sheila, don't you? You met her that night at Mary D'Arcy's party.'

Stephen smiled as he uncorked the bottle and took a drink of sweet tea. How could he forget?

'Of course I do. She wanted to be a nurse, didn't she?'

'That's right. Well, she got her wish and now she's working in the hospital above in the castle. When I heard there was trouble starting I tried to get up to see her, but a policeman turned me back. I thought I might be able to go up after it got dark, but the soldiers said there was a curfew, so I had to stay here.'

'There was some heavy fighting going on around the castle yesterday. I heard machine-gun fire coming from up there.'

'Yes. One of the soldiers told me the Citizen Army had occupied City Hall and they were trying to get them out last night.'

Stephen stopped the bottle halfway to his lips.

'The Citizen Army?'

'So he said. Apparently they're involved in this rebellion as well. About half of them are in Stephen's Green but the rest of them are up around the castle.'

'God Almighty,' he murmured, and in the brief pause that followed he heard the cracking report of Lawford's rifle from across the roof. Stephen had been in that room, and he'd seen the table pulled up to the window with clips of ammunition strewn around it. The window gave a clear shot right up Dame Street, to Dublin Castle and City Hall.

'So, what will you do now?' he asked, 'Do you still want to get up to the castle?'

'I'd like to, but I don't see how I can unless there's a ceasefire this afternoon. They're still fighting up there and I won't be let out on my own after dark.'

'I'll take you,' he offered, before he was even sure he would be allowed. But the more he thought about it, the more likely it seemed. The telephone lines were still out and they'd be keen to get messages back and forth. 'If you don't mind waiting until tonight, I'll take you up there when it gets dark.'

'Is it dark yet?'

Joe looked around at the question. Brennan's face was just a white blur in the gloom of the basement. His voice was a dry croak, little more than a whisper, and Joe licked his own cracked lips as he looked up through the grating at the dying light outside. He'd never felt more in need of a drink in all his life, but there was nothing to be done. They had no water and no hope of getting any until it was fully dark. Just their luck to end up in the basement of a haberdasher's shop – nothing but bolts of cloth and reels of thread all over the place. A few yards further and they would have made it to a pub.

'We'll give it another few minutes just to be sure,' he said, and went over to where Brennan was lying propped in the corner. 'How's the leg?'

'Not so bad.' Brennan forced a weak smile through the grime on his face, 'I think the bleeding's stopped, but I've a woeful thirst on me.'

'That makes two of us, so.' Joe slid his back down the wall, yawning as he finally sat down, 'But not to worry, there'll be plenty to drink once we get out of this hole.'

If we get out. Christ knows we've done well to get this far. He shuddered to think about those last few minutes in the office with bullets thudding up through the floorboards and plaster flying from the walls. All morning they'd had machine guns firing at them from the smouldering roof of City Hall. Then came the first charge from the castle, and they'd knocked it back. They'd hit them hard, cutting down ten, twenty of them in the street. But they came again, and again, and suddenly they were in the door, trying to force their way up the stairs – fifty of them: shouting, screaming, howling like savages. They wanted revenge. They wanted blood for the blood on the street.

But, by God, they'd made them pay for it. Shooting down the stairs through the smoke and the dust. Screaming, blood, the smell of gun smoke. And all the time more of them kept pouring in through the door. It couldn't last. They were running out of ammunition but the rifles were getting too hot to shoot anyway. Men were being hit – dying, screaming, bleeding – but the khaki kept creeping up the stairs until it was butts and bayonets, feet, fists and bodies.

In the end they broke and ran. The only way out was through the windows, a long drop into the alleys behind. Joe found Brennan leaning out of a window, hurt in the leg, afraid of the height.

'It's too far—'

'Get out, for God's sake, get out.'

The only thing holding the British forces back was the pile of dead and dying men lying on the stairs, the ominous silence with the threat of another volley through the smoke. But they were coming, picking their way slowly.

'For fuck's sake! Get out or we're dead!'

He bundled Brennan out of the window, dangling him as low

as he could by the arms before he let go. He landed in a heap on the cobbles, the leg giving out, a muffled scream. Uncaring, Joe dropped his rifle down on top of him and scrambled out, feeling the cold air flying past his face and then the thump and pain in his shins when he landed.

Behind him, he heard the crash of a door being kicked in, shouts, the crack of a shot. He picked up his rifle and Brennan by the scruff of his coat and dragged him down the alley. No plan, no thought in his mind but to get away. Then there were shouts behind him, the clatter of boots running on the cobbles, and he darted into cover, flinging his weight against the next door he saw and crashing into the narrow space behind. A gloomy corridor, stairs leading down. He gently closed the door and sat back against it, clutching the hot rifle to his chest and listening, hardly daring to breathe as the boots ran past.

That was hours ago. After his heart stopped thumping against his ribs, he'd helped Brennan down the stairs into the basement and looked at his leg. A bullet had passed clean through his thigh, but there was a lot of blood, his trousers soaked in it. Nothing to do but tie a hankie around it and wait.

'Do you think they'll have patrols out?' Brennan asked, and he gave Joe such a start that he wondered if he'd been dozing.

'What? No, no. Not after dark. Too dangerous. They'll pull them back to the castle for the night.'

Christ, you're an awful liar! He let all his breath out and tried to wash out some of the tiredness with it. He was weary, but they'd have to move. If they could get across the Liffey they might be able to get into the GPO garrison, or the Four Courts. That's if they were still there. If they'd been hit half as hard . . .

He put that thought from his mind. All the hours he'd been down in the cellar, he'd been thinking about Connolly – wondering if he were still alive. They'd had no news, nothing to tell them if the other garrisons were still standing. What little hope he'd held onto after his escape had been dashed by the slow, insistent thump that he'd heard first in the afternoon; the steady pounding of an artillery piece. That was the end, he knew – because once they started, they wouldn't stop until it was all over.

He put on his cap and picked up his rifle. No point in moping – all he could do was try. He got Brennan under the arms and helped him to his feet. Fumbling in the dark, he managed to sling the rifle across his back and pull Brennan's arm across his shoulders. Then the step and hop up the stairs to the door. He eased it open an inch and felt the blessed cool air on his face. Brennan was breathing hard, but quiet, determined.

'All clear,' he whispered, and they shuffled out into the alley. He could hear the crackle of gunfire, and now and then the heavier boom of artillery. There was an orange glow in the sky to the north, but he headed away from it for now. They had to keep off the main streets, stay in the alleys as long as they could. A turn and they were headed towards the river, past blank walls and privies, with the great grey mass of Christchurch looming above them. They were heading down now, they'd be on the quays, and then—

'Halt,' a voice barked out behind them.

'Ah, shite!' He heard Brennan hiss. They broke into a desperate, awkward run, hobbling along like a pair of cripples, until a shot rang out and Joe felt an almighty kick in his back.

The shattering boom of the field gun burst out of the darkness and echoed around the four walls of Front Square. Lillian jumped at the noise and pulled her cardigan closer around her throat. They'd been firing all day, but she still couldn't get used to it. She'd gone over to watch earlier on and found it strangely mundane. It was just a machine, worked by men stripped to their shirts, laughing and joking with each other as they passed the brass shells into the breech and then covered their ears to fire. Every time they pulled the lanyard the percussion from the muzzle flattened the daffodils. Then the breech was opened and the empty cartridge slid out, smoking, as the next was passed along. But it was no ordinary machine. Those shells it blasted out were flying over houses and shops, falling in the streets, blowing out windows and doors. She shuddered to think what happened when one met with flesh and bone.

The ringing of bootnails brought her back to the present. The sentry at the gate straightened, and she saw Stephen silhouetted against the watch fires in the square, coming towards her under the arch of the front gate. He seemed to tower over her in the darkness, his teeth flashing as he smiled. She felt her heart beginning to race.

'Good evening, Miss Bryce. Sorry I kept you waiting. Captain Lawford had some messages he wanted me to carry up to the castle.'

A nod to the guard standing by the oak doors and the wicket gate was opened. Stephen looked out and his face was bathed in an orange glow.

'I think it will be best if we go by the backstreets,' he said, in a matter of fact way. 'No point in making targets of ourselves. Now, before we go I want you to promise me that if anything . . . unfortunate happens to me, then you'll turn around and come straight back here.'

'Certainly not.'

A bemused expression came over his face. 'I beg your pardon?'

'I said: certainly not. You're asking me to run away without helping you. Would you run away if I was shot?'

'No, of course not.'

'Well, then. Let's say no more about it.' She gestured out of the door, 'After you, Mr Ryan. That is to say, Lieutenant.'

'Stephen will do, Miss B—'

'Lillian.'

'All right, then.'

He stepped out through the gate and she stepped out after him, feeling strangely exposed after being so long enclosed. They hadn't gone far before she noticed he had his revolver out of its holster. This was a different Stephen Ryan to the one she remembered. The nervous boy who had walked her home from the ball had grown up. He was still shy, still terribly quiet, but now he wore his reserve like armour. The hesitation was gone. He moved with a predatory grace, neither crouching nor running, but walking with light easy steps that carried him across the darkened street like a shadow.

She followed him across, her heart thumping. For the first few yards she was hunched in anxious expectation of the shots that must surely ring out. But there was no sound except the crunch of broken glass as she stepped up onto the kerb. She kept her eyes on the dark of his back, only darting them to one side as they passed the tram stopped in the middle of the street, oddly silent, as if it had been frozen in place. She wondered if this could possibly be real, but then an eddy in the breeze carried down the stink of burning wood and paper, and she knew it was.

He stopped suddenly at the end of Dame Lane and she cannoned into him.

'Sorry,' she whispered.

He didn't answer, but took her hand and led her along the dark laneway. The thrill of it was electric. She remembered the breathless feeling she'd had when Billy said his name that morning. It took an effort not to be too eager to take the food up to him. And then the elation when she climbed through the trapdoor and he was there! But that wasn't like her. She was as giddy as a little girl. Was this love? This ground-sliding feeling, this overpowering happiness? If it was, then she wanted it, she would not turn it away, and yet she held herself back.

Why? They stopped on the corner of George's Street and the dull orange glow from City Hall cast his face in deep contrast. His eyes were empty black sockets, his cheeks dark hollows, but still she felt the urge. One touch, one movement – to reach up and kiss his cheek. That one act would say all the things she couldn't put in words. She would no longer have to hold herself back, no longer need to pretend. But what if he rejected her? She couldn't bear that look; puzzlement – maybe even amusement. Far better to keep her dream alive than see it destroyed.

He saved her by darting across the street, still holding her hand, and they plunged into the shadow of the castle wall. Stopped again, waiting, peering into the darkness. She was breathless now, and he squeezed her hand. What was that? She squeezed back, trying to feel some of the life in him. Why was he so inscrutable? One look was all she wanted, just one chink.

'Who goes there?' The voice was harsh, nervous and edgy, cutting out of the darkness just ahead of them. He stepped back against the wall, pressing her into the shadows with his arm.

'Lieutenant Ryan, Royal Dublin Fusiliers.'

She peered past him. A shadow detached itself from the wall and stepped out into the laneway. She saw the dull dome of a helmet and the long shape of a rifle barrel glinting.

'Show yourself, then.'

Another squeeze of her hand and they stepped out into the open, Stephen holding his revolver up by the barrel. An electric torch came on, its yellow light dazzling them.

'I've come over from Trinity College. I have messages for the officer commanding,' Stephen said, shielding his eyes. 'This is Miss Bryce. Her sister's a nurse at the hospital inside.'

'Good to see you, sir. Come on . . .' The voice was much more welcoming now, and they walked towards the light, finding a gate that was barricaded with sandbags and planking and had a machine gun set up at its centre. They walked through and found the broad yard crammed with carts, gun carriages and motor lorries.

'You'll have to go to the upper yard to find the colonel, sir,' the sentry told them and, looking at Lillian, he added, 'The hospital's up there as well, though I hear they've moved the patients down into the cellars, what with the shooting and all.'

The upper yard was full of light. Two enormous watch fires blazed on the cobbles and the colonnade was dotted with storm lanterns, but over it all the cupola of City Hall was still glowing like a torch, now and then dumping great gobs of thick smoke into the yard. Lillian followed Stephen as he threaded his way between the fires and knots of soldiers, feeling dwarfed by all this and wishing that he was still holding her hand.

'There are nurses over there.' She pointed to some blue-clad women moving along the colonnade, bending over the line of bodies lying on the ground. Wounded, she thought, and her heart faltered. So many of them.

One of the nurses stood up and moved a few paces before bending down again. Lillian couldn't make out her face, but she thought she recognized her sister – the way she moved, the curve of her back.

'I think that's Sheila,' she exclaimed, surprised at the sudden rush of emotion. She'd been telling herself all along that Sheila would be fine . . . but was it really her? Now the figure was crouched down it was hard to tell. She wanted to be sure, but part of her was afraid to go over, and another part didn't want to leave Stephen.

'Why don't you go over and see,' he suggested. 'I'll come and find you after I've given—' He broke off at the sound of a commotion at the main gate. The inner gate was being opened on squealing hinges.

'Patrol coming in!' the sergeant shouted, and a squad of men came hurrying through the gap. Two of them were dragging a man between them, and two more were carrying another on a door.

'Joe! Joe!' The upright man was shouting pitifully, twisting around to try and see the man on the door. 'Joe! For God's sake, help him, will you. He's not moving.'

'Shut yer trap, mate!' The sergeant jerked his head down the yard. 'Take them over to the barracks.'

'He needs a doctor,' the wounded man shouted hysterically. 'He needs help. Joe, Joe!'

Stephen was running already, his heart beating harshly against his chest. The closer he got, the more certain he was. He felt his throat closing with fear.

'Put him down,' he shouted to the men carrying the door. They looked surprised, but obeyed him, setting down their load almost gently. He pulled the body towards him and saw his brother's face; pale, bloodless, eyes closed. 'Oh, for God's sake, Joe!' he whispered, feeling for a pulse. It was there, but only barely. His skin was cold and clammy to the touch. 'What have you done now, you stupid bastard?'

'They shot him!' the other man accused, weeping now. 'The bastards shot him in the back!'

'Who is it?' Lillian asked, and he felt her hand on his shoulder as she bent down beside him. 'Stephen, what's the matter? Do you know him?'

The soldiers who had been carrying the door had already started edging away, sensing trouble, but Stephen didn't even look at them as he nodded. His face was almost as pale as the man on the makeshift stretcher.

'He's my brother.'

VII

The fat Welshman on the train had bad feet.

'Fallen arches, see,' he explained, holding one up. 'Keeps me out of the army.'

Stephen wanted to say it was just as bloody well, but he bit his tongue. It wouldn't do to be facetious while he was in uniform. This last fact had not escaped his fellow passenger's notice when he got on at Wrexham.

'You're a soldier, are you?' he observed with a knowing wink. 'What regiment are you with then?'

'The Royal Dublin Fusiliers.'

'The Dublin Fusiliers, eh? Are you from Ireland, then?'

'Yes, I am.'

He had said this defiantly, in the hope of forestalling the conversation. The train was almost empty, and he'd been enjoying the solitude until this gregarious Welshman had come bumping into the compartment, with his threadbare carpetbag and brown-paper parcels. These last three months in England he'd found that the very fact that he was Irish – or even the sound of his accent – tended to dry up all talk in his vicinity. But no such luck in this case.

'Oh aye? I'm Welsh myself, as you may have guessed. Ifans is the name.' He held out a podgy hand. 'Griff Ifans. I'm from a little place called Trefriw, just down from Conwy, in Caernarfonshire.'

Stephen just smiled and nodded as he shook the warm hand. He could hardly make out a word of the mellifluous singsong flow that poured out of the man, but that didn't seem to put Ifans off. For two hours he kept up an endless stream of inane banter, mixing personal details – he was something in animal feed, apparently – with a tour-guide commentary on the Welsh countryside passing by the window.

'That's Bala, see. Nice place, Bala. I knew a girl there once, Elsie was her name . . .'

The train was puffing asthmatically up a steep incline. After Bala, Stephen knew the next stop was his, and he silently willed it on with every ounce of his being. To distract himself from Ifans and his bad feet he stared out of the window. It was late September, but it felt like winter was already taking hold. The slate hillsides towered above the train, slick in the drizzling rain. Grey clouds were weeping over them and the whole country looked cold and inhospitable. *Christ Almighty! Where did the summer go?*

At last the train seemed to run out of steam and shuddered to a halt, still on the incline, and apparently in the middle of nowhere.

'Frongoch!' the conductor shouted down the corridor, 'Anybody for Frongoch?'

'It was nice to meet you,' Stephen said, snatching up his parcel and darting into the corridor before Ifans could get another word in. He found the door and jumped down into the rain. As the train squealed and puffed and started to grind uphill once again he looked at his surroundings. The same slate hillsides, the same weeping clouds. Only when the train was gone did he see the handful of stocky stone cottages and a much taller building with the forbidding aspect of a reformatory. Clustered around it were some wooden huts and barbed-wire fences. Joe had said in his letter that it used to be a distillery. No wonder they turned it into a prison camp. Who ever heard of Welsh whiskey?

They clearly weren't used to visitors. The guards in their glistening gas capes eyed him suspiciously as he walked up the road with his parcel under his arm. They saluted, but they weren't quite sure what to make of him, nor of the letter he presented. After whispering to one another they sent for an officer, and a yeomanry subaltern came at a run. The lieutenant looked from the letter to Stephen's uniform, and then, with a polite 'This way please', led him to a damp room in the distillery building.

There was a rickety table with some chairs scattered around it, but Stephen stood by the window and looked at the prisoners drilling in the yard. He'd spent the summer training recruits at depots up and down the country and he knew by the look of them that these men weren't raw. They were ragged, to be sure – only one uniform between three of them, the rest in civilian coats and trousers – but they moved with the fluid ease of long practice. They looked like soldiers, even without the uniforms.

Across the yard, a door opened and Joe came out with a guard walking behind him. Stephen watched him closely as he skirted the ranks of prisoners. He had lost weight: his green overcoat hung slack from his shoulders and even with his shirt buttoned all the way up, the collar looked loose around his neck. His expression was closed, stony, staring straight ahead, and he walked with a shuffling limp.

Still, better than the last time you saw him. Would he ever forget the moans and gore in that hospital? A temporary affair, deep down in the cellars and filled with the mingled stink of cordite and ether and blood. But even getting him in there was a feat in itself. If it weren't for Lillian fetching her sister, Joe would have been left lying in the yard with the other wounded rebels. Sheila had knelt down on the cobbles and gently felt around the wound while Stephen looked on, appalled at so much blood puddling in the panels of the door.

'We'll have to get him inside,' she said at last. Then she looked directly at Stephen. 'You'd best help me get his jacket off. They won't even look at him if they think he's a rebel. Lillie, fetch a blanket. Over there, near the door.'

With a blanket thrown over him, they carried him inside, still lying curled up on the door. Down they went, down stairs and along corridors littered with blankets and bandages and wounded men. They eventually burst into a makeshift ward and set him down on the floor, Stephen and Lillian waiting in nervous silence until Sheila came back, dragging a whey-faced doctor by the arm. There was another inspection, a whispered conference, and then a stretcher was called for. One end of the room had been curtained off for operations, and the last he saw of his brother was his blood-smeared bare chest, iodine, bandages and concerned doctors in grubby white smocks.

Joe came into the room and his sombre face brightened when he saw Stephen.

'How the hell . . .' he began, but looked uncertainly at the guard, who was hovering near the door.

Stephen waved him away. 'That will be all, corporal.'

The door closed and Joe's face cracked into a broad grin as he shook his brother's hand.

'By Jesus, it's good to see you, Stephen. But how the hell did you swing this? We're not allowed any visitors.'

'I wrote a begging letter to the War Office, telling them you were my only family. Under the circumstances, they agreed to allow a visit.'

Joe's face darkened again as he pulled out a chair and sat down gingerly.

'Under what circumstances?'

'They're sending me to France next week.'

France – where the battle of the Somme was in its dying throes. They got newspapers even in this godforsaken hole.

'Oh.'

The word fell into an uneasy silence. So much to say, but most of it didn't bear saying.

'I suppose you were expecting it.'

'I'm only surprised it took this long. I passed fit ages ago.'

'Did they keep you back on my account?'

Stephen nodded. There was no doubt about that. It had caught up with him in Gravesend, not two days after he arrived from Dublin. Just a few polite questions at first; a pleasant chat with the barracks colonel over tea in the mess. Stephen was more direct than the colonel, who was clearly uncomfortable in the role of inquisitor. He'd told him out straight, confessed right there and then. For penance he got Major Moffett from Military Intelligence. At least he said he was a major, but his uniform was a size too large and looked as if it belonged to somebody else. He had a rasping voice, chain-smoked, and tipped ash down the front of his tunic when he made notes in a greasy notebook. Stephen found him repellent, but was stuck with him in a small room for the best part of a day, glad of the fresh May breeze that wafted in through the open window. He'd made up his mind to tell the truth, but he took such a dislike to Moffett that he confined himself to answering only yes and no. He could sense the exasperation in Moffett's voice, but he held his course. What could they do to him? Prison? Unlikely. Cashiering? Possibly. Well, let them do what they wanted. He was not his brother's keeper. He had done nothing wrong.

'It wasn't that bad. They asked me a few questions, that's all.' He shrugged it off. But he wondered if, by delaying, they had kept him alive. All those weeks shunted from one depot to the next, training men for the meat-grinder across the Channel, but always there to meet the next draft. Never going himself – never sent. They didn't trust him to die.

'Anyway, how are you feeling?' he asked, sitting down and putting his cap on the table.

'How do I look?'

The old game from when they were kids: answer a question with a question.

'You look shook.'

'I feel shook.' Joe grinned, 'But it's not so bad. I'm still on light duties. They've got me working in the kitchen – peeling potatoes, stirring soup. At least I get plenty to eat.'

'How are they treating you?'

'Decent enough. They don't really know what to make of us. We've all got internment orders, but they don't want to treat us as prisoners of war. Mostly they just leave us alone. The worst of it is the damp and the rats, but, sure, some of us lived in worse back in Dublin.'

'Here.' Stephen slid the parcel across the table, 'I brought you something: smokes and chocolate. Should make life more bearable.'

'Thanks.' Joe nodded and drummed his fingers on the paper parcel. There was a question preying on his mind. 'Were you there for the executions?'

No prizes for guessing where *there* was.

'No, I wasn't. I'd already been posted to Gravesend when it started. I left Dublin the day after the surrender.'

'They shot Connolly, did you hear?'

'It was all over the papers.'

'And Pearse, and McDonough, and all the rest of them. The bastards put them all in front of firing squads.'

It wasn't lost on Stephen that he was one of the bastards. He was wearing the uniform. If he hadn't got out of Dublin it could have been him in charge of a firing squad. Thank Christ for small mercies.

'That was . . . unfortunate.'

'Unfortunate? They strapped him in a chair!' Joe hissed angrily. 'Jesus, Mary and Joseph, he couldn't stand up with his wounded leg, so they strapped him in a chair and shot him sitting down.'

'Well, Jesus, Joe. What did you think they'd do? They had a rebellion in their own back yard in the middle of a war. Did you think they'd just shake hands and wish you better luck next time?'

The moment he said it, he regretted it. He didn't want another row. Not now, not after everything. But Joe just gave him a bitter smile.

'He knew they'd shoot him,' he said quietly. 'One way or another, he knew he'd be killed. I heard him say it before we marched from Liberty Hall. He didn't want the men to hear it, but I heard him say we were going out to be slaughtered.'

'They shouldn't have shot them,' Stephen admitted. 'It was a mistake.'

The first execution was a mistake. The fourteen that followed were madness, brutality, malice. He'd followed them in the news-paper with growing disbelief. He knew it was the letter of the law, but they'd gone too far. How could they do this after thousands of Irishmen had volunteered for the army? Even in England, people were horrified. That was why conversation often dried up when people heard his Irish accent. Some of them suspected him of harbouring rebel sympathies, but many of them were ashamed.

'They lost Ireland when they did that.'

Stephen nodded. Billy had written to him just after the executions started and even he was lost for words to describe the sense of outrage in Dublin. A few days later he got a letter from Lillian that seemed to sum it up. The people who had blamed the rebels for destroying their city, who had pelted them with rubbish as they were marched down the street, had turned their anger against the government, against the police and the soldiers who were murdering men for standing up to them.

'They made martyrs of them,' Joe went on, more light coming into his eyes now, 'and that'll be their undoing. They'll not beat us the next time because the next time the people will be with us. They won't put up with this murder and oppression any more.'

Stephen got up and went back to the window. He looked at the men drilling in the square. They had turned their prison into a training camp.

'The next time?' He turned a sceptical eye on his brother, 'The last time nearly killed you. Have you not had enough?'

Joe followed his gaze across the yard and then looked at his brother with a defiant tilt to his head.

'We're only getting started.'

*   *   *

4 October 1916

Another flaming training camp! Still, at least this one's in France, and I'm the one being trained. It's the same old stuff: gas-mask drill, trench clearance, musketry, bomb throwing. But there's a sharp edge to it here, because all the instructors are men getting a respite from the front. To them it's a sort of rest cure. They entertain themselves by telling blood-curdling stories and trying to scare the living daylights out of the new men.

I have some immunity because I've seen action before, but some of them still make an impression on me. The devil is in the details. Take Metcalfe, for instance, who shares my tent. He has already asked me twice if we shouldn't dig a hole for sleeping in. I assured him that we are quite safe – I've never even seen a German – but he is hard to convince. Every morning he steps out of the tent and cocks his head towards the distant rumbling in the north. Too early for thunder, he always says, and I can see the fear in his face.

Metcalfe was at Guillemont during the worst of the Somme and jokes that he was sent here because his CO couldn't tell the time. It turns out the truth is much more serious than that. His battalion was supposed to attack a German position after an artillery barrage that would lift at the last minute. But with fifteen minutes to go, the colonel looked at his watch and decided that they were already five minutes late. Nobody knew why; perhaps the CO had taken too much to drink that morning – he drank like a fish, apparently – or perhaps his orderly simply hadn't wound his watch. Whatever the reason, he flew into a terrible rage. Why had nobody told him they were late? They were skivers, cowards! And he ordered them to begin the attack immediately.

They all knew damn well that it was suicide to attack before the barrage lifted, but the colonel wasn't having any of it. He had his RSM arrested for trying to tell him the right time and then climbed up on the parapet himself and threatened the men with his revolver if they wouldn't follow him. When they still refused to come out, he shot two of them and told the others they would get the same if they didn't attack. They must have decided that they were safer out than in because the first few platoons got out of the trench and followed him into the fire. The captain on Metcalfe's right contrived to knock down his trench ladders and saved his men that way. Metcalfe led his own men over the top but then signalled them to lie down a few yards out, with the barrage bursting all around. It seemed to bother him that he let the others go off ahead without following them, but I am sure he did the right thing.

As it was, he lost about half a dozen before the barrage finished right on time. But by then the two leading platoons had vanished and the attack was cancelled. Three men were brought back in that night, all badly wounded – and there was no sign of the colonel. Somebody came down from Brigade HQ to get Metcalfe's statement so the colonel could be recommended for a medal and Metcalfe told him to get stuffed, whereupon he was deemed in need of a rest and sent here.

It's just as well, because he really is worn out. His nerves are completely shattered; he jumps a mile when somebody lets off a bomb on the practice ranges, and if a door slams he is on the ground in an instant, covering his head with his hands. God knows what will become of him when they send him back to the line.

6 November 1916

Thank God I'm leaving here at last! I have transport papers to join the Second Dublins at Locre, near Ypres, and I can't get away soon enough! It was bad enough when it was merely dull, but now things have taken a turn for the worse. I've been appointed to the court martial of a Private Kelly, who is accused of coward-ice in the face of the enemy.

If he's found guilty, the penalty is death. The penalty is death for most offences, but it is usually commuted for lesser crimes. Not this one, however. Depending upon the outcome of our delib-erations, Kelly could find himself on the wrong end of a firing squad. The worst of it is that I suspect I'm only sitting on his case because he is Irish. Since the rebellion – and in particular the execution of the leaders – the staff is terrified of a mutiny amongst the Irish regiments. It wouldn't take much to set it off, because things are pretty glum after the Somme. So I suppose if they have to shoot another Irishman they are making damn sure to have one of his own pass sentence on him this time.

However, I'm hopeful it won't come to that. It seems to me to be a pretty clear case of what they call 'shell shock'. Metcalfe, who is also sitting, agrees with me. Kelly's record was impeccable up to now and he saw some very hard fighting on the Somme. He was the only survivor of a platoon wiped out at Ginchy and I suspect his guilt at surviving preyed on his mind and eventually caused him to crack. I can sympathize with that. On a calm night like this, with no sound but the burr of the lamp and the quiet clinking of Metcalfe (he sleeps in full battle gear, with his steel helmet on and his gas mask clutched to his chest), I can somehow feel the presence of the dead men I commanded. Why them and not me? That's the big question. How long can my luck hold? This afternoon Kelly gave evidence on his own behalf, telling how he hid amongst the corpses of his friends as the German counter-attack washed over him. He was blubbing and crying and barely coherent, but I understood exactly what he meant.

10 November 1916

Tomorrow evening I leave for the front. The court martial has finished hearing evidence and all that remains is for the three of us to deliver our verdict. Metcalfe and I agree that Kelly is a genuine case and should be in hospital rather than on trial for his life. Unfortunately, the court president is not of the same mind. He is a curmudgeonly old swine who has probably never been in earshot of the front and he doesn't believe in shell shock; says Kelly is only shamming. It sickens me to think this idiot could cost the poor man his life! We argued it out for hours this afternoon, but the old bugger wouldn't budge an inch. We will *reconvene again in the morning for another go, but unless we can bring the major around to our way of thinking, poor Kelly will be taken out and shot.*

11 *November* 1916

I write this while I wait for the train to take me to Poperinghe. I'm commanding a replacement draft as far as the front and it is a relief to be on the move at last.

At least Kelly's court martial came out well. He has been sent home as medically unfit – not a very glorious end to his career but better than being shot. It was good old Metcalfe who carried the day. He went riding with the major this morning and brought him back much more amenable to our verdict. I don't know what was said but I only hope Metcalfe didn't threaten him with his revolver!

Another bright spot is the letter that came for me before I left camp. It's from Lillian – I haven't opened it yet, but I recognize her handwriting on the envelope. I'm saving it for later. This draughty bloody train station isn't exactly the nicest of places, but I'm sure I'll see worse over the next few days and I'll probably need something to cheer me up.

It is getting cold now. Sitting on this blacked-out platform, it's hard not to dwell on morbid thoughts. Dark questions chase one another through my mind. I wonder how well I will hold up against the line? How long will I last? How will it end? The odds are not good. Before this I managed not to think too much about death, but it seems much closer now. Hospital trains unload here and the detritus of war flows past us. They come packed in wagons marked Hommes 40 Chevaux 8. *Most are French, with their dull blue greatcoats draped over the stretchers and they look shattered;*

filthy, sunken-cheeked, and with deep black eyes that fix on us as they are carried past. I can't help wondering if I will end up like that.

✳   ✳   ✳

The train took all night and half the morning to reach Poperinghe. Then it was a convoy of rattling buses to the Sixteenth Division HQ in Locre, a few miles south-west of Ypres. Stephen watched the flat countryside out of the window. Belgium now, not France. The anteroom of the war: waterlogged fields dimpled with shell craters and every house turned into a billet or headquarters.

Locre was nothing but headquarters. Forms, paperwork, waiting. Evening was coming on when he finally got rid of his draft and got out. The wintry air pinched his face as he marched alone through the dusk. The sky was clear, turning gunmetal blue and starry and promising frost for the morning. Every few hundred yards he passed camouflaged artillery batteries that made the ground throb when they fired, and in the ditches between them were little groups of artillerymen living in ramshackle shelters, the smell of their evening brew wafting out on the still air.

Siege Farm loomed out of the dying light. Two big barns and half a farmhouse. A shell had demolished the other half and the remains had been picked clean for firewood. Even the farmyard gate had been pinched, though when Stephen reached the gateway he found a man sitting against the pillar, handcuffed to one of the hinge-pins. Despite the indignity, he had managed to make himself comfortable, with a folded gas cape to sit on and a mug of tea in his free hand.

'Good evening to you, sir.' He nodded, hastily setting down the mug and rattling his cuffs. 'You'll excuse me if I don't salute.'

It took Stephen a moment to realize that this was field punish-

142

ment number one in its humane form. *The prisoner shall be attached to a fixed object for two hours per day . . .* At Etaples it had been applied more rigorously, with the offenders spread-eagled across cartwheels or gun limbers for two hours at a time. The punishment was intended to humiliate rather than inflict pain, but here he detected only mild embarrassment. Still, he decided not to mention it.

'Is this C Company of the Second Dublins?' he asked, though he'd already noted the man's Irish accent, and he couldn't help thinking there was something familiar about his face.

'It is indeed, sir.' The prisoner jerked his free thumb over his shoulder, 'You'll find Captain Wilson around the back.'

Stephen thanked him and walked into the yard. He smelled the warm waft of fresh straw from the open barns and suddenly felt very sleepy. What he wouldn't give to curl up in there for a few hours. He hadn't slept more than three hours on the train, with endless stops in the middle of nowhere and so many changes in unlit sidings that he spent half the journey craning his head out of the window to make sure they were still travelling north. Nor had he had time to shave, and his only sustenance was the stale bread roll he had bought at Amiens.

There was an armchair set out beside the back door of the farm. Beside it stood a gramophone on an upturned crate, and beside that a coat-stand that leaned drunkenly against the wall because one of its legs was missing. An officer with captain's crowns sat in the armchair. He appeared to be reading, but was slouched so low with his head bent over his book that he could as easily have been asleep. He did not stir at Stephen's approach.

'I beg your pardon, sir.'

'Aye.' The single syllable was drawled without looking up, but Stephen sprang into his salute in any case.

'Lieutenant Ryan, reporting for duty, sir.'

'Is that a fact?'

The officer turned a page and twisted the book to try and catch some of the yellow lantern light that spilled out of the window above his head. He still had not looked up. Stephen studied him carefully as he waited, standing stiffly to attention. The most conspicuous thing was the purple and white ribbon of the Military Cross on his left breast. Apart from that, it was hard to make anything out. His face was half hidden under the brim of his cap, but he appeared older than Stephen, perhaps forty or so. He was very slight, with bony hands and long fingers, and what hair he could see was jet black. Was that an Ulster accent? It was hard to tell.

'Yes, sir.'

'Do you like poetry, lieutenant?'

Definitely an Ulster accent. But he still hadn't looked up. He was poring over the page intently.

'Poetry, sir?' Stephen gingerly brought down his saluting hand. 'A little. I can't say I know much about it. Mathematics is more my line.'

'Mathematics?' At last, he looked up from the book and Stephen found himself fixed by a pair of lively brown eyes set deep in a sallow face and shaded by bushy black eyebrows. He stiffened automatically as they looked him up and down attentively. 'Sure wouldn't some people say that's just poetry with numbers?'

A good analogy, he had to admit. Stephen warmed to him. 'Yes, sir, I suppose it is.'

'Well, you're very welcome, lieutenant. Mervyn Wilson, at your service.' He extended a bony hand that felt like a bundle of wires, then turned and roared into the empty doorway, 'Corporal Power! A chair for Lieutenant Ryan!'

A wizened little man with a leathery face and iron-grey hair slicked to his skull came silently out of the doorway carrying a kitchen chair and, without a word or a look at either of them, placed it behind Stephen. He was on his way back inside when Wilson stopped him with an upraised finger.

'A pot of tea and a sandwich for the lieutenant, please, corporal, and you may pack up when you're done.'

'Very good, sir,' Power murmured, bowed and vanished back inside.

'The company's gone to the divisional baths,' Wilson said, producing a pipe and stuffing it from a leather pouch. 'But they'll be back in a wee while. We're going back up to the line tonight, so you should make the best of your sandwich.'

'Thank you, sir,' Stephen said, and sat down uncertainly.

'Your accent tells me you're from Dublin, Mr Ryan. Am I right?'

'Yes, sir. Born and bred.'

'Indeed? Were you there for the rebellion?'

Well, that was blunt. He had his cap half off his head and tried to marshal his thoughts as he set it in his lap. Dangerous waters. He wondered how much Wilson already knew.

'Yes, sir, I was there.'

'What did you make of it?'

'I think it was a mistake, sir.'

'Hmm.' Wilson nodded and carefully lit his pipe, puffing contentedly for a few moments.

'I want to say, sir—' Stephen began, but Wilson held up his hand.

'Say no more, lieutenant. Politics and religion are the surest ways to a disagreement around here, and I'll not have them bandied around. Our fight is with the Germans, not each other, and I advise you to keep it that way or we'll end up with anarchy on our hands. Is that clear, lieutenant?'

'Yes, sir.'

'You said mathematics is more your line. Did you study it in Dublin?'

'I did, sir. At Trinity College.'

'Trinity?' Wilson nodded slowly, as if this fact was significant, but then his face brightened and he held up the book he had been reading. 'I like poetry myself. It's a passion I share with my wife. She sends me books from time to time, to try and alleviate the horror, as she says. This one is by a chap called Hopkins. Have you ever read anything by Hopkins, Mr Ryan?'

'The poet Hopkins, sir? I believe I did. Something about a bird, as I recall.'

'Ah yes, "The Windhover".' Wilson nodded and smiled, as if the name alone was enough to conjure up the fondest recollection. Stephen thought it safe to offer up the only other thing he knew about the poet Hopkins.

'I believe he was a Jesuit, sir. Hopkins, I mean, not the bird. It wasn't a metaphorical bird.'

Wilson's smile faded and he shifted uncomfortably in his chair. Even if he wouldn't talk about religion, it was clear enough where he stood.

'Aye, he was that,' he said, and Stephen was relieved to see Corporal Power wafting smoothly out of the kitchen, carrying an empty ammunition crate with two mugs of tea and a plate of bacon sandwiches cut in triangles. He set it down between them.

'We have no sugar, just at present, sir.' He spoke studiously to the air between Stephen and Wilson. 'But the milk is fresh this morning and I have put up the rest of the bacon to bring with us.'

'Very good, corporal. You may pack up the gramophone as well when you finish in the kitchen.'

Power vanished back inside and Wilson took one of the

triangular sandwiches, holding it up for Stephen's inspection. It was an immaculate creation of fine white bread and pink bacon, with the crusts neatly trimmed off.

'Power worked at the Savoy Grill before the war, lieutenant. His value is above rubies.' Popping the tiny sandwich into his mouth he asked, 'You think we are a little eccentric, lieutenant? Not quite as you had expected?'

'It is not exactly what I am used to, sir.'

'Aye, well, I find it's best to make use of what little advantages present themselves – there's no point in going about a thing half-arsed.'

They sat contentedly for a few moments until there was a rushing sound through the air over their heads, and then the distant crump-crump-crump of shells landing somewhere down the road. Stephen looked in that direction for a few moments, then returned to his tea.

'Counter battery fire,' Wilson observed. 'Their artillery shells our artillery. No doubt we'll return the compliment in a few minutes.' He gave Stephen a knowing look. 'Since it doesn't appear to disturb you much, I dare say you've seen action before.'

'Yes, sir, I was at Suvla Bay with the Seventh Battalion.'

'Were you, by God?' Wilson suddenly became animated, leaning forward with his eyes blazing, 'You fought against the Turks?'

'Yes, sir.'

'Some people thought they wouldn't put up much of a fight, but I reckon you know different. Would I be right in that, lieutenant?'

'Yes, sir. They fought like blazes. We lost a lot of men.'

'Aye, aye. I dare say you did. And how come—?' Wilson broke off and cocked his ear to one side. 'Here they come.'

He leapt out of his chair and Stephen stood up beside him, even though he could neither see nor hear anything. But then he heard it – the rhythmic crunch of many feet marching in step. Looking down the road, he saw a dim shape moving along it, and this gradually resolved itself into a tight phalanx of men that wheeled into the yard, bringing the faint smell of soap flakes and DDT. The two officers who stood at the head of the column came over and saluted Wilson. One wore glasses and the other didn't, but apart from that Stephen thought they might have been twins. Very young, very eager.

'Good evening, gentlemen. All went well I trust,' Wilson said, returning their salute.

'Yes, sir. All washed and deloused and ready for action,' said the one with glasses.

'Very good. Allow me to introduce Lieutenant Ryan. He will be taking over Mr Ingram's platoon. Mr Ryan, Lieutenants Hollis and Gardner.'

Stephen made a mental note. The one with the glasses was Hollis, the other one Gardner. From the 'How do you do' as they shook hands in turn, he gathered that they were both English.

'Is Mr Devereux not with you?' Wilson asked mildly.

'Devereux?' Hollis and Gardner both blushed, and Stephen realized he wasn't far behind them. At first he wondered if he'd heard right. Then, could it really be him?

'Er . . . no, sir.' Hollis answered at last, 'I'm afraid we parted company. Mr Devereux gave us to understand that he had some business to attend to at Division and that he would return here directly.'

'Probably hob-nobbing with that bloody infernal uncle of his,' Wilson growled, rolling his eyes. Stephen was certain of it now, but still he said nothing. Better to see which way the wind was blowing first.

'Well, we cannot afford to wait for him. Let the men have

something to eat and be ready to march in . . .' Wilson looked at his wristwatch by the light from the kitchen window, '. . . one hour. Mr Hollis, kindly show Mr Ryan where his platoon is quartered. Mr Gardner, have that villain Kinsella unlocked from the gate and bring him to me.'

'Very good sir!'

Hollis led him towards the larger of the two barns. He didn't say anything, but Stephen could feel his eyes on him as they crossed the yard. The options for small talk were limited, and even though he could feel one question burning in his mind, he decided to ask the more conventional one.

'What happened to Ingram, my predecessor?'

'Johnny? Oh, he was shot by one of our lot,' Hollis answered cheerfully. 'It was dreadfully bad luck, really. Ingram was an awfully nice chap. He took a patrol out one night but when the sentries changed they weren't told we had men out. One of them saw something moving and, well, that was that. Got him through both legs. Still, it's for the best if you ask me. He had a wife and a little girl, so he's better off out of it. He's back in Blighty now, and he probably won't have much of a limp.'

'And what about Lieutenant Devereux?' he asked diffidently, 'I used to know a Devereux, back in Dublin.'

'Oh really? Our Devereux's from Dublin. Stocky chap? Rugger player? Engaged to a girl, oh, what's her name . . . ?'

'Mary?'

'Yes, that's him. Is he a friend of yours?'

Stephen smiled to himself. 'I wouldn't say that.'

'Well, that's probably just as well, because the boss *hates* him.'

Here we go again.

It was the same, only different. The same slightly nauseous feeling – what he had thought was seasickness before. Butterflies in the stomach, cold feet, a nervous tension that heightened the senses. The same look in the men's faces. *They feel it too.* But everything else was different. No sun helmets or shorts here. It *was* cold, and their breath clouded the air above them as they formed up in the farmyard. He saw woollen caps, scarves and sheepskin jerkins. They were used to this. They'd lived this life for months – years, some of them. But they still got that feeling.

'All present and correct, sir,' Sergeant Curtis informed him, saluting nervously in the light of the storm lanterns. He was a young man, and seemed so uncertain of himself that Stephen wondered if he was new to the job.

'Very good, sergeant.' He picked up one of the lanterns and made the rounds of his platoon. They looked lived-in, worn – downright shabby in places – but he was perfectly satisfied. No blanco, no brass, and God knew what he would find if he looked in their haversacks – but they were ready to fight.

He stopped in front of Kinsella, the man who had been chained to the gate when he arrived. Of all of them, he looked the least nervous. If anything, there was a savage glint in his eye. Gardner had warned Stephen about him when he went back to the farmhouse kitchen to sort out his kit.

'That Kinsella is an awkward bugger,' he'd said. 'You'd do well to keep your eye on him.'

Stephen looked him over carefully. An awkward bugger, yes – but there was something about him that he couldn't put his finger on. He had a muscular frame, a thick neck and dark, heavy features. Nothing remarkable about his face except that it was maddeningly familiar. The other details were more telling. There were the ribbons of the Military Medal and the Distinguished Conduct Medal on his left breast, and three wound stripes on his cuff. His sleeve showed the double chevrons of a corporal, but above them a lighter patch where the third chevron had been.

He'd been degraded fairly recently. No wonder Curtis was so nervous, standing in his shoes.

'What are you under punishment for, corporal?' he asked.

'Drunkenness, sir,' Kinsella admitted, without a hint of resentment. No doubt when he got drunk, he did it in style.

Stephen just nodded. No point in moralizing – it wouldn't get him anywhere. He had seen men like Kinsella before: nothing but trouble when they were out of the line, but hard as nails at the front. The sort you hoped you never ran into on the other side. The sort who went out on patrol at night and came back with ears.

He handed the lantern to Curtis.

'Thank you, sergeant,' he said, and went over to the kitchen door to report his platoon ready to Wilson. Hollis and Gardner were already there, but Wilson stood a little apart from them, his teeth clenched on his pipe and his face like thunder. There was still no sign of Devereux.

'Very good, Mr Ryan.' Wilson nodded, and as he glanced towards the gate his face darkened even further. Stephen turned and saw a shadowy figure stumbling into the farmyard. His Burberry coat swung open as he steadied himself against the pillar and there was no mistaking his powerful frame. It was Devereux all right and, even though he had been expecting it, Stephen was shocked to see him. But shock quickly turned to disbelief when he realized that he was very, very drunk indeed.

'Mr Devereux!' Wilson barked, and Devereux bucked at his name and walked as steadily as he could into the circle of lantern light.

'Good evening, sir,' he said slowly, but not slowly enough to avoid slurring the words, and apparently unaware that his cap was pushed right back on his head. But he was determined to get out the speech he had memorized. 'I must apologize for my lateness. I'm afraid I was summoned to Divisional HQ while we were at the baths.' He shot an angry glance at Hollis. 'While there I was unavoidably de-detained by Brigadier— Good God! Reilly? What on earth are you doing here?'

Stephen looked at him coldly. 'My name is Ryan.'

'Yes, yes. Ryan, of course. The sizar man. Well, well! Still trying to pass for a gentleman? Eh? Jolly good! Well, don't worry, old man, your secret's safe with me!' He gave a monstrous wink and swayed on his feet as he cackled with laughter, but Wilson cut him off.

'Lieutenant Devereux!' he shouted the name with enough force to still the muttering that had started amongst the assembled soldiers. Devereux blinked and tried to focus his gaze on the furious, shockingly pale face of his company commander. Wilson was shaking with rage, but by gritting his teeth and exhaling a long breath through his nose, he managed to master himself. 'I will deal with you later, Mr Devereux, when I have the leisure to hear your explanation for this outrageous behaviour. For the moment you will march with your platoon. You will keep up and you will keep quiet or I will have you cashiered for drunkenness. Is that clear, lieutenant?'

'Yes. Yes, sir,' Devereux stammered, shaken, slack-jawed.

'Mr Gardner, your platoon will lead the way.' Wilson spoke without taking his blazing eyes off Devereux, 'I believe we are late and will have to double part of the way if we are to make a good relief. Mr Ryan, you would do well to stay close to your men until you are familiar with the lie of the land.'

'Very good, sir!' They saluted and less than a minute later the company had wheeled out of the yard and was marching in artillery formation towards the white flashes on the northern horizon.

His impressions of that first night were like a jumble of photographs; little scenes etched in his mind by the flash of a shell. He had hardly any sense of the wider landscape, just the men near him and passing things in the dark. There was no talk, only the constant rumble of artillery and the steady tramp of boots. Sometimes, when a flare went up, he saw the wider scene cast in a sharp blue-white relief that showed it weird and harsh – lumpy earth nailed with fence posts and fingers of brickwork sticking up.

As they got closer to the front line the earth seemed to swallow them up. The way grew narrower and he was aware of wooden walls and sandbags on each side. He reached out his hand and his fingers brushed corrugated iron and telegraph wire. Underfoot, his boots found slippery duckboards and sucking mud, and as they picked their way past dugouts with light glowing greenly behind the gas curtains, he realized they were in the reserve trenches. It couldn't be far now.

Suddenly the sky flashed white, there was an almighty bang, and gobs of mud rained down on them as they dropped to the bottom of the trench.

'Fucking rum jars,' Kinsella whispered at Stephen's elbow, before they got up and crept forward again, crouching now, one eye to the night sky. They passed an alcove where a doctor was bending over a stretcher by the light of a candle lantern.

'A rum jar, corporal?'

'Gerry trench mortar, sir. We calls 'em rum jars 'cos that's what they look like. There!' He pointed into the sky ahead and Stephen saw a black oblong shape about twice the size of a rugby ball sailing through the air, sparks fizzing from its tail. Another flash and a deep percussive bang and Kinsella's teeth gleamed as he grinned. 'Ain't nothing but an auld barrel full of dynamite and scrap iron. They're better 'n shells 'cos you can see them coming – but God help you if you're in the way when they land!'

A few yards further on they reached a wider trench running perpendicular to the one they were in. There was a step at the front, a couple of feet off the bottom, and earth buttresses twenty yards away in either direction. When Kinsella lit an acetylene lamp Stephen saw corrugated-iron and timber revetments, all topped by tiers and tiers of sandbags. He saw men too, shadowy shapes filing quietly past and disappearing down the communication trench.

'You took your bloody time, Jimmy,' one of them whispered to Kinsella, and he realized they had made their relief.

Haversacks were eased from aching shoulders and rifles unslung. A whispered order was passed along and half the men climbed up on the firing step as sentries, the rest stretching out where they could or settling into little niches in the walls to sleep. Stephen stood and listened for a few moments, feeling strangely at home with the dark and the smell of the earth. Then he tilted his head up to the sky, hoping for a glimpse of the stars. He felt tired, slightly dazed. It felt as if was only a few minutes since he'd left the camp at Etaples.

'Officers' dugout is a bit further along, sir,' Kinsella said, but Stephen was startled by another knot of men bumping up the communication trench. A flare soared up and he recognized Devereux's sergeant at the head of his platoon. They'd been lagging behind all the way and there was no sign of their officer.

'Where is Mr Devereux, sergeant?' he asked.

'Bringing up the rear, sir.' The sergeant jerked his thumb over his shoulder, and in the same instant the air was ripped open by a loud whizzing sound, then an ear-splitting crack that shook the earth. Half a dozen more followed, flashing orange flame and sending stones and earth rattling down on his helmet.

'Looks like the quare fellas are putting out the welcome mat for us, sir.' The sergeant chuckled, getting up and moving on. Stephen climbed to his feet and brushed the earth from his tunic. A strange sound came from the communication trench and he felt his heart begin to race. Had somebody been wounded? The sound was somewhere between a laugh and a howl, high-pitched, hysterical, and he picked up the acetylene lamp and edged towards it nervously. The light fell on a figure huddled against the side of the trench and he hurried over.

'Are you hurt?' he gasped, turning the beam onto the man's face.

'No, I'm all right,' Devereux answered, wiping his eyes with his sleeve. 'Go away, Ryan. Leave me alone.'

VIII

I don't think Devereux was pleased to see me the other night. I wasn't very happy to see him either, but there it is. He has number five platoon and I have number six. We're stuck with each other.

From what I've managed to winkle out of Hollis, I gather that Devereux has only been here a month, and this is his first stint at the front. Apparently, his illustrious uncle managed to get him a cushy job on the staff that kept him out of harm's way until now. This begs the question: what is he doing here, where people are trying to kill him, when he could be in a nice safe office ten miles behind the front? Devereux says he volunteered, but everybody else thinks he was sent. He'll need some frontline experience if he wants to get ahead on the staff, so he's been sent here to get it. Better still would be a medal or a mention in dispatches, but the chances of either of those are very slim indeed.

It wouldn't be fair to call him a coward – even after what I saw when we were shelled that night. We're all cowards at some time or another, and I wouldn't hold it against him. The real test is how he conducts himself day after day. How he stands up to it, how he handles his men, and how he gets things done. The trouble is, this is where he's sadly lacking.

Wilson has a very low opinion of him. Devereux had the watch when my predecessor, Ingram, was shot by our own sentries, and it was his responsibility to make sure they knew there was a patrol out. Wilson doesn't trust Devereux to lead a patrol himself and since there probably won't be any major actions until next spring, that means he has almost no hope of getting a medal.

It doesn't help that Devereux is such a snob. He resents being under the command of an officer who was commissioned from the ranks and he looks down his nose at Hollis and Gardner because they are temporary officers like myself, while he has a regular commission. This certainly isn't warranted because they're both fairly decent chaps, and far better soldiers than he is. Things would be much smoother without Devereux, but the situation is pretty sticky. Normally Wilson could get rid of a bad officer by dishing him in his monthly report, but with Devereux's connections he must tread carefully. He has come here for glory, and glory he must have.

Needless to say, Wilson is very curious about my relationship with him. He hasn't said anything, but I know he's watching to see if I'm tarred with the same brush. To prove my mettle, I've volunteered to take a patrol out tonight. Somewhere opposite us the Germans have a contraption for throwing those big bombs they call 'rum jars' and I am to take half a dozen men out to see if we can steal it or at least get a good look at it. I can only hope I'll still be in a position to write about the outcome tomorrow!

20 November 1916

Back to billets again after my first week at the front. I'm looking forward to a bath and a whole night's sleep.

My patrol went off quite well last night. We didn't do this sort of thing much in Turkey, and I found it quite nerve-racking. A bit like breaking into somebody's house in the middle of the night, I imagine. I think I must have held my breath for the best part of half an hour on the way out! At least this rum jar contraption was more or less where we thought it was – in a sap with only a single man guarding it. Unfortunately, stealing it was out of the question because of the sheer size of the bloody thing. It was absolutely huge! It looked like an enormous beer barrel sawn in two and banded with iron, and it must have weighed half a ton.

Since there was no way we could shift it we booby-trapped it as best we could with a few Mills bombs and some wire and started back to safety. At least we still had the guard as a prisoner – having managed to knock him out with a cosh when we surprised him in the sap. But when we were about halfway back he woke up and started making a racket and in two seconds Kinsella had killed him with a bayonet. Very useful for this sort of stunt, is Kinsella – though I wouldn't like to get on his bad side.

So I came back empty-handed. Devereux snorted a bit when I made my report (we both volunteered but he was turned down) but Wilson seemed pleased. Nobody was wounded and it wasn't my fault we couldn't shift the contraption. As it was I was able to make a decent sketch of the thing, and pinpoint it on the map, so we might be able to drop some shells on it if it starts becoming a nuisance.

It's Gardner's birthday tomorrow, so we're taking him to a pub in Locre. They call them 'estaminets' over here. He's nineteen.

* * *

By Christmas week it felt as if the whole world had turned to ice. Time passed in a slow cycle of icy blue days and clear frozen nights, with no sound but the clinking icicles on the wire and the clump of sentries stamping their feet. The cold was continuous and unrelenting and the officers' dugout near Arundel House had no stove worth talking about. It was barely warmer than the trench outside, and the walls glittered with frost, icicles hanging down from the roof beams.

Stephen sat at the table with a plate of barely warm Maconochie stew and an unfinished letter. He had just ended his watch and his fingers were still numb with the cold. He warmed them over the guttering candle in the middle of the table as he reread the last few paragraphs of his letter:

> . . . Captain Wilson is an engaging character once you get to know him. At first glance he seems to be a typical dour Ulsterman – not to mention a bit eccentric – but he grows on you quickly enough. He has a wife and two sons back in Belfast, and it would warm your heart to see how he can hardly wait for his home leave after Christmas. Also, he is a very good officer and takes great pains to look after his men. I suspect this might be because he has risen from the ranks himself. He joined the army when he was sixteen, did his seven years and then left to become a schoolteacher. When the war started he was recalled from the reserve and spent the first few months as a sergeant, distinguishing himself at the first battle of Ypres to the extent that he was awarded a DCM and given a field commission.

When he reached the end, Stephen paused to take another spoonful of stew, glancing across at the pile of blankets on the bottom bunk. Wilson was sleeping under all that and only the periodic puff of steam from his breath betrayed his presence. On the far side of the room Hollis was curled up on the other bunk, wrapped tight in a blanket and with a red woollen cap on his head. Gardner was out, bringing up the rations for the morning, and Devereux, who now had the watch, sat in the tattered armchair near the door with a blanket over his knees, chain-smoking cigarettes.

Quickly rubbing his hands together to get the circulation going, Stephen picked up his pen and unscrewed the cap.

'Who are you writing to?' Devereux asked, before the nib even touched the paper.

'Lillian – Lillian Bryce,' Stephen answered.

'Lillian Bryce?' Devereux savoured the name for a moment, then his face brightened and he gave a wry grin as he gently rubbed his cheek. 'Of course. I remember her. The suffragette. She was at Mary's . . .' he pulled himself up, as if he'd said something he shouldn't, then asked, 'Is she your girl?'

Stephen had to think for a moment before he answered. He'd never really thought of it in those terms before. He found himself smiling as he answered.

'Yes. Yes, I suppose she is.'

'Well, good for you.'

He looked like he might have said more, but there was a familiar whirring sound overhead, then the double thump of shells landing nearby. The noise brought Devereux flying out of his chair, the blanket falling to the floor, and Stephen had to snatch up his pages as the roof rattled and dropped a clutch of icicles on the table.

'Christ Almighty!' Devereux whispered, crouched and anxious, as if he was still afraid the roof might come in. Then, with an unhappy sigh, he turned and stumped outside to check for damage. Stephen swept the table clear with his sleeve and smoothed out his letter again.

. . . As for Devereux, well, he's just been asking about you.
Believe it or not, he seems to think rather highly of you(!).

Sometimes, I don't know what to make of him. If you get him on his own he isn't so bad – he drops the airs and graces and you can have a half-decent conversation with him – but mix him in with other people and he just can't resist becoming a snob and a boor. In the quieter moments I often feel a bit sorry for him, as he is very isolated here. Necessity has made friends of the rest of us. We share almost everything, be it hats and gloves, food, or little treats and bits of news from home. But Devereux remains aloof. Truth be told, he rarely gets letters from home, although he does dash off at every opportunity to see his uncle on the staff.

He also drinks rather heavily. I must take care not to sound like a hypocrite, because we all drink rather heavily by normal standards. It isn't unusual for us to have a tot of rum with breakfast – particularly with the weather we're having – and, more often than not, another to help you sleep when you turn in. Devereux is no better or worse than the rest of us when we are at the front, but when we move into a rest area he takes to the bottle with a ferocity that has been noted by his superiors. I fear it will only be a matter of time before something is said.

Now, to the workings you sent me. Your thoughts on the Goldbach have the makings of a most interesting proposition, and I have made a few further notes that you might find useful. As you will see, I believe your calculations are valid for both the weak and the strong conjectures, and I'm sure you would do well to look into Lagrange's four-square theorem . . .

He stopped writing as he heard Devereux's heavy tread approaching on the duckboards outside. There was a slide, a thump and a string of muttered curses, and then Devereux came back in through the crackling gas curtain, blowing on his hands and flopping back into his chair.

'Well?' Stephen asked.

'Bloody German bloody shells,' Devereux said, taking out another cigarette and putting it shakily to his lips. 'Bloody pain in the arse.'

The man in the basket was looking at them through binoculars. The twin discs obscured half his face and made him look like some sort of insect, hunched and small in the distance. Only when he took them down to lean over and shout something down to the ground did he become human again.

Can he see me? Stephen wondered. Does he know what I'm going to do? He'd been watching him for the last hour, studying him, getting used to the motion of the balloon. With the naked eye it appeared to be motionless, a great grey maggot painted in the sky, but through the glass he could see that it moved. It swayed regularly like an inverted pendulum, and with every gust of wind it shuddered, shook and bobbed up and down like a fishing float.

He took his eye away from the scope and adjusted the focus. Kinsella was sitting on the firing step beside him, calmly smoking a cigarette.

'How's it looking, sir?'

'The balloon is moving in the breeze.'

'Aye, it'll do that.'

Not much encouragement there. Kinsella was the best shot in the company – or had been up to now. He'd put his title on the line when he declined the shot. Too far, he said. Not even with the scope.

Funny how it was the scope that had caused the penny to drop. The captured Zeiss scope and his diary were the only things he'd managed to bring home from Turkey. God knows how they had survived, when even the clothes he'd stood up in had been destroyed at one of the hospitals. It was only when he took it out of his haversack last night that he thought of that roasting hot trench, and a man lying face down, shot as he tried to get a drink of water. Fusilier Kinsella. Of course!

He found him outside, warming himself at a brazier with some of his mates. The others melted away as he approached, until only Kinsella was left, watching him carefully.

'Corporal, did you have a brother in the Seventh Battalion?'

Kinsella looked into the fire for a few moments. Surprising how his downcast eyes looked just like a girl's, even in that brutal face.

'I did, sir,' he said gruffly, but when he went on his voice was softer. 'It was good of you to write that letter to his mother, and one of his mates said you got the bastard as shot him.'

If only you knew, Stephen thought now, looking down at him before he put his eye back to the scope. Best not tell him where *that* came from.

He was worried about the scope. Who knew what sort of knocks it had taken after all this time? Not to mention the fact that he'd never used one before. And the gun felt awkward too: a Ross rifle, longer and heavier than he was used to. They had a very bad reputation. They'd been issued to all the Canadian regiments, but they couldn't get rid of them fast enough. Kinsella had looked appalled when he asked him to find one.

'A Ross? What the 'ell do you want one of them for, sir?'

But he'd got it, and last night they'd stripped it, checked it and fitted the scope. He remembered the Canadian officer in Locre, complaining about them over his wine and *pommes frites*. They called them the worst rifle in the world. Bloody awful things. Jammed like buggery if they got dirty – and they were bloody dangerous to boot. Take your flaming eye out if they didn't kill you. Stephen hadn't believed the second part, but last night he'd seen for himself when he stripped the rifle. It really could be fired with the bolt not properly locked. The Canadian officer hadn't been exaggerating after all: 'So they carried off this poor bastard with the rifle bolt sticking out of his eye socket. We got Lee Enfields straight after that, I can tell you.'

He tried not to think about it.

The man in the basket had his binoculars up again. Stephen's finger tightened on the trigger, feeling it give a little. What have you ever done to me? he asked silently. He thought of the man standing up there, free as the air, the countryside laid out below him like a map. What did all this look like from up there? He was well wrapped up anyway. Hat and gloves, and an airman's coat. It must be cold up in the breeze.

There was an ear-splitting shriek overhead and he stiffened, easing his finger from the trigger. Christ Almighty. Here we go again. But the shells thundered over and fell a few hundred yards away. Even so, the thump of the detonations beat on his ears. Heavies. They were like a flaming earthquake when they landed. They'd been much closer yesterday. Two of them landed in the middle of a ration party and blew them to bits. Another caved in twenty yards of the main communication trench. The fourth got Hollis.

Poor bloody Hollis. He didn't even see the one that got him. It was a shrapnel shell that burst twenty feet above his head. One of the balls put a great big dent in his helmet and another penetrated his shoulder and went into his lung. It was such a small hole they couldn't even see it at first. When they found him he was thrashing around on the ground with pink blood bubbling out of his mouth. He was still alive when the bearers took him away, but then word came back that he was dead.

In his fury, Wilson ordered them to fire at the balloon. He knew damned well it was pointless, but he had to vent his rage. Every rifle they had lined up for ten rounds volley fire. Then another ten, and another. They couldn't even see that heavy battery, but the insect man was their eyes. Tethered by a slender thread, so far away and so high up, he was wreaking havoc with his binoculars and a telephone.

But the volleys were merely frustration. Every time another salvo fell, the nearest rifles cracked back angrily at the balloon – though they might as well have been shooting at the moon. Stephen reckoned the range was twelve hundred yards. At that distance most of them could barely hit the balloon, never mind the man in the basket. And it was him they wanted. The balloon could be patched, but if they killed the insect man then the Germans would think twice about putting someone in his place.

Three-quarters of a mile, and the target moving in the breeze. No wonder Kinsella had declined the shot. Even his grandfather might have baulked at it, and he'd once shot for the Queen's Cup at Wimbledon. An English mile over iron sights. Stephen remembered his pride and amazement when the old man showed him the photographs; whiskery young men with big rifles on their knees and a collection of silverware scattered through the grass at their feet. He'd picked out his grandfather immediately and realized he could easily have been looking at a picture of himself. Better yet was the actual rifle: a beautiful heavy Rigby, reverently slid from its leather case under the bed. And here he was, with the worst rifle in the world and a captured scope that had been rattled all the way around the Mediterranean.

He drew a deep breath and snugged the rifle butt into the hollow of his shoulder. As he started to squeeze the trigger again his mind was racing, calculating. Laying off for wind, allowing for trajectory, the rise and fall of the bullet. The trigger felt hard under his finger.

He could sense the shell inside the breech, gleaming brass, waiting. In his head he saw the bolt biting forward, the firing pin piercing the shell, and the explosion of gases that drove the pointed bullet forward. Twisting down the barrel and bursting out into the chilly air. It would soar up, spinning, and climb into the watery blue sky, then arc down and down towards the man in the basket, piercing layers of leather and cloth, flesh and bone, burrowing into his chest. Was this what it had come to? Was this how he fought his war? Holding another man's life by the tip of his finger?

'A fiver says he misses,' Devereux whispered from down in the trench.

Stephen let the breath gush out and turned his head to glare at him. He was standing with Gardner, and Wilson was perched above them on a ladder, quietly studying the balloon through binoculars of his own. Quite the bloody audience he had. Gardner wasn't taking the bet.

'A fiver? You must be joking. That's too much. A pound. I bet you a pound he gets him!'

Devereux shook his head. Typical – set the stake so high nobody will bet against you. Stephen was tempted to take his bet. He could afford it, just about. But then he thought better of it. He wouldn't do this for money.

'Gentlemen, do you mind?' Wilson said sharply.

Back to the scope. Another deep breath, letting half of it out. The rifle was light in his hands now. The worst rifle in the world – but not if you were careful, not if you looked after it. All he could see now was the little disc of sky inside the scope, the insect man hanging there. He started to squeeze the trigger again. It gave a little under his finger. First pressure.

'All right, two guineas,' whispered Devereux.

'You're on.'

The rifle cracked and thumped against his shoulder. At least the bolt stayed in. He saw the insect man stagger and drop his binoculars. He fell against the side of the basket and then folded over the edge, his arms hanging limply. The basket jerked and staggered and then started to descend. They were winding it down.

Wilson clapped him on the shoulder, grinning.

'Good shot, Mr Ryan.' And then, turning to the others, 'Mr Devereux, pay up.'

* * *

Frongoch Camp,
22 December 1916

Dear Stephen,

Just a note to let you know they are letting us go. The whole camp is being cleared out and they have told us we will be back in Dublin by Christmas. Everybody is delighted and we're all sitting here with our belongings wrapped up in brown paper, waiting for the word.

Nobody is sure why they decided to let us out, but most of us think it's only a stunt to impress the Americans, who they are hoping will come into the war. I don't care. This place was a miserable hole even in the summer, and I don't think I could last the whole winter. I'll be glad to see Dublin again.

I hope you keep safe and have a happy Christmas.

Best wishes,

Joe.

PS: A mate here has invited me to stay with him when we get back to Dublin. I don't know how long it will take, but I'll write to you when I get settled. For the time being you can send mail c/o the ITGWU, 31 Eden Quay.

Christmas Day and we're back in the front line. The weather is absolutely freezing but at least it's quiet. No gunfire since last night – not even a rifle. Father O'Leary came up yesterday evening and said Mass in the big dugout. Wilson didn't attend (he's a Presbyterian, as far as I know) but he came in later when the men were singing carols and issued a rum tot before they turned in.

I was at the Mass but didn't pay much attention as my mind kept turning towards home. I envy Joe being back there for Christmas. I'm not exactly short of companionship here, but it's not the same at all.

I got a nice letter from Lillian as well – and a parcel with chocolate, sweets, socks and a bottle of brandy. God bless that girl! I don't what I'd do without her. But I'd give it all back just to sit with her for an hour like we did that night in Dublin Castle. God, when I think how we talked and talked – it was as if we'd known one another all our lives. It's frustrating when all I can do now is write letters. The next time I get leave I will see her. I must see her. I won't leave it to fate like I did the last time. Life is too short.

This morning I did the rounds of the sentries – the frost is treacherous and I nearly fell on my backside twice – and when I got back I learned two interesting things. First, after my display of marksmanship with the artillery balloon the men have nick-named me the 'Assassin'! Very melodramatic, I'm sure. I believe the range and other details grow larger with every telling! Gardner told me about it over breakfast and it seems the distance has already increased to a mile.

The other thing is that Wilson has put my name forward to take command of the company when he goes on leave in January. This is a bit strange as he's only going home for two weeks. I'm pleased that he trusts me, and it will stand to me when the next vacancy for promotion comes up, but I think he has an ulterior motive. Strictly speaking, Devereux is senior to me, and his nose will be severely out of joint. He hasn't been told yet, but no doubt there will be fireworks when he finds out!

28 December 1916

Back to billets after Christmas at the front. It's Doncaster huts this time, as we are moving along the line a little bit. The huts are draughty and cold, but they're still better than the barns at Siege Farm, and they have real beds. I'm looking forward to using mine tonight.

As expected, Devereux has kicked up a fuss about my promotion. The moment we got back he was off like a shot to the infernal uncle. This was a mistake, since he should have gone to our battalion CO. The colonel was summoned to explain the situation to General Hickie himself, and needless to say he was bloody furious – not just because Devereux circumvented the chain of command, but also because he's the one who got Wilson his commission; they go back a long way, and he would take one Wilson against ten Devereuxs any day.

Apparently, Devereux complained that he had greater length of service, but it turns out there is only a few days between us and I have more frontline experience. The truth is, Devereux has a bee in his bonnet because I'm only a temporary officer while he is a regular. This cuts no ice with the colonel, who never liked having Devereux inflicted on him in the first place. He and Wilson have now hatched a scheme to get rid of Devereux, who has been a thorn in their sides for long enough.

Wilson explained it to me after we had served dinner. It's a tradition for the officers to serve the men their Christmas dinner, and although we were three days late and lacking plates and cutlery, it was appreciated all the same. We took ours out in the snow, away from the clashing of tins and the singing in the mess hut. The scheme is quite simple: when we go back to the front in the New Year Wilson will mount a raid to grab a few prisoners for intelligence. Devereux will officially be in command – although Wilson has already hand-picked the men to go with him, as well as the place. There is an isolated German sap near Arundel House that is often used as a listening post and they should be able to nab the occupants without much trouble. Wilson will write a glowing report about the operation and, with the CO's endorsement, Devereux should warrant at least a mention in dispatches and then he can be safely sent on his way.

Short of dressing up a couple of our own men as Germans, it couldn't be safer. All the same, Wilson doesn't like it – he doesn't like anything that involves Devereux bringing men in contact with the enemy – but he is willing to go along if it means getting rid of him. I'm inclined to agree. Regardless of his merits or otherwise as a soldier, Devereux's conflict with Wilson is bound to lead to trouble sooner or later.

Dublin,
31 December 1916

Dear Stephen,

I hope this letter finds you well. You were very much in my thoughts over Christmas and I hope you are keeping safe (and warm!).

As I am sure you already know, your brother is back in Dublin. A huge crowd turned out to welcome home all the interned men just before Christmas. I haven't seen him myself, but Sheila met him the other day.

To tell the truth, he gave her a bit of a turn. She was on nights all last week and it was the early hours before she got out of the castle.

She got quite a shock to find him waiting outside (actually, 'lurking' was the word she used) and she was sure she was going to be attacked! The poor lad must have been there all night because he was half frozen, but he took off his cap, introduced himself, and thanked her very civilly for helping him when he was so badly wounded. He then very politely insisted on walking her all the way home.

I have enclosed a few sheets outlining a problem I am working on at the moment. The problem is not strictly mathematical – the real problem is one of my students, a Mr MacIntyre who is a very peculiar creature. MacIntyre is no great mathematician, but he is of the opinion that he is, and he does not take kindly to being told he is wrong. I think he finds it particularly offensive being corrected by a mere woman, so perhaps a second opinion from you might help him see the error of his ways. As you can see, his contention is quite simple – it concerns the use of Fibonacci numbers to find primes – but is also quite obviously flawed. Nevertheless, MacIntyre believes it to be one of the great lost truths of mathematics, and he thinks he can make a name for himself if he can construct a proof. I thought it might amuse you to write a short counter-proof. If nothing else it will keep your mathematical faculties in trim, and I'm sure you will enjoy it.

I look forward to your next letter and I want you to know that we are all praying for you here, and hoping that this dreadful war will be over before the new year is out.

Yours truly,
Lillian.

*   *   *

Arundel House was what it was called on the trench map. Three-foot walls and a teetering chimneybreast. It hardly deserved the name, but there it stood in the inky pool of its own shadow, a clear landmark on the white blanket of snow.

Too clear by half. The moon was so bright that he could make out the bullet holes in the plaster, the black scorch marks, and the forbidding glint of the barbed-wire entanglements. The listening post was just a few yards beyond the ruin, but Devereux would not be going there tonight. Not with this moon – not with no cloud and the ground so spotless white.

But Wilson wasn't going to give up that easily. In a week he would be home on leave, and he wanted to be shot of Devereux by then. He stood in the freezing trench for over an hour, studying the ruin, the moon and the frigid indigo sky. But it was no good. The moon was full and there wasn't a scrap of cloud to cover it. Disappointment was plain on his face when he finally took his eye away from the periscope. It would be suicide for men to go out tonight. They would be like flies on a tablecloth.

'It'll never do, Mr Ryan,' he said, handing him the periscope. 'Pass the word that the raid is cancelled. Put listening parties in our two saps, changed every hour, and sentries in the fire trench as usual. I'll tell the Black Hand gang their hour of glory is post-poned.'

'Very good, sir.' Stephen stumped off along the frozen duckboards, and Wilson slipped into the officers' dugout, where Devereux had been waiting with his men for this past half-hour, all four of them muffled up in hats and gloves and with their faces blacked.

Stephen found Gardner crouched over the firing step, inspecting the bare feet of one of his men by the light of a candle.

'The stunt's off—' he began, and they both turned towards the sound of raised voices coming from the dugout. Wilson's shrill tone was partly drowned by Devereux's deep complaining rumble.

'So I see,' Gardner whispered as the argument came to an end. The gas curtain snapped open violently, and Devereux's bulky shadow emerged, snorting great clouds of steam in the freezing air. He stamped angrily towards them and stormed past without a second look, muttering under his breath.

'Breen, you must change your socks every day and stamp your feet for a minute every hour,' Gardner said, with hardly a pause. 'The blackness will clear up if you get the blood flowing again. Now, put those dry socks on.' With that, he stood up and stamped his own feet, craning his head around to look at the stars and the moon. 'Bit on the bright side, if you ask me. I don't see what Devereux's so put out about. I wouldn't fancy my chances out there tonight.'

'Me neither. But he does seem hellfire anxious to go. Maybe he thinks the boss can command the weather, eh?'

Stephen clapped him on the shoulder and moved on to post sentries and detail listening parties for the saps that lay a few yards out in no man's land. On his way back he passed the details to Gardner, who had the watch. When he returned to the dugout he found Wilson sitting alone, a mug of tea on the table in front of him. He was staring into the steam, and Stephen silently edged around the table and stretched out on the plank bunk that filled the back wall. As he lay there, a large brown rat ran out on the shelf over the table, raised his snout to sniff the air and looked at both of them with his shiny black eyes before running on into the shadows.

'I've half a mind to send him out anyway, the impudent shite,' Wilson growled a few moments later.

'You know very well you won't.'

'Oh aye? And why wouldn't I? He as near as dammit called me shy – and in front of his men, too. I should send him out and be rid of the bugger.'

'But then you'd lose three good men as well. And if he was wounded it would be your fault for sending him, no matter how badly he wants to go. Best to wait. It's bound to cloud over soon. He'll have his chance tomorrow night.'

'I hope to God you're right, Stephen. He'll not talk to his superior officer like that again. I don't care who his uncle is. I'll not stand for it – and to hell with the consequences.'

'This clear spell can't last forever. Tomorrow night or the night after. I guarantee it.'

Wilson wrapped his bony hands around the enamel mug and blew on his tea. In the flickering light of the candles his eyes were sunk in deep black sockets and he looked tired and strained. Home leave would do him a power of good.

'I hope to God you're right,' he said again, but Stephen had already nodded off.

He snapped awake, still in his greatcoat. The dugout was pitch dark and somebody had thrown a blanket over him. For a moment he couldn't think what had woken him, but then he heard the screech and pop of a rocket, followed by the rattle of machine-gun fire. He heard Wilson cursing in the dark as he flew up from the table, knocking his chair backwards, and rolled off the bunk and up the steps after him. They stumbled out to find the trench bathed in the stark white light of flares and SOS rockets, and the sentries shouting and firing in quick succession.

'What the bloody hell is going on?' Wilson roared as Kinsella came running up.

'Mr Gardner reports heavy machine-gun fire from near the house, sir, and they're letting off rockets to beat the band—'

'Get into the house sap and see if it's a raid, Mr Ryan,' Wilson shouted, and then, 'Corporal Kinsella, make contact with the company on our left. Tell Captain Clarke we may need their support. Where the hell is Mr Devereux?'

Stephen left them behind, running to the little curtained burrow that led into the house sap. He started to scramble in, but collided with somebody crawling out. It was Breen of the black feet.

'Beg parding, sir,' he touched his forehead as he tried to extricate himself from the narrow hole, 'Mr Gardner is after sending me for more ammunition. He's putting down covering fire for the patrol to get back in.'

'Patrol? What patrol?'

'Mr Devereux's patrol, sir. Sure aren't they after getting pinned down at the house.'

'Christ Almighty,' Stephen swore, 'Go and tell Captain Wilson, then hurry back with the ammunition.'

He flung himself into the tunnel through the trench parapet and scrambled along the shallow gully that led to the saphead. He found Gardner lying in the shallow saucer of earth, firing the Lewis gun in short bursts at the flashes blazing in the dark beyond the ruined house.

'What the hell is going on?' he demanded.

'Devereux's lot went out about half an hour ago, but I lost track of them until all hell broke loose and they came haring back to the house. I think they're pinned down now. Don't seem to be moving – see for yourself.'

Another flare screeched up into the night as Stephen stuck his head above the edge of the sap. There were three dark figures huddled on this side of the ruined house, about thirty yards away, but only one of them was returning fire with his revolver. Gardner fired off another burst that ended suddenly with the flat click of an empty ammunition drum.

'Wilson didn't authorize the raid,' Stephen said, and Gardner looked as if he had been kicked.

'But he told me—'

He was cut off by the ear-splitting shriek of an artillery shell, then the hard percussive crack of the detonation. Whiz-bangs. The two men pressed themselves flat as frozen earth and stones rattled down on their helmets, then Stephen glanced out to the house again. It was a German SOS marker. The moment they saw those distress flares going up, the German artillery would hit it with everything they had. Breen came crawling up with drum magazines in the crook of his arms, grinning wickedly.

'Pardon for the delay, sirs. Captain Wilson's compliments and he says you're to shoot Mr Devereux if the opportunity presents itself.'

Now that their artillery was firing, the German machine guns grew quieter. Another ear-splitting shriek as two more whiz-bangs fell on the German side of the house, silhouetting the jagged walls in white incandescent light. They had the range all right.

'If they don't get a bloody move on they'll be flattened!' Gardner shouted, hammering the drum onto the Lewis gun with the heel of his hand and loosing off another burst. 'They must be wounded.'

Wounded, or just terrified, thought Stephen. It would take a more resolute man than Devereux to run for cover through an artillery barrage.

'Keep firing at those machine guns!' he ordered, and before Gardner could answer he had pulled himself over the rim of the sap and was running for the house. Instantly, the German machine guns came to life again, throwing a glowing line of tracer through the air in front of him, but he didn't flinch; his only thought was to reach the cover of the low wall ahead. A shell landed behind him and something hit him hard in the small of the back, punching him forward, sending him sprawling on his face. But he was there and, using every ounce of his forward momentum, he scrambled into the shelter of the wall.

It didn't take long to see why they weren't moving. Devereux was stretched on his back, his head and face a bloody mess. At first glance Stephen thought he was dead, but when he laid his hand on him he groaned and moved, his arm coming up feebly.

He crawled over him to where Sergeant Dwan was sitting against the wall, trying to reload a revolver with one hand while his other clutched the wound in his thigh. Another man was lying beside him, twitching, his bloody hands held over his scorched face and smoke coming from his hair.

'Where's Tanner?' Stephen shouted, his lips almost brushing Dwan's ear. There was the crash and bang of another salvo, the earth shook, and a piece of the wall blew outwards in a cloud of dust.

'That's Tanner.' Dwan jerked his chin at the twitching man, 'Byrne's dead in the German sap.'

'What about you? Can you walk?'

Dwan shook his head and the ground heaved under them as another shell landed over the wall. A brick flew from the top and smashed into Stephen's helmet, knocking it half off his head and stunning him. But he already knew what he had to do, and he didn't have long.

'I'll come back for you,' he shouted, and dragged Tanner into a sitting position, paying no heed to his screams. Kneeling first, he managed to stand up in a wobbling crouch with Tanner draped across his back. Bullets barked and spat angrily off the top of the wall, but he turned around and grabbed Devereux by the collar of his greatcoat, dragging him along as he staggered back to the saphead. He'd only taken half a dozen steps before he thought it was too much. Tanner was doing his feeble best to help him by holding onto his waist, but the dead weight of Devereux felt like it would pull his arm off. Doggedly, he kept going; step by painful step. His knees buckled but held, and he felt dreadfully exposed as he went back to the sap, like walking through a tunnel with walls of fire and earth. It seemed to go on forever, but then there was Gardner's grave face as he came running out to help.

He dumped Tanner into his arms, dropped Devereux within reach

177

of the sap and turned back to fetch Dwan. That was quicker; a dozen long strides and he was there. The Germans must have realized that there was no attack and their fire was slackening. Nevertheless, as he staggered back to the sap with Dwan's arm about his shoulders, a shell smashed into the chimneystack, bringing it down with a dull crash. He felt the hot wind of the detonations blasting past him, something knocking into his shoulder, but then he was safe, slithering into the sap, scrambling, crawling forward after Gardner and Breen, dragging the other two to safety.

By the time he slid into the trench, the tumult was starting to die down. The machine guns were still firing, flares screeching up from the bays, but order was being restored as Stephen hurried along to find Wilson. Cease firing! Cease firing! He rounded a traverse and stumbled into a great mound of earth half-filling the trench. A shell had blown in the parapet, and by the light of a storm lantern men were digging at the fresh earth with shovels, plates, their bare hands.

Wilson was there, digging with the men. He saw Stephen and scrambled over the mound.

'Corporal Power is under that,' he said grimly, then took him by the arm and led him back the way he had come. 'What about Devereux's patrol? Is he still alive?'

'I believe so, sir. Only Byrne was killed. All the others are wounded. Mr Gardner has sent for the doctor.'

'By God, Stephen, I'll make him wish he was dead.'

But he said nothing when he saw the three survivors stretched out on the firing step, Gardner helping the whimpering Tanner onto a stretcher while the battalion's doctor crouched over Devereux. A shell splinter had opened his skull, cleaving through scalp and bone. There was a gaping slit where he had parted his hair and the brain was visible inside, a white mass oozing blood. And yet he was still alive, his breath coming in long, loud gasps.

Stephen suddenly felt his knees go weak and he slumped against the wall. Wilson was saying something to him but he could barely hear him – his voice sounded so very far away. His hands were shaking; he was shivering uncontrollably, his head spinning. Then, in a heaving rush, he felt himself being sick into the bottom of the trench.

It was nearly dawn by the time he got back to the front trench. Wilson had insisted that he go with the doctor, and Stephen had been too dazed and nauseous to disagree. He stumbled after the stretchers and found a quiet corner in the regimental aid post. An orderly brought him a mug of tea but he let it go cold, instead trying to squeeze the tremors out of his hands by making fists. He couldn't take his eyes off the doctor standing in the lantern light, soothing the wounded in a rough and ready tone and working with his bandages, needles and swabs. Devereux was the worst. As the doctor examined his head, he twitched and writhed as if somebody was applying electric shocks. Finally, he threw off his blanket and brayed wetly with the pain, and Stephen was relieved when they took him away at last and the aid post fell silent. The doctor wiped his hands on a bloody rag and sank tiredly into a canvas chair.

'How are you feeling, Ryan?'

'Fine – better now,' he nodded to the spot where Devereux's stretcher had been. 'What about him? Will he survive?'

'I really couldn't say,' the doctor shrugged as he pulled out a silver cigarette case. 'I've given up trying to second-guess the Almighty on that score. He's young, he's fit; he may pull through. It's all a question of will power.' He opened the cigarette case, 'Smoke?'

Stephen shook his head. 'No, thank you. I'd best be getting back.'

He'd already seen the first carrying parties going past, bringing up food and ammunition for the day. It would be light soon, and the morning stand-to would be ordered. He stood up and walked along the communication trench, suddenly feeling stiff with the cold. Everything seemed eerily quiet; there was no firing now, and not a soul moved except the sentries, who turned and nodded to him as he passed.

'All right, sir?' Kinsella asked, rising up out of the shadows like a wraith.

'Yes, I'm fine now, thank you, sergeant.' Stephen answered with a weary smile. 'All quiet, I see.'

'All quiet, sir. Captain Wilson's in the dugout.'

Stephen passed through the gas curtain and breathed in the familiar fuggy reek of paraffin and sweat and earth. Wilson was sitting at the table with pen and paper, and the contents of Devereux's haversack emptied out in front of him. His face was grim as he looked up, but then he smiled.

'Come in, Stephen, sit down. How are you now? Feeling better?'

'Yes, I'm fine, thank you,' Stephen took the other chair and set his helmet down on the table. 'Is everything all right here? What about Corporal Power?'

Wilson shook his head, 'Dead, I'm afraid. Blast killed him, most likely. But, however, it could have been worse. I've already drafted my official report,' he gestured at the page in front of him, 'needless to say, you feature prominently. Mr Gardner told me what you did. Quite a feat, if you ask me.'

'Well . . .' Stephen felt himself blushing, not sure how to reply, 'it all happened so fast, I hardly had time to think.'

'Aye, well these things often happen that way.' Wilson nodded, sensing that Stephen wasn't of a mind to talk about it just then. 'Unfortunately, I've also got to explain Mr Devereux's actions in my report, and I can't say I'm looking forward to that. I was just, well . . .' He gestured at the pile of belongings on the table, plainly embarrassed. 'Well, I don't know. I thought I should write to his next of kin anyway. I'm not even sure who to write to. I'd rather not write to his uncle, who'll get the official report anyway. I don't suppose you know any of his family?'

It came as a shock to Stephen to realize that he knew almost nothing about Devereux. Three months living together and they'd probably had ten minutes of conversation.

'I knew his fiancée, after a fashion,' he admitted. 'But I never met his family. They were in the newspaper business, and I believe they had an estate in County Wexford.'

'He was writing a letter,' Wilson held up an open envelope, 'There's no address on it, but it begins "Dear Father", and it goes on about the raid he was going to lead. He had high hopes about it, you know. He talks about "restoring the honour of our family" – what do you make of that?'

Stephen shrugged. He sensed a conflict in Wilson's emotions despite his earlier harsh words. Devereux had disobeyed a direct order and got two men killed and three more seriously wounded. Wilson was perfectly within his rights to tell the truth – to blame everything on Devereux – and yet Stephen felt he wouldn't. Devereux had paid for his folly. There was no point in heaping ignominy on top.

Not waiting for an answer, Wilson shook his head and started stuffing Devereux's things back in his haversack.

'What honour will he bring them now?' he asked in a tone of disgust, 'Even if he lives he'll be a cripple. It'll eat him up for the rest of his life, Stephen – him and those who love him. He'll not thank you for what you've done, lad. You mark my words, he'll not thank you for it at all.'

From the *London Gazette*

His Majesty the KING has been graciously pleased to confer the Military Cross on the undermentioned Officers and Warrant Officers in recognition of their gallantry and devotion to duty in the field:–

T./ LT. STEPHEN JAMES RYAN, R.D.F.

For conspicuous gallantry and devotion to duty. He shewed the greatest courage and disregard for danger while rescuing wounded men in full view of the enemy positions. Unable to bring all the wounded to safety on his first attempt, he returned to their position while under very heavy enemy fire and completed the evacuation without further casualties. His gallantry and determination set a fine example to his men.

IX

My first day in command and our first turn in new trenches. I lost my first man just hours after we got here. I hope that isn't the shape of things to come.

A sniper got him early this morning just after stand-to. The weather is bloody freezing (as usual) and after making my rounds I was looking forward to a nice hot mug of tea when I heard the shot. I knew it was close by and when I ran around a traverse to investigate I cannoned into Kinsella running to fetch me. His face doesn't lend itself to showing emotion, but he looked shocked.

He brought me to young McCarthy – a boy from Carlow who came up with the last draft of replacements. He had been shot in the face; there was a neat little hole just beside his nose, and the back of his head was a mess. It's hard to find good things to say at these times, but at least it was quick – he literally didn't know what hit him. But that was no consolation to his friend, who was crying his eyes out a few feet away. His name was Dalton and they had grown up together, joined the army together and trained together. They did everything together until this morning, when curiosity got the better of McCarthy and he looked over the parapet into no man's land. The low sun must have shone on his face like a mirror.

It's my own rotten fault. The warning was right there in the divisional intelligence summary, but I didn't see it until it was too late. Wilson must be even more efficient than I thought, because I don't know how he finds the time for all the paperwork. There are returns to be filled in for everything, maps to study, and the divisional intelligence summaries (known as the comic cuts) to read. Most of it isn't too bad, but the comic cuts are hard-going. They are written in the most stuffy, impenetrable language, and usually contain dire statements about the political situation in Russia. Right at the end of the current one is a warning about a German sniper operating 'with great effectiveness' in this area. Unfortunately, by the time I was able to read that far, it was too late for poor McCarthy.

Of course, even if I'd known, there was little I could have done to stop McCarthy exposing himself like that. Over the course of the day, I've managed to glean a bit of local knowledge about this German sniper. He's been working in this sector for months and he's killed upwards of a hundred men. He's got such a grisly reputation that he even has a nickname – the 'Phantom'. It seems our taste for melodrama knows no bounds.

But I have quite a reputation myself. I am the Assassin! I'm deadly at a mile! Day or night makes no difference to me, apparently. I left my Ross rifle back in our billet (the Canadian was right – they are too unreliable for everyday use) but another one has miraculously appeared and stands on the firing step outside the dugout even as I write.

I can take a hint as well as the next man but I'm not sure how to break it to them that it just won't do. Range isn't the problem here. This chap isn't shooting at more than four or five hundred yards, but he's well concealed and he's probably working from a specially built hideout with an armoured steel loophole. The Germans are very scientific about sniping. We have some gifted amateurs, but theirs are trained at a special sniping school and they are very hard to find and kill. I've heard of chaps having success against them with big-game rifles, but it would take days to track down this Phantom and by then we'll probably have moved to a different sector. I think our best bet is just to keep our heads down until we move on.

21 January 1917

Bloody awful night last night. All the men were on edge after the business with the sniper. The tension should have relaxed after dark, but it just got worse. I can't really describe the sinister fear that snipers instil. They don't kill half as many men as shells or machine guns, but their effect is almost supernatural. I suppose it's because the other things are more or less random. They are directed, up to a point, but whether or not they kill you is a matter of luck. On the other hand, a sniper picks out his target, takes aim, and coldly reaches out to snuff out a life. It's rather chilling by comparison. And who knows that better than I do?

Anyhow, last night this Phantom got another notch on his rifle without even having to pull the trigger. It was young Dalton, the friend of McCarthy, who was shot that morning. He was badly shocked after seeing his friend killed right beside him, and I had Gardner put him in a shelter and give him a hot drink. I even told Sergeant Curtis to excuse him from duty for the day, but he kept getting out of the shelter and going back to the spot where McCarthy was killed. Three times I was called to talk to him and the third time, with him weeping and sobbing and shaking, I almost sent him to the doctor.

In hindsight, that's what I should have done. But when he turned out for the evening stand-to he was dry-eyed and in better form. I was sure he'd got over it.

Then, just after midnight, I heard a shot and I knew straight away what it was. A shot in the dark isn't unusual – there is always a fixed rifle or two working the night shift, to make sure we keep our heads down – but there was something about this one that gave me a terrible feeling in my gut. I hurried along the trench, and sure enough there he was, right at the spot where McCarthy was killed. He was hunched in a corner like a rag doll, almost out of sight, but there was no mystery about what had happened. It was plain from the way the rifle lay against his chest and the bare foot sticking out, one toe still hooked in the trigger guard.

How can I describe the feeling I had when I saw him? It wasn't anger or pity – I have been here too long for that. And it wasn't quite fear either, but something closer to despair, as if there can be no end to this. I thought I had seen the worst there was, I thought I was hardened to it, but I was wrong. I didn't sleep a wink for seeing his poor bloody miserable face every time I closed my eyes.

*   *   *

Vengeance is mine saith the Lord. That phrase kept running through Stephen's head. It was the first thing Wilson had said after Stephen explained his plan. They were in reserve and he needed his permission to go back up to the front. He'd listened silently, looked at the map with the carefully pencilled lines all over it, then nodded slowly as he muttered the words under his breath.

'You think you can do it with this gun?'

The gun was the most solid part of his plan. It was a massive thing, a Holland and Holland double rifle, a .444 nitro express.

It would stop a charging elephant in its tracks. Kinsella had managed to borrow it from the Munster Fusiliers, who had been in India when the war broke out. Usually when Kinsella said he'd borrowed something you could rest assured it was stolen, but in this case he was telling the truth. The gun came with a polite note from the owner, wishing him luck and apologizing for the fact that he only had three of the enormous sausage-sized shells to go with it.

'If I can get close enough, yes. I believe I can.'

'What if he sees you first?'

'Then he'll kill me.'

That went without saying. He wouldn't be the first one to try to beat the Phantom at his own game. He knew two men had already gone out to get him and had never been seen again.

Wilson leaned back and looked at him candidly. 'This is about those two lads you lost when I was away, isn't it?'

'Yes, it is.'

'It's vengeance.'

'No, I don't—' he began to disagree, but Wilson cut him off.

'In fact, it smacks of pride, Stephen.'

'But he's still at it. He's killing men every other day. They can only send carrying parties up there at night now, and the men are getting windy about going out on patrol. He's destroying morale. Somebody has to stop him.'

'Aye, but why does it have to be you? This is more than just some fancy shooting match – this is bloody dangerous, and it's not your job! You're a King's officer, and your job is to lead your men as best you can. God knows, you won't be any use to them dead.'

There was no denying that, so Stephen just stood there stiffly. Wilson shook his head and carried on in a more conciliatory voice: 'They're not your children, Stephen. They're soldiers, they know the risks. You can only do what you can for them.'

'This is what I can do.'

Wilson smiled bleakly. 'I don't doubt it, lieutenant. And if you want my permission, you can have it, but remember that we lose men every week. Don't let it eat you up, and don't let yourself be the next.'

'I'll do my best.'

'Vengeance is mine, saith the Lord. You remember that, now.'

And revenge is a dish best served cold, thought Stephen, as another shiver racked his body. The sun would be up soon – maybe that would warm him. The sky was already turning grey, and he longed for daylight with every fibre. How many hours since he had last moved? Three? Four? He felt as if he had frozen into the icy earth and he had to clench his teeth to stop them from chattering. But it would be fatal to move now. The only thing he could do to keep warm was to tense the muscles in each limb until they ached; one leg at a time, then each arm, and finally his fingers, squeezing them against the walnut stock of the gun.

Vengeance is mine. He repeated it to himself to take his mind off the cold. Anything but think about his situation. A shallow ditch in no man's land with nothing but a mud-daubed bed sheet to cover him. It was getting light and he was lying about twenty yards in front of a German sniping post. Right in his line of sight. He couldn't move, couldn't make a sound. He had to breathe into the crook of his arm in case the steam of his breath gave him away. *Vengeance is mine, saith the Lord.* Why the bloody hell did Wilson have to say that? As if he hadn't got enough to worry about.

But it was coming now. Five minutes more. His eyes darted to the right and there was a visible band of pink low on the horizon. He could see the stars starting to fade. Five more minutes and he would know if he was right.

At least he would know if it was really a sniping post. All he could see in front of him was a low mound with a splintered tree trunk lying on top. In this gloom it looked innocuous enough, but he was convinced it was the sniping post. He'd studied every inch of this ground, crawling out at night to check sightlines and wire thickets, and marking his map with a tiny cross for each of the Phantom's victims. All this painstaking work had given him three definite positions, three clusters of crosses fanning out from three nondescript spots in no man's land. But there was no way to tell which one the Phantom would use on any given day. He'd agonized over it for a day and a night, until the answer finally came to him with such a start that he sat bolt upright in his cot. The moon! It was the moon. The other two posts were used more or less at random around the full of the moon, but this one was only used at the dark. Why? Did he need the cover of darkness to get in, or did it offer a better shot in the first rays of the sun? It didn't matter. Tonight was the dark of the moon. The Phantom was a creature of habit, and that would be his downfall. *Vengeance is mine, saith the Lord.*

A finger of orange light slid across the snow directly in front of him. It crawled over the snowy hump of the sniping post and he knew then that he was right. In this most unnatural of places, with its fence posts and shell holes and wire, it was too natural. It was too smooth, too perfect. He knew he was right.

He'd better be. He'd worn every stitch of clothing he had, but still he was numb with the cold. The sun was warming his bed sheet and he thought he felt a tiny patch of heat on the back of his neck. He tried to focus on it and urge it through the rest of his body. This would be hard enough without being frozen half to death. A breath of breeze picked up a little flurry of snow that whispered across the bare ground in front of him. The air was beginning to move, it would have to be soon.

Patience, patience, he told himself, and thought of his grandfather. What would he have made of this kind of hunting? He would have approved of the gun, that was for sure. It was a beautiful piece of workmanship, smooth and heavy. Swirling acanthus leaves engraved all over the metal and a fine walnut stock the colour of good whiskey. Pity he didn't have enough shells to test it. One in each barrel and one in his pocket, just in case. But it wouldn't come to that. If the first one didn't fire he would be dead. If . . .

His heart gave a leap when something moved on the mound. He stared at it, clear in the sunlight now, and held his breath. What was it? Something in the shadow, only half seen. Then he saw it again and relief flooded through him. There was a hollow under the tree trunk, a small pocket of shadow, and something was moving in there. Flapping in the fitful breeze. The gathering light penetrated the hollow and he saw it was a piece of cloth, a little curtain. Not natural in any case. He let out his breath in a long silent sigh and tightened his grip on the gun. Patience, patience.

He tried to picture what was going on inside the post. There wouldn't be much room – just enough for two men – and it would be almost as cold as outside. They probably had a sap running back to the German trench, but they would have crawled up early in any case. They'd be waiting for the sun, just the same as he was. He'd been trying all night, but he couldn't quite picture the Phantom in his mind. It was impossible to give him a face – all he could see was the monstrous glass eye of his scope. But he would be older, he reasoned. His sort of coolness doesn't come easy in the young. Grey hair at his temples and solid, strong hands on the rifle as he settled himself to his work. His spotter would be younger, keen-eyed, working with a scope of his own. There wouldn't be very much talk between them – just a few whispered numbers and directions. No jokes, no laughing. Death was a serious business.

He was staring so hard at the curtain that his eyes were watering in the cold. He blinked. Had it moved again? He willed it to move. He needed proof.

A gloved hand appeared, pulling the white cloth aside, and he suddenly felt his heart thumping against his ribs. *Vengeance is mine, saith the Lord.* He could see the flatness and the dull gleam of the steel plate they had planted below the tree trunk. Gently, gently, he eased the gun out of the crook of his arm. Christ, it was heavy! But the weight was reassuring. If it could stop an elephant dead in its tracks, it could do this – if only it would fire. But how long since it had last been used? How long had it been jumbled around with dusty baggage dragged all the way from India? Buried among tennis racquets and polo mallets and sun helmets, relics of a dead age.

The faint smell of Rangoon oil calmed him a little. The gun had been well cared for. It would fire. It was already loaded and cocked. All he had to do was slide it along his arm. Slowly, slowly. He was revealing himself too. If they thought to look this close they would see the barrel. But now he was ready. He settled his cheek against the walnut stock and watched the plate over the 'V' of the sights. He could see a small dark circle on the plate, and something started to grow out of it: a rifle barrel sliding out of the loophole. It had been wrapped in rags and dried grass, but there was no disguising the long, deadly shape. He peered into the back-sight and brought the bright dot of the foresight into line on the plate. Patience, patience. He felt his grandfather lying beside him now, patience incarnate. *Take your time, ease your breath. Don't stare at your target. Hold it firm, squeeze the trigger.*

Stephen let out a long sigh, felt the trigger give under the pressure of his finger, and kept gently squeezing. There was an enormous noise in his ear and the gun kicked his shoulder as hard as a horse. A half-second later the metallic clang like a fairground bell as the massive bullet smashed into the loophole with tons of force, driving it backwards like a hammer. He waited, not breathing, as the acrid fumes from the nitrous shell stung his eyes. Patience, patience. He gently slipped his finger to the second trigger. He could still see the rifle barrel under the tree trunk, but it had shrunk to just a few inches and stuck up like a broken limb. He let the words run through his head again. *Vengeance is mine.*

But patience, patience. He drew a measured breath. His right ear was still ringing with the shock of the report, but he could hear something in the sniping post. Frightened cries and thumping, like a trapped animal. A hand waved momentarily at the back of the snowy hummock, then a human shape emerged, stumbling onto its knees. He was dressed in a white smock with a hood pushed back off his head, blood spattered all down one side. As he fell, Stephen saw the telescope jiggling on its cord around his neck, panic plain on his face. He was too young to be the Phantom: the Sorcerer's Apprentice, then. Following him with the stubby barrels, Stephen took aim on his chest. The mighty gun boomed and kicked; the shot knocked him clean off his feet and flung him down in the snow.

Broken, just like Dalton, Stephen thought, slowly edging backwards into the ditch. Vengeance is mine, saith the lord. *But I am the avenging bloody angel.*

It was dark by the time he got back to the billet. Another farmhouse, but this one was almost intact. Wilson was leaning out of an upstairs window, watching him as he trudged tiredly into the farmyard. The rifle felt like a field gun slung over his shoulder and his stomach was hollow and empty. Hot food, a hot bath and a dry place to sleep were all he wanted, but Wilson was grinning at him as he knocked out his pipe on the windowsill.

'The hero returns,' he cried. 'Well, Ahab? I heard you got your whale. Is it true?'

So the news had travelled this far. The angry shouting from the German trench had started as soon as they realized what he'd done. Snatches of it carried to him as he inched his way back to safety. Once he caught the word 'murder' in a harsh accent, countered by ribald laughter and jeers from the British lines. Then the recrimination started. They knew he had to be close by and they vented their fury with mortars, machine guns and volleys and volleys of rifle fire. But all that did was show their impotence. They couldn't see him, and they wouldn't risk coming out after him in daylight. After half an hour the fire died down and Stephen continued creeping back, pressed into the snow, pushing the rifle in front of him as he slid from one crater to the next.

He stopped in the yard, swaying on his feet. No sleep last night, and even after half an hour's brisk march he still hadn't got the cold out of his bones.

'It's true.'

'And are ye happy now?'

Happy? All the way back he'd been haunted by the sight of the spotter, picked up and flung down in the snow. Sometimes he could even feel him crawling after him, the freezing air spitting and bubbling through the hole in his shattered chest. As if it wasn't bad enough to be stuck out there in broad daylight, with a whole division of bloody Germans dying to take a crack at him, he was menaced by ghosts. Well, it was his own fault. That's all he was good for now: shooting boys as they ran away. No wonder he felt so wretched.

'Not really, no.'

'Aye, well, everybody else is. You're the talk of the division. They're calling you the Phantom Killer. General Hickie sent down a case of wine with your name on it. I dare say you'll soon be doing theatrical engagements in the West End, shooting the pips out of playing cards.'

Stephen managed a weak smile. This was a change from Wilson's sombre mood. Had he been at the wine already?

'Come on up and have a drink, Stephen. We've got a new man just arrived, and you've got reason to celebrate. Something that'll cheer you up. Here, catch . . .'

He threw down a little package no bigger than the palm of his hand and Stephen had to dart forward to catch it, turning it over in his hands, curious. A jewellery box? He was so jaded he couldn't think what it was until he opened it and found a big silver cross gleaming on a bed of red velvet. He didn't even have to see the purple and white ribbon to know what it was. Suddenly, his fatigue was gone, and he couldn't stop the grin that spread across his face.

'Thank you,' he called up, childishly pleased.

'Well, don't just stand there, Ahab. We can't open this case of wine without you and we're dying with the thirst.'

The new man was Second Lieutenant Nightingale, a tall tubular boy with the nascent fluff of his regulation moustache barely showing on his upper lip. His shyness was palpable from the way he stood crouched under the low ceiling with his hands clasped behind his back. When Stephen introduced himself he shook hands and bowed very formally, all the while eyeing the heavy rifle as Stephen unslung it and stood it in the corner. Wilson was by the window, trying to push the cork into a bottle of wine with a round of rifle ammunition and the heel of his hand.

'That's a very fine gun,' Nightingale said, nodding into the corner, 'it's not standard issue is it?'

'No, it's not. As a matter of fact it's an elephant gun.'

'Oh, really?' Nightingale nodded his head, as if that were the most normal thing in the world, and lapsed into silence once again.

Stephen tried to mask his smile. *D'you get many elephants around here?* God! Had he ever been that young?

'You need them for the snipers.'

'Oh, I see.'

'Do you need a hand?' Stephen asked Wilson, who was writhing around the bottle with his bony limbs and growing quite red in the face.

'A corkscrew would be better,' he gasped, but with a squeak and a pop the cork finally gave way and he poured the wine into three enamel mugs lined up on the windowsill.

'A toast!' Wilson began, handing around the mugs. Then he peered at the left breast of Stephen's tunic, 'Where the devil is it?'

'It's in my pocket.'

'Give it here,' he demanded, and Stephen flushed as he pulled the jewellery box from his pocket and handed it over. Wilson set down his mug and deftly pinned the cross onto his filthy tunic.

'Here's to you, Mr Ryan,' he said and they drank. The wine tasted sweet and sharp in his clammy mouth. Then Nightingale leaned across and shook his hand again.

'Congratulations, lieutenant.'

'Thank you very much.'

Wilson drained his mug and picked up the bottle again. He emptied it between the three of them.

'And here's to Mr Devereux,' he said, with a cold look in his eye.

Nightingale looked uncertainly between the two of them.

'Any news?' Stephen asked.

'He'll live.'

'Then here's to him!' Nightingale blurted. The wine was telling already. Wilson gave Stephen an amused look and raised his mug.

'Aye! Here's to staying alive, Mr Nightingale.'

* * *

I slept the sleep of the dead last night. I only had a couple of blankets on bare floorboards for my bed, but I could have slept on broken glass. I went ten hours straight through and, by God, I feel much better for it now! When I woke up, my tunic had been cleaned, the buttons polished, and the little purple and white ribbon sewn over the pocket. I felt like a new man when I put it on!

Devereux has been transferred to a hospital in England. It appears he will live, but he is to be discharged wounded – a cripple for the rest of his life. I'm not sure how I feel about that. On the one hand I feel sorry for him – I wouldn't wish it on anybody – but on the other hand, I'm glad he won't be back.

Wilson went over to Battalion HQ this morning and he was in a right old taking when he came back. It appears I've become a bit too famous for my own good. What with Devereux kicking up a stink about me, and then Wilson recommending me for the MC – not to mention the business with the sniper – my name has become known to the divisional staff. This is not a good thing because being known to the brass hats makes you liable to be volunteered for the next hare-brained scheme they dream up.

In my case, the scheme is not one of their own devising, which is some comfort, at least. The Royal Engineers want to borrow officers for a big tunnelling job they have on near Messines. I don't know the first thing about tunnelling, but my name has been put forward anyway.

Wilson is put out because he's short of officers. He's always been short of officers – as long as I've been here, we've never had a full complement – but if I go we really will be cutting it a bit fine. Gardner is all right, but Nightingale has literally only been here a day. The CO has promised him a couple more, but God knows where he thinks he might find them.

Of course, they can't make me go. It puts Wilson in such a fix that I suggested I might refuse the posting, but he told me not to be a bloody fool. With over two years served I am due a promotion but I can kiss that goodbye if I say no. On the other hand, if I do take the posting then it will be a sort of dry run: I will be in command of a tunnelling company, which will make me an acting captain. Provided I don't make a complete mess of it, that rank should be made permanent when I come back in a couple of months.

(Later)

Now it turns out that I leave tomorrow. I hadn't expected it to be so quick, but I was summoned to HQ just before teatime and told to pack my kit and report for training to the Engineers first thing in the morning. Just like that. The battalion is going back up the line tonight, but I am left behind. I shook hands with everybody as they left and they all wished me luck. It surprised me how sad I was to see them go. I've only been here a few months, but it's like leaving home all over again.

Part Three

X

Silence. It was so intense that he could *hear* the candle burning, the wick hissing and spitting in its little pool of fat. It flickered on the pale, strained face of Sergeant Page, who knelt with his eyes closed and his whole being focused on the tubes that snaked out of his ears. He looked like he was listening for a heartbeat in the earth, and Stephen wondered how he could hear it over the thunder of his own. The others were as bad – all frozen with picks and shovels in their hands, all afraid to breathe, all rolling their eyes to the ceiling, waiting for it to come crashing down. They had all heard the voice too, as clear and crisp as if it had come from just down the tunnel. But speaking in German.

He raised his eyes to the roof. Ninety feet of earth held up with a few planks and boards. Ninety feet above, men were walking around in the open air; shells were falling, feet marching, guns pounding. But no sound penetrated this deep. The tunnel was as silent as the grave.

Don't bloody say that.

He shivered and swallowed his nausea. The revolver was heavy in his hand, his palm sweaty on the grip, but the air was cold and clammy against his skin, and the miserable candle gave no warmth at all. It was stale too; they'd stopped the windjammer the moment they heard it, and now he could get the stink of fear.

If Page was afraid, he gave no sign. His face was like marble until he opened his eyes and the whites showed up the grime. Slowly, deliberately, he picked up the bell and moved it a foot to his left. He closed his eyes again to listen, and Stephen silently willed him to hurry up, for Christ's sake. The muscles in his legs were burning with cramp, and he thought if he didn't hear something soon, say something, feel something other than this awful bloody tension, he would explode in a fit.

But Page wouldn't be rushed. He'd been a miner before the war and he knew what he was at. He looked like a miner too: short and stocky and hewn from stone himself. Stephen envied him his coolness. He could never be so at home down here – the best he could do was endure it and hope the men didn't notice. But these alarms were testing his nerve. This was the third one in as many days. Yesterday it had been a prolonged scraping sound, like something being dragged through the earth, and the day before it was muffled footfalls thumping overhead.

He tried to console himself with the thought that nothing would happen as long as they could hear them. Page had been through all this before on the Somme, and he'd tried to reassure Stephen after the first alarm.

'Ain't nowt to worry about if tha can 'ear the buggers moving about,' he explained in his hoarse Yorkshire whisper. 'But when tha' can't 'ear 'em, that means they've scarpered, an' probably lit thon fuses!'

That's what they were all afraid of. Not a break-in – they were ready for that – but a countermine. No warning, just a shattering thump and the roof would come crashing down on top of them. Ninety feet of solid earth. He shuddered again.

Page's stony features slowly gave way to a smile. He opened his eyes and shook his head.

'Miles away,' he said in a whisper that seemed like a shout after such profound silence.

Long-held breath came out in a gush. Men chuckled and clapped each other on the back while Stephen rolled back and stretched out his aching legs. Even his hand was cramped around the revolver, and he flexed his fingers, feeling the sweat cool between them. Christ, it was good to move again.

'Come on then, lads. Let's be having you,' Page whispered, and some of the men crawled forward to the face of blue clay at the end of the tunnel. One of them settled his back against the wooden frame and took the spade from his mate. The others stood with their sandbags, ready to take the spoil.

Stephen felt Page looking at him. He had the keen-eyed look of a terrier at a burrow.

'Carry on, sergeant,' Stephen nodded, and the man at the frame kicked the spade into the earth with a loud snick. A curling sod of clay fell away from the wall and the tunnel grew a few inches longer, a few inches closer to the enemy line.

*   *   *

15 April 1917

This is all supposed to be top secret, but the scale of it is so huge that I have to write these figures down or I will never believe them myself! I've been working underground for nearly two months, but I had no idea of the size of the project until I went to an officers' meeting at General Plumer's HQ yesterday.

Plumer himself was in charge of the meeting, and handed around some typed pages listing the progress on the various tunnels and the amount of explosives we plan to use. I must say, I was aware there were other tunnels, but I had no idea there were so many – and absolutely no inkling of the sheer tonnage of explosives we will be using. When I read my sheet I nearly put my hand up to ask if there was a typing error!

The fact is that my tunnel is only one of twenty-four that we are digging under the Messines Ridge. Twenty-four! And mine is by no means the largest! The scheme has been in the works for nearly two years now and should be completed in another two months.

Our objective is nothing less than the ridge itself. The Germans have held it almost since the start of the war and it gives us nothing but trouble. It dominates the entire sector, and from the top they have a clear view not only of our lines, but also of our rear areas and all our movements around Ypres. It is too easily defended to give us any hope of taking it with a frontal assault, so we are digging all these tunnels and filling them with nearly five hundred tons of explosives. Then, one fine morning in June, we're going to detonate the explosives and blow the Messines Ridge right off the map.

This is all very easy to write down, but the reality is damned hard work. Even though we have finished digging, it will take thirty tons of ammonal to fill the blasting galleries in our mine alone. That's thirty tons in waterproof bags and cans that all have to be lowered down on ropes and then carried hundreds of yards to the minehead. Thirty tons! And then there is the wiring and tamping that still has to be done. Two months sounds like a long time, but I think it will be barely enough.

The Boche blew a countermine against our tunnel yesterday. It was my day off, so I was above ground, but it still put the wind up me.

I saw the damage when I went down this morning. They blew in a small side gallery and caused a partial collapse in the main tunnel. It's not very serious: we didn't lose anybody and it only took a couple of hours to shore up the damaged section – but now there can be no doubt that they know exactly where we are.

The strain is intense. Every time I go underground I count the minutes to the end of my shift. I yearn for my days off. The weather is getting warmer and there is nothing better than to go to an estaminet *and sit outside with a mug of beer and a plate of* pommes frites. *But always outside. This bloody tunnelling is making me claustrophobic.*

I also yearn to go home. It's just over a year since I left Ireland and I miss the place. I never thought I would be so sentimental about it – I certainly don't think I was this homesick when I was in Turkey. I get letters every week from Lillian and Billy – and even the odd one from Joe – but sometimes they just make it worse. Every night I go to sleep thinking about Lillian, and when I wake up my first thought is how much I miss her. I can't believe it's a year since I saw her, and even though I look forward to her letters every day, I can't wait to get back and see her again. But there's no point crying about it. Even though I'm overdue for leave, there's no hope of it coming before we blow the mine. Still, that's only a few weeks off, and then I'll be on my way. A fortnight in Ireland at the height of summer! Sometimes it's all that keeps me going.

We just put the last of the ammonal in the blasting gallery. It makes quite a sight – a bit like a cavernous greengrocer's with all the bags and tins stretching away into the dark. I'm glad it's done because the bloody stuff smells pretty foul and whenever we come up after a shift we always seem to reek of fish.

Everybody shook hands when the last bag went in. There could be no talking or cheering, of course, but I knew damned well what all the lads were thinking: They won't know what hit them.

Even so, there wasn't much time for celebration. Now we have to tamp the charge – meaning block up the tunnel with tons and tons of sandbags – and the whole lot has to be wired. This is a bit technical for a poor bloody infantry officer like me, so we are getting an RE major in to supervise. His name is Macmillan and he came down and walked the gallery with me this evening. On the way, we passed the site of the collapse and he stopped and whispered to me: 'That looks fresh!'

I didn't say anything because even thinking about it gives me the willies. The Boche will be listening and, if they think we're still working they'll blow another mine, and another, until they bury us all alive. Our only hope is to get the job done and blow them all to kingdom come before they stop us. The strain is very bad. Another four weeks left and then I'll be out of this hellish place and back above ground, where I belong. But every minute I'm down here I'll have those words running through my head:

They won't know what hit them.

And I'm not thinking about the Boche.

*   *   *

Stephen scrambled into the bright daylight with the desperate urgency of a newborn. The shock of it was overpowering. The sun stung his eyes and the air felt sharp against his skin, and he collapsed on the grimy duckboards with his chest heaving and his head spinning. He couldn't breathe. He was choking and retching as he threshed around on the ground, but he could get no air. Then, at last, he coughed up a great gob of slimy mud and his throat was clear. He sucked the air into his lungs with an enormous heaving gasp.

Still he wasn't right. There was grit under his tongue, earth in his nose, his clothes, his ears. He tried to get rid of it, shaking himself like a dog, spitting, pulling at his clothes. His ears were the worst. They felt blocked, muffled. He could hear his breath sawing in his chest, but everything else was muted, distant. Christ Almighty. Had he gone deaf?

He saw a pair of boots running silently towards him. It was Macmillan. He felt his hand on his shoulder and looked up into his worried, fearful face. His lips were moving.

'What?' Stephen bellowed, and even the sound of his own voice was muffled. He shook his head again, trying to dull the loud ringing in his ears.

'What happened?' Macmillan shouted. He was so close that Stephen felt spittle splash his cheek, but he could hear him. Barely, but he could hear him. Thank Christ! Another shake and something seemed to give way inside his head. There was a pop and he felt air in his ears.

'I said, what happened?' Macmillan shouted again, so loud it hurt.

'I heard you!' Stephen rolled away and pushed himself into a sitting position, still doggedly shaking his head. Behind Macmillan, he saw Page and Murphy lying together against the wall of the trench. Page had his round face turned up to the sky, blood oozing from his eyes. 'I don't know what happened.'

'What do you mean? You must know what happened! Did it collapse?'

'Of course it fucking collapsed!'

'But what caused it? Think, man! Was it a camouflet? Did you hear an explosion?'

'I can't . . .' he shook his head again, frowning. All he could remember was the sudden dark. The awful bloody blackness falling down on them. 'I don't remember what happened. I just . . . I don't know. The lights went out.'

'Oh, fucking hell,' Macmillan rocked back on his heels and held his head in his hands. He was only a year or two older than Stephen, but he looked gaunt and aged. The work was wearing him out. Three of these mines were his, and the closer they came to completion, the more strain came onto him. Christ knew when he'd last slept. All he did was check wiring, test connections and fret about the damp in the galleries. He'd come so close to being finished – the mines were due to blow in the early hours of tomorrow morning. Thirteen more hours and his work would have been done. But now . . .

'We must go down and see if the wires have been cut,' he said decisively, and Stephen looked at the hole he'd crawled out of. There used to be a door, but the compressed air from the collapse had blown it off its hinges. The naked opening gaped at him like a wound in the earth, black and uninviting.

'All right. I'll go with you,' he offered, though his stomach churned at the mere thought of it. Macmillan smiled and clapped him on the shoulder.

'Good man. Back in a tick.'

When he ran off, Stephen sagged against the wall of the trench. The summer sun was warm on his face but he was seized by uncontrollable fits of shivering. Now that his hearing had returned all he could hear was the noise of shells thundering across the sky. It was the final bombardment, a prolonged battering that would keep the Boche in their deep dugouts. But anybody who was underground when those mines went up would almost certainly be killed. If their dugouts didn't collapse then the concussion would kill them, and any survivors would be deafened, stunned and insensible when the assault troops charged across the craters.

Two stretcher-bearers came running down the trench. 'Can you 'ear me, mate?' one shouted at Page. Page just looked at him blankly, his head lolling. What the hell had happened? He'd had twelve men down there. If Page and Murphy got out that left ten unaccounted for. But they didn't bear thinking about. He remembered the roof coming down, timbers hitting him, crumbling earth spilling over his shoulders. He could hardly believe he'd got out himself. Anybody behind him must have been buried.

Macmillan came back with his tool bag and a pair of electric flashlights in his hand, a rope coiled over his shoulders. 'All set?' he asked, and pushed a gas mask into Stephen's hands. Stephen looked at it and felt his courage ebbing. Sometimes the Germans pumped gas into a breach – as if suffocation wasn't bad enough.

When he stood up his knees were trembling, but Macmillan wasn't much better.

'After you,' he cried with forced levity, and Stephen clenched his teeth as he stepped into the hole. His feet found the familiar top step and he started to descend mechanically. It was only when his feet thumped onto solid earth at the bottom that he realized he was holding his breath, and that he had his eyes closed.

Macmillan missed the last two rungs and stumbled against him. 'Sorry, old man,' he panted, and they switched on their lamps. The beams cut through the still air, motes flashing and disappearing as they swept the gallery. Not a breath, not a sound. The brand-new detonating wires hung from the roof like bundles of sinews, but otherwise it looked as if it hadn't been disturbed for years. Stephen slipped his revolver from its holster and nodded to Macmillan before he set off along the tunnel.

Down they went, down and down, deep into the earth, cleaving the darkness with their lamps. How many times had he walked this path in the last four months? But it felt different now, more hostile. Even the air seemed menacing and black; cold on his face and closing in again behind him. Every few minutes he stopped and listened to the dark, but the only sound was the pounding of his heart in his chest. He could feel cold sweat running down his back and with every step forward he had to fight the urge to turn and flee.

Quite suddenly they came to the site of the collapse. A dense, uneven wall of blue soil filled the tunnel and swallowed the tangle of detonating wires dragged down by the collapse. Splintered timbers stuck out like straws, and the moment he stopped he could hear the roof creaking and groaning as if it hadn't made up its mind whether to fall in.

'Christ Almighty,' Macmillan whispered. 'How far are we from the charge, would you say?'

How the hell should I know? Stephen wondered silently, but he shrugged and found his voice after a moment. 'I'm not sure. A hundred feet, maybe? It's hard to tell.'

'All right. I'll test the circuit here. If it's broken we'll have to dig.'

He set to work and, for want of anything better to do, Stephen held his flashlight for him and watched his nimble fingers as they connected the battery and voltmeter. He saw the needle on the voltmeter stay doggedly still and knew what it meant when Macmillan shook his head.

'Blast,' he hissed, and the roof cracked and showered them with stones and lumps of clay. Stephen felt his knees go weak, but Macmillan just looked up and smiled, 'I'll get to work. Do you think you can find something to shore that up?'

They had passed some shoring timbers not twenty yards back.

Stephen walked up the tunnel to fetch them, dry in the mouth and sorely tempted to keep walking. But he couldn't, he wouldn't, leave somebody down here alone in the dark. When he came back he had three stout timbers under one arm and a paraffin lamp in his free hand. Macmillan was kneeling at the wall, gently parting the earth around the wires. Stephen lit the lamp and eased the tallest timber under the sagging roof, inching it sideways until it was almost vertical. When he stood back in the circle of light it looked like a match in the mouth of a crocodile.

Macmillan looked up and nodded. Then back to his meagre excavation. 'You wouldn't give us a hand here, old chap?'

As he knelt down beside him the roof groaned again, but then seemed to settle onto the timber. It took an effort to look away – his throat felt tight and he shuddered as he thrust his hands into the cool earth.

It was easier if he concentrated on the work. They both dug until their fingers bled. Eventually, they had excavated a little burrow around the vanishing wires that was only big enough for one, and then they took turns until it was so deep that one had to pull the other out by the ankles.

When he wasn't digging Stephen sat in the yellow globe of lamplight and stared into the darkness. The light gleamed on the leather of Macmillan's boots sticking out of the earth as he worked at full stretch inside. Suddenly he heard muffled cries and Macmillan's feet flailed wildly. Stephen dragged him out gasping for breath, shock all over his grimy face.

'What is it?' he demanded, and Macmillan made a sign that he should look for himself.

One flash of the torch and he could see what had startled him. Three fingers stuck out of the earth at the end of the burrow, curled upwards as if they were beckoning him on. They were white and lifeless, like the hand of a Greek statue freed from the earth. Stephen looked at Macmillan, holding his ashen face in his hands, and then took a deep breath and crawled in. It was one of his men, after all. Gently, he scraped away at the soil beneath the hand, folded it back into the earth, and placed a scrap of timber over it. He was suddenly aware that he was inside the earth, a burrow in a burrow, cold clay pressing all around him. He felt panic rising in his chest but fought it back and started to dig furiously, chasing the wires. Beads of sweat rolled down into his eyes and the heat of his breath huffed around his ears, but he dug harder, deeper. All at once his scraping hands felt something solid, and he quailed at the thought of an arm or a leg, an ivory face in the throes of suffocating death. But it was timber – a solid baulk, one of the main roof beams. He pulled at the wires, plunging down underneath, and saw clean copper ends glinting in the soil like traces of gold. That had to be it. He scrambled back out on his elbows and let Macmillan in with his battery and wire cutters.

Waiting again, he thought of the hand he had seen, following the limb to the elbow, the shoulder, finally finding the face. Whose was it? He hardly knew his men to look at. He was so used to seeing them in the half-dark that he knew them better by sound of voice. But that one wouldn't speak again. And there must be others, all jumbled in with the earth and timbers. With a jolt, he realized it might be worse – they might be still alive and lying in pitch black on the other side, breathing shallow to spin out the dying air.

Eventually Macmillan scrambled back out, pouring sweat, but grinning. 'All set,' he said. 'We've only got four out of five circuits, but the last one will go up when we blow the others. Come on, we've got two hours left. Best make sure of the wiring from here to the surface.'

Two hours? Stephen looked at him dully. He had no idea of the time because his watch had stopped. He pointed to the wall of earth, suddenly barely able to string the words together. 'What if there are men still alive?' he asked. 'What if they're trapped on the other side?'

Macmillan shook his head and the silver discs of his spectacles glinted in the light of the paraffin lamp.

'There's no reason to think they are,' he said sympathetically, 'and besides, we simply don't have the time to dig them out. This mine is going up in two hours, whether we like it or not. On the bright side, if they are alive, then at least it will be better than asphyxiation. One moment, and it'll be all over. They won't know what hit them.'

It took them over an hour to get back out, Macmillan brushing the wires where they hung low, like Theseus and his silken thread. Every time they reached a turn he would stop and connect his battery. Then he would nod, satisfied, and they would move on again. Stephen kept looking back into the darkness as they went, listening keenly. Hearing nothing.

They emerged to find the trench packed with soldiers. Some of them parted to make way, but Stephen stopped for a moment and stood among them, feeling the jostling human warmth and drinking in the wide open sky. He could hardly credit that he'd been down so long. Night had come and gone, but the morning was only waking up. The eastern horizon was tinted orange, the blue-streaked sky still flecked with silver stars. In the dull, milky light the men looked like ghosts, as if they weren't fully there. But he clearly saw the shamrocks on their shoulders and heard the familiar murmur of Irish accents.

'Are you Sixteenth Division?' he asked a small group, and a young man with red hair and a thick Cork accent answered.

'Why yes, sir. Second Battalion, Munster Fusiliers.'

'Are the Dublins in this attack?'

'Sure, of course they are, sir,' he nodded towards the rising sun, 'They're over that way, on our right.'

Stephen looked wistfully in that direction, thinking of Wilson, Kinsella and all the others. They were in for quite a show.

'Well, the best of luck to you, lads.'

'Are you going to blow the mine, sir?' the soldier asked, and his mates were all agog to know too.

'Is it big? They told us it'll be like a heavy bombardment, only all in one go.'

'Oh, it's big all right,' he assured them. 'They won't know what hit them.'

He passed along to the firing station. Even though they were only whispering, these men seemed very noisy after the dead silence of the tunnel. They were in high spirits, almost ebullient, chatting and whispering to one another. Somewhere behind him a hoarse laugh barked out and just as he reached the station he passed a group of men saying the rosary.

Macmillan was already at the station, kneeling to his boxes and batteries. The place was packed with senior officers – divisional staff, engineers, artillerymen, brass of every description. Suddenly Stephen was aware of the extreme filth of his uniform, to say nothing of the grime streaking his face. But they paid him scant attention. All eyes were on Macmillan, who was screwing snaking wires to the terminals on a little wooden box. They peered over his shoulder, intrigued, excited. Stephen shielded his eyes as the sun peeked over the horizon and flooded the crowded trench with warm yellow rays.

'We might not change history, but we shall certainly change the landscape, eh?' a colonel cracked, and everybody laughed. Stephen found himself following the rosary, muttering the half-remembered words under his breath, but before long it finished with a final emphatic *amen*. The troops turned to face the rising sun, contented, ready to do their work. *They won't know what hit them.*

'I make it a minute to zero,' the same colonel said, staring intently at his wristwatch. Macmillan nodded, licked his gritty lips, and twisted the handle out of his little wooden box.

'Stand by!' The signal was shouted down the trench in both directions. The troops shouldered their rifles and put their fingers in their ears, then stood waiting with their mouths hanging open, trying to make each other laugh. Stephen covered his ears and waited. The colonel never took his eyes off his watch.

'Fire!' he barked, and with a wrench and a grunt Macmillan plunged the firing handle back into the box.

XI

He woke with a start, instinctively curling up and huddling on the edge of the bed. He never heard the blast – the dream never got that far. But it was bad enough while it lasted: shapeless things chasing him, cleaving out of the earth to hound him down endless gloomy tunnels. On silent wings they flew, reaching out their blanched white hands to grab him and pull him back into the ground. Sometimes they caught him and he woke suffocating as the earth swallowed him up. Sometimes he escaped to the surface where they could not follow, but they sent their screams instead, unearthly noises that wrapped around him like smoking tendrils, stinking of the shattered ground and pulling him back. Then he would beg Macmillan to fire, for God's sake, to blow the mine, to save him. And Macmillan would smile behind his opaque silver spectacles as he pushed the plunger, and the invisible electricity in the wires would jolt him awake.

He gasped, and instantly the memories of the explosion crowded in on him. The sound of the detonation was deep and muffled, felt as much as heard as the ground bucked beneath his feet. Then came the hot breath of wind on his face as the whole hillside bulged up into the air, slowly, slowly, like a great green balloon, until it finally cracked and burst into a towering cloud of smoke and fire that blotted out the rising sun. It took a moment for the roar of the blast to reach him, but when it came it washed over him like a wave, and brought with it a shower of stones and sods of fractured earth.

He could still hear it when he opened his eyes. The room was strange – he was in a big bed, well sprung, with smooth sheets and soft pillows. So soft it was as if they were holding him down. He thought he was still dreaming – a dream within a dream – but then he heard the insistent ticking of the clock, the twittering of birds outside the window. He raised his head and saw a shaft of white light piercing the gloom through a chink in the curtains. A horse and cart clip-clopped down the road outside and the delicate rattle of china on a tray came from downstairs. He sagged back against the pillows and waited for his heart to stop racing. It was real, he was safe.

Safely home. He remembered last night – coming in on the Holyhead packet and the thrill as the land suddenly loomed out of the darkness ahead. No lights with the blackout – just an absence of stars low on the horizon, and then the sense of safety as the arms of Dublin Bay reached out to pull him in. It had taken him a night and a day to get from France, and now that he'd finally arrived he couldn't quite believe he was home. It was nearly midnight when he finally came down the gangplank, but there was Billy, leaning on his cane with a crooked smile and a tip of his hat.

'There was no need to come and meet me,' Stephen chided after they'd shaken hands. 'It's the middle of the night. I could have got a cab.'

'Oh, shush, Stephen. It's the least I could do. You are my guest, after all. Besides, I wanted to show you my motor car.'

He gestured at the black Ford parked on the quay, and Stephen gave him a disbelieving look. A junior barrister could hardly afford a motor car. But Billy knew this as well as he did.

'Actually, it's not mine, as such. It's Uncle Tom's – but I have the use of it. In fact, I have the run of the place now that they've decamped to Galway for the summer.'

'Galway?'

'Yes, they're staying with my parents. Auntie Joan thought it would be safer there. She seems to think Dublin is liable to be bombed by Zeppelins.' He gave his friend a wicked grin. 'Heaven knows how she got that idea into her head. But, anyway, off they've gone down to the country, leaving yours truly holding the fort. I have the house to myself, and you are my first houseguest. So let's have none of your complaining, lieutenant.'

'Captain, actually.' He heaved his valise into the back seat and then brandished his cuff at Billy, showing him the triple crowns.

'Captain? Since when?'

'Since last week.'

'Blimey, Stephen. Medals, promotions.' He gave him a playful nudge, 'You're not half bad at this soldiering lark after all.'

After he'd admired the car, Stephen helped Billy start it by winding the handle, and then sat up beside him as they chugged into the city. They reached O'Connell Bridge and swung across it, but Stephen twisted around in his seat to look back at Sackville Street.

'Jesus, Mary and Joseph!'

Even after a year, the ruins had still not been cleared. Piles of shattered masonry lined the roadway, broken windows gaping blackly from the few remaining buildings. He knew the damage was bad – the place had still been burning when he left Ireland just after the rebellion, but somehow this was worse. The more unsound buildings had been knocked down and their absence seemed to reveal a gaping hole at the heart of the city. He stared at it, aghast, remembering the elegant boulevard that used to be there, with its bright shop windows and criss-crossing tramlines. Now it just reminded him of Ypres.

'Quite a sight, isn't it?' said Billy, changing gear with a loud grinding crash. 'Oops, sorry about that. Our very own war zone, right in the middle of the city. It'll turn into a bloody shrine to the rebellion if they don't watch out. Not that they need one. The fickle folk of Dublin have already taken the rebels to their hearts.'

Stephen detected a note of bitterness and turned back around in his seat. 'Why? Are they popular?'

'Popular? I'll say. They're flaming heroes. I'm afraid they make old Johnny Redmond and his high hopes for Home Rule look rather anaemic by comparison. It's independence or nothing now, and the Unionists will just have to lump it!'

Billy's aunt's house was a big Victorian villa on the Rathgar Road. Stephen had a vague impression of high ceilings and heavy furniture, but it was one in the morning and he could hardly stop yawning. After Billy had shown him to his bedroom and wished him goodnight he'd practically fallen into bed. Now he pushed himself up and looked blearily around. There was a bedside table, an armchair with his uniform draped across it and a *chinoiserie* screen in the fireplace. He was a million miles from plank beds and bombed-out farmhouses, but his eyes were still gritty, and there was a throbbing in his temples.

He felt better after a bath and a shave. More wonders: a proper bathtub, and hot water on tap. When he dressed and went downstairs, Billy was in the dining room, sitting at the end of a long polished mahogany table with a steaming cup of coffee and a newspaper. In the next room, a clock told the hour with musical chimes.

'Stephen, there you are. Did you sleep all right?'

'Yes, quite well, thanks.'

Billy set down his newspaper and gave him a stern look over the top of his spectacles.

'Are you sure, Stephen?'

He had pulled out his chair and sat down a little self-consciously. He felt his cheeks beginning to glow.

'Yes, why?'

'Well, you look a bit peaky and, if you don't mind my saying so, you made a bit of a racket last night. Are you sure you're all right?'

'What sort of racket?'

'Shouting and whatnot. I wouldn't have mentioned it, only it sounded like you were having a right old time of it.'

'Oh, I beg your pardon.' Stephen cast his eyes down and squirmed in his chair. They all did it back in France. It was so commonplace that nobody ever said anything. 'I didn't realize I was making a noise. I'm sorry if I disturbed you.'

'Well, it's not *me* I'm worried about. Are you sure you're all right?'

'Oh, I'll be fine. It's probably the bed. I'm not used to such a soft mattress – I'm not used to any mattress, to tell the truth. I dare say I'll get used to it.'

Mentioning the mattress seemed to do the trick. Billy gave him a consoling grin as he lifted the coffee pot.

'I shudder to think what you have to put up with over there,' he said. 'Is coffee all right, or would you prefer tea?'

'Coffee would be fine.' Stephen got up to the sideboard and helped himself to some bacon and toast, 'We don't get much of that either, as it happens.'

Billy looked at him aghast. 'Good God. And we're supposed to be fighting for civilization. What *do* you get, then?'

'Tea. Endless cups of tea – usually stewed and, as often as not, cold. Sometimes cocoa if we're lucky.'

'And what do you eat?'

'That depends on where we are. At the front it's mostly stew of some description.' He held up a rasher on a fork, 'And bacon sandwiches. Lots of bacon sandwiches. I've developed quite a taste for them.'

'Well, me too, as it happens,' Billy admitted. 'Bacon's about the only thing we can get, what with all these shortages. Even coffee's become a luxury thanks to these flaming submarines. Still, I suppose it hasn't done me much harm.' He proudly patted his belly, which was much reduced from the last time Stephen had seen him. He was by no means slim, but he was much more solid now, more of a man than the chubby schoolboy he used to resemble. A serious man, too, in his black suit and tie.

'You're off to work, then,' Stephen observed, chewing on a piece of bacon and sipping some of the strong, bitter coffee to wash it down.

'Yes, must earn a crust, you know. I'm not in court today, otherwise I'd invite you along to watch the fun. What about you? Any plans for your week in the old country?'

Stephen shrugged. How long had he been looking forward to this leave? And yet, in the end, it had rushed up on him. He wasn't sure what to do with himself. There was so much he wanted to see, and yet he was unprepared. What with everything that went on, he hadn't had time to send telegrams or letters. Apart from Billy, nobody knew he was home.

'I'm not sure. I thought I'd drop in on Joe this morning. After that I think I'll . . .'

'Go and see Lillian Bryce?' Billy asked avidly.

'Perhaps,' he answered coyly.

'Oh, for God's sake, Stephen, you don't have to pretend with me. I saw her not a fortnight ago and she told me all about the letters you've been sending one another. She said she couldn't wait to see you, so stop dragging your heels. Go and see her. When you do, you can invite her to dinner.'

Stephen felt his friend was pushing him. One part of him resented it, but the rest of him wanted him to push harder. He looked at him with growing interest. 'Dinner?' he asked.

'Yes, you know, the evening meal. I'm in an entertaining mood, and I'm not going to send you back without at least one decent dinner inside you. But the last thing I want is to have to sit here all evening looking at your ugly mug. Some female company would do us both the world of good. Invite her to dinner here, just the three of us. Say on Sunday? I'll see what Mrs Walsh can find. She's a wonder, is Mrs Walsh.'

The reflected sun was warm on his face and the sound of the breeze rustling through the trees was soothing. Stephen sat with his eyes closed, feeling the sweat cooling in the small of his back. He was in St Stephen's Green, sitting on a bench near the duck-pond, and he didn't know what had just happened to him. His hands were still shaking and he pressed them together in his lap, willing them to stop.

Another fit. Was that what it was? A fit of the vapours? He didn't know what it was, to tell the truth – had hardly realized it was happening the first time. That was on the train to Boulogne, but he'd been sleeping then and thought it was just another night-mare. This one was in broad daylight – it had come on him as he walked down the street, tipping his hat to ladies and thinking how well the meeting with his brother had gone.

He turned his mind back to the meeting, thinking he'd been all right then. There hadn't been the pain in his head, the dryness in his throat, the thumping heart and the shaking hands. He felt fit and happy, and it was only as he climbed the dusty stairs to the union offices that he realized his uniform might not be a welcome sight. They were probably all Citizen Army men with good reason to be wary of soldiers. The girl outside certainly gave him a hard stare before she asked him to take a seat and went back. She was gone quite a while, and he had a vision of panic, of men scrambling out of the window. But eventually the door opened again and Joe stuck his head out, his guarded look dissolving into a broad grin when he recognized his brother.

'Jesus, Mary and Joseph,' he whispered, and came all the way out, shutting the door behind him. 'Look who's back! It's good to see you, Stephen.'

There was an unaffected joy in his greeting, real warmth in his handshake, and Stephen felt his anxiety melting away. His brother looked well in his brown suit and tie. Quite the man – no longer the boy he remembered – and a healthy man at that, with none of the shuffling stiffness he'd seen at the camp. He sat down and they chatted for a few minutes, but Stephen had the feeling he was making him uncomfortable, and didn't object when Joe suggested that they go out for a cup of tea. When they came out onto the street, Joe cast a glance over his shoulder and asked, 'See that fella across the road?'

Stephen darted a look and saw a burly young man in shirtsleeves and a waistcoat with his jacket slung over his shoulder. He was peering intently into the window of a dressmaker's.

'The one who's interested in women's clothes?'

'He's G Division – from Dublin Castle. They have a watch on the office. I wonder what they'll make of me going for a cup of tea with one of His Majesty's officers.'

Stephen wondered that too – particularly when he spotted the man again from the window of the Lyon's tea shop – but Joe didn't seem to be too bothered. He chatted away for over an hour, curious about the war, the medal, working underground, and what life was like at the front. It was only as they finished their tea that Stephen realized his brother had told him hardly anything about himself. His union work seemed to be an endless round of meetings, minor confrontations with employers and squabbles over rates of pay. But that was exactly as he had imagined it would be – Joe had used hardly any names or hard figures, and he wondered if it was really that dull, or if he was being evasive. The one thing he opened up about was the trip he'd be taking in a few days.

'Myself and a few of the boys are off down to Clare,' he said with obvious relish. 'We'll be doing a bit of campaigning for the by-election.'

'Clare?' Stephen was puzzled. Clare was in the west of Ireland, and predominantly rural. No cities, and not many towns. 'Is the Labour Party running a candidate in Clare?'

'Not Labour,' Joe answered, picking a shred of tobacco from his teeth, 'Sinn Fein. De Valera is running against the Parliamentary Party.'

Although he didn't say anything, this troubled Stephen. Eamon De Valera was the senior surviving leader of the Easter Rising. And lucky to survive at all, if what he heard was true. Some question over his citizenship: he had been born in America, or his mother was American. Whatever it was, it had saved him from the firing squad. And now, here he was, not a week out of an English jail and standing for election to Westminster – with Joe helping to drum up votes. Small wonder the police were following him.

But they parted amicably enough, shaking hands and promising to meet again in a day or two. Stephen hadn't gone very far before the thumping in his head grew stronger. The sun hurt his eyes and the rush and press of people on the pavement jangled his nerves. Fear gripped him – fear of what? He couldn't say, there was nothing to be afraid of, but it bloomed inside him, filling him with dread. Somebody bumped into him and he turned sharply, frightened, his heart tripping. Then a tram rushed past, the bell clanging, and he almost dived for cover.

The pain in his head made it hard to think. It almost blinded him as he pushed his way forward, desperately trying to escape from something he couldn't even see, let alone name. Was he going mad? Was this how it happened? Was this how they cracked up? Panting and frightened, he saw the green of the trees and hurried towards them. Cover, quiet. He plunged into the park and steered a winding course, away from the strollers and couples. He was walking as fast as he could, almost running, until eventually, something snapped and he asked himself what he was doing. What was driving him? It was like waking up. He looked over his shoulder and there was nobody there. Nothing to be afraid of. He bent double, trying to catch his breath, and then walked to the bench and flopped down.

The physical symptoms passed within a few minutes, but he was still frightened. Not filled with horror as he had been earlier, but afraid of himself, of what was happening to him. That it had happened to him before meant it was more than just a passing weakness. But it didn't explain what was wrong with him, or how he might help himself. What was causing it? What could he do?

He closed his eyes for a few moments, basking in the sunlight reflected from the water. There was a noise to his right – a rustle, and then a shriek. Laughter followed and two young boys darted from the bushes. Not the well-kept little boys who were strolling with their nannies or mothers, but two scrawny little gurriers with dirty knees and torn jerseys, each carrying a wooden rifle. Stephen smiled to himself. They were on an adventure to the posh part of town. Many was the time he and his brother had done the same when the weather was this fine.

'A soldier! A soldier!' one of them cried, and they ducked behind a tree and then popped out again, covering him with their rifles. He held up his hands in mock surrender.

'Take that, you Brit bastard!' the other one shouted, and

pretended to fire. The smile died on his lips as they ran away, laughing. He looked down at the little purple and white ribbon on his breast. Billy was right; the rebels were the heroes now.

After a while, he stood up. His legs were weak and his head was light, but he forced himself to start walking. He knew where he was going, but he felt he was only drifting in that direction. People passed him, smiling politely, nodding, but he saw them as if they were through plate glass. When he left the Green and walked down Grafton Street, the crowds grew thicker. They frightened him. He felt his heart begin to palpitate again as he skirted them, darting to and fro with quick steps to avoid them. He kept his head down, hardly seeing them, aware only of his own reflection as he passed the windows of jewellers and clothes shops. This was another world; it was alien to him – or rather, he was alien to it. These people were all perfumed and pretty, but he was still stinking of the shattered earth in Messines. He was an underground creature thrown out blinking and blinded into the light. He didn't belong here, these people didn't know him, didn't see things the way he did . . .

Before he knew it, he was at the college gate. How did he get here? It was as if he was in a daze and had just woken up. This was happening too often. He looked behind him, but he couldn't remember crossing the road, he couldn't remember the last part of Grafton Street. He didn't know what made him stop here. His hands were starting to shake again.

He thrust them into his pockets and pressed on. The air under the deep arch was cool on his skin and he shivered and felt a dry bolt of nausea clawing its way up his throat. It was like going down again. But there was the sun on the other side. He lengthened his step and gasped when he stepped out into the light. Warm air, flies buzzing, the smell of grass and roses. A couple of students were running across the square. A few more were drowsing in the grass, reading. There was no danger, and yet, and yet . . .

His feet carried him forward again. Familiar cobbles, the tall tower of the campanile. How many times had he walked across here? Threading his way along the path and around the side of the Rubrics. New Square opened out before him. The high steps leading up to the double doors of the mathematics department. He suddenly realized how close she was, and it checked him again. All the way home he'd been thinking about her, dreaming about her, reading her letters over and over again. But now that she was close, *this close*, he was unsure of himself. How much did he rely on those letters? Every week they brought a little glimmer of light from the life he used to know – the life he aspired to know again. Normality, sanity. But what if meeting her in the flesh somehow broke the spell? What if he disappointed her? What if she saw what he was really like?

His resolution crumbled and he started to think the worst. What if the letters were just letters – a war duty, like knitting socks for men at the front? They didn't have to *mean* anything. Why should she keep herself for him? Why would she be interested in this miserable creature with shaking hands and a shortness of breath? She wasn't stupid. She wouldn't waste herself on him.

Despite his doubts, he reached the top of the steps before he stopped. He peered in through the doorway like a stranger. He recognized the floorboards, the dusty staircase, the noticeboard, but again he felt separated from them. They were like museum exhibits – familiar but under glass. He knew he couldn't go in. With all his momentum gone he suddenly felt weak and lost. Defeated, he turned away and went back down the steps.

'Mr Ryan, Mr Ryan.'

Five paces from the bottom of the steps, he stopped dead, hunched as if he'd been caught in the act. He recognized the voice, but he was almost afraid to look.

'Mr Ryan. Stephen!' she called again, breathless, and he heard her shoes clicking down the steps behind him. He turned to face her, already trying to swallow his shame.

'Oh my goodness! It is you. When did you get home?' She was standing on the bottom step. She was taller than he remembered, and she had changed her spectacles for a lighter pair with wire rims – but there was no mistaking the planes of her face and the light in it as she smiled. Time had been kind to her: it had knitted her frame together, rounded her features, given her the strength of maturity. Everybody was growing up without him.

'I . . . Er, yesterday – last night,' he said uncertainly, and plucked the cap from his head.

'You said in your letter you would be getting leave, but I didn't think it would be so soon. Why didn't you come in and say hello?'

He hesitated, fumbling for some explanation, but she didn't wait to hear it. She ran forward and, with an easy movement, kissed him on the cheek. 'Oh, it's so good to see you. How are you? What's this?' She plucked at his sleeve and laughed, 'Have you been promoted and you didn't tell me?'

Relief flooded through him so suddenly he thought he might faint. As if sensing this, she took him by the arm and led him to the bench underneath the window of the senior common room. She must have seen him from there. They sat side by side, she still holding his arm, and he felt the strength and warmth in her hands. It was his first real human touch in how long? And his cheek still glowed where she had kissed him. He willed her not to let go, but there was little danger of that; she was keen to hear everything about him. When had he been promoted? How did his mine go off? It had been all over the papers – the Messines attack, the greatest success of the war. He slowly felt himself unwinding as he talked, but just as he felt the last shreds of discomfort falling away, she squeezed his arm and asked: 'Stephen, forgive me, but what time is it?'

He looked at his wristwatch, 'Two o'clock.'

'Oh, dash it anyway!' she exclaimed, 'I've got a tutorial at two. Senior freshmen – Mr MacIntyre and his cohorts. Do you remember I told you about him in a letter?'

Remember? Of course he remembered. He nearly had them all off by heart.

'The Fibonacci sequence.'

'That's him. Though he's given up on that at long last. He's taken more of an interest in politics – which is just as well, because he really doesn't have much talent for mathematics. I wonder . . .'

The Fibonacci sequence. The name echoed in his head. He was surprised at the dart of pleasure that he got when he thought of it. Each number the sum of the two before. Why was that important? It wasn't really – it was just numbers. But how he used to play with them, toy with them, roll them around in his head! He followed Lillian's gaze up to the window, remembering the common room, with its threadbare carpets and creaking armchairs. He remembered sunbeams streaming in the windows and watching the dust motes swirling. The first time he sat in a tutorial there, he thought it was the nearest thing to heaven. Nothing but pure mathematical argument; ideas, theories, proofs. He could happily have spent his life in that room, chasing the elusive proofs through untold labyrinths.

'Won't you come inside, Stephen? I'm sure they'd love to meet you.'

'I wouldn't like to spoil your tutorial!' he said, suddenly nervous at the thought of going inside. Even though he wanted to go in, he was trying to find reasons not to. 'I doubt they'd want to see a soldier in their class.'

'Oh nonsense! Mr MacIntyre might get his republican hackles up, but I wouldn't mind him. The others would be delighted to see you. I've told them all about you before – especially your work with Professor Barrett on the Riemann hypothesis. They'd be fascinated to talk to you. And would you believe we were going to discuss the Mersenne primes? Your particular subject – now there's kismet for you! You *must* come inside . . .'

She took him by the arm again and led him up the steps. They were inside before he realized it, and suddenly it was just the same as it had been before. The same creaking floorboards, the same dusty smell, the same yellowing paper pinned to the board. Lillian still had him by the arm and she smiled at him as they came to the door of the common room.

'Good afternoon, everybody,' she said, and her students all stood up politely as she came in. Some things had changed after all. 'This is my friend, Captain Ryan. He was a student here before the war and he is an outstanding mathematician, particularly in the field of number theory. He has kindly agreed to join us for today's tutorial. I'm sure you'll make him feel very welcome.'

He smiled at them. About a dozen in all – but they were so young. Had the war aged him that much? They were barely two years younger than him – some even less – but they looked like children. Despite the warm introduction, they looked back at him with a mixture of curiosity and suspicion. Here was the war come into their room, the ghost at the banquet. But they smiled back politely and as they made to sit down the young man nearest the door turned to Stephen, offered him his chair, and took a place on the settee nearby. Stephen sat, feeling the clamminess of his own hatband as he fidgeted with it between his knees.

When everybody else was settled, one young man stayed standing on the other side of the room and Stephen felt his eye on him. He was a lean and stringy individual with long bony wrists that hung out of the cuffs of his jacket. His sallow face was thin and pale and already in need of a shave. As he stood up, he thrust his hands deep in his pockets and leaned forward belligerently. This was MacIntyre. Stephen knew it even before he opened his mouth.

'Good afternoon, *Captain* Ryan,' he said, in a harsh reedy voice.

Stephen looked at him charily. This was no ordinary welcome. The sinewy young man had paused to look around the room and make sure his audience was watching. From the way the others averted their eyes it was clear they were afraid of him. He was the class bully, warming up for a performance.

'Sit down, please, Mr MacIntyre,' Lillian said wearily, as she crossed to the chair by the window, where she had left a stack of papers.

'I'll not sit down with a warmonger,' MacIntyre said, shooting her an ugly glance. Stephen felt his face hardening. His hands clenched into fists.

'Very well then,' she returned to the door and pulled it open. 'You may leave.'

MacIntyre stood his ground. His mean face took on a dogged look. 'I will not leave on account of an imperial officer,' he said indignantly. 'I'll not make way for an Irish mercenary in the King's service.'

The others gasped at his audacity. MacIntyre was pleased with himself, leaning back with a sly smile twitching at the corners of his mouth, the height of smug insolence. How long had he been rehearsing that?

'That is your prerogative, Mr MacIntyre,' Lillian said, and strode quickly across to where he stood. Stephen could see no trace of the shy girl who used to come into class early to avoid making a fuss. She seemed to have grown in stature; now standing taller than her student, her face pale and furious, her head upright. She had the formidable grace of a square-rigged battleship with all its sails unfurled, bearing down upon the enemy. 'But let me tell you what else you will not do. You will not insult my friends, and you will not obstruct my classes with your political ranting. We have no place for politics in this class, as you well know. Nor do we have a place for obnoxious young men who lack the common courtesy to welcome a guest. This is a class for mathematics and mathematics alone – we leave all other concerns outside. Which is where you are going, Mr MacIntyre.' There was another gasp as she seized him by the arm, no face so shocked as his, and before he could utter a word of protest she was dragging him to the door. 'You may return after you have apologized to the class and to Captain Ryan.'

With that she thrust him into the hallway and shut the door behind him. Stephen saw poorly disguised smiles as he turned back to the students sitting around the room. MacIntyre was clearly more feared than admired. Lillian took her seat near the window and smoothed her skirt.

'Now, I believe we were discussing the Mersenne primes and Brother Mersenne's method for finding them,' she said pleasantly. 'Like Mersenne himself, Captain Ryan has a particular affinity for prime numbers. I have no doubt he will be able to explain the technique far better than I can.'

There was a light burning in the drawing room when he came back. Billy was sitting in an armchair with a book and a brandy. He was still in his dinner jacket and a cigarette was slowly burning itself out in the ashtray beside him.

'I thought you'd be gone to bed,' said Stephen when he came in. 'I hope you didn't stay up on my account.'

'Not at all,' Billy smiled and closed his book. 'It was such a wonderful evening that I didn't want to just slide off to bed. I thought I'd savour it for a bit.'

Stephen unbuckled his Sam Browne and opened the top buttons of his tunic.

'Good idea,' he sighed. He was in such good humour that he'd made the walk home at a brisk pace and was slightly out of breath. He threw his cap on the sofa and went to the sideboard, where he poured himself a brandy.

'I take it you got her home safely.'

'I did,' he grinned and eased himself into an armchair. 'She asked me to thank you again for a very pleasant evening.'

'The dear girl. The pleasure was all mine.' Billy took a drag from his cigarette and blew a long plume of smoke into the air. The meal had gone far better than he had expected. Three was such an awkward number and he had been extremely conscious of being the gooseberry, but in the end it was the most gratifying evening he'd had in a long time. 'I congratulate you, Stephen. That is a very fine young lady you have there: witty, charming and sharp as a pin.'

Stephen nodded agreeably, his mind still half on the walk down through Rathmines and then along the canal to her house in Percy Place. The pleasant feeling that he was floating through the warm night air, with only her hand on his arm to anchor him, and yet the dread of it ending: the knowledge that soon they would reach her house and he would be coming back without her.

'Isn't she?' He raised his glass, 'Here's to her!'

'Yes, indeed. God bless her!'

They drank their toast and fell into a companionable silence. It had indeed been a very pleasant evening – far better than if it had just been the two of them. It was as if Lillian had been a catalyst, transforming the atmosphere and freeing them from the bonds of long acquaintance. Everything was discussed anew, and as the evening wore on Billy found he was surprised at the changes wrought in his friend.

'You don't mean to tell me,' he said to Stephen as they finished their soup, 'that you actually agree with the rebels. And you sitting there in your uniform.'

'I didn't say I necessarily agreed with them,' Stephen answered carefully. 'I said they've changed everything, and I think people should understand that and stop dreaming about what might have been. Because we haven't heard the last of Sinn Fein – not by a long chalk. Now that they've gone into politics, it looks like they're here to stay.'

'Oh, hardly! They've only won two by-elections on the back of the executions of Pearse and his men. And both of them have refused to take their seats in Westminster. Yes, they're enjoying the run of public sentiment, but that never lasts. No politician can survive on a political idea alone. Sooner or later the people who elected them will want their voice heard in Parliament and then they will elect somebody who will speak up for them.'

'But are people not tired of talking?' Lillian asked, 'I mean, look at this convention that John Redmond is running above in the college. It's supposed to gather together all the Irish politicians so they can resolve the Irish problem, but half of them wouldn't even go – including Sinn Fein. Not that it stopped the rest of them from sitting down and talking, which proves nothing, except that talk is cheap. And what do they think they will achieve? Home Rule? Sure, Home Rule is dead. Didn't Lloyd George offer it only last month and was turned down, because even Johnny Redmond knows it's not enough any more, and that Welsh divil was only offering it to keep us quiet.'

These last words were delivered with such passionate vehemence that they all froze, looked at each other and then burst out laughing.

'Well,' Billy said, 'to think that the pair of you used to be so quiet. I can hardly believe my ears. But everything you say is true. It looks as if I shall have to modify my outlook to suit these changing times.' He picked up his glass, 'May I propose a toast? *Tempora mutantur*. To the changing times!'

Now that they were alone again, Billy reflected that not all the changes were for the better. He watched his friend through half-closed eyes and remembered the worrying things he'd spotted during dinner; how Stephen's hand shook when he lifted a cube of sugar into his coffee, and the way he often lapsed into morose silence. True, he had never been the most talkative creature, but this evening he'd clearly been making an effort to be pleasant company – and yet sometimes he had simply dropped out of the conversation, as if he'd fallen into a trance. Billy wasn't the only one to notice it either. When it happened, Lillian would give him a concerned look, then take a breath and turn to Stephen directly with a question, or pat his hand – anything to bring him back to the land of the living.

Stephen had noticed it too. He was aware of his own behaviour just as he was aware of the war; it was pushed back, suppressed. He'd struggled with it, tried to keep his mind on the meal, tried to be witty – but the war cast its shadow even here. Time was slipping through his fingers. Another three days and it would be back to France. This day next week he would be back to tinned jam and bully beef, living from one letter to the next, waiting for *that* bullet or *that* shell. The one that would blot him out, end it all. Every time his mind turned in that direction he stopped it, but it always went back, like an obstinate dog on a scent. He didn't want to, but when he started thinking like that he couldn't help himself. That was why he stayed silent. He bound it to himself, buttoned it up, and tried to keep it down. Because if he let it out, even a little bit, it would end in tears.

'I want to thank you too,' he said, slowly swirling the brandy under his nose and inhaling the sharp scent. 'Not just for the dinner – for having me to stay. It's been unbelievably pleasant to get out of barracks.'

'Don't mention it, old man.'

'I'm afraid I haven't been much of a houseguest.'

'Nonsense. You're more than welcome.'

'And I'm afraid I'm rather making a pig's ear of it with Lillian.'

Billy sat up and looked at him sharply. 'Why? Did she say something when you left her home?'

'No, not at all.' His mind turned to the pavement outside her house. The dim glow of a lamp behind the sitting room curtains. When he called to collect Lillian she'd brought him in there and introduced him to her mother, a handsome woman with greying hair and shrewd eyes. Then Lillian had gone upstairs to change and it was half an hour of tea and Eccles cakes, answering quick-fire questions about the war, the front, what life was like over there. Her motive soon became clear: Sheila wanted to go to France to work in a hospital near the front. Did he ever hear the likes of it? As if there wasn't enough for her to be doing in Dublin. Sure wasn't she working even now – on a Sunday, God love her – otherwise she'd have been here to meet him.

'Well, here we are then,' he said to Lillian as they stopped at the gate at the end of the evening. It was silent save for the distant thunder of water in the canal lock down the street.

'Yes, here we are,' she smiled. 'Thank you for walking me home.'

'It was my pleasure.' He'd been steeling himself for so long that he hardly noticed when she let go of his arm. Now there was a gap between them, he knew it would only get wider. But his mind was a muddle; he genuinely didn't know what to do next. 'Well, goodnight then.'

He was on the point of turning away when she laughed.

'Stephen Ryan, you really are quite insufferable.'

He felt himself begin to blush. He'd put his foot in it somehow. What had he done wrong? In some ways, the war was simpler.

'I'm sorry . . .'

'You walk me all this way and then leave me on the doorstep without so much as a goodnight kiss.'

'Ah, yes. Sorry.'

She moved closer, but his eye went to the light in the living room window.

'Won't your mother be . . . ?'

'My mother?' She looked at the window and shook her head, 'Don't you worry about her. Ever since I was a girl, she's been afraid I'll turn into an old maid. I thought you'd have guessed as much from the interrogation she gave you this afternoon. Anyway, it's long past her bedtime. I doubt she's watching, but if she is then I shouldn't be surprised if we get a round of applause.'

The kiss. It was so easy, as if they naturally fit together. The warmth in her lips was surprising. The strength in her hands on his shoulders, the scent in her hair. It was overpowering, but when they finally parted his heart was beating madly and he could hardly find the breath to speak.

'Goodnight, then,' he said, and watched her go up the path and open the door. A final wave and a smile and she was gone. He lingered with one hand on the cold iron of the gate, his lips still warm, and with the urge to laugh and run madly down the deserted street. But in the end he just whispered the words again and walked away with his hands in his pockets.

'I didn't think so,' Billy said complacently. 'That girl is clearly quite mad about you.'

'It's not her, it's me,' Stephen said glumly. 'I mean, she's wonderful but, God, I don't know. I get the feeling there's something I'm not saying or doing. But on the other hand . . .' he broke off, not sure how to say it.

Billy glared at him through his cigarette smoke. 'But? But what? Are you mad about her or not? You just said you were.'

'I am. But it's not fair on her, is what I'm trying to say.'

'Stephen, Stephen . . .'

'It's not fair. I don't want to burden her.'

'You mean if you get killed?'

Well, there it was in so many words. Stephen had already opened his mouth to explain, but he caught himself. Billy knew more than he thought.

'Yes. Precisely.'

'You said that before.'

'What?'

'Don't you remember? It was in the Empire that morning before the Rising. I asked you why you hadn't written to her and you said you didn't want to burden her. I must say, I thought it was utter tosh then, and it's utter tosh now.'

'You wouldn't understand.'

'Understand what? Understand what it's like over there? Of course I don't. But I can see the effect it's had on you and I can read the newspapers. I also know you've been fighting for three years now, and you haven't been killed yet. That's got to mean something, hasn't it?'

Stephen swallowed some brandy, wincing as it burned his throat. 'I wish it did, but if I've learned anything, it's that skill or talent has very little to do with it. It's all a matter of luck – and what worries me more than anything is that in three years I've used up more than my fair share.'

Billy measured his next words carefully. This conversation had become very unreal and he couldn't quite believe that they were discussing his friend's life with such complete detachment.

'So you think your luck's going to run out?'

'I'm sure of it.' He allowed himself a bitter smile. 'Do you want

238

me to do the maths for you? It can all be worked out quite accurately, I assure you. But there's a simpler proof,' he held up his sleeve so Billy could see the three crowns, 'I'm a captain with three years' service. It used to take a man ten years to reach that rank. Why do you think I got there so quickly? Is it because I'm such a good soldier, or is it because most of the men I joined up with are already dead or wounded? Even bloody Devereux, for God's sake. Christ knows what sort of state he's in.'

Billy watched him steadily, nodding slowly to himself as he prepared his reply. 'Let us leave aside for the moment that, from what you told me, Devereux was a liability to himself and others. Let us assume that you were promoted at least in part because you're good at your job, and not just because they were scraping the bottom of the barrel. So, all that being said, you have discovered you are mortal. Well, which of us isn't? Which of us isn't afraid of dying?'

'That's not what I'm talking about, Billy.'

'No, you're talking about not wishing to burden Lillian with your death. You don't want her to mourn for you.'

'That's right, I don't.'

'Well, while I admire the sentiment, I'm sorry to have to tell you that it's still utter tosh. You're only codding yourself.'

'Billy . . .'

'What? Do you think it wouldn't break her heart now if something happened to you? The fact is, the girl is mad about you, and you're mad about her, so why don't you just bloody well get on with it.'

Despite the gravity, Stephen laughed and shook his head. 'You once said you were the last person who should be giving me advice about women.'

'Well, more fool you for listening to me. But while we're throwing one another's words back in our faces, let me remind you of

239

something you said to me just after you joined the army. You said you wanted to live before you die.' Billy drained his glass and ground the butt of his cigarette into the ashtray before pushing himself up out of his chair. 'We all die sooner or later, old man. Personally, if I thought it was going to be sooner rather than later, then I'd damn well make the most of what I had left.' He clapped a friendly hand on Stephen's shoulder. 'Goodnight to you, now. I'll see you in the morning.'

He had some time in hand so he sat on the bench and read his newspaper. The window above was open, and now and then snatches of conversation drifted down to him, but no voice he recognized. He concentrated on his newspaper: the new Russian government was standing firm with the Allies, but there were reports of mutinies in half a dozen Russian regiments. They'd be in a right fix if the Russians packed it in. On the other hand, the Americans were starting to arrive. General Pershing had landed in Liverpool and would be received by the King. Maybe they would turn the tide. Maybe even the sight of them would push the Germans to sue for peace. It couldn't go on like this forever. Somebody had to get an advantage sometime, and when that happened the whole bloody thing would crumble. If the Russians went first, the Germans would have it. If they held on and the Americans came in, then it would be the Allies. It was all about holding on. But the French had already had a mutiny. How long before the British army had one too? How long before somebody decided enough was bloody well enough?

He took a breath and carefully folded the paper and set it down beside him. This wasn't the time to be getting worked up about it. He slit his eyes against the sun and watched the swifts whirling around the sky for a few moments, and then the door to No. 39 opened and a tide of students flowed down the steps.

The ones who recognized him from last week nodded their acknowledgement. A few moments later a solitary figure came out; there was mutual recognition, but no polite nods. MacIntyre loped down the steps two at a time, pulling his jacket on and scowling at Stephen as he tramped past him on his long, bony shanks.

Then Lillian came out, pinning her hat and smiling as she came down the steps. Her face darkened as she caught sight of MacIntyre's retreating back. 'Sorry I kept you. I had to have a word with Mr MacIntyre.'

Stephen stood up and watched him walk out of the square. 'Is he still smarting from the other day?'

'He's threatening to complain to the dean.'

'Oh? I'm sorry if I got you into trouble.'

'Oh, not at all.' She took his arm and they started to walk across the square, 'If it wasn't you it'd be something else. His real problem is that he doesn't like being taught by a woman. But I wouldn't worry about it. Professor Barrett already has the measure of him. If he's going to start raising ructions he'll find himself out on his backside soon enough.'

They walked out of the college and past the provost's house to Nassau Street. As they reached the Empire Café he had a rather queer feeling when he looked in the window and remembered sitting in there with Billy on Easter Monday. *I don't want to burden her* came ringing back to him. Then they were inside, amidst a hubbub of voices and clattering crockery.

'I'm afraid this won't be quite what you remember,' Lillian warned him, as they found a table near the window. A waitress passed bearing plates with translucent rashers of bacon and yellowish pats of potato. 'You need to have relatives in the country to get any decent food these days. I don't know how Billy managed such a fine dinner the other night.'

'Some of his clients are farmers,' Stephen explained. 'He says he's not above taking payment in kind.'

Lillian smiled, but then her eyes widened and her voice dropped to a whisper. 'Oh my goodness. Isn't that Alfred Devereux?'

The name hit him like a blow and his mouth went dry. Slowly turning in his chair, he followed her gaze towards the back of the café. Devereux was in a wheelchair, hunched and slumped sideways, but there was no mistaking his powerful frame and his uniform. He was facing them – his head tilted to one side as if he had fallen asleep – but his eyes were open and his lips were moving in an irregular pursing motion, as if he was trying to whistle.

'Christ Almighty,' Stephen muttered under his breath. He didn't know which was more shocking: the mere sight of him or the frightful scar that cleaved his forehead. He remembered the last time he had seen him – jolting down the trench on a stretcher, his head a lumpy mass of field dressings, and he himself still with the sour taste of vomit in his mouth, his knees trembling. In the light of a dying flare the doctor's hands were black with blood, as if he was wearing gloves. He was wiping them on a rag like a butcher would.

He felt the blood drain from his face as Devereux's eyes rolled lazily around and met his. The scar had puckered the skin of his forehead, twisting his face into an unwholesome leer, with a flat, glabrous cast to it. The flesh seemed pale and lifeless, but the eyes were strangely alive, darting up and down as if they were trapped in a dead face. Stephen met them as best he could, but then a woman moved between them, crouching down with her back to him and offering a spoon to Devereux's moving lips. She was wearing white kid gloves and her lustrous black hair was coiled up under a dainty hat.

'The poor man,' Lillian whispered, 'you said he was wounded, but I never pictured him in a wheelchair. God love him. He was always so athletic, so fit, but look at him now.'

Stephen turned back to face her, glad she had spoken. He could feel the cold sweat rolling down the small of his back and his throat was dry. Suddenly the café seemed very loud, the clatter and noise beating on his ears and the sun glaring in the window at him. It was very warm, and yet he felt a shiver shake his spine. His trembling hand found a glass of water and he gulped half of it down.

Lillian was frowning at him. 'Stephen, are you all right? You look very pale.'

'Yes, I'm fine.' He set the glass down and clamped both his hands around it to keep them from shaking.

'Are you sure? Do you want to get some—?'

'It'll pass.' He tried to grin but it came out more like a grimace. He could feel the sweat on his forehead now. He was trying to breathe normally, but his chest felt constricted. *Talk, you fool.*

'Is that . . . ?' he began, then coughed as the words caught in his throat. 'Is that Mary D'Arcy with him?'

'Oh no! That's his sister – I think her name is Susan. She looks after him now. They must be staying at their town house up on Earlsfort Terrace. Did you not hear about Mary? She took off to London when she broke off the engagement.'

'She broke it off?' He laughed giddily. Should have guessed. Mary was hardly the type to be pushing a wheelchair and spoon-feeding. 'When did that happen?'

'A few months after the rebellion. She— Stephen, are you sure you're all right? You're as white as a sheet.'

'I'm fine, I'm fine, I'm fine.' He wiped his mouth with the back of his hand, feeling the metallic taste rising in his throat. His mind was racing, seeing flares screeching up, shells thumping into earth and snow, and bits of brick blown into dust. Some small part of him managed to latch onto what she had said.

'You mean last year? Before he was wounded?'

'Yes. September or October, I think. Didn't you hear about it?'

He tried to think back to that time. Christ, it seemed a lifetime ago! September or October? That would have been about the time Devereux transferred to the front.

'No, not a word. What happened?'

Lillian was still looking at him warily, but she explained: 'There was a dreadful scandal. She had an affair with a major who was charged with committing atrocities during the rebellion – an older man with a wife,' she broke off and looked around, as if she was embarrassed to be gossiping. 'I'm telling you, Stephen, you wouldn't see the likes of it in a penny dreadful. God knows how she got involved with him. He was a very good-looking man, by all accounts, but quite mad. After the rebellion he was charged with murdering some prisoners, but his defence claimed he was shell-shocked and he had a good war record, so they reduced the charges to brutality and conduct unbecoming. Nobody knew a thing about him and Mary until she turned up at his trial and got into a fight with his wife. After that her father stepped in and packed her off to London as quickly as he could. I imagine her poor fiancé only found out about it in a letter.'

Stephen followed all this as best he could while casting glances over his shoulder and at the same time trying to calm himself. Poor bastard. No bloody doubt he got a letter, and no bloody doubt that was what made him give up his cushy berth on the staff. He hadn't been lying after all, when he said he volunteered.

'Was he injured in the same raid where you got your medal?' Lillian asked.

'I beg your pardon?' He'd been looking towards Devereux, watching his sister stand up and hand her bowl to the waitress with a grateful smile. She was a young girl, quite good-looking. Was this her life now? Wheeling her crippled brother around and feeding him soup? Looking into that dreadful face and trying to brighten it with a smile?

'I'm sorry, I wasn't listening.' He sighed as he turned back. It was passing. His mind was calmer, though the metallic tang was still in his mouth and there was a mild throbbing in his head.

'Was it the same raid where you got your medal?'

'Yes, as a matter of fact it was.'

How much more could he tell her? Did she really want to know that Devereux was the one who went looking for a medal, but he was the one who got it? That Devereux had ended up lying on the firing step with his brains hanging out, twitching like a dying fish. What would she think if he told her? But maybe if he did it would be easier. Maybe then he wouldn't hear Devereux's breathing snorting in his ears, loud and wet as if he was drowning. 'He wasn't supposed to be—' he began, but stopped as a waitress appeared beside the table.

'I do beg your pardon. Are you Lieutenant Reilly?' The voice was young but sounded tired. Not a waitress, but Susan Devereux. Stephen looked up sharply. Viewed this close she had the look of her brother, but more kindly, softer. She seemed hesitant, embarrassed, as she bobbed her head to Lillian, 'Forgive me if I'm interrupting your lunch.'

'It's Captain Ryan, actually,' Stephen answered, and as he started to stand up her gloved hand restrained him.

'No, please, don't get up, captain. I won't detain you. You see, I saw you come in, and the colour of your hatband is the same . . .' She gave a nervous laugh and more words tumbled out. 'I'm terribly sorry to intrude. My name is Susan Devereux. I wonder do you know my brother, Alfred?' She pointed to the wheelchair. Devereux was staring at them in his lopsided way, one eye fixed, the other moving. 'He was with the Dublin Fusiliers, you see, and he seems to think he knows you.' She opened her hands to reveal a little notebook with odd words and sentences scrawled across it in pencil. Just above her finger he could see the words 'Tell Reilly' written in an uneven, childlike hand.

'Do you remember him at all? Ryan, you say? Perhaps he has made a mistake, but you can see he has written Reilly here quite clearly. I dare say he's mistaken you for somebody else. The poor soul often gets confused. Sometimes he doesn't even know where he is.' Again the nervous laugh, betraying the horror. 'Look,' she turned the notebook around so he could read the whole message, 'he's got it into his head that you came here especially to see him. He says you shouldn't have bothered!'

XII

The loud crack of the shot brought him awake with a start. His eyes snapped open and he cast around wildly before he saw it was only Nightingale glaring angrily over the sights of his revolver. The tiny dugout was half filled with gun smoke, but Nightingale wasn't finished. He followed the sleek black rat as it bounded along the back wall and jumped into the knee-deep puddle that covered the floor. It started to swim for shelter under the rudimentary plank bed where Stephen was lying, but Nightingale fired again and the rat disappeared with a splash.

'For Christ's sake! Do you mind?'

'Sorry, old man!' Nightingale grinned sheepishly, 'I thought you were asleep.'

Asleep? He couldn't remember the last time he'd slept properly. The best he could manage was a fitful doze. Seven days they'd been here, seven days of continuous shelling. The noise was unbearable – the constant thunder of shells roaring overhead had stretched his nerves to breaking point. That they were British shells made no difference. Hour after hour, day and night, they ripped through the sodden sky. As he lay in the leaky dugout he could feel the thumping, pulsing air pressing him into the mud, pushing him down and down until he gasped involuntarily, unable to breathe.

He didn't say anything more, but rolled back on his plank,

staring up at the roof. Rough-hewn logs and corrugated iron – it couldn't even keep out the rain, let alone the shells. Water dribbled in through the holes, splashing and plinking into the puddle that covered the floor. It had been raining for seven days too – non-stop, day and night. Everything was sopping wet. The wooden walls of the dugout, cobbled together from Huntley and Palmer biscuit boxes, were starting to swell and warp. One had cracked earlier on, and a black tongue of mud was oozing down towards the floor.

This was the price of their success. When they detonated the mines at Messines they had attacked from well-built trenches of three years' standing. The ground they had taken was the very ground they had been shelling for all that time and the intricate network of streams and ditches that had kept it dry had long since disappeared. While the Germans had fallen back on a carefully prepared line of concrete outposts, the Allies now had to face them from a morass, sheltering in a broken chain of shell craters that were slowly filling with the unending rain.

The rats were the worst he had seen. They were big and fat and seemed to know no fear. Out of the corner of his eye he saw another one scramble in under the gas curtain and plunge into the yellow scum that floated on top of the puddle. Gas residue – he might live to regret that little dip. But he swam on, scrambled out, and darted through the gap between two boards. Nightingale let him pass because he was busy painting his feet. Now that he'd taken his boots off – no easy task in itself – Stephen could see how bad they were. They looked like the feet of a corpse, blanched dead white with mottled patches of green and brown. Nightingale was painting them with the gentian violet the doctor had given him. The smell was horrendous.

Stephen closed his eyes again. The need for sleep was overpowering but he knew it wouldn't come – not even now that there was a lull in the shelling. His nerves were stretched to breaking point and even in the near silence it was all he could do to lie still without grinding his teeth. He slid his hand down to his pocket and felt for the little square box. Still there. He'd had it in that same pocket ever since he came back to France, carrying it like a touchstone, a reminder of what he'd missed. Or worse, he thought bitterly, a reminder that you're a bloody coward.

Sometimes he almost convinced himself that it wasn't really his fault. He tried to blame it on Devereux – poor bloody Devereux with his crooked face and his long-suffering sister. That's what had kicked him off – seeing them in the café that day. Just when he thought he was the better of it, a fit came on him again. He saw the wounded and the maimed, their grey, bloodless faces at every table, leering at him like Devereux, beckoning to come and join them. Then the fear deadening his limbs: the cold hands, cold feet, the shakes. It was worse than going into bloody action. Susan Devereux was still prattling away when he suddenly stood up and said he had to leave. As he marched to the door he heard Lillian apologizing for him, then running after him. She caught his arm outside.

'Stephen, are you all right?'

'Yes – no, I . . .' The headache had him in its grip now. The bright sun seemed to magnify it. He felt his temples throbbing. The pain was intense, but there was anger there too, a sort of giddy malevolence. He felt the urge to lash out, to strike something. Maybe that would make it go away. 'I'm just not feeling . . . can you leave me alone for a few minutes, please? I just need some peace and quiet.'

And he walked away, just like that. It was so easy it made him sick to think about it. When he thought of her standing there on the pavement, watching him leave, he wanted to cry. His hand came back up and clutched the gas mask against his chest, holding it like a child's toy. Flaming awful thing. More like a hideous rubber parasite than a toy. The thought of putting that obscene snout back on – the sweaty heat and the faint smell of death – turned his stomach. He had lived in it half the night and he could hardly bear to put it back on. His throat was raw and his ears and neck were chafed and bloody from the straps. It wasn't worth it. If the whistles blew for another gas attack he would throw it away and take a lungful. Get it bloody well over with.

But he knew he would never do that. Not with mustard gas. If ever there was a fate worse than death, it was a dose of that stuff. It burned the skin and seared the throat, melting the lungs inside your chest. Even with the mask on and every inch of flesh covered up you could feel it prickling, tingling, burning. It lingered in corners and oozed out of the ground in a foul yellow mist. He had seen what it did to Gardner. Poor bloody Gardner – he'd held him in his arms as he thrashed and screamed through his scorched throat, clawing at the sleeve of his coat in his agony. When he finally stopped, the glass eyes of the mask were splashed with his spittle, flecked yellow and red. That was no way to go.

He'd become so used to the noise of the shelling that when it stopped – or paused, for it was only a lull – the near silence made him uncomfortable. The little sounds irritated him; the drumming of the rain and the plink-plink of it dribbling into the puddle, the tuneless whistle as Nightingale painted his feet. He was relieved to hear squelching footsteps approach, and then the gas curtain flapped open and Wilson splashed in, pouring water from the creases in his cape. Acting major now – he was supposed to be the battalion adjutant but they'd been hit so hard he was running the whole bloody show. The number of men they'd lost just sitting here was appalling – and they hadn't even started the attack yet. Only Wilson knew when that would be, but if he'd heard anything over at Brigade HQ, he wasn't saying. He took off his helmet and

Stephen realized he looked bloody shattered. It had been a long week's wait, but he still managed to smile. He sniffed deeply and wrinkled his nose.

'Och, has something died here?' he asked.

'I believe my feet have actually started to rot,' Nightingale replied, looking at one of his toes with some distaste.

'Aye, well, they're giving us a day's rest in camp tomorrow, so you can get the doctor—' Wilson broke off and looked to the roof. Outside, there was the whiz and thump of incoming artillery. Five-nines, with the distinctive wobbling sound of gas shells. One, two, three, four. They all looked at one another, then Nightingale started pulling on his socks.

'Hell and death!' Wilson cursed, as the whistles started to shrill.

'Gas! Gas! Gas!' bellowed a distant voice and Stephen sat up groggily, water lapping around his legs. Then he stumbled out through the curtain after Wilson, gagging as he dragged the mask on.

They only lost two men getting back to camp. One killed and one wounded, both by the same shell. The wounded one was Kinsella – pierced through the shoulder by a splinter that stuck out like a jagged dagger. From the way his arm hung loose, it must have broken his collarbone, but no amount of pain could wipe the grin off Kinsella's grimy face. It was the very model of a Blighty wound. He was going home.

The survivors paraded when they got back to camp. Barely a couple of hundred left from a nominal strength of over a thousand. As if to mock them, the sun came out as they formed up and raised faint clouds of steam from their sodden clothes. Stephen looked at them standing in their pitifully short ranks; muddy, filthy, wet and worn out. If they were going to attack anything, it had better be soon, because they couldn't hang on much longer.

Wilson knew it as well as he did. When the men were dismissed he took him to one side.

'It's tomorrow,' he said, stuffing his pipe, 'we go back up tonight, attack in the morning.'

'Where?'

'Vampire Farm.'

'Vampire Farm?' He looked over his shoulder at the dissolving ranks, 'We don't have enough men for that!'

Wilson just nodded. They'd both been watching Vampire Farm this last week – a squat concrete blockhouse set into the crest of the ridge and ringed by wire entanglements. They'd both seen the machine guns coming back up during lulls in the barrage, and they'd both counted them. Five machine guns.

'You'd best get some rest,' Wilson said, and lit his pipe with a match. 'Try to sleep. I'll brief you and Nightingale after lunch.'

Nightingale came hobbling up to catch him before he reached his tent. He was shouting his name, but Stephen hardly noticed as he shuffled across the camp, thinking only of his bed. He was dead tired: three gas alarms last night had kept them all on edge. He couldn't believe that Nightingale still had the energy to run on his swollen feet, still less the good-natured smile plastered across his face.

'A letter!' he shouted breathlessly. 'Stephen! You got a letter.'

Stephen looked at him dully, thinking he wouldn't get that excited if the letter was for somebody else. But he took it with a polite 'Thank you' and then his heart tripped. He recognized the envelope without even having to see whose hand the address was in. Nightingale ran on with another letter for Wilson, and Stephen swayed on his feet as he turned the envelope over in his fingers. *At last.*

He couldn't wait to get to his tent, but found a quiet spot and sat down on the grass. Mud crumbled under his fingers as he wearily unbuttoned his tunic. Six weeks since he'd been back and no letters save an indignant one from Billy. *Dear Stephen, what the bloody hell do you mean by taking off without even a word of goodbye* . . . He knew he didn't deserve one, but he'd always hoped. His hands were shaking as he opened the envelope and slid out the single sheet of notepaper.

*   *   *

Dublin
5 August 1917

Dear Stephen,

I hope this letter finds you well and I hope you do not mind me writing to you. When we last parted I could see you were quite upset and I wondered if it was something I had said or done. It was only afterwards that I realized what a shock it must have been for you to see Alfred Devereux like that. I know the war has put a tremendous strain on you and I am very sorry that I didn't make more of an effort to help you. In my defence, I had thought I might be able to see you again before you went back to France. It came as quite a shock when Billy called on me the next day to say that you had gone back early.

Having said that, I am still unsure where I stand. I write to you in the hope that we can still be friends. If you think this letter is an imposition then please throw it away and think no more about it. However, I want you to know that I think of myself as your friend and I care very deeply about you. If you feel the same way then please, please, write to me and let me know that you are safe.

I remain,

Your friend,

Lillian

*   *   *

He read the letter twice, then sat for a while, staring at it. At once he wished there was more, but it was still more than he had hoped. What else could she have said? More than he hoped, and more than he deserved. A chink of light beckoning him on. He looked up from the page and shielded his eyes from the sun, feeling the warmth on his face. The tiredness was gone from his bones, misery lifting in the heat. Where was she now? Probably preparing her lectures, getting ready for the new term. He pictured some quiet room in the college, Lillian sitting at a desk, a picture of concentration as her hand moved gracefully across the paper. He sagged forward over her letter, his tired muscles unravelling, releasing the cramped tension in the pit of his stomach. He hardly moved when a hand touched his shoulder.

'We're going to have a bite of breakfast before we turn in,' Nightingale said, and Stephen sat up and folded the letter back into its envelope. 'Do you want to join us?'

'Yes, yes, I will. In a minute. I'll be along a minute,' he answered, confused. 'I think . . . I want to just write a letter first.'

'All right.' Nightingale still had his hand on Stephen's shoulder. He leaned closer, concerned, 'Are you sure, Stephen? You look like you've had a shock. Not bad news, I hope?'

'What? Oh, no, not at all. Not bad news.' Stephen forced a smile as he wiped his eyes on his sleeve. 'Just something . . . somebody I know. A friend from home wants me to write to her, that's all. I'll be along in a few minutes, don't worry.'

The briefing took place in Wilson's tent. Stephen and Nightingale sat on the edge of Wilson's cot while Wilson sat in the chair. That was it: all the battalion's surviving officers. The three of them were going to organize and lead an attack against a fortified blockhouse that had five machine guns.

Even after their first proper sleep in days, they were all still muzzy and weary. They had changed out of their filthy uniforms, but still managed to look scruffy and bedraggled. Nightingale was in his socks, hoping his feet might dry out a bit before he had to put his boots back on. He'd been to the doctor and shown him the damage – the swelling, the discoloration, the sloughing skin. The doctor gave him another bottle of gentian violet and told him to try and keep his feet dry.

When Wilson ducked in through the door, Stephen thought that, for the first time since he'd known him, he looked like an old man. Old and tired. They all were. Even Nightingale kept yawning and blinking and staring at the map that Wilson laid down on the floor.

Wilson himself never even referred to it. They all knew the ground, and the plan was simple enough.

'The Ulster Division will be attacking on our left,' he began, talking softly. 'When they are fully engaged we will join the attack. Stephen, you shall take A Company up on our left flank and try to join up with the Royal Irish Fusiliers before pressing home your attack on the farm. I shall take C Company and try to get them up to the crest of the ridge before we come down on the farm from the right. If everything goes well, we should then be attacking from two sides.'

If, should, try. The plan was simple, but it was peppered with all these hopeful conjunctions. Even Wilson didn't believe in it – that was plain from his face as he finished talking, waited for a few moments, and then produced his pipe from his pocket.

'Questions?'

'What about the barrage?' Stephen asked.

'Well, the main barrage has been going on for a week, as we know. I think we all know how effective that's been.'

No bloody use was what they all knew. Every time there was a lull in the barrage those machine guns came up from their hiding place deep, deep underground. They had watched through binoculars, counting the grey helmets popping up under the heavy concrete slabs, and timing them to see how long they took to prepare their defence. It never took more than five minutes.

Wilson consulted his notebook before he went on.

'They'll be firing nothing but high explosive tonight,' he said. 'With any luck, the wire should be well and truly cut up by the time we get there.'

There it was again – *with any luck*. Meaning: not a chance in hell. What sort of luck had they ever had? Not that it made any difference. Before they even got to the wire there were five hundred yards of ground to cross – five hundred yards of sucking mud, knee-deep and worse. And five minutes after they started out, the machine guns would be up and sweeping down all before them.

'What about me?' Nightingale asked, 'What do I do?'

'You will hold B Company in reserve, Mr Nightingale. I will transfer what remains of D Company to your command as well.'

'But—'

Wilson held up his hand. 'No buts, lad. We must have a reserve. You will bring your men up and push through when we take the strongpoint.'

Nightingale opened his mouth to protest again but thought better of it. It was a reprieve – they all knew that. *When* we take the strongpoint? Wilson was only trying to sweeten the pill. *Not that it needs much sugar!* But Stephen didn't begrudge Nightingale his good fortune. He would have to hold the line if the Germans counterattacked, and even if they didn't they were bound to shell the bejesus out of the British line to break up reinforcements. But by that time he'd probably be past caring.

There were no more questions. The three of them sat there in silence for almost a minute, feeling the heat of the sun through the heavy white canvas. Stephen's hand moved to his tunic pocket and patted the letters. There were two of them now. He'd been thinking about changing what he had written, but now he decided to send it as it was. It might be a bit raw, but it was true. It said what he wanted to say. He looked at his watch. Mid-afternoon – suddenly time was pressing. He'd have to drop it off with the clerk before they went back up.

Wilson might have been reading his mind.

'I'm sure you've both got things to do,' he said, taking his still-unlit pipe from his mouth. 'I for one have some writing to do. So if you don't mind . . .'

'Very good, sir.' They both rose and put their caps on, saluting awkwardly under the conical roof of the tent. Wilson didn't look up as they walked stiffly out into the sunshine and left him to his letter.

They managed to get back up the line without losing any more men. It helped that it was dark, though they ended up cursing the night as they got closer to the front and found themselves stumbling and slopping through the cratered ground like blind men or drunks.

They had marched through Ypres itself, with its tottering cathedral and mounds of shattered bricks. Somewhere around Hellfire Corner it started raining again and by the time they turned off the Menin road they were soaked through once more. An Irish bloody bog in Belgium, Stephen thought, looking at the low line of the Frezenberg Ridge that crossed the sodden sky before him. Only in Ireland it wouldn't have been sparking with the orange flashes of bursting shells.

It was almost midnight before they were back in their position. The same waterlogged dugout with the leaky roof, the same plank benches, and the same rats. Only they were even saucier in the dark: Stephen had to kick one off the bench before he sat down. The water was higher than he remembered. The three of them had to sit with their feet on the benches, knees up under their chins, like survivors in a sinking lifeboat.

Once they were settled in, there was little to do but wait. The shelling was sporadic and light, waiting for the break of day to begin in earnest once more. They drank whiskey to ward off the damp, and Stephen read Lillian's letter over and over again by the light of a candle that bobbed around the floor in the upturned lid of a dixie. Wilson took out his tattered copy of Hopkins, but instead of reading it he kept it clutched to his chest, like a keepsake. The rain pattered and dribbled into the puddle on the floor.

It was surprisingly peaceful. Now that he had time to reflect, Stephen realized he wasn't afraid of what the morning might bring. In some way, he recognized that he belonged here. He'd only had two fits since he came back to France, and both of those were while he was in the rear areas. It seemed that the closer he was to the front, the less chance there was that he would lose a grip on himself. Maybe because there was more at stake. Maybe because he knew all the others were in the same boat. Whatever it was, he was here now, and he was not afraid. He'd sent his letter, and when he read it through in his mind's eye, he was satisfied. It was a good thing. If this was to be the day, then at least he would have set things right. He was happy with that at least.

Wilson was also in a peculiar mood. He hummed a tune to himself for a while, and then he suddenly lifted his head and asked Nightingale, 'Did you ever hear the stories of Cuchulain?'

Nightingale looked bemused and shook his head.

'Cuchulain? I can't say I've heard of him. Was he an Irish fellow?'

'He certainly was. In fact, he was the greatest warrior Ireland ever knew – he was an Ulsterman like myself.'

'Oh, for God's sake!' Stephen laughed and rolled his eyes to the roof.

'Well, it's true!' Wilson answered tartly. 'I don't remember hearing of any heroes who came from Dublin!'

Nightingale's interest was piqued now. 'Who did he fight, then?'

'Everybody,' muttered Stephen, thinking of the long roll of feats and battles he'd been forced to memorize at school. He hated it: could hardly pronounce the names, still less remember them. But that was no use to Brother Michael, who patrolled the classroom with the leather strap hanging from his belt, and God help those who couldn't name all the sons of Queen Maeve.

'There were many battles.' Wilson paused to gather his thoughts, 'My favourite is the battle at the ford. You see, Queen Maeve sent her six greatest champions to fight Cuchulain and he beat every one of them. So she summoned Ferdia, who was Cuchulain's best friend, and poisoned his mind against him. She appealed to his pride by telling him Cuchulain couldn't be bothered fighting him since he'd already seen off six of the best. So the two of them met at a ford and fought it out as a matter of honour, even though neither of them really wanted to fight.'

'So who won?' Nightingale asked, clearly less than impressed with Wilson's storytelling.

'Why, Cuchulain did, of course. But it wasn't who won that mattered, it was the way they fought. They were such great friends and warriors that they fought all day and then ate and drank and tended their wounds together at night. But on the third day—'

'Three days? They fought for three days? You're pulling my leg!'

Stephen laughed at the disbelieving look on Nightingale's face, 'It's only a legend, a fairy tale!'

'—But on the third day they were both nearly worn out. They

were both wounded and battered, but neither of them was able to strike a killing blow. Ferdia realized he was doomed. He knew his friend was stronger than he was, and if he got even the smallest chance he would win. But there was nothing he could do because he couldn't end the combat and keep his honour. So they fought on and on until Ferdia pierced Cuchulain's breast with his sword. Then Cuchulain flew into a rage and killed him stone dead with his spear. His best friend, whom he loved like a brother. He wept.'

'Oh,' Nightingale said, shocked at the abrupt end of the story, 'that's very sad.'

'All war is sad,' Wilson replied, looking at Stephen, and they both nodded.

*   *   *

BRITISH OFFICIAL – 16 August 1917
At 4.35 this morning Allied troops attacked again on a wide front north and east of Ypres. Steady fighting is taking place and progress is being made on all points in spite of stubborn resistance on the part of the enemy.

*   *   *

In such murky weather there was no sunrise. At around four the sky started to lighten and a milky mist gathered low on the ground. The artillery barrage suddenly doubled its intensity, and as the British bit harder, so the Germans bit back. Three salvoes rained down on them in as many minutes and after the third they sat uneasily in their waterlogged hole, gas masks at the ready, waiting for the next one.

But suddenly it stopped. As if a switch had been thrown, the

260

sky fell silent and there was no sound but the drip-drip-drip of settling rainwater. Then, in the distance, there was a crackling volley of rifle fire. The Ulster Division was starting its attack. The Dublins knew their objectives as well as their own: Iberian Farm, Somme Farm, Hill 35. After a few minutes the clacking of machine guns started up, followed by the pop of trench mortars and underscored by the rumbling artillery.

'God speed, boys,' Wilson murmured, and the others nodded silently.

An hour later Wilson went off to Brigade HQ and Stephen looked to his men. Whatever the shortcomings of his shelter, they had had none, and lay in the open, wet and bedraggled in their gas capes. But as he crept from one crater to the next they welcomed him with muddy grins.

'Any sign of the fleet, sir?' they asked. All week it had been a standing joke that if this rain kept up, the North Sea Fleet would support their attack.

'It's not deep enough yet for the Dreadnoughts,' he joked back, trying to be more reassuring than he felt. Just after he left the dugout the noise of firing from their left had started to die away and now had finally fallen silent. He doubted it was because the Ulster Division had taken all their objectives.

Wilson confirmed as much when he came back from Brigade HQ. He was leading the carrying party with the rum ration, slipping and stumbling under the sloshing weight of their carboys. He didn't even need to be asked: just one look and he shook his head.

Their attack was set for nine o'clock, and at seven the artillery opened its barrage on the German lines. Stephen wormed in among his men, breakfasting with them on undiluted rum and hard tack, and watched the shells falling on the crest of the ridge. Each one flashed orange at its heart and spat up a thin black cloud of earth. They seemed to smoke less than he remembered, perhaps because the ground was so soft. But no matter how many fell, they made no difference to the blocky grey edifice that crowned the ridge. The shells threw up a curtain of earth, but each time it subsided, the scene behind was unchanged.

With less than an hour to zero, Wilson summoned him back to the dugout to discuss the final details of the attack. Little had changed since the day before except that things had become more uncertain. The Royal Irish were believed to have been stopped somewhere between Borry Farm and Vampire Farm. Their exact disposition was unknown, but they were last reported taking heavy enemy fire. Stephen was to try to link up with them if he could, but whether he did or not he was to press on with the attack on Vampire Farm. Wilson's part was as before. The signal for Nightingale to advance would be three flares fired in quick succession from the farm.

'Three flares, right you are,' Nightingale noted it down in his pocketbook and as he did, Stephen looked past him at Wilson. Wilson shrugged.

At the end of the meeting he looked at his watch and then shook hands with each of them in turn. Ten minutes to go. They wished each other good luck and went outside, where the sun was trying to break through the thick, gunmetal clouds. Without looking back, Stephen scrambled into the broad shell crater where his company waited. Only thirty-four of them left – less than half strength. He nodded at Sergeant Devlin, who tipped his helmet in reply. He hardly knew Devlin and wished Kinsella hadn't been wounded. He never needed him more than he did now.

'All set, lads?' he called out.

'All set, sir,' they murmured in reply. He sat down alongside them and emptied the shells out of his revolver into the palm of his hand. He looked down at them for a moment, bright and new in the gloomy wet, and then reached under his cape and patted the pocket with the letter. His good-luck charm. Just as he took his hand away the roar of the shelling stopped and they all instinctively looked up into the sky. As if to fill the sudden silence, the rain gathered strength and started to beat down on them in big heavy drops that pinked on their helmets and drummed on the canvas of their capes.

As he started to reload he saw Wilson climb up to the rim of the crater on the right, standing out in the open with his arms outstretched, like a priest saying Mass. He had taken off his cape and his helmet and stood bareheaded under the rain, unholstering his revolver. His reedy voice carried clearly across the churned earth.

'Would you look at this lovely weather, boys!' he roared. 'Sure isn't it just like being at home?' Muted laughter drifted up from the crater below.

Stephen felt the anxious eyes of his men on him. 'You must keep moving, whatever happens, lads,' he said, scanning the pinched faces for something better than lost hope and bovine weariness. 'No matter what – forward, forward all the time. You all know where we're headed and we must get there before they know we're coming. If we get in close enough they can't touch us. You must keep—'

He was cut short by a sharp noise like tearing cloth. German shells came crashing down around them, whiz-bangs bracketing the crater and shaking the soft earth where they lay. They cowered down, pushing themselves deeper into the mud, but the next salvo passed overhead, falling deeper into the lines.

'Steady, lads,' he called out as they craned their necks to the sky, waiting for the next one. 'Our friends must be expecting us.' His weak crack raised not even a smile. They hunkered and knelt in the mud, grimmer than ever.

'*Erin go brea*,' Wilson bellowed, still out in the open – he hadn't even taken cover from the shells. Now he turned around to face up the hill, gesticulating wildly at the German positions. 'We're coming to get you, boys. You'll not keep us out today!'

Licking his lips, Stephen looked down at his watch. It was a minute to nine. Dead on time another salvo from the British artillery screamed overhead, drowning Wilson's words. He was dancing now, doing a little jig as his men crawled out of the crater to stand beside him. Stephen felt for the whistle on its little cord, then crawled forward to the rim of the crater, gazing across the brown expanse of sodden earth curving gently up towards the ridge. The men slithered up beside him, forming a ragged arc on either side. The second hand on his watch swept upwards. His mouth was dry, his heart going fit to burst. He wasn't able to get his breath. What if he couldn't blow? Five seconds.

'Come on the Dubs!' Wilson cried, and his men gave a blood-thirsty howl as they followed him out. He was almost lost amongst them, a slight figure in the throng of heavily laden men. It was time. With a last deep breath, Stephen bit down on the metal of the whistle and blew for all he was worth.

XIII

Nightingale slowly let the discs of the binoculars slide down the dreary landscape. Viewed through the glass it looked like a painting – flat, achromatic, unreal. When he could see nothing more than the blurred earth a few yards in front, he put down the glasses and looked up. The sky was low and grey and the ashy clouds seemed almost to brush the earth. It would be dark soon: the day was almost over.

He'd been lying out in this spot so long that he was nearly submerged in the mud. After the others started their attack he had sat in the trench for an hour, listening as the firing grew to a crescendo and then died away altogether. By then he was completely certain that the flares wouldn't go up, but he couldn't just sit there. There was no sign of anybody coming back, no counterattack, no artillery barrage, nothing. When the rain clouds settled on top of the ridge he crawled forward to try and see what was going on, but all he could see was the squat grey hump of the strongpoint. Nothing moved. A half-dozen khaki lumps dotted the grass in front of him, but they were clearly dead. Otherwise the slope was eerily empty. It was as if the rest had vanished into thin air.

If the Germans wanted to counterattack they would have done it straight away. It occurred to him that they might be waiting for nightfall, but he knew they wouldn't come then either. Why would they? All they had to do was hold their line. It was well made and well sited: strong concrete shelters dug deep into the ground, and each one placed to support the others. They'd be mad to leave those behind just for the sake of a few hundred yards of bog. Why would they come down here when all they had to do was sit in their strongpoints and let the British attacks break on them like waves on rocks?

This much had occurred to him hours ago, but still he lay out by himself, only dimly aware of his men waiting fifty yards behind. Part of it was hope – if anybody was alive he might see him, he might be able to help him. But another part was fear. He was alone now, and he didn't know what to do next. Who did he report to? What did he say? How could he explain that they'd all just disappeared? It was his responsibility – he was in charge. Why had he just let them go?

But he couldn't stay out all night. He slowly pushed himself up out of the mud and started to crawl back to the trench. Every foot of ground felt cold and repellent to him and he found himself shivering, his teeth chattering. When he finally slithered in, Sergeant Dunne pressed a tin mug into his hands. The tea wasn't very hot but it seemed to roast his fingers through the metal.

'Any sign, sir?' Dunne asked, and Nightingale just shook his head as he took a mouthful of tea.

'There's a runner here from Brigade HQ. Wants to know how the attack went, sir.' He nodded to a whippet-looking man crouched in the trench a few yards away, soaked to the skin with no helmet and only his collar turned up against the rain. 'What shall I tell him?'

It took an effort to speak. The cold had cramped his muscles and his jaw felt locked tight. When at last he managed it, the words came out in a croak.

'Tell him the attack failed, sergeant.'

'And what about our losses, sir?'
'Total losses, sergeant. Tell him they're all gone.'

* * *

TO: MR JOSEPH RYAN, 31 EDEN QUAY, DUBLIN.
DEEPLY REGRET TO INFORM YOU THAT CAPT. S RYAN,
2ND DUBLIN FUSILIERS IS REPORTED MISSING BELIEVED
KILLED IN ACTION ON THE 16TH OF AUGUST. LORD
DERBY EXPRESSES HIS SYMPATHY.

* * *

Stephen felt as if he was coming out of a long tunnel. He had no sense of place or time, just an icy cold inside that was numbing his chest and arms. The only feeling was in his legs, where hot pain burned, blazing up from time to time as consciousness lapped at him. He came to himself in fits and starts: now he could feel his face pressed into the earth, now see a patch of weeping grey sky, and then nothing at all. All at once he was fully alive again, moving his fingers, shivering.

He lifted his head with a groan and looked around. He was lying in a shell crater, filthy brown water lapping at his thighs and a red stain around his left knee. No wonder he couldn't feel his feet. It was so quiet he could hear the breeze whispering through the grass above his head. Time – how long? He looked at his wristwatch, wiped the mud off it, tried to focus his eyes on the dial. Then he put it to his ear to make sure of the whirring movement. Quarter past six. He let his head fall back and stared up at the sky. It was grey and mottled purple, like the colour of old bruises. But at least the rain had stopped.

The cold had dulled him so much that it took him a moment

to realize that he was still shivering, that his teeth were chattering. He had to move – at least to get out of the water. Digging his hands into the cold mud above his head, he tried to haul himself up. At the first pull, pain speared up his leg like an electric shock and he cried out. Suddenly he wasn't shivering any more, but he had to rest a minute to get his breath. It took two more pulls to drag himself out, and then he lay on the sloping side of the crater, gasping, his leg throbbing, blood and water running into the brown earth. But he was lying awkwardly, and it took another effort to roll over onto his back. Then he had to wait for the spasms of pain to subside before he could sit up and examine the wound.

His trouser leg was torn just below the knee, exposing blackened skin and a deep cut with white bone gleaming at the bottom. The steeped flesh was corpse white and macerated, the edges of the wound gaping at him like obscene lips. Shivering once again, he pulled the soaked shell dressing from inside his tunic and wrapped it around his knee, wincing as he tied it. Then he had to rest. He lay back in the mud and his fingers automatically went to his breast pocket. It was still there. That was something, anyway.

He tried to remember what had happened. The pain was coming at him harder now, and the effort of remembering took his mind off it. Start at the beginning: the very first step, sinking knee-deep into the mud. Bloody hell! If it was like this all the way they were stuffed. But there was no firing yet. It was so quiet he could hear the splashing and sucking and cursing of the men staggering after him. After fifty yards he was panting for breath, sweating, his leg muscles dead with the effort. Glancing to his right, he saw Wilson's men strung out in a broken arc, struggling uphill against the grip of the sodden earth. He knew they should have been advancing by rushes, but running was out of the question in this muck. Anybody who lay down would never get up again.

As they plunged onwards one of his men started saying the Hail Mary and Stephen found himself muttering the words under his breath. *Hail Mary, full of grace* . . . Speed was of the essence, and yet they were stumbling, crawling, almost swimming forward at times. Their precious five minutes was wasting away. If they weren't in close when the Germans came up then they would be caught at the gaps in the wire and that would be that. The wire, the bloody wire. He dreaded it; the first line was coming up, but it was cut and broken by the shells and he directed his men into the gaps with hoarse, breathless shouts.

Then they were through and the fear receded a little. They might do it, they just bloody might. There was more wire to come, but the ground was rising – it was drier, firmer, and they only sank halfway to their knees. And still not a shot from the Germans. If only it would hold just a little longer. He darted a look at Wilson's company, ahead of him now, moving faster. *Holy Mary, mother of God* . . . They just bloody might!

'Come on, lads, come on! Spread out there. Forward, forward!' he shouted, half-turning, and out of the corner of his eye he saw Fusilier Doyle topple over backwards, his hand flying to his chest. Then he heard the swish of bullets flying past, thudding, splashing brown mud all around him. He hardly had to look back up the hill; the sinister grey hump was spitting yellow now. He counted the flashes; five machine guns. *Pray for us sinners* . . .

'Keep going, lads,' he cried, struggling forward as fast as he could, his hoarse breath rushing in his ears. Bullets whipped overhead, hissing and cracking, but he didn't even hear the first shell falling until the blast almost knocked him off his feet. He reeled, half-deafened. No mistake there. More followed, falling so fast that the noise of detonation was one continuous pulsing boom. They were pouring them in, trying to break up the attack before it got in among them. He felt the heat on his face and found himself on hands and knees, mud up to the elbows, ears ringing. Staggering up again, he cast around wildly for the rest of his men, urging them on in a harsh, inhuman voice. Then he stumbled forward with them.

The second band of wire had not been touched, but when he looked over at Wilson's company he saw that they were already through. Stephen's men had to cut; the wire hard and taut under their hands, pecking and twisting and cursing with the wire-cutters. *Holy Mary, Holy Mary! Oh bloody fucking Christ!* They worked feverishly in a spitting hail of bullets. The man beside him was hit and sagged lifelessly against the wire. Then one strand parted with a twang, and another, and they could crawl through. Wriggling forward, he glimpsed Wilson's company again, half-hidden by the smoke as shells fell amongst them. Scrambling up, he saw half a dozen men scattered across the ground, the rest darting forward, pausing to fire. Panting, he kept running as hard as he could with the spongy, yielding earth pulling at his feet.

Suddenly, through the smoke, he saw Wilson standing clear in the open, firing his revolver at the angular hump of the blockhouse. A shell burst beside him and he fell down on his knees, but he stayed up and raised his revolver, still firing until another shell burst right in front of him and knocked him over backwards. Stephen stood rooted, aghast. He cast around and saw there was nobody following him any more – nobody left but the sagging man on the wire. The grey bulk of Vampire Farm loomed over him. He was almost there. *Forward, forward!* But it was no use. His lungs were bursting with the effort and he felt his strength failing him. He was alone. Sick, dazed and unimaginably tired, it took all his strength to pull his leg out of the mud and take another step forward. What was the bloody point? He let his revolver fall from his hand, felt its weight on the lanyard around his neck and as his knees sagged he heard the shriek of a shell falling, growing higher and higher as it came, until the ground burst up beside him and then he felt nothing at all.

When the postman's knock came at the door, Sheila was up first to answer it. It never ceased to surprise Mrs Bryce how much energy that girl had. Working late again at the hospital last night, and yet there she was, up with the lark and fresher than the milk. She wasn't entirely unaffected, though – she looked older than her nineteen years, and her mother knew very well that she was never as carefree as she liked other people to think. Her uniform was gone quite dull with wear, and Mrs Bryce dearly wished she would take a holiday – even a week or two for herself, anything so she wouldn't look as if she was carrying the cares of the world on her shoulders.

As she listened to the muffled words passing from the hallway, Mrs Bryce contemplated her eldest daughter, who sat at the far end of the table, poring intently over her newspaper.

Poor Lillian, she . . . Mrs Bryce stopped herself in mid-thought. Why did she always think of Lillian as if she was to be pitied? She was not unhappy, though there was always a trace of sadness about her, even when she smiled. True, her father's death had cut her deeper than it had Sheila – though she hadn't shown it at the time. She had been much closer to him than her sister. Mr Bryce had loved them both, but there was no denying that he'd had a special affinity for his eldest girl. She was the one who brought the light to his face when he came home from the sea. He'd known she was precocious and he'd revelled in it. Lord, the conversations they'd had when she was just eleven or twelve. Mrs Bryce could hardly follow it herself. But Lillian took after him in other ways, too. She was stoic, tough, always with a brave face. Her mother had not seen her cry since she was three years old. Which wasn't to say that she hadn't cried. But she was her father's daughter, his rock, and she wouldn't cry in front of anybody.

Mrs Bryce sighed and swirled the dregs of tea in her cup. Poor Lillian, she thought, for strength was her weakness. Few men would put up with her intellect, and fewer still would suffer her self-sufficiency – she did not have the vulnerability they craved. But she could be full of surprises too. There was that young man she'd brought home a few weeks back. Mrs Bryce had all but given up hope she might find one – particularly now they were in such short supply – but then she suddenly brings one to tea. And not just any young man either, but a perfectly agreeable one, in an army uniform and medals.

'It's for you, Lillie,' Sheila said, resting the letter against her teacup, and with a knowing look at her mother. 'It's got an army postmark.'

Mrs Bryce hid a secret smile in her teacup. All was not lost. Something had happened with that young man; something dis-agreeable, though wild horses wouldn't have dragged it out of Lillian. It pained her to think they'd had a row – he'd seemed such a nice lad – but then there was no telling with Lillian. She wasn't the sort to take up with very ordinary, uninteresting people. Maybe that was why she was ignoring the letter. She did not move, but remained bowed over her newspaper, peering at something, her eyes only inches from the page.

'Lillie? Are you not going to open it?' Sheila said at last, speaking for them both. But her sister seemed hardly to pay her any heed. She had gone rigid. Almost a minute passed before she slowly looked up from the page, and they could see her face was pale with shock. Mrs Bryce could tell from the set of her jaw that she was steeling herself against something, and she instinctively started to reach across the narrow table.

'Lillie, dear, what—?' she began, but before she could get the question out her daughter stood up from the table, threw down her newspaper, and ran from the room with her hand over her mouth.

It was about as dark as it was ever going to get in August. Over the rim of the crater, he could see the ground sweeping downhill, gradually dissolving into the night. Somewhere in the distance a machine gun was chattering, like a mechanical bird singing in the dusk. Closer by all was quiet; no sound but the sucking of the mud as he moved, sat up, tried to organize himself.

He was lying on his revolver, the lanyard stretching over his shoulder, and it was caked in mud. With trembling hands he wiped it clean and broke open the barrel. The shells tinkled to the ground, glittering like gold in the dying gleam of the day. He reloaded and snapped the gun shut, picking some more mud from the end of the barrel, and resting it in his lap. He felt more secure now, but the gathering darkness felt sinister. He could feel the strongpoint looming over him. It was barely thirty yards away – he hadn't thought he was so close; he'd nearly had a bloody heart attack when he saw it. So he could forget about stretcher-bearers; he would have to get back under his own steam.

How easy it would have been to just lie there under the brow of the hill and wait for death. He'd thought about it earlier, while he was waiting for the dark. When the pain in his leg started to gnaw at him he had pulled out the tube of morphine tablets the MO had given him. Enough there to put him out of his misery. Or there was always the revolver if he wanted to be more certain. He'd tipped the pills out into his hand and stared at them, little grey discs, hardly anything to look at. Then he slowly started to pop them back into the tube – all but one, which he swallowed. Not yet, he thought, you can always do it later.

That was two hours ago, and he could feel the effects starting to wear off. But he couldn't take another yet. What if it was too strong? What if the last one was still in his system? He needed his head clear if he was to do this. The quickest way to the downhill side of the crater was through the water, but he was shivering with the cold and he had a horror of the slimy feel of that yellowish pool and what it might hide. So he had to slither around the edge of the crater, clawing with his hands and pushing with his good leg. Every movement brought sharp pains stabbing up from his wounded knee, every foot gained brought his hand to the tube with its promised relief. But he couldn't, he couldn't. And he forced himself to go on. By the time he reached the other side he was in a muck sweat and panting as if he'd run a mile.

The moon was hidden in cloud. With the black silhouette of the strongpoint hanging over his shoulder he peered down the slope and tried to gauge the distance back. Four or five hundred yards – a long crawl through thick mud and broken wire and God knew what. The throb in his leg was a hard reminder of what it had cost him just to get to the other side of the crater, but he didn't have the luxury of time: he needed the darkness for cover. If he didn't make the distance by sunrise, a sniper or machine gun would pick him off. Better get bloody on with it, then. He holstered his pistol and took a deep breath, and then gritted his teeth as he dragged himself out of the crater.

Pain had sharpened his senses and there was a dreadful clarity about what followed. Every moment was sharp and cutting and burned in his memory by the pain in his leg. At first, he was sure he would never be able to do it. When he crawled over the lip of the crater and started pulling himself downhill, digging his hands into the soft earth for grip, it was excruciating. It clawed at him like a savage animal, twisting nerves and tearing at his flesh. But gradually, the screaming pain subsided and it just became wearing, tiring him out so he had to stop every few yards, panting for breath.

At least his head was clear. The throbbing, congested feeling was gone and he was alive to the night, the touch of the air like cold water on his skin. But if he was more lucid, he felt the loneliness all the more sharply. He knew many of his men were scattered about this ground, blown down like straws in the wind, and the thought that he had led them to their deaths weighed on him like lead in his chest. He thought of Wilson: he knew he was dead, though he had barely glimpsed it, and as he pushed himself through the cold mud he heard the wind whistling in the wire and remembered the banshees in his grandfather's stories. Keening death into the house, he said, though it was the silence that followed that was more terrible, falling like a shadow on the face of the moon. He pictured him lying cold on the ground with only the wind wailing over him, and sobbed as he crawled forward, dumb tears scalding his face. Was he crawling to an empty trench? Or one that was manned only by corpses, their faces turned to the dark sky, the wind tugging at their hair, and just the burrowing rats to animate them.

Rats! He heard a noise and froze, gripping the revolver in his fist. Something brushed his leg and he recoiled, only to get a fleeting touch of fur across his face that made him curl up in horror, heedless of the hurt screaming out of his leg. He lay in a ball, arms over his head for protection, feeling the disgust flowing through him. Then, slowly, pain won out and the clarity came back. He straightened his legs, panting with the effort, gulping deep breaths to soothe the burning in his chest, and then the smell rose up on him like a wave, filling his nostrils, clinging to his skin. Putrefaction, decay, rotting flesh. He must have interrupted their feast. With his stomach heaving, bile rising in his throat, he scrambled forward on his elbows, desperate to escape the charnel pit he had crawled into.

Panic carried him a few hurried yards before he collapsed, the pain in his leg overpowering. When it became bearable, he rolled over on his good side, holding his knee out of the wet, and peered at the dial of his watch to try to get some idea of the time. It was too dark to see, and he didn't dare light a match, but after a few minutes a passing gap in the clouds revealed a glowing half moon and he saw it was past midnight. Then, in the waning light, he saw fence posts standing up all around, filaments of broken wire waving and glinting between them. As darkness closed about him once more he had a feeling of despair, that he was trapped in a cage. And to think this had once been open fields, with sheep grazing among the summer flowers. What on earth had they done?

It took an effort to get moving again, but he forced himself to roll over and start crawling. He was tired now, could feel fatigue overtaking him, and he was losing track of time. Crawl and stop, crawl and stop. He had no idea where he was, no sense of direction; he was floating in a void, with nothing but the pain in his leg and the cold, clinging mud to fix him in the world. He had to struggle with the urge to stop and rest his head on his arms, let sleep take him. Twice, he felt his head nodding, and then caught his breath as he snapped awake, eyes raw and closing. But then it happened again, and as he came awake he realized he'd been sleeping, not just dozing off.

He knew he had to move again, but he couldn't find the strength. He'd had it. He was utterly past all caring, and he let his head sink back down on the ground with a low sob. Self-pity welled up. It wasn't bloody fair. What sort of life had he had? What chance had he had? He thought of Lillian. God, he wished he could have seen her again. He wished he could have said everything he wanted to say. With his own words, and not just in a paltry letter. He wished he could have kissed her again, just once. He thought of how she would receive his letter and the news of his death, probably on the same day. Christ! He hadn't wanted that, of all things. He felt tears start to sting his cheeks. Not bloody fair. Not bloody . . .

Without even realizing it, he had stretched out his arm and dragged himself forward a few inches. He groaned with pain and pulled back his arm to wipe the tears on his sleeve. And again, and again. He gritted his teeth, but still the groans escaped. Maybe another pill. But he had momentum now. The pain was keeping him going. Five more pulls and then . . .

He froze, listening, hastily fumbling for the revolver that was dragging behind him on its lanyard. The pain faded and he cocked his head towards the sound. It was a sound – he'd heard it. Again! A sigh – just a few yards ahead. He strained his eyes towards it, holding his breath, sliding his thumb over the hammer of the revolver. A shadow seemed to move, there was a loud metallic click, and then the words, 'Who goes there?'

He wanted to answer. He strained his throat, working his lips furiously, but it seemed his mouth was parched and his throat had shrunken. All he could manage was a dull croak. A light blinked on, blinding him, and indistinct whispers followed. Through shielded eyes, he saw a man crawling towards him, then felt strong hands on his shoulder. He must have cried out as they pulled him over the rim of the crater: whispered apologies followed and he saw lanterns and men hurrying up, encircling him with worried, wondering faces. These parted a few moments later and Nightingale looked down at him in consternation.

'Bloody hell,' he cried, blinking back tears and taking Stephen's hand in his. 'Look who's come back from the bloody dead.'

Stephen squeezed his hand for all he was worth, only half sure it was real. He squeezed and squeezed and tried to speak, but nothing came out – only a strangled sob. Then another, and another, until his whole body was racked and he could hardly breathe.

'There, there, old man,' Nightingale laughed, still holding his hand. 'It's all right now, you're safe. You're safe, Stephen.'

XIV

'What about a nice cup of tea?' Nurse Winslow asked and, with hardly a pause, she answered for him, 'You'd like that, wouldn't you? Of course you would.'

Stephen watched her fussing around the little room, shifting the water pitcher half an inch to the left, fidgeting with the curtains. He knew his silence made her nervous. She was like a trapped bird, flitting to and fro and chattering incessantly. But if she stopped, she'd have to face up to the fact that he couldn't answer.

'You must be tired after all your exercise. A cup of tea would be just the thing.' She tugged at an invisible crease in the coverlet and smiled at him. He smiled back. It was all he could do. Grin and nod, or shake his head. No words would come – not since they'd dragged him into that trench three weeks ago and he'd tried to gather the last of his strength to answer Nightingale. He'd been so desperate to speak, to say something, anything, but nothing would come, not even a grunt. Nothing when the stretcher-bearers came to carry him to the regimental aid post, and then dropped him as the morning hate from the Germans caught them in the open. Nothing when Nightingale came to see him at the casualty clearing station and fell fast asleep in the chair beside his bed. But by then he'd given up trying to speak and just fumbled for his pocketbook and pen. He wrote a note and then thumped

Nightingale's knee to wake him up. Nightingale yawned and looked blearily at the grubby piece of paper, then nodded.

'Right you are,' he said, and stood up, looking like a lost child in the middle of all the cots and stretchers, 'I'll let her know, don't you worry.' And then he'd bent down to shake Stephen's hand, and that was the last time he'd seen him.

Three weeks on and he was in London. His leg had been washed and stitched and bandaged and now stuck stiffly out in front of his wheelchair. Sometimes it hurt – a deep, throbbing pain, like a pulse inside his knee – and sometimes it itched furiously. But the doctors said there was no infection and it was healing. With that knowledge he put up with the morning exercises they made him do, back and forth along the parallel bars, back and forth until his arms ached with the effort and sweat was dripping off his brow. But the muteness was beginning to trouble him. It was beginning to look recalcitrant. Sometimes even Nurse Winslow let her mask slip and he would catch her looking at him with a mixture of pity and exasperation.

'A cup of tea, then,' she said, half to herself. 'A cup of tea, and then a wash and a shave. We'll have to have you looking your best for when that nice girl comes to see you.'

He smiled again – but there was nothing forced about it this time. Lillian was coming. It was true. He hadn't dreamed it yesterday, or the day before. She came every day, on the tube from Holland Park. Every day for the last two weeks. Just to think of it put joy in his heart. As long as she was there, he didn't care if he never spoke again.

'Why don't I leave you sitting by the window while I fetch your tea?' Nurse Winslow asked, 'Then you can look out at the gardens. You'd like that, wouldn't you? Of course you would.'

She pushed his chair over to the window and went out, closing the door gently behind her. The hospital was in London, but the view across the broad green swath of Kensington Gardens made it feel like the countryside. The hospital had its own spacious gardens too, with a neatly tended lawn sprinkled with patients lounging in deckchairs or walking in the late autumn sun. It should have been a comforting scene, except he saw the war in everything now. The straight privet hedges were like built-up trenches, and the newly dug earth in the flowerbeds had the same spewy texture as a fresh shell crater. With a sinking feeling, he tried to push these images from his mind, but he knew he wouldn't escape. Next came the throbbing in his head, the metallic taste in his mouth. These were the harbingers, and with them the bursting sensation, as if he was going to explode in a fit. He closed his eyes, trying to ward it off, but it was too late. In his mind's eye was the same peaceful scene, but then a cluster of shells whistled down into the grounds. Five-nines, puffing black smoke with a little orange heart of fire. One, two, three. The manicured turf was torn to pieces, divots flying in every direction. The men were ripped apart, broken and shredded and flung into the air, and his hands flew to his mouth, trying to stifle a silent scream.

The matron tapped twice on the door and, without waiting for an answer, stuck her head inside.

'Miss Bryce is here to see you, doctor,' she said, and Hardcastle grunted and looked up at the clock as he screwed the top back on his pen. Punctual to the minute, as usual.

'Very well. Send her in,' he stood up as Lillian walked in, reaching across to shake her hand. 'Miss Bryce, how nice to see you again. Please, have a seat.'

Lillian sat and watched Hardcastle subside into his chair on the other side of his desk. Despite his outward politeness, she knew he wasn't really pleased to see her. There was a mutual, if respectful, loathing. He thought she was a busybody and she, for her part, thought he was a very poor psychiatrist. He didn't even look right: big and beefy, with a red face and thick, stubby fingers. In short, she thought he looked too stupid to be good at his job.

'Well? How did you find him today?' Hardcastle asked, though he knew from the look on her face what the answer would be. She wasn't like the usual round of relatives who asked to see him. No yes doctor, no doctor, whatever you say doctor from her. A university lecturer, apparently – clever and completely self-possessed. She'd taken a leave of absence and come straight over the moment she found out where he was. An admirable show of devotion, he had to admit, but these weekly meetings were starting to become a bit of a pain in the arse.

'Much the same as before,' Lillian answered, making it sound like an accusation.

'Well, as I'm sure you understand, it's a very slow process.'

'I'm sure it is, doctor.'

She was trying not to sound impatient – and she didn't wish to appear ungrateful, because she was not. The relief, the blessed relief, of that telegram was still with her. She'd opened it with shaking hands and almost fainted when she read the two short lines. Then joy seized her and she ran to tell her mother and sister, hugging them both. It was only later that she thought of the letter, Stephen's letter, still sitting unopened on her dressing table. After reading the notice in the newspaper she'd felt sick even to look at it, but now she ran upstairs like a girl, tore it open and laughed out loud to herself as she read it again and again.

'A very slow process,' Hardcastle said again, 'but I'm sure we'll get there eventually, if we all keep at it. Our man is a hero, after all. He'll find his voice in the fullness of time.'

'I'm sure you're right, doctor,' Lillian agreed. 'It's just that I wonder . . .'

'Yes, Miss Bryce?'

281

She paused to gather her thoughts. How to tell this man that she didn't think he was up to the job. That was the problem.

'I wonder if we've explored every possible avenue. I mean, I'm sure there are alternative treatments that we haven't tried.'

'Alternative treatments? Of course there are alternatives. I understand Doctor Yealland is having remarkable success with his electric shock treatment.'

'No,' Lillian said flatly. 'I've looked into Doctor Yealland's so-called treatment. It's nothing more than torture.'

Hardcastle was loath to agree with her, but he had to admit she had a point. He had seen Yealland administering his treatment and it had sickened him. Tying a man to a chair and applying electric shocks to the back of his throat until he started to speak was a long way from his idea of medicine.

'Well then, I'm afraid . . .' Hardcastle began, but he was thrown off by the piercing stare she gave him. 'Look here,' he said, spreading his hands on the desk, 'I'll admit, I've gone about as far as I can. Sometimes, in these cases, it's just a question of waiting. Time heals all. But I'll tell you what, there's a chap I know who might be able to help. He's done well with some of the more . . . intractable cases. Why don't I give him a call and see if he can pop over?'

Lillian was pleased to see him blush when she smiled at him.

'That would be very kind of you, doctor.'

That night he lay awake and thought about Lillian. Even when she wasn't there, he liked to imagine what she might be doing. He thought about her walking under the trees, sitting on the train, or letting herself into her aunt's house in Holland Park. He tried to recount to himself every second of her visit, from the moment he saw her come into the common room, to the moment she kissed him and left.

He knew he hadn't been in good form when she arrived. That episode looking out across the garden had put him out of sorts. But it was a fine afternoon, and she'd suggested that they go and sit in the garden. Stephen had stiffened in his wheelchair, gripping the arms uneasily, but he hadn't tried to stop her. He'd let her push him out onto the lawn, but when she stopped in the open air he had motioned her on towards a chestnut tree.

'You'd prefer to sit in the shade?' she asked, and dutifully pushed him there. He still sat uneasily, looking up now and then at the canopy of five-fingered leaves, only starting to yellow around the edges. It wasn't shade he craved; it was cover.

Once they were settled, she'd brought out her writing pad. It was a big artist's sketchbook that she brought with her every day, together with a handful of pencils. But she didn't use it for drawing. Instead, she turned to a blank page, placed it in his lap and wrote a short formula:

$$2n + 1 = p + 2q$$

He'd frowned, trying to make sense of it. Numbers, letters, what did it mean? He shook his head and looked at her questioningly. She looked astonished.

'Oh, Stephen, don't tell me you don't remember it. You must. It's Lemoine's conjecture.'

He shook his head. It was as if he'd never seen it before.

But she'd patiently written it out again, and added a few examples using real numbers. Somewhere, in the back of his mind, a light came on. He took a pencil and wrote a few more himself, and then a similar formula. He wasn't sure what it meant at first, it just popped into his head. But Lillian smiled and squeezed his arm.

'Yes, yes. That's it exactly. Very good, Stephen.'

283

And they went on like that for the rest of the afternoon. It bothered Stephen that he sometimes made mistakes, that sometimes he didn't know what he was writing down. He felt like he was walking in a labyrinth, and at every turn he was presented with an array of doors to pass through. Most of the time he picked the right door to go through, but sometimes he didn't, and Lillian had to correct him. Then disappointment settled over him like a cloud, and it was hard to shake. It didn't used to be like that. He used to know the right door, instinctively, before he even tried to open it. He used to know not only the next door, but the three that came after it.

Of course, he'd already tried to explain this to Hardcastle, but he was sure he didn't understand. He wrote on his notepad and showed him: 'Not good at maths.'

Bemusement clouded Hardcastle's heavy face, until Stephen added: 'Used to be.'

Hardcastle had just shrugged.

'It'll pass,' was all he said, before he pressed on with his analysis. It had turned into a routine: endless questions about the minutiae of the attack. His preparations, his men, what he saw, what he did. Crucially, what did he remember about the last few moments before the shell knocked him down? He'd been speaking before that, had he not? He'd been shouting orders, encouragement to his men. What had happened in those few seconds? He had to know. It had to be in there somewhere.

Stephen smiled bitterly to himself in the dark. He didn't know. He'd been awake one moment, unconscious the next. That's all he could remember. Hardcastle was blundering about and he knew it. All he could do was keep leading Stephen down the path to the same point, the same dead end. Every session was the same, and Stephen had started to resent those afternoons in his office. It wasn't just Hardcastle's lack of imagination, nor his inability to effect a cure – or just bloody *fix* him – but also the fact that Hardcastle wasn't a soldier. Oh, he wore the uniform all right, but what the hell did he know? He'd never been to the front, he'd never been under fire. He didn't know what it was *like*. How could he, when the horror he saw was second-hand? All he could do was tell him to try and put it out of his mind, but they both knew that was no bloody use.

Sleep usually wouldn't come until the small hours. The nights were too quiet here and the silence took on an ominous weight, as if something dreadful were just about to happen. It helped to focus on the little sounds that were close by. As he lay awake with his fists clenched on the coverlet, he listened to Redfern snoring. His room-mate was an artillery captain who always slept underneath his bed, and his light, regular snore was soothing to Stephen's ears, though he sometimes snorted awake with a little mewing cry. Sometimes too, he wet himself, but he mostly kept his madness safely bottled up under the bed.

Redfern was a slight man with receding fair hair and watery blue eyes, and he had been blown up on three separate occasions. Miraculously, apart from the concussion, he had not received so much as a scratch – not even the last time, when his entire battery was destroyed and he was thrown twenty feet through the air after a German shell hit their ammunition dump. On the surface, he exhibited no obvious symptoms – at least not in the daytime. He neither stammered nor twitched and, apart from biting his nails constantly, he appeared to have no other nervous affliction.

Redfern's problem was that he had no memory whatsoever of his life before the war. He could recite chapter and verse about his movements at the front: where his battery had been, fire plans, ranges, elevations, even the number of shells fired in any given day. But he couldn't remember that he had been married for years. When his wife and teenage daughter came to see him they were complete strangers to him. Every week it was the same pantomime – and what made it worse was that he was so anxious to be polite to these people. After all, they had taken the trouble to come all this way to visit him; it was the least he could do. They brought him pots of homemade jam and knitted socks and the three of them would take tea on the lawn and spread the jam on thin slices of hard bread. Redfern always played along for all he was worth, sipping his tea in a genteel fashion, with his little finger extended. But when he looked at his wife and daughter he seemed to gaze right through them as if they weren't there. His watery blue eyes betrayed the yawning gulf in his mind, and mother and daughter always left in silent tears, supporting each other down the long gravel drive.

But at least he was quiet, and that was why he shared a room with Stephen. The screamers were kept upstairs, and they were what really set his nerves on edge. It was worst on the quiet nights, when they would suddenly rip the silence apart with a long, piercing shriek, like the noise of a shell going over. Strangely, it seemed to relieve the pressure in him – as if the pent-up demons had been released – and once it was over he felt more at ease, the danger past.

But sometimes it was a longer process; he could hear the screams and shouts bubbling upstairs, gradually building to a crescendo. Tonight, it started with a series of low, shuddering sobs, as if some poor soul was suffocating. Christ! He twisted the coverlet under his chin, wishing he were deaf instead of dumb. Then came the howling, shattering the stillness as it rose in pitch and ended, quite abruptly, with an audible thump. He flinched, knowing the poor bastard had flung himself against a wall. He heard sobbing afterwards, then the hurried footfalls of the night nurse. There were worse things than not sleeping.

* * *

The next day, Hardcastle came to see him in his room. Redfern had gone to breakfast but Stephen was still in bed. His breakfast lay untouched on the tray Nurse Winslow had brought. It had been one thing after another last night. Another bout of screaming in the small hours had kept him awake most of the night, and now he felt groggy and slightly nauseous. Hardcastle seemed equally uneasy. He knocked politely on the door and then poked his head inside, grinning nervously, like a schoolboy sent to the headmaster.

'Ah, Ryan. Thought I'd find you here. Mind if I come in?'

Stephen shook his head, and Hardcastle came in and sat gingerly on Redfern's untouched bed.

'How's the leg?' he asked, and when Stephen shrugged, he scratched his head absently and said, 'Yes, yes . . .' his voice trailing off. But then he seemed to remember himself and went on; 'I had a meeting with that girl of yours yesterday. Quite a formidable young lady, is your Miss Bryce. I mean that in the nicest possible way, of course, but I'm sure you already know that, eh?' Hardcastle grinned and Stephen smiled back politely.

'Anyhow, I promised her I'd get a pal of mine to look at you. We were at Cambridge together, would you believe? Name of Rivers – he's working with the Royal Flying Corps at the moment, but apparently he had quite a good run of it working at a hospital up in Scotland. Quite a lot of success with chaps who . . . who have problems similar to yours. So I rang him up and, lo and behold, he's free this afternoon. Said he'd pop over to have a look – as a favour, you know. You don't have any objection, do you?'

Stephen shook his head.

'Good, good. Thought you'd say . . . Well, you know what I mean. Let's say three o'clock then. I'll have the orderlies bring you up.'

A new head-shrinker at three o'clock. Well, it couldn't hurt

– but before that he had to undergo the ordeal of the parallel bars. Nurse Winslow wheeled him down to the gymnasium and left him in the care of Jardine, a huge Scot who was strong enough to lift him bodily out of the wheelchair. Before they began, Stephen looked at the bars as a prisoner might regard the rack. Even though he knew he was making progress, it was slow and painful progress. The splinter had cut tendons in his knee that were slow to heal, and there was nerve damage that made it feel as if he was walking with somebody else's leg. After half an hour he was exhausted, and when he fell on the floor, pain seared through his leg and right up his spine. More than once Jardine had to haul him up by the scruff of his pyjamas – but he never flagged, he never stopped his musical flow of encouraging banter. The last time he fell he thought he was at the end of his tether. Exhausted, he lay with his face on the floorboards, feeling tears starting to well up into his eyes. Jardine hauled him up with a cheery bellow.

'Come along now, Mr Ryan. This is no time for lying about. Up you get!'

Stephen wanted to lash out at him, kick him with his good leg, slap that bloody smile off his face. But instead his hands found the bars, the blisters burning on his palms, and he held himself upright until the shooting pain became bearable. Jardine winked at him.

'That's a good lad!'

Jardine was also an incurable gossip and, like most people, he seemed to think Stephen's muteness somehow affected his hearing as well. He often interrupted himself to offer, in a loud rasping voice, whatever little scraps of gossip were going around the hospital. Today, the news was bad.

'You heard about wee Mr Mitchell, the other Irish gentleman? Och! Terrible, terrible! The poor wee man!'

Stephen knew Mitchell only by sight. He was a small, dark-haired young man with an unnaturally pale face and piercing eyes. While most of the men at the hospital were withdrawn to one degree or another, Mitchell was the worst he had seen. He took his meals alone and said hardly a word to anybody – not to the nurses, not to his room-mate. In the evenings he would take a book or a magazine and sit by himself in the corner of the common room. If anybody sat near him, he would get up and go to bed.

Most of what Stephen knew about him, he had overheard. He was, as Jardine said, the other Irish gentleman; he had been a second lieutenant in the Royal Irish Fusiliers. This struck a chord with Stephen, because it was the Royal Irish who led the attack on the left flank, and Mitchell had been with the first wave. He was only a replacement officer, rushed into the thick of it after barely a week in France and the phrase baptism of fire hardly did it justice. Every other officer in his company was killed within the first fifteen minutes. Two of them were close friends of Mitchell, and were blown apart in front of him by the same shell. In spite of this, he had kept his cool, gathering up the remnants of his shattered company and leading them to safety. He seemed to have passed the hardest test; he was mentioned in dispatches and made acting company commander – but when his battalion mustered to move into reserve he was nowhere to be found. They eventually discovered him in a communication trench, sawing the head off a German corpse with a bayonet, singing softly to himself as he worked.

'He tried to kill hiself,' Jardine whispered, tears in his voice. 'Poor lad was near dead when they found him. Hanged hiself with a pillowcase. Och, I don't know what they're going to do with him, the poor wee man.'

Jardine tried to lead him to the end of the bars, but Stephen stiffened, pushing him away. *Christ!* It was this place. He felt the walls pressing in on him, cold nausea, and tremors ravaging his body. *Christ Almighty!* Blackness dimmed the edge of his vision and he lost his grip on the bars, feeling shards of pain piercing his knee. Jardine held him and gently dragged him back to the wheelchair, but it didn't matter, it didn't matter. He sat there, racked by sobs, shivering. Jardine looked distraught.

'There, there, son! It'll be all right now, don't you worry.'

At lunchtime, Nurse Winslow came to his room with his shaving kit and he wrote two lines on his notepad and showed it to her:

Want to wear my uniform.
Don't want to go in wheelchair.

She pursed her lips doubtfully, 'Hmm, we'll just have to see about the second one. I suppose we can get you into your uniform, and then we'll see if you can manage with a stick.'

Redfern came in and sat on the other bed, biting his nails vigorously as she helped Stephen on with his breeches and boots. He could have managed the rest himself, but here at last was something that she could do for him, and she fussed over him, brushing his tunic and straightening his tie. At last, when he was almost ready, he sat on the bed, buttoning up his tunic, and she sat on the bed beside him, buckling his Sam Browne.

'I've never seen one of those before.' Her fingers touched the little purple and white ribbon over his left breast pocket, 'What is it?'

He picked up the notepad and wrote:

Military Cross

'Oh goodness me!' Her eyes widened, 'Is that what it is? I really didn't know. What a terrible ninny I am! You must be awfully brave!'

Stephen smiled, blushing deeply. Redfern stopped biting his nails for a moment to give him the thumbs up and a wink.

Hardcastle's office was on the first floor. Usually Stephen was carried up in his wheelchair by a pair of porters, but this time he hauled himself up the banister, leaning heavily on Nurse Winslow, and wondering with each wincing step if he'd let his pride get the better of him. By the time they reached the landing his forehead was beaded with sweat and his hands were shaking. Nurse Winslow gave him a worried look as she pressed the stick into his hand and straightened his tunic.

'Are you sure you're all right?' she asked, and he nodded vigorously. He put his arm around her narrow shoulders and they set off along the landing. When they reached the door, Stephen leaned against the wall and put all his weight on his good leg. Nurse Winslow knocked on the door and pushed it open for him. 'Good luck!' she whispered and he stumped hastily towards the desk under his own steam.

Rivers was standing at the window, gazing out over the lawns. Between them stood the desk, a big ornate affair with a green leather top, and Stephen fetched up against it with a loud clank of his stick, quickly shifting his weight to his free hand. He straightened as best he could when Rivers turned from the window and looked him up and down. 'Captain Ryan, isn't it? How's the leg? Getting about on it, I see. Good, good. Please, take a seat. No need to flog it too hard, what?'

Stephen lowered himself carefully into the armchair and rested the stick against the front of the desk. While Rivers seated himself and opened his file, he looked around the office. He liked it in here; it was all wood panelling and bookcases, heavy with the odour of beeswax polish, and it reminded him of the study in Billy Standing's house. The tall window was filled with treetops and blue sky and he could clearly read the spines in the book-cases; quality stuff – gold lettering in tooled leather. Gibbon's *Decline and Fall*, Aristotle's *Poetics*, Lucretius, Ovid, Homer. Familiar names, but from another life. Nevertheless, he could picture himself spending a pleasant afternoon in here with a glass of good whiskey, reading and savouring the silence and the slow ticking of the clock.

Rivers's head was bowed, intent on the file, and Stephen studied him for a moment. He was short and chubby; thinning grey hair and a pencil moustache lending him a somewhat trim look in his captain's uniform, with its bronze caduceus on his lapel. Short-sighted, too – the afternoon sun glowing white in the flat, vitreous discs of his spectacles as he finally lifted his head and took them off, his eyes flickering towards the little purple and white ribbon.

Not shirking, Stephen thought and, as if he had read his mind, Rivers looked at him and smiled.

'I see more of those than you might think in my line of work,' he said, 'and the other sort, too. There is no shortage of heroes in hospital.' He had the air of a pleasant schoolmaster and Stephen realized he was paying compliments to put him at his ease. Maybe it was part of the new technique. He smiled back, but let his eye travel down to his file, lying open between them on the desk. The page was filled with short paragraphs of dense handwriting. Furthest away, he could see the last paragraph contained only two words, but he couldn't read them. Barking Mad, perhaps?

Rivers leaned back in his chair and steepled his fingers together. 'I wonder, do you happen to know the clinical term for your condition, captain?'

He shook his head, though he was thinking of those two words at the bottom of the page.

'It's called aphasia,' said Rivers. 'Do you know what that means?'

Once again, he shook his head. *You won't catch me out that easily.*

'It's from the Greek. Literally, it means without speech. A curious state, don't you think? After all, it is the power of speech that set us apart from the apes. So, it's fair to say that losing one's ability to speak is a fairly serious turn of events.' Rivers got up and went to the window. 'And, when we examine your case, captain, it is also quite curious. Aphasia is a rather common symptom of repressed trauma – but it is usually only seen in enlisted men. Officers almost always develop a stammer rather than being struck completely dumb, as you have. A remarkable division of class, don't you think?'

Stephen's eyes followed him to the window as he rubbed a sore spot above his knee. *Must be my lowly origins showing through.*

'Sorry if I'm boring you.' Rivers turned from the window and grinned, his hands in his pockets, 'I do drone on a bit, at times. Comes of having been a teacher. I find it often helps if the patient understands a bit about his condition. All part of the therapy, in a way. But let's not get bogged down in generalities.' He took a silver cigarette case from his pocket and opened it to Stephen, who shook his head. Rivers put a cigarette between his lips and spoke into his cupped hands as he lit it, 'Because it would be unwise to concentrate on the more peculiar aspects of your case. We would do better to look for the cause. I see from your file that you served with a tunnelling company for a while. Must have taken a bit of getting used to for an infantry officer, working underground. Miss the open spaces, did you?'

Well, this was a change from Hardcastle's approach. Stephen didn't know what he was getting at, but at least it was different. He nodded, following Rivers as he paced back and forth across the window. He found comfort in the sunlight that was pouring in around Rivers. It was strange, but even the mere mention of tunnelling had brought back sharp memories. Sitting in this airy room, with its bookcases and bright windows, he could visualize himself in the tunnel again. It was a very vivid sensation; he could even smell the earth.

Rivers nodded too. 'I'll bet you did. Nobody likes being closed in. It's unnatural. I dare say Dr Freud would say it has something to do with the birth trauma. But that doesn't concern me just at the moment. The really interesting thing, captain, is that in cases like yours the peccant trauma is often interment.'

Peccant. Now there's a word.

Rivers eased himself back down in his chair. He sat back and took a long pull from his cigarette. In the stillness of the room, Stephen could hear the tobacco hissing as it turned to ash.

'Interment,' he repeated. 'Burial. Have you ever been buried, captain?'

Buried. The word hit him like a slap. He must have jumped an inch out of his chair.

'I'll take that as a yes, shall I?' Rivers was looking at him keenly as he scribbled a hurried note in the file. Stephen felt as if the blood had drained from his face. His skin had that cold, clammy, crawling feeling. He hadn't felt that in a while. The smell of earth became overpowering. All at once he felt his throat dry up, his senses deserting him. For a moment his eyes rolled upwards and the suffocating black engulfed him once again. He had the image of lifeless white fingers sticking out from fresh earth. It took an effort to bring himself back to the office, and when he opened his eyes again Rivers's look had changed to one of concern. He was leaning forward, gazing at him.

'Stay with me, captain. It might be unpleasant, but I think we're making progress. And so quickly, too. I think we've hit the nail on the head. I should tell you that your experience is not as uncommon as you might think. Many of the cases I have seen have been buried at one time or another. Not as deep as you were, I dare say: usually a shell falling nearby, sometimes a trench or a dugout collapsing. But it always has a much deeper effect than it seems at first. Most men carry the trauma with them for months or even years before it finally declares itself.'

He stubbed his cigarette out in the brass ashtray at the corner of the desk and made another note in the file, then leaned back again, a satisfied look on his round face. 'That's half the battle, you see, recognizing the cause. Now, I want you to think back again. Ask yourself what happened. You may think you can't remember, but that's precisely the problem. It's repressed, you see. It's perfectly natural. Your own mind is trying to protect you by hiding the memory, but you must remember. You must bring it out into the light.'

He went on, but Stephen was hardly listening. He was back in the dark. It seemed a thousand years ago – was it really only a few months? The other side of the summer. He remembered the dank musky smell that built up when the ventilator was shut off. The smell of sweat and fear. They had stopped pumping and doused the lights. One of the listeners had heard something. Stephen crouched in the dark, straining his eyes and ears into the endless void. Terrified. And he was in charge, damn it, they were expecting him to tell them what to do.

The rush, when it came, was shocking. A flash of panic; he felt the breath knocked out of him as one of them cannoned into him in the dark.

'Run!' he hissed, 'Jesus Christ! Run! They're going to blow it!'

He was dazed, on his back, in pitch black. What had they heard? What tiny sound had transmitted all that information?

They were crawling over him now, hurrying knees and hands. An electric lamp came on and he picked himself up and ran to the flickering light. Grotesque shadows filled the tunnel in front of him. Then he tripped over some inert body, fell headlong, and kept crawling on towards the light with the panted curses behind him. He knew he ought to take command, but flight was in the air now. There was no stopping it. He had to get out. He stumbled into a taller gallery, where he could stand up in a low crouch. Around he went, his mouth open to call back to the men behind him, and then it came; a dull thump, and the rending crash of falling earth.

'... Most men are ashamed of their reaction,' Rivers was saying, 'but it really is the bravest ones who are the worst. A coward has no problem expressing the emotion of fear, although he may also feel shame. No, I have seen the stoutest hearts . . .'

It was closing in around him. The air vanishing as the earth dropped its cloak over his face. Still he thrashed forward, desperate, driven by the sight of the men in front of him staggering under the weight of tumbling soil. He was down on his hands and knees when he saw the light go out. The solid weight of a man came down beside him, and still he hurried forward, a frightened rabbit in a shrinking burrow. It enveloped him and he flailed wildly in the blackness, feeling the crushing weight, suffocating, until at last he felt air on his face and scrambled into it and ran, ran, headlong into the dark. Then he made the connection. The man going down beside him, engulfed by the falling earth. The hand, white fingers in the earth. A timber must have caught him. Stephen remembered the words. He had heard them above the rending noise; a cry, a little mewing voice as he fell, but the Irish accent plain even in the tumult.

Oh Jesus, Mary and Joseph!

'The flower of English youth has often crumbled . . .'

'Irish,' Stephen said.

Rivers stopped in mid-sentence. 'What was that?'

'I said, I'm Irish,' he repeated in a stronger voice, tears scalding his cheeks.

extracts reading groups
competitions books new
discounts extracts
competitions
books
new
events books
new extracts
new reading groups
interviews
events extracts
discounts
new books events
events new
discounts extracts discounts

www.panmacmillan.com

extracts events reading groups
competitions books extracts new

MALPAS

10 . 1 . 14